DEATH ON A TRAIN

THE FLORA MAGUIRE MYSTERIES BOOK 5

ANITA DAVISON

B
Boldwood

First published in 2018 as The Bloomsbury Affair. This edition published in Great Britain in 2024 by Boldwood Books Ltd.

Copyright © Anita Davison, 2018

Cover Design by Head Design

Cover Illustration: Shutterstock and Adobe Stock

A CIP catalogue record for this book is available from the British Library.

Paperback ISBN 978-1-83518-880-4

Large Print ISBN 978-1-83518-879-8

Hardback ISBN 978-1-83518-878-1

Ebook ISBN 978-1-83518-881-1

Kindle ISBN 978-1-83518-882-8

Audio CD ISBN 978-1-83518-873-6

MP3 CD ISBN 978-1-83518-874-3

Digital audio download ISBN 978-1-83518-877-4

Boldwood Books Ltd
23 Bowerdean Street
London SW6 3TN
www.boldwoodbooks.com

Dedicated to my agent, Kate Nash, who has been with me all the way, offering encouragement without expectation and understands exactly what this writing life is all about.

1

EATON PLACE, LONDON, APRIL 1905

'Good evening, Stokes.' Bunny's voice from the hall brought Flora to her feet. Issuing a brief apology to her two dinner guests, she left the dining room, shivering in the blast of cold air that rushed through the open front door.

Tall and muscular with slightly boyish looks which sent females of all ages checking their hair in nearby mirrors, his lightly tanned skin was flushed from the cool night air, his blue eyes bright behind rimless spectacles.

'I'm horribly late for dinner, Stokes. Is your mistress furious?'

He handed the butler his hat and then shrugged out of his overcoat.

'I would rather not speculate, sir.' Stokes placed the hat on a hook, took his coat and gave it a shake, scattering raindrops on the tiled floor. 'I've laid out your dinner suit in your dressing room. Will you require my assistance to change?'

'Unnecessary, thank you. I'll manage. If you could just tell my wife, I'll be down as quickly as I can.'

Flora stepped from the cover of the archway from where she had observed them.

The butler froze, the overcoat held out in front of him.

'Ah, Flora.' Bunny cleared his throat and summoned a conciliatory smile. 'I intended to be here on time, but it couldn't be avoided.' He lifted his arms intent on a hug, but she sidestepped him. 'I see I'm not forgiven?'

'You've almost missed dinner!' Her fierce whisper held the mounting irritation she had nursed all evening.

'If you'll excuse me, sir, madam. I must see to my duties.' Stokes divested himself of the coat and, head down, fled towards the kitchens.

'How's the reunion going?' Bunny fingered an arm of his spectacles nervously, his gaze going to the closed dining room door.

'Don't change the subject.' Flora brushed a hank

of damp hair from his forehead. 'Better than I could have imagined, actually.' Her attempt to stay cross was ruined as his cologne stirred her senses. 'It's as if they have never been apart. I doubt they'll even notice I'm gone.'

As if on cue, a baritone chuckle drifted into the hall, followed by a gale of relaxed feminine laughter.

'Then why the sad face?' Bunny ran a finger along her cheek. 'Sounds to me like your parents are getting along splendidly.'

'I'm delighted, of course. It's just – oh, never mind, we'll talk later. I should get back to our guests.'

How could she explain? William and Alice might have put the past behind them, but theirs weren't the only lives disrupted by twenty years of lies and secrets.

'*Your* guests – this was all your idea, remember?' Bunny planted a swift kiss on her forehead and headed for the stairs. 'By the way,' he halted halfway up and leaned over the handrail, 'your trip to Harvey Nichols was very much worth it. That gown is magnificent. I love that shade of blue on you.'

She waved him off impatiently, but her steps lightened as she returned to the dining room, relieved he was home and that the weight of the dinner party no longer lay entirely on her shoulders.

'I'm sorry about that.' Flora resumed her seat in a

room where soft golden light reflected off crystal and gilt, the crackle of flames and shift of coals in the Adam fireplace completing the cosy ambience. 'Bunny promises to be with us shortly.'

'You've no need to apologise, my darling,' William patted her hand. 'I haven't enjoyed a dinner this much for a long time.' His gaze shifted from Flora to the lady opposite. 'Although Flora insisted under no circumstances was I to cry off—'

'Which you have done on two previous occasions,' Flora added.

He had kept a muscular physique in his mid-forties, honed from years spent in the saddle on the horse ranches of far-flung continents. Tiny lines carved into his tanned skin beside intelligent dark eyes that sparkled with private amusement. His dark hair sported half-inch wide silver wings at his temples.

'It's been a wonderful surprise.' Alice's cheeks warmed to a becoming pink. 'I reconciled myself long ago to never seeing William again.' She tore her gaze away from him only long enough to rearrange her napkin on her lap. 'He was a secret I imagined keeping forever. I could hardly believe it when Flora told me you lived in London and she saw you regularly.'

Alice too wore the years lightly, with girlish slenderness, unblemished porcelain skin and the same wide, hazel eyes Flora saw in her own mirror every morning.

Stokes had shown William into the room where Alice waited, then his soft murmur of her original name, Lily, followed by Alice's sharp exhalation of breath, spared Flora having to explain her reasons for deceiving them.

Had they been alone, Flora was convinced they would have rushed into each other's arms; only keeping a respectable distance between them for form's sake.

'Had I known what you had planned, Flora,' William said, 'I would have cancelled my trip to Moscow and told Balfour to go to blazes.'

'You've been in Russia?' Flora set down her wineglass with a heavy thump. 'When you said you were taking a northern holiday, I imagined Scotland, or Belgium. Not Russia. Why didn't you tell me?'

'I couldn't, my sweet. It was all very clandestine.'

William's work was closely covered by the Official Secrets Act, and he would never discuss the details. He seemed oblivious to the fact his secrecy made her worry all the more.

'What is Russia like?' Flora asked, aware a more

intrusive question would be glossed over. That William could summon several armed men at a moment's notice and his driver was a burly six feet four who sat in the lobby of his apartment at night contradicted his claim he was 'a lowly diplomat'.

During Flora's childhood, 'Uncle' William descended on Cleeve Abbey several times a year laden with gifts for his nieces and nephew. He always brought something for Flora; the butler's daughter, when she was invited to join them on cold evenings in front of the fire to listen to him recount his adventures. He would stay a few memorable weeks, then disappear again as quickly as he had come. In adulthood, she discovered William was her natural father; a truth she was still coming to terms with.

More recently, Flora had been reunited with her mother and bringing them together for the first time in twenty years was an enormous gamble; one she had not told either of them in advance. Was matchmaking your parents socially acceptable, or would she forever be a pariah for interfering?

'Colder than anywhere on earth.' William accompanied his broad smile with a contrived shiver. 'St Petersburg lay under several feet of snow when I left, and—' he broke off as the door clicked open to admit Bunny.

'Good evening, everyone. Forgive my tardiness.' Bunny strode to the table where he shook William's hand then kissed Alice's cheek before taking the remaining empty chair. 'Something came up, so I couldn't get away.'

'We're in no hurry, are we?' Alice interrupted Flora's signal for Stokes to serve the next course with a restraining hand on her forearm. 'Perhaps we might allow Bunny to eat his entrée? After a hard day at work, he deserves his dinner.'

'As long as no one minds.' Bunny raised his eyebrows in appeal at Flora. 'I *am* rather hungry.'

'Not at all, old fellow,' William said, before Flora could react. 'Gives us time to let that excellent meal settle. Besides,' he continued when the butler had withdrawn, 'Lily, I mean Alice, has been keeping us entertained with stories of her work at St Philomena's Hospital.' He broke off with a shy grin. 'I'm sorry. It will take a while to become accustomed to that name, although it suits you.'

'I've been Alice Finch for twenty years, so in effect, Lily Maguire no longer exists,' she replied, her gaze fixed on William's face, a look he returned with an almost dazed expression.

Flora directed an exasperated look at Bunny,

whose lips twitched. He grabbed the water jug and poured himself a glass.

Flora fidgeted, uneasy with the way they stared into each other's eyes like prospective lovers. Lily, or rather Alice, had run away from her life, which included Flora, years before. Despite their recent apologies and explanations, Flora's feelings of abandonment had not been entirely banished. Being lied to for most of her life was hard to forgive; something for which William took responsibility. Although the hurt still erupted without warning, Flora still hoped she could put aside her resentment and make peace with the past.

'William was about to tell us about his recent trip to St Petersburg.' Flora steered the conversation back to firmer ground.

'That must have been quite an expedition?' Bunny looked up from adjusting the position of his chair. 'I've always wanted to go there. I've heard it's a beautiful city with amenable people.'

'Not so amenable at the moment, apparently.' Flora's hard look at William dared him to change the subject. 'The newspapers talk about nothing but strikes and riots.'

'It's true, I'm afraid.' William cradled his wineglass in both hands. 'The factory workers suffer harsh, unsafe conditions. All attempts to form trade unions are fiercely put down by the factory owners, who are strongly backed by the government. The situation is – sensitive.' A shadow crossed his features, as if he conducted an internal debate on how much to reveal. 'It will take more than a lowly diplomat like me to sort out. I was only there as an official observer.'

'I thought Tsar Nicholas's father, Alexander, had abolished the serf system? Or am I being naïve?' Flora looked to Bunny who absent-mindedly broke apart a bread roll, his attention elsewhere.

'I find the Russian combination of eastern mysticism and western society fascinating.' Alice's tone was overbright, as if conscious of a sudden tension in the room. 'The Russians worship the Imperial family like gods.'

'True. It's a cultural thing,' William said, thoughtfully. 'A somewhat medieval one. Nicholas's grandfather, Alexander, embraced the principles of western living. However, Russian workers are still little more than serfs working long days in harsh, unsafe conditions. Tsar Nicholas is the richest ruler in the world, yet he prefers the life of a country squire with his wife and children. Matters of state take low priority and he avoids making decisions unless forced to.' He drank half his glass of wine in one draught and set the glass down hard on the table, his eyes troubled.

The conversation trailed off when Stokes reappeared with a covered plate he set before Bunny. He lifted the lid with a flourish, releasing a savoury aroma of roasted meat.

'This looks wonderful, Stokes.' Bunny rubbed his hands together over his plate. Stokes inclined his head with a wry smile, as if taking credit.

'I heard about that protest march in St Petersburg when those workers were shot,' Bunny spoke between mouthfuls. 'The newspapers are calling it "Red Sunday".'

'Not so much a protest as a massacre. They weren't given a chance to submit their petition before the Imperial guard opened fire. Whether it was Tsar Nicholas's orders, or the high-handedness of the police and his Cossacks. They shot and killed over a hundred people, with three times that number injured.' William twisted the stem of his wineglass and stared at the tablecloth. 'The Tsar isn't a wicked man, simply weak. He's terrified of being assassinated like his grandfather, so he overreacts at any sign of discontent.'

'Is everything all right?' Flora whispered to Bunny,

who had stopped listening and resorted to picking at his food. 'You seem distracted.'

'Of course, why shouldn't it be?' Bunny recovered quickly. 'This lamb is delicious, Flora. It certainly hasn't suffered from being kept warm.' His smile did not reach his eyes, convincing Flora something was bothering him.

'The Tsar and Tsarina must be delighted about the new baby.' She attempted to lighten an atmosphere that had grown sombre. 'A male heir after four daughters must be such a relief for Alexandra.'

'I'm afraid the child is a mixed blessing,' William said carefully. 'Tsarevich Alexei shows signs of having the bleeding disease. He might not live long.'

'I had no idea,' Alice said, horrified. 'I've not seen any reports in the newspapers.'

'You wouldn't have.' William shook his head. 'It's being kept quiet; though for how long is anyone's guess.'

'Is it true the Imperial family refuse to go anywhere these days without guards?' Alice enquired into the brief silence. 'Wasn't one of their grand dukes assassinated recently?'

'Tsar Nicolas's uncle, Grand Duke Sergei.' William's voice dropped. 'I was there.' Flora gasped, and he covered her hand on the table. 'I was in no danger, my darling, I promise. They moved into the Nicholas Palace at the Kremlin for safety, where I stayed with him and Duchess Elisabeth.'

'Doesn't sound as if that was very successful,' Alice offered.

'It wasn't.' William cleared his throat. 'Sergei left to attend to some business at the mansion. He took his driver but refused to allow his adjutant to go as the man had a family and he didn't want to put him in unnecessary danger.'

'He sounds like a courageous and compassionate man,' Alice murmured.

'In some ways, yes, but he was also reserved and autocratic. Very Russian, in fact.'

'I liked Sergei, even if I did not agree with his politics.' William continued his story, oblivious to Bunny's preoccupation. 'That day, his carriage had passed through the Nikolsky Gate when a bomb landed in his lap.' William's fingernails drew grooves in the tablecloth. 'The blast shook the ground and rattled the windows where Ella, I mean the duchess, and I sat drinking coffee.'

'I tried to stop her, but Ella rushed outside. It was a terrible sight. Sergei's carriage lay in burning pieces all over the courtyard. She did not say a word, but simply knelt in the bloody snow and picked up what was left of her husband.' William snatched up his glass and downed half the contents, dabbing his napkin hastily at a spilled drop on his sleeve.

'Oh, my goodness!' Flora whispered, her throat tight.

'How horrible! Poor Duchess Ella,' Alice whispered. 'Did they catch the assassin?'

William nodded. 'He was found injured beside the rear wheels. He said he expected to die in the explosion, but he'll probably be hanged.'

'How horrible.' Flora squeezed her eyes shut as the room stilled. The only sound was the tick of a clock on the mantelpiece, broken by Stokes with another bottle of wine.

'I'll do that, Stokes.' Dismissing him, Bunny circled the table and refilled their glasses.

'What will happen now?' Alice broke a heavy silence that had descended on the table.

'I don't know.' William's eyes darkened. 'It's not only the workers who are angry. Universities have closed because the student body has issued complaints about the lack of civil liberties. It's getting out of hand and bullets won't keep them quiet forever, but you never know—' He caught Flora's look and lifted his voice an octave. 'I imagine the Tsar will keep the upper hand for a while yet and it all might die down.'

'Are all the Eastern European royals going to be bombed or stabbed by their own people?' Flora shuddered. 'It's like the French revolution all over again.'

'I don't like the situation any more than you do, but my role is to avoid exacerbating conflict. Besides, the Romanovs have no obligation to listen to our government.'

'Then I would make an inadequate diplomat.' Flora sniffed. 'I would get them all in the same room and allow no one to leave until they agreed, and killing no one.' She turned to Bunny for his reaction, but his blue eyes behind his spectacles had darkened to navy and he appeared not to have heard.

'That's enough talk about killings and wars.' Flora adopted her role as hostess to bring the conversation back to less disturbing subjects. 'Alice, I hear Raymond Buchanan has resigned from the hospital board?'

'Er – yes. He has.' Alice fiddled with a pearl pendant at her throat, the subject evidently an uncomfortable one.

'The scandal last year affected him badly, and he's not in the best of health.'

'Raymond Buchanan?' William narrowed his eyes and stared off, as if searching his memory. 'Wasn't he involved in that child trafficking ring you single-handedly broke up last winter, Flora?' His grin was half-teasing, though the look in his eyes said he wanted to know more.

'I cannot take *all* the credit,' Flora said. 'Had Alice not brought their activities to my attention, no one would have known about those missing children.'

'And yet you omitted having found Alice again after all these years, Flora?' The accusation in William's eyes made Flora's insides shrivel. 'We spent Christmas together, and you said not a word.'

'I'm sorry. I should have explained,' Flora began. 'But Alice didn't want you to know everything at once. We thought—'

'Please don't blame Flora,' Alice gripped Flora's forearm, silencing her. 'I asked her to wait until I could tell you myself. Flora thought I was dead and to discover I had run away came as a shock. I doubt she's forgiven me.'

'Oh, no, I...' Flora stammered, but Alice was close to the truth.

'I understand, Flora.' William's eyes darkened. 'When you discovered I was your father and not Riordan Maguire, you couldn't look at me for weeks.'

'We're both responsible for that deception.' Alice massaged Flora's hand on the table. 'I contacted Riordan several times asking to see Flora, but he always refused. He was legally her father with the law on his side.' Alice blinked away sudden tears. 'I'm so glad to have found her again.'

'I knew who you were that first day at St Philomena's Hospital.' Flora turned her hand over and laced her fingers with Alice's. 'The hard part was telling you, William. The purpose of this dinner was to bring you together.' A plan more successful than she imagined. Maybe too successful.

'I told her not everyone likes surprises, but she can be stubborn.' Bunny pushed his plate away and relaxed back in his chair.

'Are you and Mr Buchanan close, Alice?' William could not prevent a glint of possessiveness in his eyes.

'It's – complicated.' Alice took a moment to gather herself. 'When I first came to London, Raymond and his wife became my family; even more so since his wife died. When the scandal of the child trafficking got into the newspapers, and he discovered his son was... that is—' she broke off, unwilling to voice the words. 'As a nurse, he asked me to care for him. He is fatigued a good deal and the slightest exertion leaves him breathless. I'm sure the stress of the court case made it worse.'

'Sounds like angina,' Bunny interjected, attracting enquiring looks his way. 'My father had it.' Bunny shrugged. 'The medics couldn't agree on how to treat it, and it killed him eventually. The workings of the human heart are still a mystery.'

'Forgive me asking, Alice,' William began, 'but how did a respectable man like Buchanan become involved in the dire practice of child abduction?'

Flora cast her mind back to the dramatic events that reunited her and her mother. A ruthless group of people sold children from impoverished families to childless couples in North America with the promise of a better future.

Alice recruited Flora's help and after her maid, Sally, was kidnapped, they searched the deserted Tower Subway, which led to a frantic race on the River Thames to rescue the children before they were shipped abroad.

'He believed they were helping families emigrate and Raymond cooperated to keep his son Victor out of prison. He became suspicious, but it had gone too far. His complicity still haunts him.'

'You're quite the heroine, Flora,' William said. 'Enough of sad things. What hostess allows her guest's glass to remain empty?' He held up his wineglass.

'Oh, of course, I'm, sorry.' Flora scrambled to her feet, but Bunny beat her to it and retrieved the wine bottle from the sideboard. Unsmiling, he refilled everyone's glass but his own, his expression tense as if his thoughts were elsewhere.

'Are you sure there's nothing wrong?' Flora whispered when he resumed his seat. 'You've been miles away since you arrived.'

'Um, no, it's nothing important. Now.' He rubbed his hands together. 'Who's for pudding?'

Flora tugged her shawl tighter around her exposed shoulders and shivered in the cool wind gusting across the porch. It had been a warm day for April, but as night drew in, splatters of rain streaked the windows from air cooled to a wintry chill. She raised a hand to wave at Alice who occupied the seat beside William in his two-seater Spyker motor car.

'She's a real beauty, isn't she?' Bunny sighed.

'Indeed, she is.' Flora leaned into her husband's one-armed hug. 'I hope I'll look as good when I reach Alice's age.'

'I meant William's motor car.'

Flora tutted, nudging him. 'Our Berliet is perfectly adequate and far more practical. Besides, there would be no need for a chauffeur and you would have to discharge Timms.'

'Hmm, I hadn't thought of that.' He followed the gleaming green vehicle with his eyes until it disappeared round the corner.

Timms, a keen motor enthusiast and former employee of the solicitors Bunny worked for had been jailed unfairly for fraud. Prompted by guilt he could not get him off, Bunny installed him in the mews behind the house where the two of them spent hours tinkering with the engine of Bunny's beloved motor car; more like friends than employer and chauffeur. In their brown coveralls and with their heads ducked beneath the metal hood, even Flora was hard put to tell them apart.

'Well, despite the host's unexplained absence, I think the evening was a success.' Flora returned to the relative warmth of the hallway.

'I've already apologised for that.' Bunny tightened his arm round her and nuzzled her hair just above her ear before guiding her back into the sitting room, where Stokes was clearing away the coffee cups and empty brandy glasses. 'You realise that bringing them together without warning like that could have gone horribly wrong? Suppose they had harboured some long-buried resentment in the intervening years, or worse, didn't like the person they had each become?'

'That didn't occur to me,' Flora lied. 'I was confident they would behave as if the last twenty years had never happened.'

'William couldn't keep the smile off his face, and all those long looks.' Bunny chuckled.

'He was like a young boy with his first tendre.'

'On which has produced a grown-up daughter.' Flora summoned a distracted smile, her thoughts still on William and whether he was likely to be recalled to Russia if the situation there worsened.

'Stokes,' Bunny halted the butler on his way out with a loaded tray. 'Before you retire, would you kindly bring us some fresh coffee?'

'Of course, sir.' Stokes bowed and left.

'None for me, thank you.' Flora frowned. 'Any more and I won't sleep. After such a long day, I would have thought cocoa would have been more appropriate?'

'Coffee.' Bunny's eyes hardened, and he caressed her shoulder. 'I have a feeling we might need it.'

'You've been very distracted tonight,' Flora dragged her thoughts back to the present. 'Are you sure something isn't bothering you?'

'Don't change the subject. We were talking about

your parents.' Bunny took the place beside Flora on the sofa. 'I sensed you became somewhat tense towards the end of the evening.'

She sighed, hoping he had not noticed. 'It might seem selfish, but they appeared so delighted to be together again that the past – my past – was overlooked. Why did Riordan tell me Alice, or Lily as she was known, had died?'

'She left him, Flora. Which must have hurt his pride. As a widower, it meant no one would whisper about him behind his back.'

Flora silently acknowledged he was probably right. Her mother had married the head butler at Cleeve Abbey to save her reputation when she had fallen pregnant by William. The family had made it clear a marriage between Lily and William was out of the question and sent him abroad. Too young and overawed by their respective families to fight back, they had both obeyed. However, William pined thousands of miles away and Lily was miserable until she could stand no more and ran away, leaving Flora behind.

Riordan Maguire had adored Flora and despite Lily's urging, had refused to let her see Flora again, preferring to explain away her absence by spinning a story acceptable for a child.

'Wouldn't it be wonderful if William and Alice found happiness together after all this time? It's just —' she broke off, smothering a yawn at the reappearance of Stokes who set down a tray in front of them, wished them both good evening and withdrew.

'I'm going up to bed. Enjoy your coffee.' As she rose to leave, he grasped her hand and tugged her gently onto the squab.

'Wait a moment, Flora. There's something I need to tell you. Well, more show you, actually.'

'Something which explains why you were late for dinner?' She yawned again, but complied.

'In a way.' He stood; one hand held palm downwards in a command for her to stay. 'Wait here. I'll be back in a moment.'

'Can't whatever it is keep until morn—' she broke off with a sigh as she addressed an empty room.

More for something to do than a desire for some coffee. She poured herself a cup and stirred in milk, the gentle ticking of silver against china the only sound in the room as the hot, aromatic coffee triggered her senses.

The evening she anticipated with such pleasure should have been one for celebration, but observing her parents smile at each other across her dining table, all her unresolved feelings resurfaced.

The knowledge that Lily Maguire had cared for other people's children in a London hospital while her own daughter grew up without her remained a cruel irony. That Alice had instigated contact again went some way to compensating for the past, although a deep-seated antipathy persisted for all the lost years in between.

Flora's childhood had been far from unhappy with Riordan Maguire, who had always been a loving parent, if an uncompromising one. His halo had slipped slightly when she discovered he had known Lily had been alive all this time. He had even destroyed the letters she sent him pleading for forgiveness. Letters Flora had known nothing about, but which Alice had told her she had written to see her again. That he had been killed protecting Flora made it impossible to harbour bitterness against him, but also meant he could never explain.

At the sound of the rear hall door closing, she returned her cup to its saucer. The smile she had summoned in anticipation of Bunny's return faded instantly when she realised he was not alone. A young man with light brown hair hovered a pace behind him, his head down and shoulders hunched as if unsure of his welcome. He lifted his head, his eyes meeting Flora's for a second before he ducked away, his cheeks flushed red.

'Eddy!' A shaft of delighted recognition ran through her and she leapt to her feet, crossed the room in two strides. 'How lovely to see you! But why are you here this late? Has something happened?'

'Hello, Flora.' Eddy slumped onto the centre squab of the closest sofa, ignoring the fact she remained standing. The cheeky-faced boy she had been a governess to five years before had changed into a handsome young man. His angular frame had filled out into a sturdy athletic build, and his eyes, so similar to his Uncle William's, were red-rimmed. His suit was rumpled as if he had slept in it, his collar half undone and his hair stuck up on one side.

'Eddy, whatever's wrong?' Flora dropped her arms, mildly hurt he had avoided her welcome hug. 'Has something happened? Is it your parents?'

'As far as we know, Lord and Lady Trent are still enjoying their trip to New York,' Bunny answered for him.

'Oh, yes, of course.' Flora frowned as she recalled the Trents had sailed to America two months before to see their eldest daughter, Lady Amelia, and her American husband for the first time since her marriage five years before. They planned to bring them back to England with their children for the summer.

'Eddy arrived at my office this afternoon.' Bunny lifted the coffee pot towards Eddy in enquiry, but was waved away. 'He wasn't making much sense at first, so I sat him down with a brandy until he grew calmer and could tell his story.' Bunny poured a cup for himself and strolled to the mantelpiece, taking an occasional sip. 'Knowing William would be here tonight, I felt it wise to take him to the chauffeur's room until he and Alice had left.'

'What story, Eddy?' Flora eased down onto the seat beside him, her arm loosely wrapped round his stiff shoulders. 'What has happened?' And why wouldn't he want his Uncle William to know he was in London?

'My name is Ed.' He adjusted his jacket flaps and loosened his tie, possibly to disguise the fact his lip trembled when he spoke. 'I'm nineteen. Too old to be called by my nursery name.'

'Ed then.' Worry knotted Flora's insides as she waited for him to speak.

'Go on, Ed,' Bunny prompted when he stayed silent. 'Tell Flora exactly what you told me, Ed. Take your time and don't leave anything out.'

'I... I got bored at Cleeve Abbey with everyone

away,' Ed began, then swallowed. 'Term doesn't start for a couple of weeks, so I planned to spend a few days in town at my sister Jocasta's. You know, take in a show with a few chums, maybe.' He shrugged, as if the idea seemed nonsensical now. 'Anyway, I took the afternoon train from Cheltenham and got into a compartment with another chap.'

'What chap?' Flora asked, impatient for him to get to the point.

Bunny shushed her, and pointed his coffee cup at Ed, prompting him to continue.

'We chatted for most of the journey.' Ed rocked on his chair, his hands clenched between his knees. 'Then he fell asleep. Just dozing, you know. Maybe I did too, I can't be sure. When the train arrived at Paddington, I shook him. Told him it was time to get off, but he didn't wake up.' He massaged his forehead with one hand. 'The guard arrived and said we had to leave the train. He tried to shake the man to wake him, but he did not respond. I tried to explain he must be ill and I had already tried that, but he cut me off. He said he was dead.'

'What?' Flora brought a hand to her throat. 'What could have happened to him?'

'I don't know. The guard demanded what I had

done, then shouted for the police. Everything went haywire after that with lots of shouting.'

'That's outrageous!' Flora said, angry that anyone could make such an assumption. 'How could they think *you* were responsible?'

'I tried to tell him it wasn't me, but the guard refused to listen. I – I made a run for it.'

'You ran away?' Flora stared at him as the full horror of his situation sank in.

'I didn't know what else to do.' He cupped his chin in his hands, his elbows on his knees.

Flora bit her lip as a pang of nostalgia for the boy she had once cared for arose. 'I couldn't go to Jocasta's, and you were the first people I thought of who wouldn't call the police.'

'We might have no choice, Ed,' Bunny said gravely. 'We cannot pretend—'

'I'm glad you came to us, Eddy. I mean Ed.' Flora interrupted her husband with a warning look. 'First things first. Will Jocasta raise the alarm when you don't arrive?'

'I doubt it.' He kept his head down, muffling his voice. 'I didn't tell her I was coming, but she never minds when I turn up whenever I feel like it.'

Flora sighed, relieved she would not have to deal with a frantic Lady Jocasta demanding they instigate a search for her lost brother. 'Bunny's right, Ed. We must call the police.'

'No!' He jerked his head up and stared at each of them. 'They'll lock me up. I know they will.'

'See it from their point of view.' Bunny stroked his chin with one hand, something he always did when thinking. 'A dead man in a compartment, you bent over him with blood on your hand – literally. Think how it must have looked?'

'Blood?' Flora gasped. 'What blood? You didn't mention any blood.'

'Ed said there was a small amount on his shirt,' Bunny said.

'Not much,' Ed qualified. 'Only a spot no bigger than a half-crown. I didn't notice it until I touched him.' Ed rubbed the palm of his right hand with the fingers of his left, as if rubbing an imaginary stain.

'This man didn't die of natural causes then?' Flora said.

'Which is what I don't understand.' Ed's voice was almost a whine. 'I was in the compartment the entire time and didn't see a thing.'

'You must have seen *something* if you were the only one there.' She darted a look at Bunny, who gave a warning shake of his head. 'Sorry, I didn't mean to sound accusing, but that doesn't make sense.'

Had Ed been responsible, he wouldn't have tried to wake the man. He would have simply left the train at the first opportunity, not wait for a guard to come along and challenge him. She had known Ed his whole life and there was not a malicious bone in his body.

'The guard made an assumption based purely on what he saw,' Bunny said, his arms crossed over his chest. 'Or thought he saw. Ed, I'm afraid you made the situation worse by bolting.'

'You're not in a courtroom now, Bunny.' Flora narrowed her eyes at him. 'This is Ed we're talking about, not a common criminal.'

'I *can't* be accused of murder.' Ed's voice rose in panic. 'Even if I'm found innocent, the accusation will follow me for the rest of my life.' He rubbed his hands up and down his thighs again. 'I'm to take a seat in the House of Lords one day.'

'The situation is hardly favourable for the young man either,' Bunny snapped. 'He's dead.'

'Bunny!' Flora glared at him, which he returned with a, 'what can you expect?' look.

'Oh, Lord.' Ed stopped rocking and chewed at a thumbnail. 'I cannot believe this is happening. I didn't hurt him, honestly!'

'We know you didn't!' Flora smoothed his messy

brown hair down on one side. 'What can you tell us about the dead man?'

'What do you mean?' Ed straightened; his tone was sharp.

'Describe him. Tall, short, fair or dark-haired?'

'Ah, I see, yes.' He relaxed again, chewing his bottom lip as he gave her question some thought. 'Um, about my age, an inch taller perhaps. Brown hair, but darker than mine. His eyes were brown too, again darker. He wore a black suit but no waistcoat. I remember because the red bloodstain against his white shirt was such a shock.'

'Do you have any idea what could have caused the blood?' Flora asked.

'Did I overlook the dagger sticking out of his chest do you mean?' Ed curled his upper lip. His fear had apparently not spoiled his capacity for sarcasm. 'No. Just the red spot.'

'This stain, was it wet or dry?' Bunny asked.

'Er... damp, but looked fresh.'

'Could he have been ill?' Flora asked. 'Consumption makes you spit blood, doesn't it?'

'How should I know?' Ed snapped with barely restrained impatience. Or was it panic? 'He seemed healthy to me.'

Chastised, Flora eased away, giving Bunny a 'you try' look.

Bunny replaced his cup on the table and took the seat on the sofa beside Ed. 'Let's go back a bit. Did this chap introduce himself?'

'Yes. He said his name was Leo. Leo Thompson.' Ed worried a loose strand of cotton protruding from a button on his cuff.

'Now we're getting somewhere.' Bunny kept his voice low. 'You said you talked during the journey?'

'Sort of.' Ed shrugged. 'Trivial stuff, mostly. Polite passing of the time, that sort of thing.'

'Did he say where he was going in town and why?' Bunny asked.

'Um... I'm not sure.'

'It was a two-hour journey, Ed. You must have talked about *something* more than the weather.' Flora tried to stay calm.

'We didn't mention the weather,' Ed said dully.

Flora bit back a sharp remark, losing patience. She admired Bunny's calm tone, but then, as a lawyer, he was used to extracting information from witnesses. Left to her, she would have shaken the details out of Ed.

'Did Leo say anything which might show where he came from?' Bunny asked.

'He mentioned the shop.'

'Which shop, Ed?' Flora took a deep breath to calm her growing frustration.

'His mother owns Thompson's. Not that I've ever been there.' His expression implied the notion was ridiculous.

'You mean the haberdashery in the Promenade?' Flora asked. 'Why didn't you say that before?'

Ed shrugged.

'He was a local to Cheltenham then, which is definitely something we can work with.' Bunny nodded, thoughtful. 'There were just the two of you in the carriage for the entire journey?'

'Yes. We had the compartment to ourselves.'

'You came first class?' Flora asked.

'Well, of course!' Ed glared at her as if affronted. 'How else?'

'How crass of me to suggest otherwise!' She rolled her eyes, but was intrigued. Thompson's was a medium-sized establishment selling needlework supplies and fabrics, not a vast emporium. Would a haberdasher travel first class?

'I'm sorry to be vague.' Ed held his hands out, palms upwards. Then he straightened, eyes wide and put a hand to his forehead. 'Blast! I completely forgot.' He stared at each of them. 'I left my suitcase on the overhead rack in the compartment. My name and address are inside.'

'Oh, Ed.' Flora closed her eyes and tried not to sigh. 'Maybe someone won't make the connection and take it to the lost property office?'

'I doubt it.' Bunny raised a cynical eyebrow. 'The police will most likely have it by now.' He got up to check the clock on the mantelpiece. 'It's after midnight, so I'll telephone Inspector Maddox first thing tomorrow. Hopefully, he'll be sympathetic.'

'Do you have to?' Ed pleaded.

'He knows us, Ed, so he'll help you,' Flora said with more confidence than she felt.

'Maddox is our best chance at the moment.' Bunny smiled reassuringly. 'I'm not a criminal lawyer, at least not yet, but I might know someone in my firm who can help.'

'I'll need a lawyer?' Ed swallowed nervously.

'As a precaution only.' Bunny's tone remained gentle, but doubt filled his eyes. 'And, Flora, don't mention to the inspector we've been going through Ed's story, or he'll think we've coached him. His version needs to sound spontaneous.'

'All I care about is helping Ed,' Flora insisted. 'What Maddox might think is the least of my concerns.'

'Why?' Ed's frown held suspicion. 'What *does* he think of you?'

'That I'm a meddling amateur.' Flora sniffed. 'Worse, a female, one of the most reprehensible kind.' Flora enjoyed an amicable, yet competitive relationship with the inspector, who issued regular warnings about the perils of meddling in police business, while benefitting from her investigative skills.

'Actually, he thinks a good deal of you, Flora.' Bunny shoved both hands in his pockets, grinning. 'The night you were locked inside that barge by the child smugglers with Ruth Lazarus, Maddox became frantic at the idea you might be hurt.'

'He has an odd way of showing it.' Flora muttered, sceptical. The notion of the handsome, if supercilious, Inspector Maddox being sentimental had never occurred to her. She stared up at Bunny through her lashes. 'Was he really worried about me?'

'It took two constables to restrain him from hitting the woman when they finally caught her. What do *you* think?'

'Really? And how many did it take to stop you from dashing to my aid?'

'Oh, at least five. But I put up a good fight.'

'I'm still here, you know!' Ed's impatient protest cut across them. 'And exactly how many policemen do the two of you know?' He shrugged off Flora's comforting arm and split a fearful look between them.

'Please don't tell Papa what's happened?'

'When do your parents return from New York?' Bunny asked, ignoring his request.

'I'm not sure, though I expect they'll be back in time to arrange the house party next month. Mama likes to fuss over every detail, even though the staff do all the work.'

'That gives us a week to ten days.' Flora had almost forgotten about the house party at Cleeve Abbey to celebrate Lady Amelia's first summer in England since her marriage. Lady Emerald, their second daughter, would also be there with her husband and two young sons, as well as the youngest, Lady Jocasta, with her husband, Jeremy, and their toddler daughter, Mabel. Flora had been looking forward to it, not least because it would give her a chance to show off their baby son, Arthur, now a year old and taking his first steps.

'You look as worn out as I feel, Ed. We'll let you get some sleep and we'll talk again in the morning.' Flora eased him to his feet. 'Take the blue guest room. You know where it is. There hasn't been time to air it properly, but I'll ask Stokes to make sure you have plenty of linens.' Reverting to practical matters distracted her briefly from Ed's frightening situation.

Bunny opened the convex glass door of the clock on the mantelpiece at his elbow. 'Flora's right, Ed. All this might look less daunting in the morning.' He inserted the key into the hole in the centre of the face and wound the mechanism; the sound of the ratchets clicking into place was always his last routine task of the day.

'Thank you, both of you,' Ed said as they entered the hall. 'It's been such an awful day. Nor did I relish spending the night in the chauffeur's room, either,' he added, answering Flora's question of where he had been hiding all evening. 'Timms was obliging, but he's too tall for that sofa, his knees barely fit inside the arms.' It wouldn't have occurred to Edward, Viscount Trent, to volunteer to take the sofa and leave the bed to the chauffeur.

'You go on up,' Bunny whispered, hanging back. 'I'll go through my list of criminal lawyers and select a couple. Just in case.' He squeezed Flora's arm before he strode along the hall to his study.

As Ed disappeared onto the landing, Flora lifted her foot onto the first step to follow, and caught sight of her reflection in the hall mirror. The dress Bunny had said flattered her earlier made her skin sallow and her eyes dull with anxiety. Unless they could find out exactly what had happened to Leo Thompson on that train, it seemed likely the police would accept the most obvious explanation. In which case, she and Bunny were Ed's only chance.

Sighing, she arched her neck, easing the stiffness that had worsened since Ed's arrival, and dragged her feet wearily up to her room.

3

Ed lacked his usual good humour at breakfast the next morning, with dragging feet and eyes as dull as brown paint. He wore the same suit he had on the day before over a freshly laundered and ironed shirt Stokes had obligingly fetched from Bunny's tailor that morning. Flora told Stokes Ed had lost his luggage and sent the butler shopping for fresh shirts, socks, and undergarments. At least Ed would look respectable for his interview with the police.

'How are you this morning?' Flora asked, knowing the answer. 'Did you get any sleep?'

'Not much, though I must have dropped off, eventually.' He dragged out a chair, removed a magazine from beneath his arm, and slapped it onto the table.

'I'm starving. I hardly ate anything yesterday.' He continued on to the sideboard and helped himself from the row of bain-maries lined up.

'This inspector chap.' Ed swiped a bread roll from the basket, breaking it open on his side plate. 'Is he a straight arrow? Will he hear my story then arrest me, anyway?'

'We'll have to wait and see, Ed,' Flora replied. 'But he's smarter than he looks, so be respectful and he'll give you a fair hearing.'

'Flora's right,' Bunny entered the dining room in time to hear this last remark. 'Maddox won't do anything until he's sure of the facts.' He patted Ed's shoulder on his way to the sideboard where he loaded a plate with fried bacon and tomatoes.

'Did you get through to the inspector?' Flora accepted the kiss he pressed to her cheek on his way back to the table.

'I did. He knew all about the body on the train but has agreed to keep an open mind until he hears what Ed has to say.' Bunny scraped his chair closer to the table and opened the neatly folded copy of *The Times* Stokes had set beside his place. 'Ed, have you remembered anything else from yesterday?' he asked behind the broadsheet.

'Like what?' Ed replied, setting a plate of miniature sausages and scrambled eggs on the table.

'Anything,' Flora said. 'The smallest detail could make a difference.'

'I've told you everything.' He speared a sausage with his fork, twisting it from side to side. 'Are these the real things? They're tiny.'

Flora smiled, relieved Ed could still be distracted by food. 'They're called chipolatas. They come from Italy, or France?' She shrugged. 'I doubt it matters. Mrs Cope likes them because they cook much quicker than ordinary sausages.'

Ed peered at the fork before shoving the meat into his mouth and chewed. 'They're good. A little spicy too.'

Bunny clicked his tongue, causing Ed to look up quickly from his plate, a bulge in one cheek and his eyes huge. 'I'm afraid you've made the newspapers.' He folded it to the page and slid it across the table.

'I don't want to read it.' Ed's knuckles whitened on his cutlery.

'Let me see.' Flora slid the paper towards her, where beneath a heading of 'Police Seek Killer Who Fled Scene at Paddington', a paragraph outlined what they already knew. The report had not included Ed's name, only that a young man had been pursued inside the station by the Transport Police but fled the scene. An appeal had been made for witnesses to come forward. She flicked a look at Bunny, then laid down the paper. 'I suggest we change the subject.'

Bunny poured himself coffee, then held the pot up in enquiry. 'What shall we talk about?'

'We have a wedding to go to later this week,' Flora said. 'You remember my friend, Lydia Grey, Ed? She's marrying Harry Flynn, at last.'

'Lydia,' Ed tried the word out on his tongue. 'Ah, I remember now. She's the schoolteacher who helps you with your crime-fighting exploits.'

'A slight exaggeration, but essentially correct.' Flora recalled Ed had sported a permanent blush when they had been introduced that had lasted most of the afternoon.

'Have I met this Harry chap?' Ed asked.

'I doubt it. He was Evangeline Lange's fiancé, the young woman whose murder Flora and Lydia investigated two years ago,' Bunny said. 'Harry and Lydia were always friends, but since then they have grown close. Lydia has also been made headmistress at the school after the former incumbent was imprisoned for spying.'

'What an exciting life you lead, Flora.' Ed attempted a smile which did not reach his eyes. 'Better than having to teach me about the repeal of the Corn Laws.'

'It's a shame Lydia will have to give it up.' Bunny kept his attention on the broadsheet. 'I hear she's done an excellent job at the academy.'

'Actually, she doesn't plan to,' Flora said. 'When they return from their honeymoon in Ambleside, she intends to continue running the school. All with Harry's approval, I might add.'

'The Lake District in April?' Ed crumbled the remains of his bread roll in his fingers, none of which reached his mouth. 'Huh, I'll wager it will rain every day.'

'Sounds like a perfect honeymoon to me,' Bunny muttered, raising the paper again. 'Harry had recently taken an interest in the Labour Party.'

'Your friends are socialists?' Ed asked, a mock horrified expression on his face.

'Horrible, isn't it?' Bunny winked at him. 'He might even stand for Parliament one day.'

'Not the Belgravia constituency,' Flora said, smiling. 'I think it's admirable that he has developed an interest in the plight of the working man. Most young men in his position simply enjoy their privilege without giving the fate of others a thought. Lydia is very proud of him. Oh, and Lydia has invited

William and Alice to the wedding. Separately, of course.'

'Hmm. Be careful, Flora,' Bunny peered at her over the top of his newspaper. 'This scheme to get your parents together again could backfire.'

'I don't agree. The more time William and Alice spend together, the better. And talking of weddings,' she added quickly, 'Sally is officially walking out with Abel Cain.'

'Who?' Ed frowned. 'Ah, you mean the man moun- tain who has to turn sideways to get through a door?' His lips twitched, but not enough to be called a smile as he reached for the toast rack. 'They must make an unusual couple, what with your maid being so tiny.'

'Sally's determined to keep predatory females at bay until she can get him down the aisle.' Flora slid the butter dish towards Ed, dismayed at the sight of his bitten fingernails.

'Any particular predatory female?' Bunny snapped his newspaper, his eyes sparkling behind his spectacles.

'Yes, the new housemaid,' Flora said, aware she was talking for the sake of it, but it was an improvement in tense silence. 'She has this soft voice and the face of a china doll, which prompts men to rush round her with offers of help. I employed Abel to work in the garden and Sally caught her talking to him. Now she comes to me at least once a day with some spurious complaint. The most recent being the girl hums too loudly. I'm sure the poor creature doesn't understand what she's done wrong.'

'What's Abel doing with your garden?' Ed dipped the butter knife into the jam and spread a thick layer of blackcurrant conserve on his toast. 'If you can call a handkerchief of grass behind a seven-foot-high brick wall a garden.'

'It's more than adequate for a town garden,' Flora replied, mildly hurt as she discreetly picked globs of butter out of the conserve. 'I wanted a safe place for Arthur to play, and somewhere to sit on sunny days.'

'Safe?' Ed rolled his eyes as he took a large bite of his toast. 'There's nothing more dangerous there than a lily pond.' He snorted. 'My playground was a thousand acres of countryside littered with plough shares, bad-tempered cows and unbroken ponies.'

'And you've not lived until you've fallen out of a hayloft,' Bunny added.

Flora rolled her eyes at the men's mutual burst of loud laughter and went back to her breakfast. She knew when she was being ganged up on.

'I see you have a copy of *The Graphic* there, Ed.'

Bunny pointed to the magazine beside Ed's plate. 'Are you reading anything of interest?'

'What? Oh, yes.' He blinked as if he had never seen it before. 'Timms lent it to me. There's an article about an American who has brought an entire dinosaur to London. It's called the Diplodocus.' He opened the magazine to the page and slid it across the table towards him. 'There's an impressive drawing of it there. They say it's the largest animal ever found.'

'The skeleton isn't real, Ed.' Bunny left his chair and strolled to the sideboard to re-load his plate. 'Andrew Carnegie had a replica made which he is sending on a world tour.'

'I'd love to see it in the British Museum while I'm here. I don't suppose there's much chance now,' Ed muttered under his breath.

'It isn't one dinosaur either.' Flora was determined not to allow the atmosphere to deteriorate into gloom and despondency. 'They put it together from five which were dug up in Arizona.'

'Trust you to know that.' Bunny raised an admiring eyebrow as he returned to his seat. 'Anyway, there's still time, Ed. It won't be open to the public until later this month. You can see it then.'

'If I'm still a free man,' Ed mumbled.

'Stop it, Ed. I refuse to let you talk that way!' Flora snapped.

A persistent buzz began inside her head. The thought of having to inform Earl Trent his son had been arrested for murder brought a sour taste to her mouth.

'We'll sort out this dreadful affair. I promise.'

4

Stokes appeared at the dining room door and coughed discreetly into a fist. 'Detective Inspector Maddox is here, sir, madam. He claims you're expecting him.'

'We are indeed, Stokes. Would you show him into the study?' Bunny's gaze held Flora's over the napkin he used to wipe his mouth. 'Goodness, he didn't waste any time.'

Between bites of toast, Ed muttered something Flora couldn't hear.

'All you have to do is tell the truth.' She scraped back her chair and prepared to follow Bunny.

'That's what I *have* been doing.'

'And preferably not in that tone of voice.' He showed no signs of moving. Sighing, Flora tucked her arm through his and hauled him to his feet, propelling him to where Bunny shook hands with the policeman at the study door.

'Shall we go in?' Bunny ushered them into the masculine room and closed the door on a curious Stokes.

Flora had forgotten how handsome Inspector Maddox was, although why she should think policeman could not be good-looking escaped her. Slightly taller than Bunny, he was well built: broad shouldered but carried no surplus fat; a square-jawed face had expressive brown eyes which turned to flint in an instant.

He greeted Flora with a curt, but respectful nod and removed his bowler hat, leaving a ridge in his wavy black hair above his ears. 'How nice to see you again, Mrs Harrington.'

Flora summoned a polite smile. 'Allow me to introduce you to Edward, Viscount Trent.'

'I gather this young man is the cause of all the trouble?' The inspector eyed Ed with open suspicion. 'Viscount, eh?' His eyes narrowed. 'We haven't had one of those in the cells for a while.' At Flora's strangled protest, he held up his hand. 'Just my little joke.'

Ed muttered a vague greeting and, after a brief handshake, thrust his hands into his pockets.

Inspector Maddox reached for a tan suitcase at his feet – bound in brass and sporting the initials 'EV' in gold cursive script above the lock – and heaved it onto Bunny's desk with no regard for the polished surface.

'I rescued it from the transport police.' He aimed a sceptical look in Ed's direction. 'We had to search it, of course, but I assure you everything is still there.'

'Thank you,' Ed muttered through gritted teeth, but made no move to touch it.

'I'm sure you'll discover this was simply an unfortunate misunderstanding by the guards at Paddington, Inspector.' Flora took one of the pair of upholstered chairs next to the fireplace and gestured him into the one opposite. 'One we're confident you'll be able to sort out.'

'That's for me to decide, Mrs Harrington.' He flicked open one side of his jacket and removed a notebook from an inside pocket. 'I suggest you sit down, young ma— my lord. This could take a while.'

Bunny gestured Ed into the empty chair at the desk.

'I'd like to hear what you have to say for yourself about this affair, my lord, before I make anything official,' the inspector's manner set the tone of the coming interview.

'Please drop the "my lord" stuff, or we'll be here

for hours.' Ed's voice was steady, but his hands shook slightly in his lap.

'As you wish.' Maddox cleared his throat, withdrew a pencil from the recess in the notebook, and held it poised above the page. 'Before we begin, I ought to inform you that a post-mortem was carried out last evening and the conclusion was that the young man was stabbed through the heart with a slim-bladed knife.'

Flora suppressed a sigh, her faint hopes for a natural death removed completely.

Ed blanched but made no comment.

'Now, sir,' Maddox continued. 'Kindly start at the beginning and tell me exactly what occurred on the train, whether or not you believe it to be relevant.'

Ed swallowed. 'I... I boarded the early afternoon train to Paddington at Cheltenham Spa and entered a compartment occupied by a man a little older than me.'

'Were you previously acquainted with this man?'

'No. I... I'd never seen him before.' Ed picked at a thumbnail; his eyes averted.

'Did he board the train with you, or was he already in the compartment?'

'He was placing his bag on the overhead rack

when I entered the carriage, so I assume he got on the same time I did.'

'Did the young man give his name?' Maddox continued in a calm monotone Flora found somehow disturbing.

'His name was Leo, Leo Thompson,' Ed replied.

'Did he display nervousness or agitation?'

'No, not that I noticed.' Ed frowned. 'He was reading a book most of the time. Why do you ask?'

'If he was aware someone wanted him dead, he had reason to be worried. Did he keep checking the corridor or jump when someone spoke to him?'

'We were alone in the carriage. I'm sure I would have noticed if he had been nervous. He wasn't.' Ed shrugged.

'Did you and Mr Thompson conduct a conversation? If so, did he instigate it, or did you?'

'*He* did. Although you couldn't call it a conversation. Some children in the next carriage were making an unholy row, er – I mean a noise. He said he hoped their parents would quieten them. I agreed, and we got talking. It was Dickens.' Maddox glanced up at him in enquiry at which Ed added, 'The book.'

'Ah, yes, I see.' Maddox continued to write, though his frown persisted. 'Anything else?'

'Like I told Flora and Bunny, trivial stuff, mostly. I

asked his reason for going to town, but he seemed reluctant to tell me at first.'

'Reluctant in what way?'

'You know. When someone has to think about everything they say before they say it. It was a perfectly ordinary question, but he just mumbled something and went back to his book.'

'Could you hear what he said?'

'Not all of it. Something about "from a spark a fire will flare up", or something like that.' Ed shrugged. 'It made no sense, so I didn't pursue it.'

'I see. Did he mention where he lived or anything about his family?'

'No, he didn't.'

'Ed, tell him about the shop.' Flora nudged him gently.

'What shop would this be?' Maddox glanced up; his pencil poised above the page.

'He mentioned his mother ran a shop in the Promenade in Cheltenham.' Ed's neck flushed a deep red and he fiddled with a shirt cuff.

'Mr Thompson was a local gentleman then?' Maddox resumed writing. 'You might have mentioned that at the start.'

'Sorry,' Ed murmured. 'I forgot.'

'Why would Ed harm a stranger on a train?' Flora blurted.

'Might I proceed?' Maddox raised an eyebrow at Flora. Chastened, she resolved to show more restraint, marvelling at how Bunny stayed so detached.

'There was something!' Ed held up a finger. 'Mr Thompson was going to interview for a job.' He shook his head slowly. 'How did that slip my mind?'

'Never mind, Ed. Did he say where?' Flora asked.

'A job in a department store. Boodles or Beamish.' Ed rubbed his flattened hands rhythmically along his thighs, then his eyes widened and he inhaled sharply. 'Beadles. That was it! I don't know where.'

'Did anyone else enter the compartment during the journey?' Maddox added another line of scrawl to the page.

'No, I've already said. There were only the two of us. Oh, there was the waiter who served tea, but he stayed only a moment or two.'

'Was this at the beginning of the journey or part way through?'

'Um, it was just after we left Reading.'

Maddox consulted his notebook. 'Which would make it roughly half an hour before the train arrived at Paddington.' He rested his elbow on his thigh and brought his face close to Ed's. 'Think about the time between the waiter's departure and your arrival at Paddington? You drank the tea he brought. Then what did you do?'

'Did Mr Thompson drink the tea?' Flora asked, adding, 'Which isn't relevant, as we know he wasn't poisoned.'

'Not necessarily.' Maddox raised one eyebrow. 'The killer might have drugged Mr Thompson, thus rendering him incapable of fighting back when he stabbed him.'

'I didn't think of that.' Flora smiled in apology and relaxed back in her chair.

'Which is why *I'm* the detective, Mrs Harrington.' His eyes glinted with mischief, which reminded Flora that her contribution, though tolerated, was rarely required. 'Perhaps we would get a lot further if you would allow *me* to do the questioning?'

'Yes, of course. I'm sorry.'

Bunny directed a sympathetic smile her way, together with a brief wink which helped lift her spirits.

'Did Mr Thompson leave the carriage?' the Inspector continued. 'To go to the facilities, perhaps?'

'No, not as I recall.' Ed frowned, then immediately his eyes widened. '*I* did though. After I had drunk my tea, which tasted fine by the way, I went along to the lavatory. It was occupied, so I had to wait in the cor-

ridor for a few minutes. No one came past me and entered the compartment. If they had, I would have seen
them.'

'How long were you away from the carriage?'

'About ten minutes. I stood in the corridor for a
while and watched the scenery. Just to stretch my legs
after sitting still for so long.'

'What about the cups?'

'Beg pardon?' Ed's brow furrowed.

'You said the waiter brought you tea,' Maddox said
slowly, as if addressing a child. 'Do you recall him returning to collect the dirty crockery?'

'I – I don't know. I suppose he must have done.
The cups weren't there when we reached Paddington.
I didn't really notice.'

'Did you see any of your fellow passengers apart
from Mr Thompson and the children in the next
carriage?'

'We didn't see the children, we only heard them.
There was a couple in the carriage next door who
sounded as if they were arguing.'

'Could you hear what they were saying?'

'Not really.' Ed tugged at his collar, easing it away
from his throat. 'Is it important?'

'At this stage, sir, *everything* is important,' Maddox

insisted. 'Now about this argument – exactly what did you hear?'

'A man and a woman's voices. They weren't shouting, so I couldn't make out the words. More like intense indistinct murmurs, but it didn't last long.'

'And this occurred when?'

'After I came back from the lavatory.' He frowned. 'No, before. I remember, because I tried to look into the carriage as I passed, but they had the blinds pulled down.'

'I see.' Maddox drew a line through the writing he had just completed. 'Was there anything odd about Mr Thompson when you returned to the compartment?'

'He was dozing. At least I assumed he was. I suppose he could have already been dead, but I cannot be sure.'

Maddox sighed. 'We'll ignore that for the time being, sir. What happened then?'

'The train pulled into the station and I stood up ready to get off. Mr Thompson hadn't moved, so I punched his arm. Only playfully, to tell him it was time to leave the train.' Ed swallowed and licked his lips. 'It sort of flopped to one side and his jacket gaped open. That's when I saw the blood on his shirt.'

'And then?' Maddox prompted.

'The guard arrived. He saw the blood and demanded to know what I had done to him.' His voice dropped to a mumble. 'Stupid man.'

'Perhaps Mr Thompson suffered a nosebleed?' Flora suggested.

'In which case, there would have been some on the inside of his nose and certainly more on his clothing,' Bunny interjected. 'I take it there was none, Inspector?'

'Correct, Mr Harrington.' Maddox's voice held barely restrained patience. 'Exactly the point I had been about to make.' He turned back to Ed. 'Now, sir—'

'What about Mr Thompson's personal effects?' Flora asked, partly to give Ed time to compose himself. 'Did they provide any information about where he was going and why?'

Maddox consulted his notebook. 'He had a first-class rail ticket, a Baedeker's guide with a cross marked against the British Museum, but no forms of identification.'

'He had no money on him?' Bunny asked.

'No, sir.' Maddox raised an eyebrow. 'That detail aroused our suspicions as well. He carried no cheques or money orders. He would certainly have required funds for even a short stay in the city.'

'What about the letter?' Ed straightened in his seat. 'He had one from the hotel. They confirmed his booking and sent him the train ticket.'

'What letter?' Maddox asked, frowning.

'I didn't actually see it, but he patted his pocket, like you do to reassure yourself it's there.'

'And the name of this hotel?' Maddox scribbled something in his notebook.

'Oh, bother, I can't remember other than it was a flower that began with a "B" or maybe a "D".' His eyes dulled. 'I didn't pay much attention. Sorry.'

'Have you considered this might have been a simple robbery which went wrong?' Bunny suggested. 'Mr Thompson might have tried to fight off the robber, who then killed him in the struggle. It would explain the lack of money and possessions.'

'Possibly, sir,' Maddox said. 'It's too early to say.'

'What about Mr Thompson's bag?' Flora asked, encouraged by the fact Maddox had treated Bunny's questions as valid. 'Did you find it on the train?'

'We did.' Maddox consulted his notebook again, but did not explain further. Maddox's eyes narrowed, and he leaned a forearm on his knee, his chin jutted. 'Is there something you've neglected to tell me?'

Ed hesitated, prompting Flora to interject. 'Not everyone is accustomed to being cross-examined, Inspector. I know you reasonably well, and yet I still find you intimidating. Goodness knows how poor Eddy must feel.'

'It's Ed,' he said through gritted teeth. 'And there were other people on the train, so why am *I* the only one being interrogated?'

'Simply, because you were discovered bent over the body and you ran from the Transport Police when they attempted to question you, sir.'

'Question me?' Ed snorted. 'Lynch me more like. They were waving their batons about ready to brain me.'

'One question no one has asked yet,' Bunny began slowly. 'Mr Thompson was stabbed, you say. Was a weapon found?'

'No, Mr Harrington.' Maddox snapped the notebook shut and replaced it in his pocket. 'The tracks within a mile of the station are being searched as we speak. The Transport Police handed the case over to my division as a favour. I've gained you a few days' respite, but they expect an arrest by the end of the week. In the meantime, sir,' he pointed a finger at Ed, 'you'll not leave these premises under any circumstances. Do you understand?'

'What?' Ed's eyes widened. 'I can't stay here! I've things to do in town. I've got theatre tickets and restaurant bookings with friends. My parents are holding a house party in Gloucestershire soon. They'll expect me to be there.'

'Then you'll have to make your excuses. I'll keep you informed, Mr Harrington, Mrs Harrington.' Nodding briefly to each of them, Maddox pushed both palms against his knees and rose. 'Incidentally,' he turned back before reaching the door, 'do you know any Latin? Do the words *Deus Dat Incrementum*, mean anything to you?'

Flora shook her head. Bunny said nothing. Ed fiddled with his shirt cuff, his foot jiggling rhythmically.

'What about *Iskra*?' Maddox again received no response. 'Ah, well, it's probably unimportant. There was a foreign newssheet in Mr Thompson's suitcase. Most likely it was used to line the case, which was fairly old. However, if the young gentleman remembers anything else, I trust you'll contact me?'

'Of course, he'll be sure to let you know straight away. Won't you?' Flora aimed a hard look at Ed, who nodded.

Bunny moved to the bellpull to summon Stokes, who appeared immediately, suggesting he had been hovering outside in the hall.

'Make excuses to my mother?' Ed muttered once

Inspector Maddox had been shown out. 'The man doesn't know what he's saying.'

'At least you got your suitcase back,' Flora said, although his answering shrug implied this was little consolation. 'What do you suggest we do now, Bunny?'

'My guess would be to try to find out more about this Leo Thompson. Specifically, who might have wanted him dead?' He stroked his chin, his brows drawn together. 'We need to start at the beginning.'

'At Paddington Station?' Flora asked. 'There won't be anything to find now, surely?'

'I meant Cheltenham. We'll pay a visit to this shop Ed mentioned.' He glanced at the clock, then back at Flora. 'If we hurry, we'll make the morning train.'

'I'll get my things.' She rose, her gaze on Ed's brooding expression as she left the room, unable to shake off the feeling there was something he had not told them. But what?

5

They caught the Great Western Railway train at Paddington with minutes to spare; while Flora fretted about having no time to spend with Arthur before they left, she promised herself she would make it up to him when she returned. At Cheltenham, Bunny engaged one of the few hansom cabs that idled on the forecourt.

'The town reminds me of London with its classical Georgian town houses set around garden squares,' Bunny said as the driver lowered the wooden flaps over their knees. 'Which is probably why I feel at home in both places.'

'I had forgotten how pretty it is here. I didn't re-alise how much I had missed it,' Flora said as they set off through streets lined with houses built in the Georgian style for which the town was famous. Wrought-iron railings enclosed neat, narrow gardens where daffodils, tulips and purple crocuses proliferated. Ancient trees formed a canopy punctured with shafts of spring sunlight that shone onto the packed dirt road.

'Would you prefer we lived here instead of London?' Bunny rested his hand on the overhead strap as if he expected a more adventurous ride, but the horse maintained a steady, leisurely pace.

'I don't think so, but doesn't everyone have feelings of nostalgia for the place they grew up in and which holds so many memories? Perhaps not for the way it really is, but how you saw it when young?'

'Perhaps I'll buy a house in Wellington Square, where we'll spend our old age with a decrepit Stokes and a bent and grumpy Sally, hosting card parties for retired admirals and colonels.' He nodded to where two old soldiers watched the world go by from a bench set against the Imperial Garden railings.

'I wish you hadn't put that picture into my head.' She gave an involuntary shudder as the hansom entered the wide, tree-lined thoroughfare that was the Promenade. The dirt road contained few vehicles other than a few horse-drawn tradesmen's carts loaded with various goods from cut wood to vegetables, a solitary motor car and a milk van.

'That didn't take long,' Bunny said as their cab pulled into the side of the road. 'There must be a race meeting today, as I don't see many people about.'

'The festival was last month,' Flora said as he handed her down. 'Most Cheltonians would regard this as a normal day. It's not exactly Knightsbridge.'

Thompson's Haberdashery was a narrow shopfront; its façade of grey stonework above a bow window with a frame painted dark navy blue was squeezed between a bookshop and a hardware merchant. A tapestry landscape of the famous Pump Rooms had been propped on a wooden easel in the window, an arrangement of embroidery threads forming an artistic rainbow.

'I'm surprised Cavendish House hasn't put them out of business,' Bunny observed.

The department store spanned several shop fronts; its plate glass frontage, frieze of leaded windows and ornamental wrought-iron balconies as impressive as any seen in London.

'Which makes me feel guilty for not having patronised the smaller businesses in town when I lived here. Lady Trent had an account at Cavendish House, which made it easier to shop there instead. I imagine she still does.'

Flora took his hand to descend into the road, crossing the pavement while he paid the driver. The shop door displayed neither a wreath, nor even a black mourning ribbon.

'It appears news of Leo's death has not yet reached the town,' she whispered as Bunny gave the door a gentle push, their arrival announced by a jangling bell attached to the inside of the door.

Flora allowed her eyes to adjust to the interior gloom as a plump woman in a ruched cream blouse bunched over an ample chest appeared from the rear, her shapeless black skirt falling straight to her ankles.

'May I help you?' A pair of disinterested eyes, like brown pebbles, scrutinised each of them. A waist-high glass-fronted cabinet separated the space in half, behind which shelves lined the walls, each one tightly packed with bolts of fabric. A dark wooden cabinet ran along a wall to one side, filled with square wooden drawers, each with a window showing the buttons, pins and embroidery silks stored inside.

'We were wondering...' Flora halted, unsure how to approach the subject. 'Might we speak to Mrs Thompson?'

'I'm sorry, madam, but I'm afraid Mrs Thompson

is deceased.' The woman's smile faded. 'However, I'm sure I can help with whatever it is you're wanting.'

'I didn't realise. I'm sorry to hear that.' Flora exchanged a perplexed look with Bunny. Had they come all this way for nothing?

'Last Christmas, it was. Such a sad time to lose anyone, don't you agree? Not here though,' she added, as if they might baulk at the idea of a death on the premises. 'She passed away in the hospital on Sandford Road.'

'Was it a long illness?' Flora fondled a silk handkerchief on a display on the counter.

'Oh, she weren't ill. She had an accident with a pair of scissors. She cut her hand. Terrible thing.'

She gestured to a cabinet to one side of the counter where pairs in various sizes were displayed. 'The kind we sell here are very sharp. I've a few scars myself from careless handling, I...' Her puzzled expression dissolved, replaced by a gentle smile. 'Wait, I know you, don't I? Why, it's Miss Flora, Flora Maguire? You used to be governess up at the Abbey?'

'I'm sorry, but I don't—' Flora hesitated, her mind a complete blank.

'You wouldn't remember me, and why should you, dear? I'm Mary Drake, from Clayton village. My eldest daughter used to be a housemaid at the Abbey before she married the head gardener.' Her already ample chest puffed up a little more in pride at her daughter's elevated status.

'Oh, yes, of course, it is. Look dear, it's Mrs Drake,' Flora lied. 'I'm Mrs Harrington now and live in London.'

Bunny looked up from his perusal of an arrangement of gentlemen's gloves. His mouth twitched as he moved on to a display of buttons.

'Come to visit the family up at the Abbey, have you?' she asked. 'I thought they were away?' She leaned an ample hip against the counter, her arms folded as if prepared for a long session.

'No, we're just here for the day.' It appeared the local grapevine remained in excellent order. 'I'm so sorry about Mrs Thompson,' Flora added, surprised at how convincing she sounded. 'You weren't here when it happened?'

'No, dear. I was in Bristol' – which she pronounced, 'Brissol' – 'at my sister's. Sylvia was alone in the shop all day.'

'Mrs Thompson's injury must have been severe to require her having to go to the hospital?' Flora examined a pair of the shop's apparently lethal scissors, careful to avoid touching the blades.

'It was. When I got back next day, her hand was all

bandaged up. Sylvia seemed perfectly cheerful in her-self, even said she had sold one of our needlework cases. Then two days later, her son came to tell me she was feverish and couldn't leave her bed. I went to Tivoli Road to see her, and she looked right poorly. I sent for Dr Grace, who took one look at her and sent her to the hospital.'

'Dr Grace Billings?' Flora brightened at the name. She had crossed paths with Gloucestershire's first fe-male doctor before; a competent, no-nonsense woman.

'That's her, though from what I've heard, the doc-tors her don't give her an easy time of it. Them all being men.'

Flora nodded, assuming Mrs Drake was not one of Dr Billings' patients.

'My husband don't hold with lady doctors,' she added, answering that question. 'Says it's not natural. Anyway, poor Sylvia passed away the next day. Dreadful it were. And she was so pleased about having sold the box too.' Her lower lip trembled as she pointed to the glass case beneath Flora's hand. Several wooden boxes rested on a length of cloth, each of a different polished wood, with domed lids hand-painted with floral designs.

'You can't buy *these* in Cavendish House,' Mrs

Drake said proudly. 'Sylvia commissioned them from a carpenter in Nailsworth. We don't sell many. What with them being a bit pricey.'

'They're beautiful. Might I see one?'

'Of course, dear.' Mrs Drake withdrew one with red peonies on the lid and laid it reverently on the counter. The compartmentalised tray inside contained darning and embroidery needles, stitch rippers, three pairs of scissors in different sizes, a thimble and a tiny box of pearl-headed pins, bobbins and crochet hooks, all of which nestled in indentations in the dark blue velvet lining.

'The one Sylvia sold had white flowers on the lid.' Mrs Drake's eyes gleamed as she sensed a lucrative sale. 'Though I prefer these red ones myself.'

'It's lovely craftsmanship.' Flora ran a hand over the smooth wood, her excuse to elicit information rapidly becoming a desire to possess the item for herself. 'I think I'll take it.'

Flora shot a half-pleading, half-determined look at Bunny. He rolled his eyes, but smiled in silent approval and retired to a chair at the end of a counter, no doubt provided for elderly customers and bored husbands.

Mrs Drake took down a roll of thick brown paper from a shelf above her head.

'It must have been hard for her son, losing his mother like that,' Flora said, watching as she unrolled the brown paper onto the counter with her blunt fingers.

'Indeed yes, such a nice young man, is Leo.' She sighed. 'Lovely manners. But then he went to one of those posh schools in the country, so it shouldn't be wondered at.'

'Did you know Mrs Thompson's husband as well?'

'Oh, no, dear.' Her lips puckered with disapproval; the idea was apparently unthinkable. 'He died when Leo was only a toddler.' She lowered her voice to the conspiratorial tone of the habitual gossip. 'I don't think the marriage was happy, because she never mentioned him, not once.' She ran the edge of a pair of scissors along the paper, dividing it in two with a light swishing sound.

'This shop is charming.' Flora gave the rows of neatly packed shelves a long, appraising glance. 'I imagine Mrs Thompson found it a challenge to run on her own?'

'What with Cavendish House almost next door, you mean?' Mrs Drake nodded sagely. 'Well, she didn't depend on the shop to live, but it suited her to have something to do.'

'Mrs Thompson had an alternative source of income?' Bunny asked, bringing her attention sharply towards him.

'Well... um,' she hesitated, as if caught out in an indiscretion. 'Well, it stands to reason doesn't it, sir? I mean, Sylvia always had nice things. And could afford to send Leo away to school.'

'I assume her son owns the shop now? Although I imagine it's your own sterling efforts which have kept the place going since Mrs Thompson's death?' Bunny graced her with his most charming smile. 'I cannot imagine a young man flourishing in such an environment.'

'I do my best, sir.' A deep flush appeared in response to his blatant flattery. 'Funny you should say that, sir, because Leo is selling the shop and moving away. I suspect he only stayed in the town so as not to upset Sylvia. She doted on him, you see.' Mrs Drake released a sad sigh. 'He doesn't have to worry though now, does he?' She wrapped a length of string expertly round the box, tied it into a neat bow, and snipped the ends with a flourish.

'Where will he go?' Flora grew mildly uneasy, knowing the 'nice young man' was dead.

'He has few friends round here and spends most of his time in London since his mother died. He's there now, in fact, making plans, like as not.' She set down the scissors and pushed the parcel across the counter.

Bunny idly studied the passers-by in the street from his chair as Flora talked, his attention caught by something outside.

'What will you do when the shop is sold?' Flora handed Mrs Drake a folded white five-pound note.

'Don't you go worrying about me, dear.' She counted change into Flora's palm. 'If the new owners don't want to keep me on, I'll find something soon enough.'

Bunny abruptly scraped back the chair and grabbed Flora's arm. He grabbed the wrapped parcel from the counter, pushed it into her hands and ushered her towards the door. 'Thank you, Mrs Drake. This has been most enjoyable,' he said over his shoulder, 'but we ought to be going. We don't want to be late for our appointment, do we, my dear?'

'Um... no. It was so nice seeing you again, Mrs Drake.' Flora said as the shop door banged shut behind them.

'What appointment?' The parcel beneath Flora's arm gave a satisfying crackle of paper.

'It was the first thing I could think of.' He took a swift look over one shoulder. 'Don't look now, but we have company.'

Despite Bunny's warning, she glanced back, and inhaled sharply. Two police officers stood at the haberdashers, removing their helmets before they entered.

'Oh, dear, poor woman. What should we do?' The wooden needlework case bounced against her ribs as Flora hurried to keep up with him.

'About Mrs Drake? Nothing. I vote we go for luncheon at the Queen's Hotel. I'm starving.' He side-stepped pedestrians who chattered in groups and obstructed the wide, tree-lined pavement. 'You did an excellent job of questioning her, by the way. She might have become suspicious if it had gone on much longer.'

'Let's hope she's too occupied with what the police tell her to mention us.' Flora cast the shop a final backwards look, then stepped off the kerb into the road, only for Bunny to haul her roughly back onto the pavement just as a drayman's cart swept past them in a thunder of hooves.

'Are you all right?' His hand slid round her waist and he leaned close, his eyes behind his spectacles dark with concern.

'Yes, of course. I should have been paying more attention.' Her heartbeat quickened to a painful thump, and she tightened her hold on her new acquisition. 'I'm still distracted by the fate of that poor woman.' She smoothed down her skirt with her free hand and allowed her breathing to slow.

'Which one, Mrs Drake or Sylvia Thompson?'

'Both, I suppose.' She reminded herself Mrs Thompson was beyond sympathy now. 'It's a shame Mrs Drake didn't know more about Leo's plans. Perhaps Inspector Maddox has had more luck?'

6

They entered the hotel between a pair of Corinthian columns that flanked the doors into an entrance lobby dominated by a Georgian staircase that wound up to a crowned glass roof. The scent of spring flowers mixed with beeswax polish and a tang of vinegar greeted them; familiar smells of wealth and comfort, borrowed during Flora's life as a governess but which since her marriage to Bunny had become her own.

'Earl Trent once told me this building was modelled on the Temple of Jupiter in Rome,' she dropped her voice to a whisper in the hushed atmosphere as they headed into the dining room. 'It opened the same year Queen Victoria came to the throne.'

'That doesn't surprise me.' Bunny flicked a look at

a wing-back chair in a corner. 'That chair over there looks as if Lord Melbourne might have sat in it.'

'Hush. The town is very proud of this hotel,' Flora whispered as the maître d' held out her chair in a dining room while around them the clink of cutlery, tinkle of crystal and the low murmur of conversation created a calm and affluent ambience.

Bunny flicked up the back of his jacket and took the seat opposite before accepting a menu the size of a broadsheet. 'You've gone all wistful, Flora. What are you thinking?'

'Only that this room contains so many memories. The girls attended the Ladies College, and every Thursday afternoon, Lady Trent would bring the four of us here for tea. I didn't go the college, of course, but I was enrolled at Miss Bostock's on Bays Hill Road. I loved that school.' She sighed as her head crowded with more memories. 'We'd sit at the same table in the corner over there where Lady Trent would pour and Lady Amelia doled out the fancies. I never got to have the vanilla one, which was Jocasta's favourite.'

'You could have one now if you like.' Bunny raised a hand to summon a waiter.

'No, don't.' She gestured for him to lower his hand. 'It wouldn't be the same. Ignore me, I'm wallowing.' Bunny would never understand how, for one blissful afternoon a week, she would forget she was simply the butler's daughter. 'Now,' she opened her menu, 'what shall we have?'

* * *

After an excellent meal of tender roast beef followed by lemon sorbet decorated with chocolate swirls, they adjourned to the lounge, where they occupied twin chairs flooded with light from the double-height arched windows overlooking Imperial Gardens.

'I shall need only consommé and crackers for supper tonight.' Flora sank into the wing-back chair with a tiny, self-satisfied sigh and tucked the wrapped needlework case beneath her seat. 'Should we have asked Mrs Drake if Leo had any enemies?'

She broke off as a waiter brought their coffee, together with a plate of petits fours shaped like miniature pieces of fruit. He offered them a copy of the *Examiner* which Bunny pounced on as if he had not seen a newspaper for a week.

'She would have thought it a strange question when she didn't yet know Leo was dead.' He offered her the plate.

'I suppose so. And she said Leo didn't have many friends in the town, so no one local would have a reason to kill him?' She declined the marzipan treats reluctantly. 'Apart from the shop, I doubt he has much money and with no living relatives, what would be the point of killing him?'

'No money that we know of,' Bunny murmured. He slapped the newspaper with one hand, making Flora jump. 'Some former military chap called Elwes was prosecuted for what is described here as "driving furiously" along the Promenade at twenty miles an hour.' He frowned and peered closer at the page. 'I should be interested to know what sort of motor it was, but it doesn't say.'

Sighing, she glanced up from her cup. 'Bunny, did you hear what I said?'

'What? Oh, yes, of course I did.' He lowered the paper and gave her his full attention. 'The possibility Sylvia Thompson had an alternative income could be relevant. I doubt that the shop could have supported them both and provided enough for private school.'

'There's always your suggestion of a robbery gone wrong.'

'I've rejected that theory,' Bunny crumpled the paper in his lap. 'Had there been a struggle in the compartment, someone would have heard or seen something. And why were Leo's pockets empty when he was found?'

'That fits with the robbery idea,' Flora said.

'Or his assailant deliberately stripped him of anything which might have identified him.'

'Why kill him on the train? He would have had to wait until it arrived at the station before he could get away, either that or jump off when it was still moving?'

'My guess is the murderer planned to be off the train and well away by the time the body was found.' He refolded the newspaper and discarded it on a nearby chair. 'What he didn't count on was Ed being there, firstly to prevent him carrying out the deed, then to raise the alarm sooner than planned.' He plucked a pear-shaped marzipan decorated with angelica leaves from the plate. 'It's not looking good for Ed. All he has in his favour so far is his lack of motive.'

'Don't say that!' A tremor of fear ran through her. 'He's relying on us to help him out of this mess.'

'I don't believe Ed is a murderer any more than you do.' Bunny demolished the petit four in one bite. 'However, nor do I possess a layman's faith in the police. I see too many of their mistakes in my profession.'

'Mrs Drake must know about Leo by now,' Flora said. 'Do you think she'll tell those policemen we were at the shop asking questions?'

'I hope not. If our name does come up, things could become awkward with Inspector Maddox. I don't relish another lecture from him about interference from amateurs and civilians.'

'Thus far,' Flora mused. 'All we have is a department store we know nothing about, a letter which may or may not exist confirming a booking at a hotel which may or may not be a flower beginning with a B or maybe a D.'

'It's not much, is it?' He crossed one ankle over the other, rested his head against the back of the chair and popped another marzipan into his mouth before reaching for another.

Flora watched his hand hover over the last remaining petit fours, and unable to resist any longer, swiped the marzipan delicacy from between his reaching fingers. His mouth opened in surprise as she sank her teeth into the almond paste, closing her eyes as she relished the thick sweetness on her tongue. When she opened them again, she found him grinning at her.

'Leo could have been looking for answers why his mother died?' Flora licked sugar from her fingers. 'Blame is part of grief, isn't it?' She recalled how unwilling she had been to accept the man who had raised her had died in a riding accident. Her tenacious search for the truth when everyone told her she was merely being unreasonable finally proved he had been murdered.

'If he believed Sylvia's death was suspicious, surely he would have contacted the local police?' Bunny sounded sceptical.

'Perhaps he did, but maybe no one listened, so he might have gone to London to see someone with more authority?' Flora sat forward in her seat, while turning the idea over in her head. 'The story he gave Ed about the job could have been subterfuge. He would hardly admit to a stranger he was looking for answers as to why his mother died?'

'Possibly not, but it would certainly have made Maddox's investigation more interesting.'

'Leo might have appealed to the hospital for answers as well.'

'The hospital isn't likely to tell *us* anything. Especially if they were culpable.'

'I wasn't thinking of the hospital.' She searched the room for a clock, but the only one she found was located too far away to make out. 'What time is our train?'

He consulted his half-hunter. 'Another hour and a half yet. Why?'

'While we are here, why don't we pay a visit to Dr Billings? No, don't look at me like that. If your mother died in similar circumstances, wouldn't *you* demand every detail of her case from her doctor to ensure no mistakes were made?'

'Hah! It would take more than a cut hand to take off *my* mother,' he muttered under his breath and signalled for their bill from a passing waiter.

'There might be more to it.' Flora gathered her gloves and bag. 'I mean, what are the chances of a perfectly healthy mother and son both dying within four months of each other?'

'Probably higher than you would imagine.' Bunny fastened his coat. 'And don't be disappointed if the good doctor has nothing interesting to add.'

Flora smiled, nursing a quiet conviction that Dr Grace would be far more forthcoming.

* * *

While she waited for Bunny to locate a hansom on Montpellier Street, Flora lifted her face to a shaft of early spring sunshine that had broken through a canopy of grey clouds. Despite her worry over Ed, the prospect of lighter, warmer days held promise, the smell of spring flowers and newly-mown grass reaching her from the garden square opposite.

'No luck, I'm afraid.' Bunny returned to her side. 'I suggest we wander farther along the Promenade to see if there are any cabs there. Or we could always take a tram.'

'Pittville Parade isn't far. Let's walk. I could do with some exercise after that luncheon.' She thrust the parcel towards him. 'Would you mind taking this for me? It's getting heavy.'

Their route took them past a fountain with a stone statue of Neptune surrounded by prancing horses that Bunny greatly admired. Halfway along the Promenade, with its various shops with their inviting window displays, a spatter of rain brought them to a halt on the pavement.

'And we didn't bring an umbrella,' Flora said, dismayed as dark spots appeared on the flagstones, while benches emptied rapidly as their occupants made a dash for cover.

'Come on, this way.' Bunny shifted the parcel beneath one arm, grabbed her hand with the other and pulled her beneath the red and white striped awning of a gentlemen's outfitters. 'It doesn't look as if it will last long. We'll wait here until it passes.'

Flora brushed raindrops from the shoulders of her powder blue coat, huddling closer to Bunny as more people crowded into their temporary shelter. A young woman in a black skirt and jacket with a straw boater on her brown curls joined them, breathless from her run to get out of the rain.

'Amy? Amy Coombe?' Flora raised her voice above the steady thrum of rain on the awning above their heads.

The woman's startled frown changed instantly to a broad smile of delighted recognition. 'Miss Flora! Well, this is a surprise. I wasn't expecting to see you.'

'We're only here for the day to, er, visit friends.' She drew Bunny closer to include him in the conversation. 'You remember Amy don't you, Bunny? The housekeeper at Cleeve Abbey where I used to live?'

'Of course I do. How are you, Miss Coombe?' Bunny tipped his hat.

'You look as if you are on an errand.' Flora indicated the beribboned box that hung from Amy's hand. 'As you can see, I've been shopping.' She nodded to where Bunny kept a firm grip on the needlework case, the brown paper wrapping darkened in places by raindrops.

'It's my afternoon off, so I'm going to visit my sister who's in service in Fauconberg Road. She recently got engaged to their butler.'

'That's such good news, Amy. You must be excited?' It seemed Amy's sister too had risen above the abuses ad-

ministered by their drunken father, whom many believed had killed Lily Maguire after an argument about
the way he treated his children. Three years previously,
when Flora was at Cleeve Abbey looking for the truth
about Riordan's death, Amy had told her the story of her
mother's disappearance as well as her own childhood at
the hands of an abusive father. Lily Maguire, as she was
known then, had tried to help Amy escape Sam Coombe,
whose attack on Lily had resulted in her disappearance.

'I am, Miss Flora. I've bought her a little something to celebrate.' She held up a small parcel
wrapped in candy-striped paper tied with a pink bow.

'Have you considered marriage yourself, Amy? I
can recommend it.' She smiled at Bunny, who winked.

'Not me, Miss Flora, I'm happy as I am.' Amy's
pursed lips displayed her opinion of the idea. 'I'm
head housekeeper now, since Hetty died,' she said,
referring to her predecessor.

'I heard. Such sad news.' Hetty had been the
Cleeve Abbey chatelaine for three generations who
had finally lost her grip on reality and spent her last
weeks frightened and disoriented.

'Indeed, though perhaps for the best,' Amy said
gently before her face brightened. 'Oh, and thank you
so much for your letter, Miss Flora. Who would have
guessed Lily Maguire was alive after all these years? I

spent half my life thinking my father had killed her. It was such a tonic hearing you've been in contact with her again.'

'I knew you would want to know, as you were very fond of her all those years ago.'

'Where had she been all this time?' Amy's eager expression rapidly faded. 'Oh, beg pardon, Miss, it's not my place to ask, but I've always wondered what happened to her. Has she changed much?'

'I cannot tell, Amy. I was only six when she disappeared. I barely knew her.'

'Ah, yes of course.' Amy flushed a deep red. 'I'm thrilled for you both. And you have a baby now. A little boy?'

'Arthur, yes. He's a year old and growing every day.'

'How lovely. Are we to expect you up at the Abbey today? We had no word you were coming?'

'Er, no, not with Lord and Lady Trent away. We only came for the day.'

'Indeed?' Amy's brown eyes widened, her head on one side inviting further explanation.

'Actually, we called in at Thompson's Haberdashery, only to discover Sylvia Thompson had died recently.' Beside her, Bunny gave an expressive cough, but she refused to look at him.

'I heard about that.' Amy shook her head sadly. 'Such a shame, and so sudden.'

'It must have been a terrible blow to her son.' Flora adopted a vague expression she hoped was convincing. 'Did you know him at all?'

'I knew Mrs Thompson, but only saw Leo from a distance when he came to the summer fair with his mother. She was nice to me, but he didn't pay me much attention. As you might imagine, a handsome young man like him wouldn't pass the time with a housekeeper.' Her tone might have been sarcastic coming from anyone else, but this pronouncement was delivered without resentment.

'Was this at last year's fair?' Flora asked.

In August each year, Lord Trent threw open the grounds of Cleeve Abbey to the townsfolk for a summer fair, a tradition begun during the previous incumbent's time. Intended as an afternoon of outdoor games with a beer tent for estate workers, it had expanded over the years into an annual festival with sideshows, art exhibitions, pet shows and cake competitions attended by the entire district.

Amy bit her lip as she searched her memory. 'Could have been the one before, I'm not sure.'

'Did Mrs Thompson talk about Leo much? Who his friends were and what he was interested in?'

Bunny gave another cough, louder this time, but again Flora ignored him.

Amy cast him a slightly worried look. 'Are you all right, sir?'

'Quite well thank you, Amy. Must be motor car fumes getting to my chest.'

Flora bit her lip to prevent a smile. Only two motors had passed them in all the time they had stood there. 'You were saying, Amy?'

'She never said so, but I sensed Mrs Thompson didn't think much of his friends. If anyone asked, she'd change the subject.'

'Really? Why do you suppose that was?' Her pulse quickened as she waited for her answer.

'I couldn't say.' Amy shrugged. 'Why the interest, Miss Flora, if you don't mind my asking. I had no idea you knew the Thompsons?'

'Only in passing. Her death struck me as rather sudden.'

'You know what Flora is like when presented with a puzzle,' Bunny interjected, his eyes widening in warning.

'You don't think there was something odd about her death, do you?' Amy's eyes sharpened. 'Last time you were here, Sally Pond told us all about you breaking up a trafficking ring. Sylvia Thompson isn't another one of your murder cases, is she?'

'No, Amy. I was simply curious.' Flora gave a thin, nervous laugh, resolving to have a word with Sally when she got home about below-stairs gossip.

'I'll tell you what, though.' Amy stepped closer, lowering her voice. 'Sylvia Thompson was close with a lady named Kitty Tilney. She helped Leo arrange his mother's funeral, what with him not having anyone else in the world.'

'Really? And where does Mrs Tilney live?' Flora asked.

'One of those big houses in Clarence Square, but since her daughters married, it's too big for her, so she rents out the top two floors.'

'Do you know her well?' Flora asked.

'I've never met her.' Amy's eyes flashed with mischief. 'Only I hear things. She lives at number twenty-four, should you be thinking of asking her about how Mrs Thompson died.' She confided the information with a large dose of scepticism. 'I doubt there's any mystery there though. Mrs Thompson was taken to the hospital and everything.'

Bunny coughed into a fist and nudged Flora discreetly with a well-aimed elbow.

'Thank you, Amy. You've been very – informative,' she said, ignoring him.

With Amy's penchant for gossip, Flora wondered how she had kept the secret of Lily Maguire for so long.

'We're so busy up at the Abbey,' Amy began, changing the subject. 'What with all the arrangements for the house party next month? Even the lodge house is being opened up to accommodate the single gentlemen.'

'We're looking forward to it.' Flora hoped they would have cleared Ed's name by then or the house party would be a dismal one. Either that or it would be cancelled.

'Looks like the rain has stopped.' Amy poked her head out from beneath the canvas. The other people sheltering had slowly drifted away, leaving only the three of them.

'I should be on my way, or I won't have any time with Anne before I have to get the tram back to the Abbey.' Amy backed away. 'It was nice to see you, Miss Flora, Mr Harrington.'

'You too, Amy.' Flora watched Amy walk away. 'Oh dear. I might have made her suspicious.'

'Your questioning wasn't exactly subtle, and Amy's

no fool.' He hefted the parcel beneath one arm, the other extended for her to take.

'Her comment about the summer fair was interesting. Ed might have met Leo there.'

'Ed said he didn't know him. Besides, the whole town attends the Cleeve Abbey summer fair, so their paths might never have crossed. The fact Mrs Thompson disapproved of the company Leo kept is a more promising avenue to pursue.'

Their leisurely walk took them into the less grand streets of Pittville, which contained smaller versions of the grand residences in the town centre. Flora skirted around a baby carriage pushed by a young matron, following the wrapped occupant with her eyes while conjuring Arthur's smile in her head.

'Mrs Drake said nothing about Mrs Tilney,' Flora said, thoughtful. 'Which is odd if she and Mrs Thompson were close. Or she was being discreet regarding her employer?'

'I doubt it, when she was happy to gossip about Mrs Thompson's accident. Perhaps Leo had a young lady in his life, and Sylvia felt threatened?'

'At the prospect of losing her only child to a wife?' Flora knew all about that kind of rivalry. Her mother-in-law's attempts to keep Bunny's exclusive affection were only relieved when they bought a home of their own. 'Which doesn't explain why he was killed.'

'A jealous rival possibly?' Bunny leaned close to whisper.

'Too far-fetched. That only happens in cheap novels.' Flora hugged his arm to her side. 'We had better walk faster if we want to talk to Dr Billings before we catch our train home.'

7

The surly man who opened the door at Pittville Parade answered Bunny's enquiry after Dr Billings with a disdainful snort. 'If you are referring to the woman with the effrontery to call herself a doctor, she moved to Sussex Lodge in Winchcombe Street.'

Bunny's polite thanks were abruptly cut off by the hard slam of the front door.

'It appears five years has done little to alter the opinions of the locals regarding female medics,' he observed as they set off again.

'How Dr Grace tolerates such prejudice I'll never know.' Flora glared uselessly over her shoulder at the closed door. 'At least her new address isn't far. It's just around the corner near the Pittville Gates.'

Sussex Lodge was a tall, thin terraced house ranged over four storeys identical to its neighbours, built in the Georgian style with a white stuccoed façade, full-height windows, and a railed area in front with steps leading to a lower-ground floor.

The woman who answered their knock informed them in an imperious tone that afternoon surgery was between three and five o'clock.

Suspecting they were about to face another slammed door, Bunny placed a firm hand on the wood. 'Then would you kindly inform Dr Billings that Mr and Mrs Harrington are here on a personal matter?'

'You'd better come in then.' She jerked her chin in a gesture for them to enter. 'I'll tell her you're here.'

While they waited, Flora took in her surroundings, which included a hall table displaying pamphlets detailing various complaints aimed at women and nursing mothers. The housekeeper returned in due course and led them up a steep staircase to the first floor, where Dr Grace greeted them in a neat private sitting room that Flora guessed she used as her consulting room.

'Ah, Mrs Harrington, Mr Harrington. What a pleasure it is to see you both again.' She shook hands with each of them before inviting them to sit.

A tall, well-built woman in her early thirties, Dr Grace possessed penetrating dark eyes and strong, handsome features that took on warmth and animation when she smiled. Her appearance matched her surroundings, neat and professional in a white blouse ruched at the front over a dark, straight skirt. Handsome rather than pretty, her strong features became warm and animated when she smiled.

'I gather it's still an uphill fight against prejudice and mistrust, Doctor?' Ignoring the arrangement of chairs, Bunny took up a position beside the long window which gave a view onto the street of the trams which glided by.

'I'm prepared for the long haul.' Dr Grace sounded resigned, if not reconciled. 'Lord Trent has been incredibly kind, recommending me to his friends. I recently treated a retired septuagenarian army colonel who lives on Pittville Lawn. Perhaps the good people of this town are accepting me.'

'It must be hard to be so unappreciated.' Flora chose a low, buttoned velvet chair to Bunny's left. 'I wish you lived in London, so you might be our physician.'

'How kind of you to say so? When I first opened my practice, there were forty doctors in the town, none of them women. I called on each one personally to introduce myself and was treated largely as a strange novelty. Most still feel I'm only good enough to hand out cough syrup and colic water to women and children, but I have no intention of giving up and I'm confident the town will accept me, eventually. Now,' she took a seat opposite, both hands clasped in her lap, 'I'm sure you haven't come here to ask about the trials of being a female doctor. What can I do for you?'

'We wanted to ask you about one of your patients,' Bunny began.

Dr Grace's eyes flickered, accompanied by an almost imperceptible stiffening of her shoulders.

'Not a living patient,' Flora added quickly. 'This one died several months ago.'

'Ah, I see.' Dr Grace relaxed slightly. 'That changes things somewhat. This patient's name?'

'Mrs Sylvia Thompson,' Bunny replied. 'We were told you treated her in her last illness.'

'I did. Poor Sylvia. An unfortunate case indeed.' A small frown appeared between her heavy eyebrows and she sighed. 'I have to say I'm reluctant to discuss her without her son's permission. He's her closest and, in fact, her only relative.'

'In normal circumstances, I would agree,' Bunny said in his best solicitor tone used to impart grave news. 'However, this is a special case. Her son was murdered yesterday.'

'Leo?' She bolted upright in her chair, her eyes wide. 'Murdered? Are you sure?' In response to Bunny's slow nod, the colour drained from her face and she stared off, her mouth working as if unable to comprehend what she had been told. 'Yesterday, you say? How did this happen? And where? I haven't heard of any deaths in the town.'

'It happened in London,' Bunny replied. 'We came from there this morning.'

'We're sorry to have brought such news,' Flora winced, feeling woefully inadequate.

'Such a nice young man. I can hardly believe it. Murdered you say?' Dr Grace repeated in disbelief. 'What with his mother having died so recently this makes it doubly tragic.' Her eyes darkened in confusion. 'I don't understand. If it happened in London, what brings you to me?'

'Leo's body was discovered in a train compartment at Paddington Station,' Bunny began. 'The young man who shared his compartment is suspected of having killed him. At this stage, the police have no actual proof, thus we are trying to find out who was in fact responsible.'

'We hoped to find out more about Leo, only to

learn his mother had died, so we haven't been able to discover much,' Flora added.

'Ah, I think I see where this is going.' Dr Grace's expression sharpened. 'You're here on a quest to exonerate this young man, but are reluctant to explain further?'

Flora exchanged a look with Bunny, at which the doctor added, 'Discretion is an integral part of my profession.'

'Of course,' Flora said, embarrassed. 'It's just that this is difficult.'

'The young man the police suspect is Edward, Viscount Trent,' Bunny said.

'What?' Dr Grace brought a hand to her throat, her expressive eyes darkening as her mind worked. 'Earl Trent's son? That delightful boy I treated for arsenic poisoning two years ago? Surely not?' Her brow furrowed as her thoughts took another track. 'Weren't you his governess before you married, Mrs Harrington?'

'Do call me Flora, please. And yes, I was. We're certain he had nothing to do with Mr Thompson's death, but unfortunately, he was found with the body.'

'I can see why the police would make such an assumption, but cannot imagine that young man committing a murder. May I ask how Leo was killed?'

Her tone switched from disbelief to calm profes-
sionalism.

'All we know is he was stabbed.'

'What sort of weapon was used?'

'We don't know.' Bunny shook his head. 'None was
found.'

'We need some sort of evidence and at least one
other suspect before they formally arrest Ed.' Flora
blinked away sudden tears, her hands gripping her
bag so tightly her fingers cramped. 'And we don't have
much time.'

'We appreciate this is awkward for you, Dr Grace,
but Flora is extremely fond of Viscount Trent.' Bunny
brought a hand down on Flora's shoulder. 'We'll do
everything we can to avoid him being accused of a
murder he didn't commit.'

'I quite understand, but I doubt I can be of help.
Leo wasn't a patient of mine. I only knew him through
his mother.'

'Would you be willing to give us details of the accident that caused Mrs Thompson's death?' Flora asked.
'It might not be relevant at all, but we have so little
information.'

'With Leo dead, I don't suppose there is anyone
likely to object.' Dr Grace thought for a moment. 'I'll

tell you what I can to help. Lord Edward's parents must be frantic.'

'Lord and Lady Trent are in New York, therefore blissfully unaware of what has happened,' Bunny said. 'We hope not to have to deliver them bad news when they return.'

The doctor's lips pursed in regret. 'I wish I could tell you more, but there isn't much to it, I'm afraid. Sylvia was brought to the surgery because of a wound to her hand, which I treated.'

'Someone brought her?' Flora remembered Mrs Drake saying she had been in Bristol on the day of Mrs Thompson's accident and that Dr Grace had been summoned a couple of days later, but nothing about Sylvia being taken to the doctor.

'A customer to the shop who was there when Sylvia cut herself. The lady summoned a hansom and brought her here.'

'Did you know this woman?' Bunny asked.

She shook her head. 'I had never seen her before. Nor did I pay her much consideration, as Sylvia took all my attention. She was very distressed.'

'Where exactly was Mrs Thompson's injury?' Bunny asked.

Flora smiled at the way Bunny didn't react to answers, but pressed on with the next question. A technique he had learned from Inspector Maddox.

'Right here.' Dr Grace held out her hand. With the other, she drew a circle round the mound of muscle between the thumb and wrist. 'Injuries to the thenar can cause long-term nerve damage, resulting in restriction of movement. The cut was only an inch long, but deep and clean, so I expected it to heal with no residual problems. However, as I discovered, it's not always easy to tell.'

'And Sylvia didn't explain how it happened?' Flora asked.

'No. She kept mumbling about being clumsy, but then the pain, combined with the amount of blood, made her very agitated.'

'She accused *you* of being clumsy?' Bunny asked.

'I doubt it. I assumed she was rambling and referred to herself, but she was difficult to comprehend.' Dr Grace's wide mouth twitched at one corner but did not develop into anything resembling a smile. 'Sylvia was tetchy with me, although the lady who accompanied her received similar treatment. The poor woman only tried to help, and yet I found her rather annoying.'

'The lady or Sylvia?'

'Both, actually. Sylvia screamed each time I

touched her, and when I removed the binding to clean the wound, the woman kept getting in my way. She tipped my instruments onto the floor at one point. I had to send for my nurse to help calm them both.'

'Guilt at having been responsible for Sylvia's cutting herself, perhaps?' Flora suggested.

'Possibly, although that never occurred to me.' Dr Grace stared off again as she gave the idea some consideration.

'Could you describe her companion?'

Flora had no idea whether this obliging stranger was relevant to their case, but at this stage, anything might help.

'I wouldn't call her that, as Sylvia did not appear to know her. Nor did she give her name. She was about my own age.' Dr Grace tapped her lower lip with a finger. 'Light brown hair, wide cheekbones and eyes which tilted up at the corners, somewhat like a cat.' She shrugged. 'Which could have been because of the way she wore her hair, which was in a rather severe bun scraped off her face.' Flora was about to thank her, when Dr Grace raised a finger. 'One thing I remember was her extremely smart coat. It was the first thing I noticed about her. A maroon colour, like excellent red wine with a design of embroidered diamond shapes in black round the hem.' She hesitated. 'More like chevrons. I rarely take notice of what anyone wears, but she put me in mind of a tall glass of wine.' She broke off with a shaky laugh. 'She didn't strike me as the friendly sort, so it surprised me when she stayed to help Sylvia. She wasn't local, because she claimed to have a train to catch and left not long after arriving. Sylvia was being quite difficult so I was glad she had gone. Once Sylvia calmed down, I dressed the wound and she was supposed to come back in a day or so to have the dressing changed.'

'What happened after that?' Flora asked, suspecting that was not the end of the story.

'Mrs Drake, that's the lady who helps her in the shop, came to see me two days later asking if I would visit Sylvia at home. When I got there, she was running a high fever. I had her admitted to the hospital straight away, but she never recovered. She died from sepsis.' She sighed, looked from Flora to Bunny and back again. 'Not one of my successes, I'm afraid. However, I cannot see how this would help you find out who killed Leo.'

'It's possible his mother's death is a factor,' Bunny said.

'I see.' Dr Grace appeared to give this idea some thought. 'I only knew Sylvia as a patient, we didn't mix socially. You might describe her as being – delicate –

and would summon me with the mildest of symptoms. Unlike some of my patients, she never complained about my bills.'

'What about Leo?' Bunny asked. 'Did he enjoy good health?'

'Excellent, as far as I could tell. He was one of Dr Fairbrother's patients.' Her voice held resignation, as if accustomed to this attitude from the male population, despite the elderly physician's mediocre reputation.

'Is blood poisoning a common outcome of an injury like Sylvia's?' Flora asked.

'It depends. Most of the patients I treat, or rather those I may treat, live in conditions where hygiene is poor; the word "clean" subject to interpretation. It's not uncommon and, as in Sylvia's case, often lethal.'

'Although poor hygiene wasn't an issue with Sylvia,' Flora assumed by what she had already learned about the woman.

'It was not, no. Her villa in Tivoli Road was always pristine, making it all the more puzzling. But then blood poisoning can be caused by many things.'

'You said it was Mrs Drake who called you, not Leo?' Bunny asked. 'How did *he* react to Sylvia's illness?'

'He was worried, naturally. He went with her to the hospital and stayed with her until the end.'

'You said Mrs Thompson was delicate,' Flora ventured. 'Could she have been suffering an underlying condition which the injury worsened?'

'Only in temperament.' Her wry smile appeared. 'Sylvia was healthy, as far as I know. However, sepsis combined with, say, an undiagnosed heart complaint might certainly have contributed to her death.'

'Was a post-mortem carried out?' Bunny enquired.

'I suggested it, but Leo refused. I could hardly insist, so that was an end to the matter. He took her death badly. First disbelief, devastation, anger and then endless questions about what could have been done differently. All the usual reactions. By the time of the funeral, he appeared calm, accepting, even grateful to me for taking care of her.'

Silence fell as each became occupied with their own thoughts, broken only by the whine of a tram outside the window. That Leo had refused a post-mortem gave Flora pause for thought. Distress at the thought of his beloved mother being violated, or because he had something to do with her death?

'I don't wish to be inhospitable.' Dr Grace rose slowly. 'But if there's nothing else I can help you with, I have to feed my son before afternoon surgery.'

'Don't let us keep you, Dr Grace.' Bunny collected the needlework case from where he had placed it beside the fender. 'We have a train to catch if we are to reach London before midnight.'

'How is your boy?' Flora asked, recalling Dr Grace's son must be five years old by now.

'Freddie is well, very energetic and I'm happy to say healthy. He's also bright and inquisitive, which makes him a handful with all his constant questions.'

'Something I shall have to look forward to,' Flora said with a sudden rush of pride.

'Ah yes, I heard you have a son now too?' Her features softened in a way only a mother's could when children were mentioned.

'Arthur is a year old now and thriving.' Flora would like to have talked more about their relative experiences, but there was no time. Instead, she gathered her things and followed Dr Grace into the hall.

'We really appreciate you talking to us like this.' Bunny said. 'Especially when you aren't obliged to.'

'Not at all. I hope you find out who killed poor Leo. It's so sad; he has no other family to mourn him.' She turned to the housekeeper who had appeared from the rear hall. 'Kindly ask John to fetch the gig and take my guests to the station?'

The woman dipped a curtsey and retreated.

'There's really no need, Dr Billings,' Bunny said. 'We'll hail a cab on the street.'

'This isn't London,' she said, laughing, the idea plainly ridiculous. 'You'd have to walk all the way to the Promenade to find one. They don't hang about on street corners here.'

'That's kind of you, and we wouldn't want to miss our train,' Flora said as they descended the narrow staircase in single file and assembled on the front step.

'I hope you'll keep me informed of your progress,' Dr Grace said as the gig appeared round the corner driven by a tow-headed youth. 'I would wish you good luck, but you're both tenacious enough to solve this mystery. Sylvia would have appreciated your efforts, and Leo deserves it.'

'Yes, I suppose he does.' Flora murmured, climbing into the gig. She had been so focussed on Ed's plight; she had barely given a thought to the fact an innocent young man was dead. But then, how innocent was Leo Thompson? No one seemed to know much about him.

8

The savoury smell of cooked meat greeted their arrival back at Eaton Place, instantly banishing Flora's resolve to have consommé for supper.

'Well, what did you find out?' Ed bounced on his heels at Flora's shoulder, blocking her way. 'Did you speak to Mrs Thompson?'

'Give us a chance to get inside, Ed,' Bunny chided him gently. 'We'll discuss it over sherry in the sitting room before dinner. Which smells delicious, by the way.'

'I've ordered cook to roast a chicken for you, sir, and madam,' Stokes said unnecessarily, bowing them inside. 'As I always say, one can never rely on hotel cooking.'

'Very insightful of you, Stokes.' Bunny handed him his coat. 'Luncheon seems a long time ago now, and we're both ravenous.'

'What's that you've got there, Flora?' Ed pointed to the brown paper-wrapped parcel she had placed on the hall table. 'Have you brought me a present?'

'I bought myself one, actually. It's a rather beautiful needlework case from Mrs Thompson's shop. I want to catch Arthur before he falls asleep. I'll be down directly and then we can talk about what we learned today.'

Flora fled upstairs to the nursery where Arthur was fragrant and sleepy after his bath but awake enough to appreciate a cuddle from his mother.

'I've missed you today,' she whispered into his powdery cheek, rewarded by baby gurgles and laughs. Before Milly could remind her he should be settled by this time, Flora laid his chubby body in his crib, soothed his mild protests with kisses and crept away.

In her room, she changed out of her travelling dress, grateful it was Sally's day off and she wouldn't have to answer questions about their last-minute trip to Cheltenham. She had been fielding oblique questions from her maid since Ed's unexpected arrival in a way which showed her resentment at being left out of any excitement.

Flora made no attempt to re-dress her hair, only tidying up the messy bits. She peered into the mirror and rubbed the soot smuts from her cheeks. Trains might be fast and efficient, but they were also dirty.

Joining Bunny and Ed in the sitting room, she walked straight into an ongoing argument.

'What you're saying is, you went all that way for nothing?' Ed's sherry glass hit a table at his elbow with a thump.

'I said nothing of the sort.' Bunny frowned at the glass, which trembled slightly but stayed upright. 'The lady who worked for Mrs Thompson didn't mention anything about a department store. Are you sure that's where Leo told you he was going?'

'Yes, he did.' Ed perched on the edge of the armchair, his forearms on his knees. 'I didn't make it up, if that's what you're thinking.'

'Don't fret over it, Ed.' Flora accepted the glass of sherry Bunny held out. 'You weren't to know every word you and Mr Thompson exchanged would be this important.' Their glasses were almost empty, which told her she had been longer upstairs than she anticipated.

'We have little more than fragments at this stage.' Bunny withdrew a notebook from his pocket, complete with a miniature pen. 'For instance, we don't know exactly what weapon was used to kill Thompson.' He scribbled something, then held the notebook away from him as he examined what he had written. 'I've made a note here about his family, but cannot make it out.'

'You're wearing the wrong glasses.' Flora patted his shoulder on her way to the sofa. 'The reading pair is in your pocket.'

'What? Oh, yes, of course.' He withdrew a metal-framed pair and swapped them for the ones he wore. 'That's better. It's about Thompson's father. Mrs Drake said Sylvia Thompson never spoke about him.'

'Which is probably irrelevant.' Ed strode to the sideboard and poured himself more sherry. 'Didn't Leo's mother tell you what you wanted to know?'

'Er... I'm afraid not, Ed.' Flora studied her glass, mainly to avoid looking at him. 'His mother died four months ago.'

'What?' Ed swung to face them, glass in hand. 'Leo didn't mention that!' He resumed his seat, perched on the last two inches of squab, as if he was about to flee the room at any moment.

'Why would he, to a stranger?' Flora frowned.

'Oh. I didn't think of that.' Ed strolled to the sideboard and refilled his glass.

Flora thought to advise caution, but changed her mind.

'Sorry.' Ed flushed. 'It's awful that she died and all that. But doesn't it seem odd they died so close together?'

'That struck me too,' Flora said.

'One murder is enough to solve at this stage without inventing more.' Bunny crossed one leg over the other and brushed fluff from his trousers. 'We called on Dr Billings, who treated Mrs Thompson during her last illness. She said her death was pretty straightforward.'

'You saw Dr Grace?' Ed's eyes brightened with interest. 'I haven't seen her since I had tonsillitis last year. Mama disapproved, of course, and wanted me to see Dr Fairbrother. Mind you, the old boy's rumoured to be retiring soon, so what Mama will do then is anyone's guess.'

'That old quack's been threatening retirement for years.' Bunny's derisive laugh came out more of a snort. 'I imagine he's still handing out liver pills and diagnosing growing pains and hysteria. They'll have to take an axe to him to make him retire.'

'Bunny!' Flora's shocked protest was muffled by the subsequent gales of masculine laughter. Though he had a point, as Flora had clashed with the doctor over the death of Riordan Maguire. Neither she nor Bunny thought much of the man, at least professionally.

'Look, I appreciate what you are trying to do.' Ed discarded his empty glass on the table. Flora frowned at it. What was it, his second or third? 'I need an expert on this. I mean, professional detectives. Perhaps I should hire one?'

Bunny lowered the notebook and exchanged a loaded look with Flora.

'I'm sorry, I didn't mean to imply—' Ed broke off with a sigh. 'I'm just worried. In fact, I'm terrified.'

'We understand that, Ed, but you have to be patient.' Flora eased closer on the squab, encircling his shoulders with one arm. 'This is only the first day of our enquiries. Now, how have you occupied yourself today?' For a country boy like Ed, the restriction was bound to be hard.

'If you mean did I escape my incarceration and go for a walk in Hyde Park? Then, no.' Ed's sly smile told her he had read her thoughts. 'I read most of the time and visited the nursery this afternoon. Arthur is getting so big. He jumped up and down in his cot when he saw me and shook the bars so hard, I was convinced he would have the thing over.'

'He likes people, especially anyone who will give

him some attention.' Flora regretted the fact they had got home too late for their bedtime game.

'I'm not usually fond of babies, but I enjoyed it. Even when that nursery maid kept staring at me the whole time.'

'I have the same problem.' Flora enjoyed a sensitive relationship with Milly, when she often felt judged as a mother. Alice had tried to reassure her the best children's nurses always became attached. It was the disinterested ones she should be wary of.

'Not, I imagine, in the same way she stares at Ed.' Bunny exchanged the notebook for his glass. 'He and Milly are about the same age, I should imagine.'

'Oh, I see, yes, of course.' When Flora looked at Ed, she still saw the boy she had once cared for, not a wealthy, handsome and eligible young man who was bound to attract the attention of a pretty girl. The notion she would lose Arthur one day to a pair of beguiling eyes and a sweet smile saddened her a little. 'We ran into Amy Coombe in the Promenade,' Flora said, changing the subject. 'She suggested Mr Thompson attended the summer fair at the Abbey last year. I don't suppose you saw him there?'

Ed rolled his empty sherry glass between his hands but made no move to refill it, much to Flora's relief. 'The place is stacked to the gunnels on fair day.'

His face flushed slightly. 'Anyway, I wouldn't have rec-ognized him even if I had. Must you keep asking me all these questions?'

'Yes, we do, Ed,' Bunny insisted. 'The police will do the same, but worse. They'll keep asking you the same ones to see if your answers change. It's an interroga-tion technique used on suspects because it's more dif-ficult to remain consistent when lying than if telling the truth.'

'Is that what I am, a suspect?' Ed directed a hard glare at each of them before dropping his gaze to the floor.

'It's a figure of speech.' Flora shook her head at Bunny over Ed's bent head. 'And you might remember something you had overlooked before.'

'Well, I haven't.' Ed rubbed his hands down his trousers, scraped back his chair and rose. 'Would you excuse me? I'm not hungry after all. If it's all right with you, I'll go to my room.'

'Oh, dear,' Flora said when they were alone. 'He had hoped for much more from us.'

'He needs to be patient. These things take time. I'll go up and talk to him in a while.'

'Perhaps Inspector Maddox has found the hotel where Mr Thompson planned to stay?'

'If he has, there's no guarantee he'll pass the information on to us. Ah, there's the dinner gong. Let's go in, I'm starving.'

'You're always starving.' Flora brushed fluff from his lapel as they strolled the hall to the dining room. 'Bunny, do you think Ed knows more than he is telling us?' she asked as he held out her chair.

'Interesting you should say that. The same thing occurred to me. But what could it be?' Bunny shook open his napkin and laid it across his lap.

'No idea. Just a feeling.' Flora lifted the lid on the platter of roast chicken, releasing aromatic steam that made her mouth water. 'I wonder if Mrs Thompson's late husband left them an inheritance? One large enough to give someone a reason to kill them both?'

'A pertinent question. Though we haven't established her death was murder, and we aren't likely to. Where wills are concerned, estranged relatives have a tendency to crawl out of the woodwork. I could look up the register of wills, but it could be a long search. Thompson isn't an uncommon name. Nor do we know which year he died.' Bunny forked several slices of white chicken breast onto his plate. 'This looks good, really succulent. Ed will be sorry he missed it.'

'I'll ask Stokes to take him up some sandwiches later.'

'You're too soft with him, Flora. Going without

supper might do him some good and teach him some humility.'

'Is this the sort of treatment Arthur will have to expect for future misbehaviour?'

'Arthur won't misbehave.' The slow wink he aimed at her made her smile. 'Don't you think it was strange that Thompson travelled first class?'

'He told Ed the hotel sent him the train ticket.'

'Ah, yes, I had forgotten. What kind of hotel makes their guests' travel arrangements?'

Having no answer to that question, Flora handed him a dish of vegetables, debating how they were going to prove Ed's innocence before his parents returned from New York. They needed something. Or Inspector Maddox might become impatient and drag him off to a cell in Cannon Row.

Perhaps hiring a detective might not be such a bad idea after all? She brought a slice of the succulent white chicken to her mouth but lowered it to her plate again. The dinner she had anticipated with pleasure tasted like sawdust in her mouth.

9

At breakfast the next morning, Ed's continued restlessness was manifested in surly, monosyllabic responses to Flora's attempt at conversation. His irritation resulted in his clumsy manhandling of the crockery and the upending of a jug of milk over his trousers. Flora accepted without a word his complaint that the handle was too small, while Bunny merely glared at him over his newspaper.

Muttering darkly, Ed stomped off to his room to change.

Her appetite spoiled, Flora excused herself and went up to the nursery to spend time with Arthur. The sound of the doorbell, followed by the sharp tattoo of Stokes' footsteps across the hall tiles drew her attention. Vaguely wondering if the caller might be Inspector Maddox with some encouraging news, she paused on the half landing and listened to the caller's voice drift up to her vantage point, making her freeze on the spot.

'I'm not expected, Stokes,' Lady Jocasta greeted the butler. 'Though I'm sure Mrs Harrington won't mind my calling so early. I assume she's at home?'

At Stokes' murmured assent, Jocasta swept past him into the sitting room.

Flora descended the stairs, alerted to Ed's jacket draped over the banister rail. She grabbed it, and sped up the stairs, avoiding the one which creaked on the turn in the landing, and entered his room.

'Hey! I'm still changing in here,' Ed protested. He turned his back and continued fastening his trousers. 'I'm not thirteen any more, you know. A chap needs his privacy.'

'Keep your voice down!' Flora snapped, closing the door behind her. 'Your sister is downstairs.'

'Oh, cripes! She mustn't know I'm here,' he halted with his belt still undone. 'You know what's she's like. She'll get the complete story out of me in ten minutes.'

'Which is why I came to warn you not to come

down.' She held out his jacket. 'Here, you left this downstairs.'

'Thanks.' As he took the jacket and swung it onto the bed, something clattered to the floor. He bent and retrieved what at first glance appeared to be a four-inch metal spike attached to a mother-of-pearl handle. 'What's this?' Ed peered at it, frowning.

'It fell out of your pocket.' Flora took it from him. 'It's some sort of needlework tool. I didn't know you had taken up sewing?'

'That's ridiculous,' he snorted 'Why would *I* want such a thing?' Ed perched on the edge of the bed to tie his shoelaces. 'I've never seen it before. Are you sure it came from my jacket?'

'Yes, I—' At the sound of approaching footsteps, Flora placed the tool on the mantel beside an ormolu clock. 'I'd better go down and keep Jocasta occupied. You're not to leave this room until she's gone.'

'What!' Ed's shoulders slumped. 'Can't I even pass the time with Arthur in the nursery?'

'Not a good idea. Jocasta might ask to see him, so best you remain here until I tell you she's gone.'

'She'll be ages,' Ed muttered. 'You know what Jo's like when she gets talking.'

Ignoring him, Flora tugged the door closed and

descended to the first landing, almost colliding with Stokes on his way up.

'There you are, madam. Lady Jocasta Fitzhugh is—'

'Yes, I know, Stokes, I heard her arrive,' Flora interrupted him. 'Where did you put her?'

'I settled Lady Jocasta in the sitting room, madam.' His inference he wouldn't ever 'put' anyone anywhere was clear. 'I'll inform her you'll be with her directly. Oh, and the master has already left. He said to tell you he will be home for dinner this evening.'

'Thank you.' The fact Stokes could never bring himself to call his employer 'Bunny' still amused her. 'Oh, and Stokes?'

'Yes, madam?' His shoulders stiffened slightly, as if expecting an unwelcome request.

'I would appreciate it if you didn't mention our house guest to Lady Jocasta.' Her gaze flicked to Ed's bedroom door and away again.

'As you wish, madam.' Giving an acquiescent nod, he backed away.

Flora halted outside the sitting room door, ran her hands down her skirt, counted to three and pushed open the door.

'Jocasta! This *is* a surprise.' She glided forward to

receive her cousin's exuberant kiss. 'How lovely to see you! You look well.'

Flora had shared a schoolroom with Jocasta and her two elder sisters until they were old enough to attend separate schools in town; an arrangement she had never questioned, but had made sense when she discovered the Trent children were her cousins.

A year older than Flora, Jocasta's boundless enthusiasm for everything life offered was viewed by some as unbecoming in a wife and mother. Fortunately, her husband, Jeremy, as well as her family, adored everything about her. As for Flora, Jocasta was the sister she had always wanted.

'I'm in rude health, as they say.' Jocasta accepted her hug and then resumed her seat. 'I'm sorry for arriving unexpectedly, but I have some serious news to impart.'

'Really?' Apprehension sharpened Flora's voice. Had news about the body and Ed's part in it somehow reached the family?

'Nothing horrible, I assure you, so you can close your mouth, or as Nanny would say, you'll catch a passing fly.' She released a burst of delighted laughter and lowered herself onto a sofa. 'I love the way you think the worst, which means I cannot resist teasing you. I'm having another baby.'

'Oh, that's – that's wonderful. You had me worried for a moment.' Flora sank into the space beside her, a hand pressed to her chest to still her rapid heartbeat. 'Congratulations. Have you announced it yet, or is it too soon?'

'You know me, I'm no good at keeping secrets, so I don't expect you to keep it, either. Jeremy is delighted, of course, and hopes it will be a boy this time, but I don't think he minds either way. As you'd expect, his parents demanded it be a boy this time. As if I had any say in the matter.'

'Don't they regard your Mabel as an heir? Surely, she's entitled to a share of the family fortune too?'

Mabel, a chubby toddler of eighteen months with a halo of golden curls, was her father's pride, even if her mother seemed less than enamoured. Jocasta left the child to a nursery maid, in the vague hope she would become more engaging when she grew; a view of parenting considered normal in Jocasta's circle, and one which Flora had never felt confident in challenging.

'You're so, well – modern – Flora. You make me laugh.' Jocasta removed her gloves with neat, feminine movements and laid them on the sofa beside her. 'Mabel will never be left out, but you know how reluctant the landed gentry are to split up their estates.'

'I'm afraid I do,' Flora said, attempting not to sound too cynical.

'Don't worry, Flora. The day Mabel was born, I insisted she be given generous enough settlement to ensure she'll never be at the mercies of a younger brother or, worse, a spendthrift husband.'

'I apologise for underestimating you, Jocasta.' Flora felt new respect for her erstwhile irresponsible friend and cousin. 'When is this longed-for son due?'

'He'll be an October baby and we're going to name him Octavius, or maybe she'll be an Octavia?'

'Are you serious?' Flora's eyes widened.

'Not in the slightest.' Jocasta giggled. 'But it will cause a stir in the family for a while.' She giggled again.

'You shouldn't tease your poor family.' Flora shook her head slowly. 'A Libran child then, who will be lazy, but fair and appreciate the beauties of life.' Flora approached the bell pull, torn about whether to feel envy or sympathy for the unborn mite. 'May I offer you coffee?'

'Er, no thank you.' Jocasta grimaced. 'I can't stand the smell of the stuff at the moment.' Her toffee-coloured eyes widened in eager anticipation. 'I wouldn't mind some tea though, and some cake if your cook has some freshly baked. I cannot stop eating sweet things with this pregnancy.'

Flora scrutinised the ceiling, convinced she had heard Ed's heavy tread on the floor above.

'Is something wrong, Flora?' Jocasta frowned, twisting a chocolate brown curl in her finger. 'You seem unusually jumpy.'

'No, not at all. What was it you were saying?' The creak ceased, and she relaxed again.

'How is your plan to bring Lily and Uncle William back together again? You invited them to dinner, didn't you?'

'She calls herself Alice now, and yes, the dinner party went extremely well. Although I've promised Bunny not to interfere any more. He says if William and Alice wish to spend time together, they will do so with no help from me.'

'He's probably right.' Jocasta straightened in her seat, her lips forming an 'O' as an idea occurred to her. 'I know, I'll ask Mama to invite Alice to the house party next month. It would be a perfect opportunity to introduce her back into the family. She's bursting with curiosity about where she has been all this time. We talked about her often before they went to America.'

'I'm not sure that's a good idea.' Flora's stomach dropped. The gathering loomed uncomfortably on the horizon, and she and Bunny were still no closer to removing Ed from the list of suspects for Mr Thompson's murder. 'It might not be prudent to include your mother's former lady's maid in a family party,' Flora began. 'After all, your Mama persuaded William to cancel their wedding because she didn't want her younger brother marrying a servant.'

'You're worrying unnecessarily.' Jocasta waved her away. 'Grandmamma was the most fervent objector, and she's dead now. Mama is a different person these days. One could say she embraces scandal rather than avoids it.'

'Which isn't the reassurance I hoped for.' The tea had arrived and Flora busied herself with crockery and portioning out Mrs Cope's lemon sponge.

'I'm simply saying she has accepted you as her niece and doesn't think twice about introducing you.'

'I know. Sometimes it embarrasses me more than it does her.' At a recent luncheon at Fullers restaurant, Flora had become the unwelcome centre of attention for that very reason.

'I enjoy telling people you're my cousin, just so I can watch their inner debate whether they should ask me to explain. Incidentally, most of them don't, out of politeness, so you are a mystery. Besides, Mama still feels guilty about Uncle William.'

Since discovering her true parentage, Flora had often wondered what her life would have been like as William and Alice's child.

'Mama expected he would forget Lily – I mean Alice – within months and marry some American socialite,' Jocasta went on. 'That he remained single was a constant disappointment. She'll be delighted to hear they're back together.'

'William and Alice aren't together,' Flora reminded her. *At least not yet.* 'The last thing they need is gossip and criticism.'

'Don't give society too much credit, Flora,' Jocasta said through a mouthful of cake. 'We love to drag people down. It's not even malicious. We do it to shore up our own failures and insecurities to make us feel superior.' Jocasta removed the cake crumbs from the corner of her mouth with a finger. 'Believe me, no one really minds where you or Alice came from as long as the stock is good.'

The fragrance of lemon and almond from Jocasta's plate made Flora's mouth water, but she cut herself an almost transparent slice with the excuse she was keeping Jocasta company.

'Eddy will be at the house party, of course, before he returns to Oxford.' Jocasta tossed three sugar cubes into her tea and stirred noisily. 'He said he would come up to town for a few days, but the wretch hasn't so much as called me to tell me when he's arriving.'

Flora's hand stilled on the teapot as she filled her cup. 'You know what Ed is like. I expect he's busy with his friends.' Her hand shook slightly as she put the china back carefully on the tray.

'Yes, you're probably right.' Jocasta sighed and stared off as she chewed. 'He won't want to spend time with his matronly big sister. Silly of me to even expect it.' A tiny frown appeared between her eyebrows, and she tilted her head as she took another bite. 'Incidentally, since when did you call him Ed? Was that his idea or yours?'

'I, er, cannot remember.' Flora fiddled with an embroidery hoop containing a half-finished initial on a handkerchief which Sally left behind. Flora hated embroidery. 'He must have mentioned it when I last saw him.' Her gaze went to Jocasta's skirt as she searched for something to distract her. 'I do like your outfit, Jo. Where did you get it?'

'What this?' Jocasta returned her plate to the table, stood and twirled in front of Flora, displaying the café-au-lait skirt embroidered with a diamond pattern between knee and ankle, teamed with a matching jacket trimmed with turquoise piping. 'Maryanne

Fielding took me to her new couture house. Chevrons are de rigueur this season.'

'I didn't know you patronised a couture house, Jo?'

'You must let me take you there sometime.' Jocasta checked her appearance in the overmantel mirror.

'What does a couture house offer which a seamstress cannot?' Flora asked.

'Exclusivity, my dear,' she spoke over one shoulder before turning back to the mirror again. 'They offer designs unavailable anywhere else, but that are also instantly recognisable, so everyone knows who made them. It's like membership in an exclusive club where the name represents not only the tailor's skill but also how much it costs our husbands.'

'What a shallow world you live in, Jo.' Flora smiled, bemused by the aristocracy's love of private clubs and elite organisations.

'At least I'll never drown.' Her shoulders lifted briefly in a girlish gesture as she resumed her seat. 'The House of Joel is run by two delightful ladies, Miss Ruby and Miss Renee. Maryanne took me to a showing just off Bond Street. If you visit, mention my name, or better still, Maryanne Fielding's.'

'Maybe I will,' Flora replied, but had no plans to abandon her hard-working seamstress whose skill with a needle provided for four children and an out-of-work husband.

'Is there any more tea, Flora?' Jocasta frowned into her empty cup and reached for another slice of cake with her other hand.

'Oh, yes, of course.' Jocasta appeared set for the rest of the morning, sending Flora's stomach into freefall.

Jocasta spent the next half hour opining the loss of her figure during the hottest months of the summer; accompanied by three slices of cook's excellent cake and several cups of tea.

'Goodness, is that the time?' She gave the clock a horrified glance. 'I'm meeting Blanche Hemming for some shopping and then luncheon. I had better get a move on.' She scrambled to her feet. 'I expect we'll next see you at the house party. I cannot wait to meet Alice.'

Flora showed Jocasta out. She and Bunny planned to travel to Gloucestershire with Jocasta and her husband in their town coach, Jeremy, having not yet succumbed to the delights of motor travel. With another Fitzhugh baby on the way, Flora doubted he would soon.

She closed the front door on her guest and leaned against it, releasing a slow breath. Suppose they couldn't prove Ed's innocence before then? Not only would they have to break the dreadful news to his parents, but admit they had known about it at the beginning and, despite their efforts, had failed to exonerate their son.

The responsibility weighed heavily as Flora dragged her feet up the stairs, wishing Inspector Maddox would call soon with some welcome news.

10

What had been a jumble of disconnected thoughts during Jocasta's visit solidified into a plan by the time her guest had left. The first part of her strategy was to write to Mrs Tilney, the lady Amy had mentioned as being a close friend of Sylvia Thompson. While dressing, she pondered how, as a stranger she might phrase the letter in order to elicit information about the Thompsons.

'She'll most likely think I have a colossal cheek and tear it up or inform the police I'm a suspicious character who needs a visit from the constabulary,' Flora muttered under her breath as she examined her reflection in the hall mirror. Her white-on-white embroidered blouse with a fluted front yoke and a straight teal wool skirt were perfect for her planned expedition.

'Are you talking to me, madam?' Sally asked as she approached, a pile of linens in her arms most likely destined for the laundry.

'I'm simply thinking aloud.' Flora tucked a stray strand of hair behind her ear, amused at the fact her maid had finally learned to call her 'Madam' and not her habitual 'Missus', the lesson having been an arduous one. 'Have you seen Lord Edward?'

'Not since breakfast.' Sally moved closer, lowering her voice. 'He's in a lot of trouble, ain't he?'

'Whatever makes you think so?' Flora's hand stilled on her hatpin.

'Well, stands to reason, like.' Sally clutched the linens to her diminutive chest. 'The only visitor he's seen since he arrived is Inspector Maddox, and he stayed in his room while you were downstairs with Lady Jocasta. Then he spends the rest of the time moonin' about the place with his chin on the floor. You and Mr Bunny are poking about in another murder, aren't you?'

'It's a complicated situation, Sally, and hard to explain.' Flora pretended to adjust her hat, her eyes averted from her maid's reflection in the glass. She could never successfully lie to her maid. Sally was too sharp for that.

'I know what's going on, because Mr Bunny never keeps a newspaper for more'n a day.' Sally huffed an impatient breath. 'Now there's three copies of *The Times* and two *Evening Standards* on his desk, all opened to an article about a murder at Paddington Stat—'

'All right, Sally.' Flora lowered her arms, resigned. 'You mustn't say a word to anyone about murders, or mention Lord Edward is staying here. Do you understand?'

'Course I do. Stokes has already warned the staff to keep shtum. Did his lordship kill that man?' Her round brown eyes widened in excitement rather than shock. Sally's claim to notoriety was having been born in Flower and Dean Street, where two of Jack the Ripper's victims lived. That the area had been demolished before Sally was born did nothing to reduce her pride in her origins.

'He certainly did not!' Flora inhaled sharply. 'I will not discuss this with you now, as I'm about to go out. Would you ask Stokes to have the motor car brought round?' As Sally turned to go, she added, 'On second thoughts, as you're so interested, you can get your coat and accompany me.'

'That's more like it. Won't be a mo.' Grinning, Sally hurried off down the hall. Ed wasn't the only one who hated being stuck in the house all day.

Her maid's footsteps had barely receded when a noise made Flora glance up to where Ed leaned over the banister. His sandy hair flopped forward partly obscuring his face.

'Has she gone?'

'Who? Sally?' At his frustrated sigh, she gasped, 'Oh, Ed, I'm sorry. I completely forgot. Jocasta left a while ago.'

'And you left me up there?' He stomped down the remaining steps, his gaze sliding from her toes to her hat. 'You're going out? What about luncheon?'

'I'll have something later.' In response to his raised eyebrows, she added, 'Ah, I see, you meant you?' Though by his blank look, her sarcasm had been wasted. 'Don't worry, you won't starve. Stokes has his instructions, and he's been made aware you don't like cabbage.'

'I just wish I didn't have to stay here.' He slumped down onto the last step, elbows on his knees and chin in his hands. 'How many times can I read about a rabbit in a blue coat and stay sane? It's not as if Arthur appreciates it; he giggles in all the wrong places.'

'I'm sorry, Ed, but it cannot be avoided.' The distress in his voice scraped at her heart. The optimistic, fun-loving boy she once cared for had become a despondent young man in a matter of hours. Close up, she could see purple smudges beneath his eyes. Had he slept at all since his arrival?

'Where are you going anyway?' He pressed his face against the balusters.

'Your sister recommended a couture house she frequents.'

'What?' His jaw dropped. 'You're going to buy a new dress? That's rum. You might at least spend the time looking for clues or something.'

'I'm not going to buy clothes. I have an idea, but need more information before I can discuss it with you.'

'An idea about what? Come on, Flora, you cannot leave me hanging.'

She shrugged into her coat. 'Look, Ed.' Her fingers worked their way down the row of buttons as she talked. 'If I learn anything, I promise you'll be the first to know.'

'I'm not really in any position to argue, am I?'

'Precisely. And don't be so petulant. I'm doing this for you.'

'I know you are, but if you come back with an

oversized cardboard box with a pretentious name scrawled across it, I shall be most peeved.'

She was about to protest, but his cheeky grin revealed he was joking.

'Couldn't I come with you?' he wheedled. 'I'll stay in the motor car.' When she frowned at him, he added, 'I overheard Stokes tell Timms to bring the Berliet round.'

'I don't think it would be a good idea, Ed. What if Inspector Maddox found out? Look,' she sighed at his disappointed expression, 'there are some copies of *The Strand Magazine* in the study with some of Conan-Doyle's detective stories. I know you like those. You never know, you might even find something instructive which might help to prepare for your next term at Balliol.'

'You're not my governess any more, Flora.' He pushed himself to his feet and descended the last few steps, where he stood slouched against the newel post, his arms crossed over his chest.

'It's a hard habit to break. Also, I cannot believe how quickly you forgot all the things I taught you about manners and gratitude. You're behaving like a peevish child at the moment.'

'I don't mean to be, especially when you've been so kind to help me. I'll try to behave better, but have you any idea how frustrating it is being stuck here? I want to be out there helping you find out who killed Leo!'

'I sympathise, but—' She met his gaze. 'You called him Leo, not Mr Thompson. I noticed you did that before.'

'Did I?' He shrugged. 'Does it matter?'

'Not really, but – well, never mind.' Perhaps it was more common these days to use someone's first name so soon after meeting them. 'Incidentally, Jocasta thought you were staying with her this week. We don't want her calling Cleeve Abbey and finding out you aren't there.'

'Cripes, what do I do?' He pushed a hand through his hair, making the front stand on end 'I know. I'll write and say I ran into Stinky Baines and am staying with him. His parents are away in the South of France until the end of June.'

'Yes, I remember that name – funnily enough. Remind me... Stinky isn't his real name?' Flora pulled on a glove. 'Or shouldn't I ask?'

'It's a funny story, actually. He loves cheese, so his parents would send him packets of the stuff throughout the term which he always kept in—'

'I get the gist, Ed. Thank you.' She gave an exaggerated shudder, briefly pondering the strange proclivities of schoolboys. 'Do the Baines' have a telephone?'

'I expect so. Why?'

'Don't write to Jocasta. Call her and apologise for not contacting her. That you now you have a cold or something.'

'That's a spiffing idea. Jo hates germs. If she thinks I'm ill, she'll ban me from going within a mile of her. But what if she insists on calling a doctor or sends her maid round with calves' foot jelly or some equally awful concoction?'

'Calves foot jelly? Jocasta? Really, Ed.'

'Of course, I wasn't thinking.' He trailed back upstairs again, his sulky expression reminding her of the boy she spent a week with at sea on the *SS Minneapolis* in pursuit of a murderer. They had formed a strong bond as that adventure unfolded aboard ship, and now another murder had thrown them together again. Though this time it was a matter of keeping Ed's reputation intact. Not to mention his life. Lord and Lady Trent would be devastated and have every reason to accuse them of mishandling the situation. The responsibility weighed heavily on Flora.

Sally approached along the hall, her head cocked to where Ed's footsteps could still be heard above them. 'Will his lordship be all right? He's been that tetchy this morning.'

'He's frustrated. I doubt I'll be able to keep him indoors much longer.'

'I'm glad to be getting out m'self, if truth be known.' Sally pulled a soft-crowned velvet hat on over her dark curls, squashing them. 'I ain't never been to one of them *coo-chure* houses.'

'*Haven't ever* been,' Flora corrected her. Either Sally had remarkable hearing or she had eavesdropped. How else would she know about The House of Joel?

'The new girl, Jessie, is getting on me nerves.' Sally followed Flora along the tiled front path to where Timms waited at the open door of the motor car. 'She's a bit simple, if you ask me. I asked her four times this morning to make me a cup of tea and she just stared at me as if I was talking Dutch.'

'It's not her job to make you tea, Sally.' Flora climbed into the rear seat, where she waited patiently for her maid to settle before giving Timms an approximate address for The House of Joel.

'What do you hope to find at this *coo-chure* house, then?' Sally asked when Timms had pulled into the road.

She had hoped to keep Sally away from Ed's trouble, partly because he was family but mainly because their last investigation had almost cost Sally her life, not that she would not be put off easily.

'I told you it was complicated.' Flora sighed, resigned. 'A witness we spoke to mentioned a lady in a red coat similar to something Lady Jocasta wore. She said the design was exclusive to this fashion house.'

'A red coat?' Sally wrinkled her nose in mild disgust. 'Is that all the clue you've got?'

'Unfortunately, yes.' Sally's obvious disdain made her realise it was a tenuous link. 'It's worth a try. Anyway,' she slanted Sally a teasing sideways look, 'I'm surprised you're not more concerned about leaving Jessie with Abel? It's thirsty work building walls. I don't doubt he'll need to ask *her* to fetch him tea more than once.'

'What choo implyin', madam?' Sally's tone was just the right side of respect. 'My Abel's not fickle.'

'I didn't say he was. But are you willing to take the risk?'

'Hah! Don't you worry 'bout him. I've got *his* measure.' Sally jutted her chin belligerently and stared out of the side window. 'And hers.'

11

Timms guided Bunny's Berliet into a neat double-fronted Georgian house in Albemarle Street. Gleaming black railings led to a black front door; a discreet brass plaque on the wall beside the bell push proclaimed it as The House of Joel.

A fair young woman with a winsome smile answered Flora's knock. She wore a tailored grey skirt and crisp white blouse, her honey gold hair drawn back into a neat, unfussy coil at the back of her head.

'I'm Miss Renee Joel. All our patrons call me Miss Renee.' She thrust out a slender hand that Flora took after brief hesitation, having mistaken her for a junior member of staff. 'Is this your first visit, Mrs Harrington?' Miss Renee glanced at the calling card Flora handed her.

'It is. My cousin, Lady Jocasta Fitzhugh, recommended your establishment.'

'I'm sure we'll be able to assist you.' Miss Joel dimpled charmingly. 'Lady Jocasta is a frequent and valued patron.'

Flora didn't doubt it.

They were shown into a cream and white salon with an abundance of gilt mirrors and delicate French-style furniture. The only concession to business being the desk set in one corner, with an open appointment book beside a vase of fuchsias. The entire house smelled of fresh paint and beeswax polish.

Flora wandered to the full-height window that overlooked the street, which gave her a clear view of Timms, who leaned on the car bonnet, his arms folded. Two young ladies in straw hats and skirts swaying round their ankles approached. Their steps slowed as they drew level with the handsome chauffeur, heads close together and cheeks flushed pink as they whispered behind their hands. The chauffeur inclined his head and smiled at them in flirtatious acknowledgment. Flora's lips twitched, and she left the window and took a seat on the sofa. Sally perched on an upright chair in the corner, her feet together and hands clasped in her lap.

'How might we be of service today?' Miss Renee asked.

'I admired one of your designs recently, of a rather distinctive coat.' Flora described the red coat Dr Billings had told her about. 'I would like to own a similar garment.'

'The chevron motif is a feature of our autumn collection. However, the item to which you refer was a one-off piece commissioned by another client.' Her eyes softened with regret. 'It cannot be replicated.'

'How disappointing.' Her excitement dissolved. 'Would you be prepared to reveal for whom you made the coat?'

'I'm not sure I ought to—' Miss Renee broke off, flushing.

'I asked,' Flora smoothed down her skirt while conjuring a credible reason for her request, 'because I'm due to attend a house party soon. Some guests patronise your establishment. If I wore the same motif in her company, it might prove embarrassing. For both of us.'

'I can see that might be difficult.' Miss Renee worried her bottom lip with small white teeth. 'If it's for reasons of discretion, I might make an exception. We made that garment for Lady Roseberry.'

Flora recalled a suffrage meeting at which Lady Roseberry was a guest speaker. A flamboyant woman in her late forties, short and plump; not at all like the woman Dr Billings had described.

'Lady Roseberry is a very particular client,' Miss Renee fidgeted. 'Every item we make for her is exclusive. She's most insistent.' Miss Renee retrieved a leather-bound folder from a nearby table. 'Perhaps you'd like to browse our current designs? I'm confident you'll find something you like. In the meantime, I'll send Abigail to take your measurements.'

'How kind, but perhaps on this occasion I won't require—'

'Wouldn't hurt to look, would it, madam?' Sally left her chair and crept across the carpet on silent feet, eyeing the book hungrily.

Her discreet exit sabotaged; Flora hesitated. 'Well, as I'm here, I suppose not.'

Lulled into the comfortable atmosphere, and with both Sally and Miss Renee urging her on, time sped by as she browsed through the plates.

Jocasta had not exaggerated, The House of Joel produced unique and beautiful gowns which did not conform to the fashionable S-bend shape Flora found so uncomfortable. Miss Renee made skilful pencil sketches to illustrate subtle changes which could be made to suit Flora's figure.

With the use of blatant flattery and Sally's encouragement, Flora was persuaded to try on a cornflower blue organdie gown. The full skirt floated to her feet like a soft cloud.

'This suits your colouring perfectly, madam.' Miss Renee tweaked folds and adjusted buttons as she talked. 'It brings out the green tinge in your eyes, too. You are so slender; you could be one of our regular models. I doubt this gown would need much alteration to fit you.'

'It would be perfect for Miss Lydia's wedding.' Sally hunched her shoulders excitedly, her hands clasped beneath her chin.

'I admit, it's stunning. And original.' Flora fingered the bodice overlaid with delicate lace, twisting from side to side as she considered whether she dared buy it, when she knew deep down the battle was already won. 'The wedding is tomorrow. Can the alterations be done in time?'

'It's minor work, which is well within the abilities of our seamstresses. Mrs Harrington.'

'Then I'll take it.' Flora ran her hands down the skirt, hoping Bunny would regard the expense as justified in the name of investigative research.

'What about the dusky pink one, madam?' Sally hovered at her shoulder. 'It would be perfect for the earl's house party. Your uncle, the earl, would love to see you in that.'

Flora raised her eyebrows, but Sally's blatant showing off had an instant effect on Miss Renee, who, sensing another lucrative sale, fluttered and gushed round her.

'We'll have to make the orchid pink gown from scratch, which could be completed within a week.'

Flora exchanged a conspiratorial look with Sally. 'Why not?'

The sale agreed. Miss Renee wrote up the documents, booked a fitting appointment for Flora's second gown in four days and, amid thanks and gratitude all round, showed them to the door.

'I enjoyed that more than I expected to.' Flora tugged on her gloves and descended the front steps. 'It was almost worth finding out nothing about the coat.'

'Madam,' Sally nudged her. 'There's someone trying to get your attention.'

Flora followed her gaze to the area steps, where Abigail, the girl who had taken her measurements ascended to street level.

'Excuse me,' she asked, hesitant, shooting a quick

glance at the closed front door. 'I heard you ask Miss Renee about the coat.' She pressed a card into Flora's hand. 'The people here will help you for a reasonable price.' Without waiting for a response, she hurried back down the steps and disappeared through a door into the basement.

'What's it say?' Sally peered over her shoulder as Flora examined the thin, slightly greyed piece of card.

'It's an address,' she read aloud. 'M Maurice, Bespoke Tailor, Church Lane, Fulham.'

'Knock-off merchant.' Sally sniffed derisively. 'Thought as much.'

'I believe you're right, Sally.' Flora tapped the card against her bottom lip. 'It seems Lady Roseberry isn't the only one in town wearing chevrons this season.'

She strode to where the chauffeur held open the rear door of the motor car and showed him the card. 'Do you know your way to this address?'

'I could probably find it, madam.' Timms touched his cap, his wry smile of one who is accustomed to keeping secrets.

After a couple of false turns, Timms pulled the motor car to a halt in front of a row of houses that might have once been grand residences but had been split into places of business on the ground and lower floors with lodgings above. The rendered façades were cracked and stained, with flaking paint on doors and window frames. A cigar shop stood beside a sign offering legal services, and a 'For Rent' sign was displayed in an upper window. Dull paint, unsteady railings and broken paving stones proliferated, with not a tree or patch of grass in sight to break the unrelenting brick and concrete stained by years of coal smoke.

'It's number twelve,' Flora tapped the chauffeur on the shoulder. 'On our right and farther down.'

'Are you sure you want to go in there, madam?' Timms gave the street a hard glance as he held open the door for her to alight.

'I shall be as quick as I can.' She did not remind him not to leave the motor car unattended. He loved the machine as much as her husband did. 'Sally, you stay here with Timms.'

'Why can't I come with you?' Sally halted half-way out of the rear seat.

'Because I'll find out more if I'm alone. Now don't look at me like that. I know what I'm doing.'

Flora hesitated at the bottom of three worn stone steps with a dip in the centre from thousands of feet, which led to a shabby black door; an upper-ground-floor window beside it was blacked out by a faded blind. Avoiding the wrought-iron rail which threatened to topple at the slightest touch, Flora paused in front of the door and took a deep breath.

She followed a tentative knock with a firmer one, which was answered by a lanky man in a smart, if slightly threadbare suit, a pair of round spectacles perched on his head over a severely receding hairline. He slid them expertly down his forehead onto his nose to examine the card Abigail had given her, at which his expression altered from wary suspicion to surprised delight.

Flora held out her hand to retrieve it, but he slid the card into his pocket, leaving her hand in mid-air.

'Come this way, Mrs—?' he broke off with an enquiring look.

'Madam will suffice.' Flora mimicked the bored condescension her mother-in-law saved for tradesmen and recalcitrant shop assistants.

'It usually does.' He sighed and inclined his head, an arm extended in an invitation to precede him into a narrow, dimly lit dark green hallway that carried a faint smell of mildew. With the door closed, the hall was thrown into deeper gloom, making Flora feel less confident as her footsteps echoed on the cracked lino. Regretting not having brought Sally with her, Flora forced herself forward into the room he directed her to at the end of the corridor.

Gas jets hissed from the walls, lit to supplement the meagre light from one tiny window at shoulder height. A plain pine table dominated the centre of a room filled with shambolic wooden racks ending a foot below the yellowed ceiling, each one stacked with bolts of cloth.

'The garments aren't made in here,' he said quickly when he caught her staring round the dingy space. 'My seamstresses have a studio at the top of the house with better light.'

'I wondered if you could make a certain style of coat I've seen,' Flora declined the seat he offered, determined to get the unpleasant business over with quickly. 'A one-off design which the designers refuse to make for me. The young lady who gave me the card said you might oblige me.' She described the coat with the chevron pattern for a second time that morning.

'I know the garment to which you refer.' He removed his spectacles and laid them on the long table. 'I could make one to resemble the original design so closely, you wouldn't be able to tell the difference. For a considerably lower fee, I might add.'

'I see. So, you copy the designs from The House of Joel and reproduce them for ladies who do not wish to pay their prices?'

'Correct.' He flushed and coughed into a fist.

'There will be certain differences. The buttons, for instance, are manufactured and not handmade from bone, but in all other respects—'

'It will be identical.' Flora nodded slowly. 'I understand. Might I ask how many coats of this design you have made?'

'I – I beg your pardon?' He blinked, snatched the glasses from the table and put them on, either to see her more clearly or to hide behind. 'I don't understand.'

'I think you do, sir.' Flora's confidence rose in direct proportion to his nervousness. 'I would like to know the names of the clients for whom you made the coat.'

'My good lady, I really don't think that's any of your concern.' His voice remained steady, but the hand he brought to adjust his spectacles shook.

'Even if such a coat was worn by someone in the commission of a serious crime?' She had no idea if she had guessed correctly about the lady in the red coat, but something about Mrs Thompson's death niggled at her.

'What *are* you insinuating?' He pulled in his chin, his eyes wide with shock.

'Nothing at all. In fact, *I* might help *you*.'

'Help *me*?' Scepticism replaced his surprise.

'Indeed. If you give me the names and addresses of the women to whom you sold the chevron coats, I can guarantee the police won't bother you.'

'Madam, please understand,' he extended both hands in a gesture of regret, 'I have a reputation to protect. The ladies I supply expect confidentiality, therefore I am unable—'

'As you wish,' Flora interrupted him. 'I had hoped to avoid having to mention your name to the police.' She gave the room a sweeping look of disdain. 'There's also the matter of the girl.'

'Girl?'

'If the House of Joel discovers one of their seam-stresses entices customers to your establishment, I doubt she'll have her job long.'

'You cannot do that.' His eyes widened in alarm. 'Abigail is my youngest sister. She needs the job. I cannot afford to employ her here.'

Flora's stomach dropped. Had she gone too far? The one time she employed her mother-in-law's con-descension, she had threatened a man for no other reason than he tried to make a living. Even Flora knew it was not an unknown practice for tailors to copy their competitors' designs and sell them off at cheaper rates.

'I didn't mean to threaten you. All I need is information.' Guilt brought heat to her cheeks 'If you help me, I'll have no reason to mention our conversation to anyone. Especially the police.'

Why did she *say* that? Now he would really think she was threatening him.

'That is *all* you want? The names of these particular clients?' Hope flared in his flat eyes as he saw she offered a negotiation, not a confrontation.

'You have my word.'

He hesitated for a few seconds, then gave a brisk nod and strode to a rack in the corner. He pulled down a cardboard box the size of a small suitcase and laid it on the table. 'I made three coats like the one you mentioned. I have the receipts here.' He rummaged through the contents, pulled out a wad of paper and flicked through it. 'Here they are. The first was for a Mrs Walters who lives in Chelsea.'

'What did she look like?'

'I beg your pardon?' He blinked, confused.

'You have her measurements there.' Flora nodded at the paper in his hand. 'Was she tall, short, old or young?'

'Oh, er.' His lips moved as he did mental calculations. 'A short lady, and generously proportioned, as I recall. About sixty. Her husband is a grocer who—'

'No, she isn't who I'm looking for.' Dr Billings had described her as a tall, attractive woman. 'Who else?'

He selected another card. 'I made one for a Miss Ann Craft of twenty-six Courthouse Road, Finchley.' He pressed a finger to his cheek and stared off in an aid to memory. 'I remember her very well. A blonde, blue-eyed young woman of about twenty with a waist measurement of an enviable eighteen inches and she—' He broke off as he caught Flora's expression. 'Is she not of interest?'

'I'm not sure.' Flora thought for a moment. 'Possibly not, as the lady I am looking for was dark-haired.' Though she memorised the address just in case. 'And the next?'

'The only other person who bought this coat did not give her name, so I marked her down in the order book as a "Miss S".'

'Surely you know *something* about her? You took her measurements I imagine, and must have spoken to her at least twice.'

'Well, er...' He flushed a deep red. 'She wasn't particularly memorable, as I recall.'

'Really?' Flora speculated he had made some unwelcome compliment, and the memory of her uncompromising set-down put that high colour in his cheeks.

'All right. She was tall and of slender proportions, which showed the coat off to advantage. She kept her hat on so I didn't see her hair colour, but her high cheekbones gave her an exotic look.'

'It wasn't that difficult, was it?' That telling off must have been chilling. 'Anything else? An address, perhaps?'

'Uh – no. She refused to give an address and requested the coat be delivered.'

'Delivered where?' *That sounded more like it.*

He turned the copy of the bill of sale over. 'Ah yes, here it is. The Dahlia Hotel in Coptic Street, Bloomsbury. I'm afraid there's nothing else I can add.' His slow shrug displayed an air of defeat. 'I made this one at the end of last year, so I assume she stayed at a hotel, and has since moved on.'

'Thank you, Mr Maurice. You've been most helpful.' Flora quoted the name printed on the card, although he had not introduced himself.

He escorted her to the front door, where she extended her hand for a parting shake. Her gloved fingers connected with his, and she transferred a sovereign into his palm. He did not look down, but his eyes widened a fraction.

'How did you get on, madam?' Sally eased along

the rear seat to make way for her. 'You look like you've lost a half-crown and found sixpence.'

'Considerably more,' Flora murmured, as she took her seat. 'I assumed he was dishonest, so I wasn't very nice to him.'

'Feeling bad, now, are you?' Sally asked.

'Actually yes. I've just bullied a man simply for trying to make a living. His shop makes no difference at all to the Lady Roseberrys of this world. I imagine there's many a librarian or office girl pleased to own a suit or a coat similar to those worn by society ladies. Never mind the cheaper buttons or the thin lining. In a former life I would have been happy with one too.'

'Don't see anything wrong with them m'self. My mam used to make knock-offs.' Sally unfolded a cone of stiff paper and peered inside. 'Well, more like knock-offs of knock-offs, if you see what I mean.' She thrust the paper cone under Flora's nose. 'Would you like one?'

'What are they?' Flora eyed the paper suspiciously.

'Mint imperials.' Sally popped one into her mouth.

'Thank you, no.' Flora inwardly shuddered at the idea of cracking her teeth on a solid lump of sugar.

'Good at it, my mam was. Kept us kids from

starving at any rate. 'Cos me dad weren't no good at it. At least I think he was me dad.' Her voice tailed off as she peered into the paper cone, crumpled it in one hand before returning it to her pocket.

Flora bit her lip to prevent a smile, while reminding herself she shouldn't seek entertainment in her maid's underprivileged early life – something Sally made almost impossible with her pragmatism.

'Seems to me you're going to a lot of trouble madam,' Sally continued. 'There must be hundreds of red coats in London.'

'I know, but this is a particular coat, and quite distinctive. And I might have found it. That man back there delivered it to The Dahlia Hotel.'

'What's that when it's at home, then?'

'A hotel with the name of a flower that begins with a "D", Sally. As Master Bunny says, I don't believe in coincidences.'

'I've never 'eard him say that,' Sally mumbled through a bulge in her cheek.

12

Flora dressed early for dinner that evening to give her time to compose a letter to Mrs Tilney, the lady Amy claimed had been Mrs Thompson's closest friend.

After several false starts, clear by the rapidly filling wastepaper basket at her side, she began with an apology for approaching someone to whom she had not been introduced, followed by condolences on the loss of her friend, Sylvia Thompson, with whom Flora claimed a slight acquaintance. Hoping to encourage openness on Mrs Tilney's part, Flora explained her upbringing at Cleeve Abbey; how she now lived in London and had only recently been informed of Sylvia's demise, and also expressed her sympathy for Leo.

The approach of Bunny's footsteps made her slide the sealed envelope into a drawer.

'Sorry I'm late, but I lost track of time and then couldn't find a hansom.' He planted a swift kiss on her temple, tossed his jacket over a nearby chair and un-tucked his shirt from his trousers. 'How was your day?'

'Eventful, if frustrating. Jocasta called to see me this morning.'

'Did you shove Ed into the cupboard under the stairs before she spotted him?' Bunny chuckled at his own joke.

'Something like that. She told me about a couture house called The House of Joel. I paid it a visit today in search of a red coat.'

'You bought a coat?' Without unfastening the but-tons, he pulled the shirt over his head and hurled it in the general direction of the chair without looking to see where it fell.

'No, but I found the perfect dress for Lydia's wed-ding.' She watched the shirt tumble to the floor in dis-may. Three years of marriage had taught her complaints about his untidiness went nowhere. It also confirmed her decision not to mention the pink silk until it occupied space in her wardrobe.

'So, what's this about a coat?'

'Do you recall Dr Billings said the woman who

helped Sylvia Thompson when she was injured wore one?' She dragged her gaze from the crumpled shirt.

'Vaguely. Is it important?'

'I don't know – yet.' Flora selected a sapphire pendant from her jewellery box and fastened it around her neck, her chin tucked down. 'For Dr Billings to notice what she was wearing is significant. I thought finding out to whom the coat belonged might lead us to the woman.'

'Did you find out much?' He kicked off his left shoe, followed swiftly with his right.

'Frustrating. But there *is* a connection.' Flora arranged the pendant in the hollow in her throat and twisted on the stool to face him. 'A tailor in Fulham who makes copies of couture designs made an identical coat for a woman who asked for it to be delivered to The Dahlia Hotel in Bloomsbury.'

'Now that *is* interesting.' Bunny contemplated the ceiling, one hand beneath his chin. 'But hardly conclusive.'

'It's more than a coincidence, though. A woman wearing the same coat was in Cheltenham when—'

'A similar coat. You don't know it was the same one or the same woman.' He threw his socks into a corner, then pulled out three drawers in succession, looking for a clean pair.

'Spoken like a genuine man of law. Pedantic to the last. Similar then. And your socks are in the top drawer, where they always are.' She tried not to sigh. 'The tailor said he only made three coats like it.'

'Or three dozen. Flora, you cannot believe anything he said. He's hardly likely to have revealed his activities to you if he's stealing designs.' He located a pair of socks, which he held up in triumph. 'Anyway, whose murder are we investigating? Leo's or his mother's?'

'Leo's, I suppose but—'

'Exactly. And this woman, whoever she is, is probably long gone by now.' He gave her shoulders a squeeze on his way to the door. 'I'm going to have a bath before dinner.'

Flora propped her chin in her hand and stared at her reflection in the mirror. She kept recalling what Dr Billings had said about the woman's strange behaviour when she brought Sylvia to the surgery. The way she kept fussing and how clumsy she was by getting in the doctor's way. Nothing definite, but as Riordan Maguire would have said, Flora could no more ignore it than a cat after mackerel.

* * *

'That policeman is here again, sir,' the butler announced just as Flora and Bunny settled in the sitting room with a pre-prandial sherry. 'I explained this is an unsociable hour to call, but he insists on speaking with you and Lord Trent,' he added with the trace of a sneer.

'It's all right, Stokes. Show him in, would you?' Bunny waited for the door to click shut again before asking, 'Do you sometimes feel Stokes is a little too grand for us?'

'Frequently.' Flora puffed air through her pursed lips. 'I imagine him seated at the kitchen table, a pencil behind one ear as he trawls through advertisements in *The Lady* in search of more conventional employers. Preferably titled ones.'

'I'm a solicitor.' Bunny pulled a face. 'How more conventional can one be?'

'I meant me.' She leaned across the space between them on the sofa and tweaked a lock of hair from his forehead with her free hand. 'A mistress who investigates grisly murders and entertains police officers probably offends his sensibilities.'

'Well, don't tell anyone, but I enjoy your penchant for crime solving. It's exciting. Like you.' He caught her hand in mid-air and brought the tips of her fingers to his lips. 'At least if we do it together, you're less likely to venture into the houses of killers and get yourself locked in cellars at their mercy.'

She snuggled closer, recalling when she and Sally had been trapped in just such a situation. It was Sally's optimism and quick thinking that had saved them then.

'That was a mistake.' Flora's pride at having solved a crime had sent her barging into a dangerous situation without thinking.

'Inspector Maddox, sir, madam,' Stokes announced from the door, sending them springing apart.

'Good evening, Inspector.' Bunny rose, skirting the sofa to welcome the visitor.

'I apologise for disturbing you so close to the dinner hour.' Maddox accepted Bunny's handshake, then acknowledged Flora with a gracious nod.

In his customary mustard check suit, he brought an earthy smell of old leather overlaid with horse manure into the room. That he had arrived unaccompanied, she took as an encouraging sign that he was not about to arrest Ed.

'Might I offer you a sherry?' Bunny asked on his way to the sideboard.

'I don't see why not.' Maddox rubbed his hands together in anticipation. 'After all, I'm on my way home and officially off duty.' He flipped up the back of his coat and sat on the upright chair, giving the room a swift, penetrating glance. 'Where is Lord Trent this evening? Not taken himself off to some gambling den in search of excitement?'

'He's upstairs, dressing for dinner,' Flora said through gritted teeth. 'I can assure you he hasn't left this house all day.' Though, if the inspector was aware of how restless Ed had been, he might arrest him for his own protection.

'You're not here to check up on him, I trust?' Bunny frowned, the decanter hovering over a glass.

'I would rather wait until the gentleman is present to save having to repeat myself.' He took a sip of sherry, rolled it around his mouth and peered into the glass.

Ed's gaze went straight to the inspector when he arrived. 'Stokes told me you wanted to see me.'

Maddox placed his glass on a low table and stood, offering his hand, which Ed took, but released after the briefest of shakes.

'Have you discovered the weapon used to kill Mr Thompson?' Bunny asked.

Maddox folded his hands across his midriff, regarding both Ed and Bunny through half-closed eyes. 'As we surmised, the victim received a single stab wound. And not to be too specific in the presence of a lady,' he raised an eyebrow in Flora's direction, 'a thin-bladed knife was inserted between his ribs just below the heart and thrust upwards.'

'I'm grateful you weren't *too* specific, Inspector.' Flora winced.

'My apologies, dear lady. I'm simply quoting from the official report. The style of the weapon is significant, because when removed, the wound sealed, which explained the small amount of blood present. With his heart punctured, the young man bled internally and died quickly.'

'Poor man,' Flora murmured and glanced at Ed, whose face had drained of colour.

'You've seen this type of injury before?' Bunny asked.

'I have.' Maddox removed his ubiquitous notebook from an inside pocket and flicked through it. 'These thin knives or stilettos, as they are known, are favoured by Italian immigrants in areas like Somers Town and St Pancras. The victim is often unaware of what has happened until it's too late, by which time the assailant is nowhere near. We have yet to locate it and doubt we will as they are expensive and rarely discarded.'

'Have you found out anything at all?' Ed asked sulkily.

'Our enquiries are still in the early stages. We're in touch with the Gloucestershire police, who paid a call on Thompson's Haberdashery in Cheltenham. A Mrs Drake informed them Mr Thompson inherited the premises from his mother, who died in December from blood poisoning after a domestic accident.'

Flora's internal debate whether to inform him this information was not news was decided by Bunny, whose hand came down on her shoulder in warning.

'Inspector,' he said. 'My wife and I ought to reveal we visited Cheltenham the day of your last visit.'

'I was wondering when you would mention that.' Maddox sighed and shook his head. 'Mrs Drake mentioned the nice young couple from London who were so interested in Mrs Thompson and her son.' He clicked the edge of the notebook with his thumb, setting Flora's teeth on edge. 'She seemed to think you grew up in that area, Mrs Harrington. Or was that a fabrication?'

'It was not.' Flora avoided looking at him. 'I was born and raised there. But, before you ask, we didn't know Mrs Thompson, or her son. Had we done so, we would certainly have told you.'

Maddox's sceptical gaze flicked to Bunny, who added, 'That's quite true. It's possible to live in a small town and not know everyone.'

Flora chewed her bottom lip. Did Maddox also know of their visit to Dr Billings? Perhaps he was biding his time to drop it into the conversation?

'I apologise if you feel we interfered,' Bunny added. 'It seemed logical to find out what we could. I assure you we didn't reveal anything to Mrs Drake, which we shouldn't have.'

'I doubt there's any point in my protesting at this late stage.' Resigned, Maddox took another sip from his glass before consulting his notebook again. 'We have few details of her family other than Sylvia Thompson's parents are deceased, and she was an only child.' His eyes lifted to Flora's. 'Feel free to stop me if you already know all this.'

'What about Leo's father?' Flora asked, chastised but defiant. 'Do you know anything about him?'

'Only that they married abroad, and Mrs Thompson returned to England after his death.' Maddox snapped his notebook shut and slid it into his pocket. 'Have any of you come across a gentleman by the name Mr Frederick Hunter-Griggs?'

'No, I don't think so.' Flora glanced at Bunny and Ed but was met with only blank stares. 'What has this person got to do with Leo Thompson?'

'I hoped you might enlighten *me*.' Maddox retrieved his glass and examined the dark amber liquid through the cut crystal before taking a mouthful. 'He is part-owner of an establishment called The Dahlia Hotel, in Bloomsbury.'

Bunny widened his eyes at Flora, who gave him an I-told-you-so look.

'That was it!' Ed straightened. 'It was called The Dahlia. I remember now.'

'What name did you say, Inspector? Hunter-?' Flora frowned, wondering at Ed's sudden selective memory.

'Griggs,' Maddox supplied. 'I spoke to the gentleman myself and he informed me they had no one named Thompson expected at the hotel, nor had anyone of that name stayed there during the previous three months.'

'Perhaps Leo was staying at another hotel with the same name?' Ed suggested.

'There isn't one, sir, and I haven't finished.' Maddox coughed into a fist. 'When I asked Mr Hunter-Griggs if he knew anyone by the name of Thompson, he said no, but by coincidence that was his late stepmother's maiden name.'

'Sylvia Thompson was his stepmother?' Flora finished for him, a tingle of excitement working its way up her spine. 'Then Leo must have been his half-brother?'

'It appears so.' Maddox gave a smug smile on each of them before continuing. 'The gentleman informed me he had not seen his half-brother for many years. Until recently. His father, Colonel Amery Hunter-Griggs, and his stepmother separated when Leonard, was four. She changed their name back to Thompson and moved to Cheltenham where her parents lived. Leonard has recently been reconciled with the Colonel and his children since Sylvia Thompson's death.'

'The Colonel is still alive?' Flora interjected. 'Then Sylvia wasn't a widow?'

'Indeed, not.' Maddox paused as if savouring the moment. 'Which is where this case becomes interesting. When I informed them that Leo Thompson had been murdered, Mr Hunter-Griggs was most insistent that Leonard Hunter-Griggs, as he has called himself since his mother's death, is not only alive and well, but living at The Dahlia Hotel.'

'What?' Flora's shock was echoed by Bunny.

'But he can't be?' Ed leapt to his feet. 'He's dead. I saw him. Inspector, you have his body.'

'I spoke to Colonel Hunter-Griggs myself.' Maddox waved him back down again. 'He was at the hotel when I called, even though he resides elsewhere. He enjoyed a joke at my expense for some time, em-

ploying every derogatory term for a metropolitan police officer I have ever heard. Not to mention a few I
haven't.' He eased his collar with a finger, clearing his
throat.

'How uncomfortable for you.' Flora clamped her
lips together to prevent a laugh. 'Did you talk to
Leonard as well?'

'I did not.' Maddox frowned. 'However, both the
Colonel and his elder son, as well as several hotel
staff, all claim to have seen the young man that day.'

'But he told me his name was Leo Thompson.' Ed's
breathing quickened on the edge of panic. 'I didn't
make it up.'

'It's not unreasonable Thompson would adopt his
family name now they are reconciled,' Bunny said reasonably.

'Then why not tell Ed he was using a different
name?' Flora asked.

'Which is not relevant, as the young man who died
wasn't Leonard Hunter-Griggs.' Maddox shrugged.

'There's obviously been some sort of misunderstanding.' Flora lifted her arms in surrender. She gave
Ed a reassuring smile, but he turned away, his lips
moving in silent questions.

'One which I'll have to unravel if I'm to get anywhere with this case,' Maddox said. 'I have a body in

the morgue I need to identify before I can begin looking into who killed him and why.'

'Does that mean you don't think Ed is a suspect now?' Flora asked.

'It's not as simple as that, Mrs Harrington. Lord Trent was discovered bending over a corpse. Whoever the man was, questions still need to be answered.'

'But I didn't know—' Ed broke off. 'Oh, what does it matter? You don't believe anything I say.'

'*We* believe you and Inspector Maddox will do everything he can to find out what happened. Won't you, Inspector?' Flora challenged the detective with a stare.

'That's my job, Mrs Harrington.' Maddox drained his glass and pushed himself to his feet. 'But I warn you not to question any more witnesses. If you're seen anywhere near Piccadilly in the near future, I might have to have *you* arrested.'

'On what charge?' She bridled at his patronising tone. 'Loitering intending to shop?' He was becoming far too supercilious for her liking.

'Thank you for calling, Inspector.' Bunny shot Flora a warning look and opened the door, his free hand extended in an invitation for Maddox to leave. 'If there's nothing else, I'll show you out.'

Their tandem footsteps echoed on the hall tiles, followed by their low goodbyes at the front door.

'I thought you said your Inspector Maddox would sort everything out. He's got it all wrong.' Ed pulled a cushion onto his lap and plucked at the gold fringe with restless fingers.

'I don't understand it either.' Flora slumped down beside him. 'That the dead man was using someone else's name is strange.'

'The inspector was pretty angry, wasn't he?' Ed rested his chin on the edge of the cushion. 'He practically accused me of lying.'

'I'd say that's an exaggeration, but don't look so despondent, he'll get over it.' Flora tried to imagine the lambasting Maddox must have endured at the hands of this Colonel Hunter-Griggs and couldn't help sympathising.

'Did you have to tell him you and Bunny had gone to Cheltenham?' Ed snapped, tossing the cushion aside.

'You *know* we did. Mrs Drake mentioned we were there so we couldn't lie about it,' Bunny said as he returned to the room and resumed his seat, his expression thoughtful.

'You didn't say much when Inspector Maddox was here,' Flora said.

'There wasn't much I *could* say.' He retrieved his glass and rolled it slowly between his hands. 'If this Leonard Hunter-Griggs is still alive, then who was the dead man on the train?'

'There must be some sort of mistake,' Ed muttered into his chest. 'The man who died said he was Leo Thompson. Why would he lie?'

'I've no idea,' Bunny's shoulders lifted in a re-signed shrug. 'But then why would this colonel say his son was alive and well if he wasn't?'

'More importantly,' Flora added. 'Why did someone want Leo Thompson dead in the first place? And does that mean the man at the hotel is in danger?'

'No more danger than I am,' Ed muttered. 'The inspector still thinks I'm a murderer.'

13

Dinner was lukewarm, in more ways than one, with little conversation other than polite requests to pass the vegetables. The aroma of roasted pork and apples, which normally elicited enthusiastic compliments to Mrs Cope's skills, went unnoticed. When the clearing of throats, intermittent coughs, and the relentless tick of the grandmother clock grated, Bunny ventured a question.

'Why did Sylvia Thompson tell everyone her husband had died?'

'Possibly because a widow attracts more sympathy than a woman who has left her husband,' Flora replied. 'Although if Leo, or Leonard, is now living with his father and brother at their London hotel, how come Mrs Drake didn't know that? She implied he was still living in Cheltenham?'

'But is he?' Bunny nodded at Ed. 'As you pointed out earlier, Ed, Maddox didn't actually speak to him.'

Ed reached for the gravy boat, which hit the tabletop with a thump, spilling brown drops on the pristine white cloth.

'Oops, sorry. It slipped out of my hand.' He flushed a deep red and dabbed at the offending stains with his napkin.

'Leave it, Ed. You're making it worse. The staff will sort it out.' Flora waved his inept efforts away.

'To be honest, I'm at a loss.' Bunny fastidiously removed his glass away from the gravy stains. 'Why would a man pretending to be Leo Thompson end up dead and tell Ed he had a booking at The Dahlia Hotel when he was already living there?'

'What do you think, Ed?' Flora asked, sensing he wanted to say something but didn't dare.

'I'm as baffled as you are.' Ed twirled his fork over his half-eaten meal.

'Unfortunately, nothing has changed as far as Ed is concerned.' Bunny twisted the stem of his wineglass. 'The identity of the body is immaterial.'

'Does that mean you think I am guilty?' Ed split a worried glance between them.

'No, it doesn't. Although I'd like to know what Maddox really thinks,' Flora said.

'I don't care what he thinks. He's looking for a reason to arrest me, isn't he?' Ed crumpled his napkin in both hands and tossed it onto the table and scraped back his chair. 'May I be excused?'

'But, Ed, your dinner,' Flora began.

'I'm not hungry any more,' he threw over his shoulder and strode from the room.

Flora winced at the slam of the door. 'You really upset him.'

'I believe *we* are the ones who ought to be upset.' Bunny drummed his fingers on the tabletop. 'I'm aware of how fond you are of him, Flora, but I cannot get rid of a feeling there's something he's not told us.'

'You still think he's lying about something?'

'Don't *you*?' He slanted her a sideways look before taking a swig from his wineglass. 'He can't tell us because he's talked himself into an impossible situation and feels he cannot back down now.'

'Ed can be reckless but he's not dishonest,' Flora insisted. 'Perhaps we should focus on things we *do* know. For instance, Leo, or rather Leonard Hunter-Griggs, is staying at The Dahlia. Don't you agree it's rather odd the red coat was also delivered there?'

'I concede that was good sleuthing to find out the

name of the hotel, but red coats?' He clicked his tongue and shook his head. 'To my mind, we need to find out more about Leo or Leonard. The most obvious being why does he go by two names which are apparently being used by two different people?' He screwed up his napkin and tossed it onto the table, scraped back his chair and rose. 'I have a letter to write. I'll be in my study if you need me.'

'A letter related to Ed's predicament I hope?'

'Sort of, but I've no idea if it's relevant or not, so if you don't mind, I'll keep it to myself for the time being.'

The door closed with a harsh click, followed by the sound of Bunny's footsteps receding briskly along the hallway.

Flora remained at the table amongst the remains of their half-eaten dinner, the names Hunter-Griggs and Thompson circling in her head until a headache threatened. What didn't help the situation was Bunny's brusque secrecy and Ed's mood. The ceaseless ticking of the wall clock drummed in her head ever louder until she became sorely tempted to throw something at it.

* * *

Flora apologised to a perplexed Stokes for the half-eaten meal and the untouched coffee pot on the sideboard when he came to clear away. Wishing him a goodnight, she went to her room, her head full of questions to which she had no answers. She had been about to summon Sally to help her undress when her gaze caught the needlework case she had bought in Cheltenham. On impulse, she moved away from the bell pull, swept the box beneath one arm and crossed the corridor to Ed's room.

At any other time, his sullen 'come in if you must' would have discouraged her, but ignoring it, she pushed open the door and strode inside.

Ed sat at the bureau, still fully dressed, his chair set at right angles to the window through which he stared at the darkening garden. 'Have you come to tell me off for my lack of manners?' He chewed at a thumbnail but didn't look at her.

'I should, because it's not like you.' She perched on the end of his bed, placing the box on the coverlet next to her. 'I know everything seems hopeless right now, Ed, but we will find the solution, and when we do, everything will become clear.'

'But it's all such a mess.' He pushed a hand into his hair, making it stand on end. 'Flora, I feel you ought to—'

'Ed,' she cut him off, suspecting another apology was imminent. 'Where's the spike I found yesterday?'

'Spike?' Frowning, he looked at her for the first time since she had entered the room. 'Oh, the one which fell out of my jacket? It's still on the mantelpiece where you put it. Why?'

'I have a theory. Would you get it for me?'

'Is that the needlework case you bought in the Thompson's shop? It's very handsome.' He ran his fingers over the painted red peonies.

'Ed, the spike please?' she urged.

Sighing, he rose reluctantly to his feet, retrieved the item and handed it to her. 'This box gave me a reason to keep asking Mrs Drake questions, but I quite like it.' She opened the lid, revealing the neat rows of instruments lined up on a blue velvet lining.

'These tools are identical but for the handle.' About four inches with a slight curve at the end, the spike from Ed's pocket was set into a mother-of-pearl handle and appeared strong enough to cause the injury Maddox described.

Ed lowered himself onto the bed beside her and gingerly tested the end with his thumb. 'It's very sharp. Why would you need something so lethal for needlework?'

'It's used to make holes in heavy fabrics like

leather and hessian,' Flora explained. 'It occurred to me that this could have been used to kill the man on the train.'

'That thing?' He frowned, sceptical.

'A knife wound would bleed more and you said there wasn't much blood.'

Ed's eyes widened. 'Are you saying the killer used this and then put it in my pocket?' His jaw went slack.

'It looks like it. Now we know the killer was on the train because there were no stops between you using the facilities and arriving at Paddington. Did you see anyone hanging about in the corridor when you came back from the lavatory? Maybe someone came out of your compartment just before you went in? Think, Ed.'

'I didn't see anyone, at least, maybe, but there were so many passengers leaving the train. I can't think.' He massaged his forehead with one hand.

'What about after you left the train?' Flora kept her voice calm, reluctant to upset him more than necessary. 'Did you keep going until you reached the street, or did you stop at all?'

'Not likely.' Ed snorted. 'When I heard the police whistle, I kept going.'

'What about your ticket? Did no one ask you for it at the barrier?'

'I had it in my top pocket, which was just as well because I wouldn't have got through the barrier without it. I had to queue before handing it to the guard.' He removed his hand from his head and clicked his fingers. 'That's when the killer must have put the spike thing in my pocket.' His features twisted in anguish. 'He wanted me accused of murder?'

'I doubt it was personal, Ed. You were probably a convenient scapegoat,' Flora said. 'Do you recall anything about the other people in the queue?'

'I can't remember.' Ed pushed a hand through his hair. 'The station was so crowded and all I could think about was getting away.'

'Which is probably what he or they were counting on,' Flora mused.

'Flora,' his eyes clouded as his thoughts took a more serious turn. 'Could I ask you something?'

'Of course.'

'What was it like when Maguire died? I mean, he wasn't your real father, but you saw him as one.'

'In many ways I still do. He raised me, remember.' A shadow crossed his face, and she eased closer, shifting the box in her lap. 'He didn't just die, Ed, someone killed him. Which made it much worse. After the initial shock, came anger because someone had taken him from me.' She shivered and rubbed her upper arm with her opposite hand as those same emotions returned. 'When I discovered the truth about my mother's disappearance and that your uncle William was my real father, I had this sense of being let down. All those years at the Abbey with everyone knowing the truth but they said nothing to me.'

'Not everyone. I didn't. Nor did Jo. When we found out, we were delighted you were our cousin.'

'Thank you, Ed. I appreciate it.' She gave his forearm a firm squeeze.

'I've never lost anyone.' Ed picked at a ragged cuticle on his thumb. 'No one I really loved. There was Grandmamma, of course, but I was at school when she died. I'm sorry I didn't get the chance to say goodbye, but I didn't lose sleep for thinking about her. She never lingered in my head. Do you understand?'

'I think so. Where's this leading, Ed?'

'On the train. When I couldn't wake Leo, I made a joke about him looking dead to the world. I punched him on the arm and told him to stop messing about. When I realised the truth – I froze, unable to take it in. I barely noticed the guard arrive, but then he barked all these questions at me I couldn't answer. My mouth wouldn't work. I panicked, pushed him away, and ran. It was horrible, Flora,' he swallowed before continuing. 'To think we had sat chatting and laughing for two hours and I had no inkling he would die. Neither did he, which is what makes the whole thing so – shocking.'

'For you, perhaps, but it happened quickly for him.'

'I still see him in my head,' he gabbled as if he had not heard her. 'I've gone over the train journey so many times, wishing I had done *something*. If I had told him to get off the train at Reading, or I had not gone to the lavatory when I did, he—'

'Stop torturing yourself.' Her grip on his arm increased. 'How could you have known?'

'In my dreams he blames me for what happened.' Ed's eyes welled, the hazel irises bright and gold-flecked. 'He comes to me at night and asks me why he's dead.'

'Oh, Ed, I had no idea.' Although she should have... the bruises beneath his eyes, the agitation and mood changes were signs he was suffering.

'Will it stop?' His voice dropped to barely more than a whisper.

'Yes. I don't know when, but it will.'

'Maybe when we find the actual killer?'

'Possibly. Probably. All we can do for that young man now is bring whoever did this to justice.'

'His name was Leo.'

'We don't know *what* his name was.'

Ed looked as if he was about to correct her but changed his mind. His shoulders slumped, and he muttered something under his breath she didn't catch.

'Is that what people mean when they say rest in peace?' he asked after a moment. 'Not the dead's peace, because they can't feel anything. Peace for those left behind who have to come to terms with the loss?'

'I've never viewed it that way before, but you could be right.'

'You won't tell Inspector Maddox about the spike, will you?' His hand closed on her wrist, his eyes filled with panic.

'Oh, Ed, we must, don't you see? Concealing the truth is the same as lying, which will make you look guilty.'

'But I didn't do it, Flora,' distress lifted his voice an octave. 'You believe me, don't you?'

'Of course, I do.' Flora rubbed his shoulder with her free hand.

How could they discover who the man was, let alone who really killed him with a woman in a red coat their only clue?

14

'What are you two talking about?' Bunny's face appeared round the side of the door, making them both jump. 'Sorry, I didn't mean to startle you.' He dragged a chair from beneath the window up to the end of the bed and straddled it. 'I was on my way to bed, and it occurred to me I ought to apologise for being unkind earlier. Maddox caught us all by surprise, which was evidently his intention. I don't like to be blindsided.' He nodded to the object in Flora's hand. 'What have you got there?'

'It fell out of Ed's jacket pocket the day after the murder. I found it earlier today but was distracted by Jocasta's arrival. It went right out of my head until now.'

His gaze went from the item in her hand to the open box on the bed. 'It almost matches those you bought at Mrs Thompson's shop.' Bunny frowned. 'Why didn't you mention this before?'

Flora shrugged. 'I suppose I didn't understand its significance.'

'Come on, Flora, I know you better than that. This is an obvious clue.'

'I probably realised that, on some level.' Flora winced, embarrassed. 'I also knew what it would mean for Ed and hoped I was wrong.'

'It certainly looks as if it could kill someone.' Bunny held the spike up to the light and twisted it back and forth, his eyes narrowed before lowering it again. 'I cannot see any blood on it.'

'Maybe it belonged to a lady on the train who dropped it on her way out of the station?' Ed sounded hopeful.

'And straight into your pocket?' Bunny grimaced. 'Where's the jacket you were wearing, Ed?'

'It's here, why?' Ed twisted round in his chair, unhooked the garment from the back and handed it to him.

Bunny didn't answer, but turned each of the pockets inside out. 'Here, look.' He pointed to a dark smear on the otherwise immaculate yellow silk lining.

'Oh.' Flora stared at each of them, but neither Bunny nor Ed said what each of them must be thinking.

'It's an odd choice for a murder weapon.' Bunny draped the jacket over the bed and perched on the coverlet beside her.

'Not for a woman.' Flora had met female murderers before and would never assume the fairer sex was less capable of killing than men. 'Perhaps she didn't intend to kill him, but she was in a rage, grabbed the first thing to hand and plunged it into his chest.'

'I would have seen that surely?' Ed shifted beside her. 'I was there all the time.'

'Most of the time,' Bunny reminded him. 'You left the compartment for about ten to fifteen minutes.'

'Not enough time for an argument or a fight, even a brief one,' Flora said.

'Interesting thought,' Bunny mused. 'Which fits with it being a planned killing, but who were they trying to kill? Leo Thompson, or Leonard Hunter-Griggs? Or was this young man living two separate lives?' He held the spike beneath Ed's nose. 'Are you sure you didn't pick this up on the train and forget?'

'I'm sure.' Ed worried his bottom lip with his teeth.

'There were women on the train. Perhaps it could have belonged to one of them?'

'You said you didn't see any of the other passengers,' Flora said.

'I didn't. They were just shapes in the corridor; you know?'

'And you didn't see any of these passengers get off the train?' Bunny asked.

Ed shook his head. 'I was trying to wake Leo. By the time the guard arrived, the train was almost empty.'

'You should have mentioned the spike to Maddox when he was here.' Bunny split a look between them. 'Both of you.'

'I'm sorry, I—' Flora stammered.

'No, don't blame her,' Ed interrupted. 'Flora was only trying to protect me. I didn't want to give that policeman another reason to think I'm guilty.'

'That policeman, as you call him, is what's standing between you and jail right now.' Bunny fidgeted in the chair, his eyes hard behind his spectacles. 'We need to minimize the damage, or the next time he turns up here, it will be to take you off to the cells.'

'Bunny, don't.' Flora recoiled. 'Memory is a strange, contradictory thing sometimes.' She should know. An incident from Flora's childhood had haunted her in dreams for years.

'Might you have bumped into someone on the train, Ed?' Flora asked. 'Those corridors are narrow, so it's possible.'

'If that's how it happened, I don't remember.' Ed shrugged. 'What will you do with it?'

'Isn't it obvious?' Bunny wrapped the metal part of the spike in a handkerchief from his pocket and placed it with the others in the needlework box, its mother-of-pearl handle incongruous among the polished wooden ones. 'We have to give it to Inspector Maddox.' At Ed's terrified look, he added, 'I'll fudge the circumstances of when and how we found it. Make it clear we had no idea what it was and so on.'

'You would *do* that? Lie to Maddox?' Flora couldn't believe her cautious, law-abiding Bunny would suggest misleading the police.

'I prefer to think it's being economical with the truth rather than lying. We should also pay a visit to that hotel, The Dahlia, was it? I'd like to look at this Leonard Hunter-Griggs.'

'Can I come?' Ed's eager expression faded when he caught Bunny's swift look. 'Sorry, stupid question.'

'We know how frustrating this is for you, Ed, but you'll have to be patient.' Flora patted the hand that lay on his knee. 'Try to get some sleep and we'll see you in the morning.'

'Not much chance of that,' Ed muttered as Flora closed his door.

'A pity Maddox was so specific about us not interfering,' Flora said as they strolled the hallway to their room. 'And thank you, about the spike I mean.'

'He seemed a little too smug tonight for my liking,' Bunny snorted. 'As if he was trying to trap us. Besides,' he wrapped an arm around Flora's shoulders and hugged her to him, 'I don't mind taking the odd risk if it will help Ed. After all, we are family.'

'I'm glad you agree, because I shall always feel responsible for Ed.' Flora snuggled into his side, brushing her lips across his jaw as he stood aside to allow her to enter their bedroom first. 'He needs to know we're on his side.'

Following her in, he strode into his dressing room. 'I sense what he told us is essentially true, but cannot help thinking he's keeping something back.'

Flora replaced the needlework box on her dresser, her voice raised over the sounds of cupboard doors opening and closing in the next room. 'Did you see Ed's face when Maddox said Leo Thompson was still alive?'

'Leonard Hunter-Griggs you mean? Not really. What did he look like?'

'Angry, as if he was about to contradict Maddox but didn't like to.'

'I've been thinking, Flora.' Bunny reappeared tying the cords of his dressing gown, apparently not having heard her last remark. 'How about we call into The Dahlia tomorrow? We can go first thing. I have a luncheon appointment, so I'll stop by Cannon Row in the afternoon as well and give that spike to Maddox.' He moved closer and met her eyes in her reflection in the mirror. 'Flora? Did you hear me?'

'Yes, of course. The Dahlia Hotel, tomorrow morning. Good idea. I was just thinking about what Ed said.'

'What specifically?'

'When he tried to wake the man on the train, he punched his arm.'

'I doubt he could have made anything worse. The man was dead.'

'That isn't what I meant. It's something you would do when you know someone well. An intimate gesture when teasing or playing a joke.'

'I'm not sure what point you're trying to make.'

'Oh, never mind.' She pushed the thought away. 'My imagination is running wild. Young men are more informal than I'm used to. Especially public school-boys.' Her fingers reached for the bell to summon Sally, when Bunny's hand closed on hers.

'Let me be your maid tonight. You know how I enjoy it.' He undid the buttons of her gown while his lips traced a line of kisses along the side of her neck.

'All right, but take care with the laces on my corset. You're always too impatient and get them in knots. Sally complains bitterly when she has to unravel them.'

'To the devil with Sally.' He pressed his mouth to the soft flesh below her ear, making her gasp at the combination of pain and anticipation as his teeth nibbled at her earlobe. She closed her eyes, allowing her body to respond to familiar sensations while her mind emptied completely of bodies on trains, needlework spikes and red coats.

15

Flora alighted from the motor car and stared round in confusion at the narrow alley where Timms had parked. 'Couldn't we have stopped in front of the main doors?'

'I have my reasons, which will become clear later.' Bunny took her arm. 'Now, watch your feet. The cobbles are slippery and I wouldn't want you to hurt yourself.'

Grumbling lightly, Flora picked her way over the rubbish strewn on cobbles slick from something unmentionable. A flower stall at the corner provided a blaze of spring colour, its fragrance going some way to disguise the tang of manure, stale beer and rotting vegetables.

'Stop complaining,' he said with a chuckle as they entered Little Museum Street, where The Dahlia Hotel straddled the corner with Coptic Street; three storeys high, above a basement clear by half windows at pavement height, the rendered façade painted a dull cream. The windows of the hotel were covered by thick blinds obscuring the interior. A canopy as wide as the pavement hung over a pair of bevelled doors, the glass etched with the name of the hotel above a painted pink dahlia.

A doorman showed them into a mainly black interior where silver and white chandeliers hung from a bossed ceiling, ornate framed mirrors hung on every wall.

'It's sort of mysterious,' Flora said. 'As if we're only being shown what they want us to see.'

'It's a hotel,' Bunny whispered. 'Patrons expect discretion and privacy, or they would go elsewhere.'

'What do you know about discretion in hotels?' Flora lowered her voice to match his.

'Not as much as you might think. Now, where shall we sit?'

'What about over there?' Flora pointed to a purple brocade sofa and wing-back chair beneath a cantilevered staircase with intricate wrought-iron balusters.

By the time they had settled into their chosen seats, the bellboys had scattered in all directions, and the porter was busily occupied with new arrivals so Bunny's signals for attention went unnoticed.

'You stay here,' Bunny sighed, rising again. 'I'll see if I can rouse someone to fetch us some coffee.' He strode towards the main desk, where he attempted to attract the attention of a desk clerk.

A shadow crossed Flora's lap, causing her to look up into the face of a man in his mid-thirties in a dark suit and carefully styled silk cravat.

'Are you a resident, madam?' He raised a sartorial eyebrow.

'I'm not, no. My husband has gone to order coffee.' A smile tugged at her lips at the idea he disapproved of lone women in hotel lounges. Had he been about to eject her as a lady of suspect morals?

'Ah,' he visibly relaxed. 'Then allow me to introduce myself. Frederick Hunter-Griggs. If there is anything you require, feel free to call upon me.'

So this was Leonard Hunter-Griggs' half-brother. 'Er, yes, thank you.' Her words were slightly muffled by the whine of the descending elevator. With a soft bounce and a screech of metal, the contraption reached the ground, the gates opening with a resounding clang. A young man in a lurid green jacket barged his way through a small group of people waiting to go in. His belligerent expression marked him out as someone not to be trifled with. He didn't seem old, perhaps early twenties, blithely unaware or uncaring of the hard stares and low murmurs directed his way as he carved a path through the patrons gathering in the lobby, colliding with a passing porter. The man in green glared at him but did not stop, waving away the porter's mumbled apology as he approached.

'Get a chambermaid up to clean my room,' he snapped at Mr Hunter-Griggs, ignoring Flora. 'Straight away, there's a good chap. I held an intimate little party last night, and the place is a dreadful mess. Oh, and I'd like some breakfast, but some joker in the dining room refused me.'

'The maids have finished for the morning, and—' Mr Hunter-Griggs' gaze slid briefly to Flora, and he sighed. 'As you wish. I'll see to it.'

'Good man.' Belatedly the young man noticed Flora, giving her a lascivious wink before he strode away, pushing through a set of double doors with such force, they crashed against the wall. In seconds, his voice could be heard raised in angry protest at someone on the other side.

A middle-aged man who had witnessed the exchange from a few feet away came hurrying towards

Mr Hunter-Griggs. Perfectly bald apart from an inch of black hair combed across his crown, the brass badge on his lapel bore the word 'Manager' in block print.

'Forgive me, sir.' He hovered at the taller man's shoulder. 'I've explained on more than one occasion breakfast finishes at ten in order for the staff to prepare the dining room for luncheon, but—'

'It's all right, Jessup.' Mr Hunter-Griggs waved him away. 'Please attend to Mr Leonard.'

Flora's hand stilled as she reached for her handbag. *So that was Mr Leonard? He certainly didn't look very dead.*

'Of course, sir.' The manager entered the dining room where the loud voices rapidly decreased to an inaudible murmur.

'Please accept my apologies,' Mr Hunter-Griggs addressed Flora, his smile amiable though a vein pulsed at his temple.

'It's not your fault.' Flora's sympathy rose for the man as she searched for a way to prolong the conversation. 'I imagine demanding guests are a hazard of the hotel business?'

'Indeed, they are. Though I suppose we were all young and impatient at his age. I hope he hasn't spoiled your morning?'

'Not at all. And I congratulate you on your diplomacy. Does he stay here often?'

'Er... no, not really. I hope you enjoy your visit to The Dahlia.' He suppressed whatever he had been about to say next and instead inclined his head politely and strode away.

'What was all that about?' Bunny lifted an eyebrow as he flopped down beside her. 'Did I interrupt your flirtation with the manager?'

'Don't be ridiculous!' She would save her snippet about Mr Leonard for later. 'What did you find out?'

'The clerk confirmed what Maddox said about having no record of a room booked for a Leo Thompson. The only strange part about that was when the clerk consulted the ledger, the entire page referring to this week had been torn out.'

'Is that unusual?'

'Completely unheard of, apparently. He insisted mistakes were always stricken through, but never removed. And, before you ask, he doesn't know who might have done it.'

'Hmm, Maddox didn't mention that. What do you think happened?' Flora asked.

'I don't know. But if Leonard Hunter-Griggs has been living here on a semi-permanent basis, he wouldn't need to book a room, would he?'

'No, he wouldn't, but he told Ed he had. And why did you say semi-permanent?'

'Because we know Thompson's been back and forth to Cheltenham in the last few weeks. He caught the London train from there on Tuesday.'

'Perhaps he booked it before he reconciled with his father?'

'The clerk just informed me they have never sent out any train tickets.'

'Then someone else here must have. But you're right, it's all very odd.' She smiled in welcome as the waiter approached. 'Ah, here's our coffee.'

'Please excuse the delay, sir, madam.' He arranged crockery on the low table in front of them, taking care to set the handles facing the same way.

'Not at all. You were very prompt.' Bunny smiled forgivingly. 'Is the hotel always this quiet?'

'It's average for this time of day, sir,' he replied, mildly defensive. 'We'll be kept on our toes next week as we're fully booked for a Russian conference.'

'Russian?' Flora accepted the cup of weak, though hot coffee handed to her; a tiny wisp of steam struggling to rise from the surface.

'Yes, madam. Some delegates have already arrived.'

'Really?' She took a sip of her coffee, which proved as unimpressive as it looked.

'We've just had the pleasure of meeting the owner.' Bunny raised his cup at the front desk where Mr Frederick had stood a moment before. 'He seems like a nice enough chap. What's he like to work for?'

'I assume you mean Mr Frederick Hunter-Griggs, who is on duty today. He's a fair man, as long as you follow the rules and don't slack.'

'Hunter-Griggs...' Bunny said slowly, as if hearing the name for the first time. 'Is he related to Colonel Amery Hunter-Griggs?'

'That's correct, sir.' The waiter's eyes widened appreciably. 'We don't see much of him though, as he's elderly and lives elsewhere, but the twins live in.'

'Did you say there were twins?' Flora glanced up quickly.

'Yes, madam. This is a family-owned hotel, but it's the younger Hunter-Griggs who handle the day-to-day running.' He glanced to where Mr Jessup was staring at him from the front desk, his smile fading. 'Excuse me, sir, madam. I – I ought to get back to my work.'

'Of course, and if the manager reprimands you,' Bunny pressed a coin into his hand which looked suspiciously like a half guinea, 'Tell him we quizzed you on the facilities of the hotel.' His transferred smile to the manager meant to convey the waiter was doing a sterling job.

'Yes, sir. Thank you, sir,' the waiter beamed, bobbed a bow and left.

'Are you thinking what I am?' Flora asked.

'I'm too generous with my gratuities?' Bunny sipped from his cup, grimaced, and put it down again.

'No – well, yes, but I didn't mean that.' She sighed. Bunny chose such odd moments to be flippant. 'I meant about the Russians.'

'They aren't exactly strangers to these shores. Lenin lived in London for a year while he organised the printing of their newspaper.'

'How did you know that?'

'I hear things.' He winked. 'And your father let some details slip the other night. It's too dangerous for them in Moscow after their leader, Lenin, was imprisoned in Siberia for his radical activities. They hold their conferences all over Europe. It was Brussels last year, I believe, and London again the year before that.'

'I had no idea. How interesting.' She gave up on the coffee and discarded her cup. 'Coming back to our Mr Thompson. I wonder how these twins the waiter mentioned would view the sudden and possibly unexpected arrival of a long-lost half-brother into the fold?'

'Ah, I see what you're getting at.' Bunny nodded slowly. 'Leonard poses a threat to their inheritance?' He plucked a tiny sugar biscuit from a plate and nibbled it. 'But if these twins are desperate enough to murder their own brother to get him out of the way, how come they killed the wrong man?'

'Mrs Drake said Sylvia came to live in Cheltenham when Leo was four. As far as she knew, they hadn't had any contact since then. Leo must have changed a great deal between four and twenty-two, so how did they know what he looked like?'

'Maybe they didn't, and this was a case of mistaken identity?' Bunny puckered his lips in a silent whistle. 'If that's true and the wrong man was killed, it would explain why there's an unidentified dead body at the morgue.'

Bunny's speculation was accompanied by the mechanical sounds of the elevator, followed by the rattle as the gates opened once more. An iron-haired dowager emerged in a flowing black coat with wide lapels trimmed with fox fur. A broad-brimmed hat wider than her shoulders sat on her iron-grey curls. A small dog resembling a ferret trotted along beside her on a lead.

'Murder goes wrong sometimes.' Flora's raised voice fell into the sudden quiet. 'Imagine how frustrated the killer must be now. Do you think he'll try again?'

The woman gasped, halted and directed a withering stare at Flora, who stared back, offering neither apology nor explanation. The dowager inflated her chest, flung the end of a trailing fur stole over one shoulder and with an outraged 'Well!' strode away, dragging the reluctant little dog across the carpet.

'You cannot say things like that in public.' Bunny held a clenched fist against his mouth, chuckling.

'You started it.' She shrugged. 'I merely finished your train of thought.'

'Let's not frighten the other patrons, and we shouldn't jump to conclusions.' Bunny crossed one ankle over the other and relaxed back in his chair, then bolted upright again. 'Good Lord!' He stared at something past Flora's shoulder, then leapt to his feet, grabbed Flora's bag and pressed it into her hands. 'Time to go, Flora.'

'Why? We don't even know that old woman,' she protested as he hauled her roughly to her feet. Her shin glanced the edge of the table and set the crockery rattling on the tray. 'Does it matter if she heard me?'

'I didn't mean her, just accept that we need to leave before he sees us.'

'Before who sees us? Come on, Bunny, at least give me a clue.'

'Them.' He nodded to where a group of men in long black or grey coats and soft hats had entered the lobby, scarves wound round the bottom of their faces. They appeared to be escorting another man like a Pretorian guard, all in step with their gazes darting the room in search of trouble. The focus of their attention was a short man in his mid-thirties with thinning dark hair, high Slavic cheekbones and widely spaced eyes with a slight upward tilt above a full-lipped, almost feminine mouth. Their intense, brooding looks brought curious glances their way from bystanders, some of whom stepped aside to let them pass. Looking neither left nor right, they carved a path through the reception area.

'Try not to stare at them!' Bunny guided her through the main doors and onto the street.

'Will you please slow down?' She hurried to keep pace with his loping stride across the cobbles, which threatened to break an ankle. 'These boots are new and they rub.'

Timms glanced up sharply at their approach, tossed the end of his cigarette into the gutter before dashing round to open the door of the motor car.

Flora climbed into the rear, shuffling along the

seat to allow Bunny to scramble in after her. 'Are you going to tell me why we're avoiding those strange-looking men?'

'Not them. William.' He tugged his jacket flap out from beneath him, having caught it in his hurry to get inside. 'He was with them, or rather one of them.'

'William?' Flora gasped. 'Surely not!' When he didn't respond, she laughed, adding, 'Are you serious?'

'I am.' Bunny eased his collar away from his neck. 'I doubt he saw us, but I decided it was best we leave before he did.'

'Is everything all right, sir?' Timms twisted in his seat to face them, his forehead furrowed in concern.

'Perfectly, thank you, but could you get us away from here, sharpish? This motor is very recognisable, and I'd rather we weren't seen.'

'Of course, sir.' His urgency transferred to the chauffeur, who tooted the horn in warning and pulled smartly into traffic.

'Are you sure it was William? I cannot think why he would be somewhere like The Dahlia in the middle of the day.'

'I suspect it's something to do with those men, who look as if they are here for the Russian conference the waiter mentioned.'

'Which makes sense after his recent travels.' A

worm of foreboding climbed up her spine at the thought of her father putting himself in danger. 'He's doing secret work for the Foreign Office, isn't he?'

'That would be my guess.' Bunny nodded slowly. 'When we get home, I suggest you don't mention to Ed that we've seen his uncle in the company of a group of Bolsheviks.'

'I wasn't going to. And what exactly is a Bolshevik?' She settled back in her seat as the motor drew level with the British Museum, her gaze taking in a colourful banner that hung from the railings that announced the Trafalgar exhibition.

'They're the Russian and more aggressive form of the English Labour Party, responsible for organising those strikes in Moscow William told us about. They want to topple the Imperial regime and bring about a change for the labouring class. I'm guessing William is involved because our government is keeping an eye on them.'

'London's a long way to come to attend a conference,' Flora said.

'Not when the Russian government is having them watched.' He hooked a thumb at the street behind him. 'And, if I'm not mistaken, that man who appeared to fascinate you in there was Vladimir Lenin himself.'

16

'Is this Lenin person dangerous?' Flora asked, her thoughts squarely on William. His recent trip to Moscow must have been more than merely a diplomatic visit to the Imperial family. 'Would he be in danger if those men discover he works for the government?'

'I imagine he might be, yes,' Bunny replied. 'Which is why I thought it wise to get us out of there.' He patted her hand in a distracted gesture of reassurance and eased onto the edge of the seat. 'Well, how did you do, Timms?' Bunny removed his wallet from an inside pocket. 'Incidentally, how much do I owe you?'

'Not too bad actually, sir,' the chauffeur did not

take his eyes off the road. 'A chambermaid seemed happy to chat to me for a few shillings. She's a bit of a gossip, so I'm not sure you can take everything she says at face value, but she had plenty to say about Leonard Hunter-Griggs.'

'We'll settle up later.' Bunny returned the wallet to his pocket.

'You enlisted Timms to bribe the hotel staff for information?' Flora nudged him in the ribs. 'You're as bad as Sally; she thinks money solves everything.'

'And you don't?' He sliced her rueful sideways look, reminding her she was in no position to judge. 'It occurred to me that if anyone knows what's going on in The Dahlia Hotel, the staff will.'

'It *was* a good idea,' she murmured. 'And one which you might have mentioned to me.'

'I wasn't sure it would work. Timms, what did this maid say about Leonard Hunter-Griggs?'

'Well, sir. The staff were told he's the owner's half-brother, and to give him whatever he wants. Libby says he's shown no interest in the workings of the hotel and lords it about the place.'

'You might have wasted your master's money,' Flora interrupted. 'I could have told you that myself, because—'

'Hush, Flora, let him finish.' Bunny tapped her

arm, silencing her. 'What else did you find out, Timms?'

Flora slumped back in her seat, her lips clamped shut.

'Well, sir,' Timms continued. 'No one appears to know anything about him. He simply turned up without warning in January.'

'Which isn't surprising,' Bunny said. 'That they didn't know he was coming, I mean. Leo or Leonard, spent most of his life either at school or in Cheltenham. Did this maid say he was a welcome guest in the hotel or only tolerated?'

'According to Libby, the twins are delighted to have their little brother back. Whenever either of them gets impatient or critical with Mr Leonard's behaviour, the other always sets everything to rights, so there's no animosity there, sir.' The chauffeur steered the motor car skilfully between two horse-drawn vans without pausing in his account. 'Mr Frederick rolls his eyes a lot, but he excuses Mr Leonard's behaviour because of his having been spoiled by his mother.'

'Mr Frederick sounds too good to be true,' Flora said. He had handled Mr Leonard diplomatically earlier, although that might have been for her benefit.

'I had to make myself scarce then, sir, because the housekeeper came looking for Libby.'

'She's a stickler is she, this housekeeper?' Bunny asked, a smile in his voice.

'That she is, sir. Most of the domestic staff live-in and they're watched closely by this Mrs Sharpe. Terrified of her most of them.'

'Unless they are chatting to handsome chauffeurs,' Flora murmured as they negotiated a corner, narrowly avoiding a man on a bicycle who wobbled precariously in the road.

'They have to buy their own soap and aprons.' Timms steered around the cyclist in a wide arc. 'Any breakages have to be paid for, and if they swipe so much as a biscuit from a discarded plate they're dismissed without references.'

'That's harsh,' Flora pulled a face.

'A fact of life in some trades, I'm afraid,' Bunny said.

'Mary Drake described Leo, or Leonard, as a quiet young man devoted to his mother,' Flora said, growing tired of being upstaged by the chauffeur. 'Nothing like the man I saw, who was both rude and arrogant.'

'What do you mean, you saw?' Bunny's eyes narrowed.

'I met him. Well, sort of. He was in the lobby with Mr Frederick Hunter-Griggs, the man you said I was flirting with.'

'The chap in the green jacket? *He's* the half-brother?'

Flora nodded, still smiling.

'Why didn't you tell me?' Bunny's annoyed voice was sucked into the wind as he lowered the window. 'Did it not occur to you I might have liked to know that earlier?'

'I tried, but you rushed me out of there as if the lobby had caught fire.' She lowered her voice, conscious the chauffer could still hear them.

'That's no excuse for not mentioning it.'

'Why? You didn't tell me about your arrangement with Timms?' Aware she sounded sharp, she slid her arm through his, unwilling to let a minor spat develop into a row. They never argued, at least not the way Jocasta and Jeremy did, with flying china, slammed doors and injured silences which lasted for days.

'Hmph,' Bunny muttered, softening.

'Oh, sir,' the chauffeur said over his shoulder. 'There was one other thing. Mr Leonard likes to gamble. Libby says there are always playing cards and empty brandy glasses scattered about his room when she cleans.'

'Excellent. Thank you.' Bunny appeared to give this some thought. 'If you remember anything else, let me know.'

'Of course, sir. And I hope you don't mind, but Lord Trent came to help me in the mews this morning. I kept the doors closed, so he wasn't seen.'

'Quite all right, Timms. Thank you, and I'm sure it helped keep his mind off things,' Bunny said. 'Now put your foot down or we'll get caught behind that van.'

'Yes, sir.' The chauffeur threw a knowing smile over one shoulder as he gunned the engine, steering through a narrow gap between the van and a hansom.

Flora gripped the back of the seat in front and swallowed, her eyes tightly closed until the motor levelled out again.

Before dinnertime their entire household staff would know all about the Harringtons' exploits.

* * *

After luncheon, Bunny left for his meeting with Inspector Maddox, taking the needlework spike with him. Flora spent an hour with Arthur in the nursery, balancing coloured wooden blocks into towers that the baby subsequently pushed over to gales of hysterical laughter. She tried to think of a way to discover more about the Hunter-Griggs family, specifically the

Colonel, but to make it work, she would need to enlist Ed's help.

Persuading him to leave the house in secret would be the easy part. Keeping it from Bunny would be more taxing.

Arthur pulled himself upright on the arm of her chair where he wobbled on chubby legs before collapsing again onto his well-padded rear end.

'What a clever boy!' she gushed. 'Your papa will be sorry to have missed that.' She lifted him into her arms for a close hug, inhaling the heady combination of gripe water and Pears soap. 'Well, Arthur. As they say, it's easier to seek forgiveness than permission.' Planting a kiss on his soft blond head, Flora handed him back to Milly for his afternoon nap and returned to her room. To avoid a barrage of probing questions from Sally, she selected a tailored skirt in light wool and a plain cotton blouse, neither of which required her maid's help to fasten. To complete her professional look, she added a plain navy jacket with unfussy fastenings, swept her hair into a smooth chignon on the back of her head, and completed her ensemble with a plain straw hat.

Passing Stokes on her way downstairs, she requested him to have the motor car be brought to the front before poking her head round Ed's bedroom door.

'Privacy!' he called without looking to see who stood there.

'Did you know it was me, or do you talk to everyone like that?' she asked archly.

'Oh, sorry, Flora.' Ed started and had the grace to blush. 'I assumed you were the boot boy. I gave him a shilling for an errand yesterday and now he's always hanging about in the corridors.'

'Perhaps he's simply trying to be helpful. Or,' she added in an undertone, 'he's underemployed.' She checked the hall and, seeing it empty, stepped into the doorframe, whispering, 'Would you like to come out with me this afternoon?'

'Out? Really?' Ed's eyebrows lifted into his hairline. 'I'd love to. Where?'

'Never mind where. Bunny and I went to The Dahlia this morning, which I'll tell you about later. Right now, I need your help with something.'

'Won't Bunny have something to say about that?' He fastened one side of his braces with a snap.

'On this occasion, he cannot help. It has to be you.'

'That isn't what I meant.' Ed sighed theatrically; his shoulders slumped.

'I was joking, don't be so serious.' Laughing, she

tousled his hair. 'He's gone to the police station on his way to the office. I would rather he not know about this afternoon in case it doesn't work out the way I hope.'

'Oooh, secrets.' Ed smoothed down his rumpled hair with both hands, grabbed his jacket from the back of a chair, and shrugged into it. 'Are you sure I won't get into trouble with the police?'

'I'll worry about them.' She chewed her bottom lip, hoping she was right just as the growl of an engine came through the open landing window. 'Ah, there's Timms with the motor car. We'd better go down.'

* * *

'This isn't exactly discreet, Flora.' Ed stared round the Fortnum and Mason dining room, where ladies gossiped over cups of tea served with toasted cheese and tiny fancies, their conversations interspersed with the odd burst of high feminine laughter and the clink of crockery.

'Stop fidgeting, Ed. It's not as if I'm helping you to flee the country.' Flora's restlessness matched his. 'If Maddox finds out, I'll say we misunderstood the conditions of the agreement. Technically, you don't need to be physically under our roof to be under our care. At least that's what I'll claim if he challenges me.'

'Then what are we doing here? I'm not complaining though, as the food is pretty good.' He pointed at her plate with his fork. 'Aren't you going to eat that Scotch egg?'

Sighing, she slid her plate closer to his to expedite the transfer of Fortnum's famous delicacy onto his own plate. 'I remembered something Maddox said, which got me thinking.'

'Which was?' Ed cut into the sphere of golden breadcrumbs, revealing a glistening yolk thirty seconds away from being runny.

'He told me to keep away from Piccadilly.'

'I don't remember him saying that. Why is it relevant?'

'Think about it.' She cradled her teacup in both hands. 'Where would a retired colonel reside in this district?' In response to his puzzled frown, she nodded at the front window. 'Look across the road and up a little to your right.'

Following her gaze, his frown suddenly cleared. 'Albany. Of course. I should have known. You're a genius, Flora.'

'It was more an educated guess, but I'll accept the compliment. Only, I cannot simply walk in and ask if a

Colonel Hunter-Griggs lives there. I've heard the residents guard their privacy closely.'

'They do indeed. So what's your plan?' Ed swallowed his last piece of Scotch egg and dabbed crumbs off his lip with his napkin.

'If I remember correctly, your friend Stinky has a brother, doesn't he?'

'Fancy you remembering that?' Ed grinned at her, a blob of egg yolk on his lower lip. 'His name's Arnold. He's three years older than Stinky and has an apartment in—'

'Albany. Do you know exactly which one is his?'

'I do.' Ed polished off the last bite of egg. 'I've been there a few times.'

'What's this Arnold like? Amenable to an amateur detective and her assistant?'

'I don't see why not. I quite like the idea of being your assistant.'

Flora cradled her teacup in both hands. 'Tell me about this Arnold.' It might help to get an impression of him before they met. If Flora was right and the Colonel lived there, she didn't want to risk Arnold spilling all the beans before she talked to him.

'He's older than Stinky, but you'd never guess, as he's smaller and thinner. I suppose it had something to do with him being ill when younger. And for your information, they're called sets in Albany. Not apartments.'

'Noted. What was wrong with Arnold?'

Ed shrugged. 'Not sure, but he wasn't strong enough to go away to school. His parents got him a tutor. Stinky always felt sorry for him as he missed out on the fun we all had at Marlborough.' Ed coughed and eased his collar away from his neck. 'Why do you need to find this colonel, anyway? What can he tell you the police can't?'

'I shan't know unless I ask. And why the reluctance? I imagined you would be grateful for this chance to get out of the house?'

'I was. I mean I am. You cannot imagine how bored I've been. But what if Inspector Maddox finds out? It might make things worse for me.'

'You don't think being a murder suspect is the worst thing that could happen?'

'No, being found guilty is.' He crumpled his napkin and tossed it onto the table. 'Anyway, the doormen at Albany know everyone who enters the building. They're bound to demand who you are and whether you have an appointment. Give the wrong answer, or even hesitate, and you'll be shown straight out again.'

'You make Buckingham Palace sound easier to get

into. Why did you think I invited you? I'm hoping you might get me inside.'

'Well, I'm not sure. I've only been there a few times.'

'You've just said the doormen remember everyone.' Flora drummed her fingers on the table, her lips pursed. His excuses had begun to irritate her. 'If we have to sneak inside, at least you know the way.'

'You don't sneak into Albany. Trust me.' He scraped his chair back. 'Oh, all right then. If I can eat in public without the world collapsing, I can probably step across the street.'

Flora swept up her bag and followed him to the door, adding in an undertone, 'It's not as if you can get into more trouble than you already are.'

17

Ed enlisted a crossing sweeper who cleared a broom walk across the manure-strewn thoroughfare of Piccadilly. Elderly, yet still spry, the man worked steadily, immune to the honks of the carts and carriages he held up in order to complete his work.

When they had gained the opposite pavement, Ed pressed a coin into the man's hand, which he accepted with a brief touch of his battered waxed hat before another pedestrian commanded his attention.

'For such an imposing building,' Flora said when Ed joined her at the twin stone pillars that flanked Albany's U-shaped courtyard, 'I'm surprised it's tucked into little more than an alley.' She stared up at the façade of dark brick, its white stone porticoes and Romanesque arches above tall Georgian windows occupying three sides of the open space. 'I imagine it was a nobleman's private home at one time.'

'I believe it was, and if you are interested, Arnold will tell you more. Let's not linger out here, Flora.' He slipped his arm through hers and glanced farther up the crowded street. 'I'm sure that's a policeman over there.'

'Where?' She peered past him. 'Stop panicking, that's one of the Burlington Arcade beadles. And don't rush me. It's not easy to move this fast in a long skirt.'

He slowed his pace, though not by much, darting another worried look over his shoulder as they approached the steps to the double front door and into a lobby made gloomy by layers of dark brown paint and polished wood.

'Let me handle this,' Ed whispered as a doorman in a tailcoat and top hat approached them.

'Good afternoon, my lord,' the man's eyes lit with recognition, one hand raised to the rim of his hat. 'Master Baines is in residence this afternoon. Is he expecting you?'

'He is not,' Ed replied, 'but as I'm in town, I had a fancy to pay him a visit. Mr Baines likes surprises.'

'That's true, my lord.' They shared a conspiratorial smile before the man inclined his head and went back to his place. 'You know the way, I assume?'

'Of course I do, and thank you.'

'That man didn't even look at me, let alone ask my name,' Flora said, mildly peeved as Ed led her along a corridor to a bare stone staircase that curved towards an upper floor.

'He's simply being discreet.'

'What do you mean dis—Oh!' She halted, her skirt hitched in one hand, a foot raised onto the first step. 'You mean he assumed I was—That's outrageous!' Ed's snigger earned him a sharp nudge in the ribs from her elbow. 'Don't laugh. I've a good mind to complain.'

'You shouldn't feel insulted,' Ed replied still chuckling. 'He would have ignored Queen Alexandra if she turned up. It's the way they are here. Arnold's set is on the first floor, but be careful. These steps can be slippery.'

'This isn't quite what I expected.' Flora examined the unadorned wrought-iron balusters and bare light fittings set into stark, distempered walls.

'I agree it's a little different from the Baines' mansion in Kensington, but Arnold wanted to live on his own and Albany is more like a gentleman's club.

These utilitarian common areas are a tradition. Like boarding school.'

Ed paused at a heavy black door with no furniture other than a tarnished brass door knocker, his confident knock answered by a lanky young man who put Flora in mind of a dandelion having bolted and on the verge of wilting. A thin layer of fair hair lay flat against his scalp and pale skin bore testimony to a life spent indoors. A high arched nose above thin, bloodless lips completed the fragile look which fitted with Ed's comment about a childhood illness.

'Hello, Ed, old chap. What brings you to Albany?' He greeted Ed with a handshake so vigorous, Flora feared he might snap the twig-like wrists sticking out of his sleeves.

'Arnold, I'd like you to meet my cousin, Flora Harrington,' Ed said, not answering his question.

Arnold's eyebrows shot up as he exchanged Ed's hand for hers, regarding her with bright blue eyes, which shone with intelligence. 'Not the famous Cousin Flora who likes to solve murders? Well, well, this is a pleasure. Please come in.'

'Thank you.' She darted a look at Ed, who shrugged. 'I had no idea I had gained a reputation.'

'How could you not?' He ushered them into the smallest entrance lobby Flora had ever seen, which was only just large enough to accommodate the three of them. 'I've read all about the Serbian spy thing in the newspapers. Then there was the child trafficking case.' His speech was rapid and slightly high-pitched, with an enthusiasm Flora found delightful. She had never been the object of such genuine admiration before and rather enjoyed it.

'That's kind of you, but my role on both occasions was purely as an amateur,' she said, aware modesty was expected. 'The police did most of the work.'

'I'd still love to hear all about it.' Arnold waved them into a sitting room decorated with a Morris wallpaper in shades of pale lilac, green and cream, fashionable some ten years before. The room's square shape and high ceiling made it seem much larger. Overstuffed sofas shared space with low-slung chairs packed with piles of cushions. Magazines, newspapers and countless framed photographs were arranged higgledy-piggledy on tables, a bureau in one corner and a wall lined with bookcases. A floor-to-ceiling window at one end flooded the room with much-needed light, giving a view of the courtyard and Piccadilly beyond.

'Take a seat.' Arnold hovered between them like a nervous daddy-long-legs, then leapt forward and swept a two-foot pile of magazines from a chair to make room. 'Excuse the mess, I don't have many visitors.'

'Please don't concern yourself, Mr Baines. This is charming.' She lowered herself into the empty chair, resisting the urge to dust it off with her gloved hand. 'How many rooms do you have?'

'Call me Arnie, please. Everyone does.' His deprecating smile made him handsome, or he would be if he weren't so thin. 'As you see, this is the sitting room, and I have a similar sized bedroom next door, plus a bathroom on this floor. The kitchen is downstairs, along with a servant's room and washroom most residents assign to a valet. However, my allowance doesn't run to one, so I eat out a lot. I can just about manage tea and toast with Gentleman's Relish when the need arises.'

Flora was tempted to suggest he might employ a manservant to prepare weight-gaining meals at regular intervals before he disappeared altogether. 'I suggested to Ed when we arrived how this building might have once been a private house.'

'Indeed, yes. Lord Melbourne built it. Not the Prime Minister, his father. In fact, William Lamb was raised here until the family sold it to Prince Frederick in the late seventeen hundreds.'

'They probably spent too much money building it and had no option,' Flora said.

'Something of the sort, I imagine. And like most royal princes, Prince Frederick proved no less extravagant than the rest of the Hanoverians, and his creditors forced him to sell. The new owners, being more economically minded, extended the building before turning the whole thing into sixty-nine sets.'

'Are all the residents here single gentlemen?' Flora tugged off her gloves and laid them on a table at her elbow. 'We didn't see any ladies in the halls when we arrived.'

'Ladies were strictly forbidden some forty years ago. In fact, they say Lord Byron used to sneak Lady Caroline Lamb into his set at night.' In response to Flora's sideways look, Arnold added, 'But that story might be apocryphal.'

'Poor Lord Melbourne,' Flora said with a smile, 'cuckolded in his parents' former home.'

'Precisely.' Arnold stared at her with a mixture of surprise and admiration.

'Did I mention Flora used to be my governess?' Ed straddled the arm of a sofa, one ankle swinging.

'Ah, yes of course.' Arnold's eyes sparkled with humour. 'Anyway, as I was saying, the trustees amended the regulations some years ago to allow ladies to live here, but few have taken it up, apart from some married couples. Lady visitors are welcome, of course. I gather the doorman didn't try to eject you?' He laughed at his own joke; the high, discordant laugh of the privileged who had never had to concern themselves with how they sounded in public. 'Might I offer you some tea?' He rubbed his hands together. 'I'm afraid it's the only beverage I have, so I hope it's adequate.'

'That would be delightful,' Flora said. 'I see you are interested in sports, Mr Baines.' She studied a display of sepia photographs in various styles of frames on a sideboard. Some in silver filigree ovals, plain brass and plain polished ebony. Some were standard family portraits and baby pictures, though the majority comprised groups of young men aiming wide smiles at the camera while holding aloft a variety of tennis rackets, polo sticks and rugby balls.

'As a spectator only. I've never been strong enough to take part.' His eyes darkened briefly, but his smile returned immediately. 'As a child I was stuck in my bedroom for weeks at a time, which was when I became interested in photography. Those on the desk in the corner are landscapes and pictures of my parents' country house in Wiltshire, while those on the far wall are of the events my brother, Stinky, took part in at Marlborough.'

'They're very good.' Flora admired an informal composition of a group of cricketers in crisp white trousers and cable-knit sweaters, bats piled haphazardly at their feet, and all with wide smiles aimed at the camera.

'Thank you. I'm proud of the one in the ebony frame of Stinky at the rugby championships. He's second from the left.' He pointed to a stocky boy of medium height with muscular shoulders and legs, a muddy rugby ball tucked under one bulging arm. The physical contrast to himself marked, and sad, although he appeared proud of his fitter, healthier sibling. 'I fear I shall soon run out of space to display them all,' Arnold continued. 'Now, if I can get the gas heater to cooperate, I'll fetch the tea. It can be temperamental sometimes. Won't be a minute.'

Once Arnold had left the room, Flora rose and wandered to the desk, its leather inlay covered with more framed photographs, each one labelled in stylish script with the date and description of the event. A photograph of the test match at Kennington Oval two years previously jostled beside one labelled, 'The 60th University Boat Race 1903'. It was of the winning team in pale shirts with wide smiles on their faces, compared to the stoic, fixed expressions of the disappointed challengers in their darker colours.

'I remember this race.' Flora held it up for Ed to see. 'Bunny watched from Putney Bridge with Jeremy Fitzhugh and came home grumbling about the umpire having misfired the starter's pistol.'

'I saw it with some chums.' Ed gave the photograph a cursory nod before going back to his perusal of a magazine. 'I'm convinced the pistol thing gave Cambridge an unfair advantage.'

'There's one here of you playing rugby,' Flora pointed to another one. 'And here you are in the swimming team.'

'Don't remind me, Flora.' Ed squirmed. 'I always hated having my photograph taken at school.'

'I cannot think why. You always look very handsome.' She found a delightful one of Ed at a cricket match, where both teams formed a guard of honour, cricket bats held aloft over a curly-haired boy, presumably their captain.

She moved on to a frame with the heading 'Cross-Country 1902' written in cursive script below the emblem of Marlborough College. A group of smiling young men in white shirts and tweed plus fours, their heads close together round a silver trophy. Behind them stood those she assumed were their proud parents and relatives, all sporting proud smiles.

'Ed, didn't you take part in the '02 Cross-Country?' she asked over her shoulder.

'I, er, I might have done, but I cannot recall. Why?' Ed muttered, his head still buried in a magazine.

'Because I can't see you anywhere in this picture.'

'Arnie takes scads of photographs. He goes to all the school sports events. I'm probably in one of the others.' He tossed the magazine on the chair behind him, rubbed his hands along his thighs. 'I think I'll see if he needs a hand. That water heater is probably playing up again.' He rose quickly and moved to the door. 'You'll be all right here on your own won't you, Flora?'

'Um, yes of course,' she replied, running a finger along the list of printed names at the bottom of the picture from where the name 'Leo Thompson' jumped out at her. Her heart raced as she located its corresponding owner in the photograph; a pleasant-looking young man with unremarkable features holding a trophy and smiling into the camera. A face which was similar to the one she had seen that morning at The Dahlia. The sepia tint picture made it impossible to discern the exact shade of his hair, but Leo's was of a similar colour. The youth in the photograph had different eyes; rounder and not as heavily browed as the man at the hotel. Would someone's eyes change so much in three years?

The more she studied the face in the picture, the more certain she became that the man on the train was the real Leo Thompson.

Then who was the man calling himself Leonard Hunter-Griggs at The Dahlia Hotel?

18

'Well, that didn't take too long, did it?' Arnold's strident voice in the quiet room made Flora jump. 'Hot water heater worked first time.'

'Not at all, I hardly noticed you were gone.' She replaced the picture and summoned a bright smile.

'Ed will be along in a minute. I've left him in charge of the tray.' He set an ornate teapot on a low table between them; with its intricate gilt curlicues and sinewy spout she assumed it to be a contribution from his parents. She couldn't imagine any young man purchasing such a delicate and expensive object.

'Your photographs are very interesting, Mr Baines, er, Arnie. Do you know the young man the third from the right in this one?' She darted a look at the half-closed door, listening for Ed's tread on the staircase.

Arnold skirted the table and peered at the picture. 'No idea, sorry. I was asked to take that one by Lady Egerton.' At her enquiring expression, he added, 'She's a friend of my mater's. She sent me a copy afterwards out of politeness, but I'm afraid I'm not acquainted with most of the people in it. Why do you ask?'

'I thought I had seen him before, but perhaps not. Er... which one is Lady Egerton?' Not that she really wished to know, but hoped to steer the conversation back to Leo.

'That's her.' He tapped the glass with a finger against a woman who looked to be in her early fifties in a light-coloured suit, the jacket cut in the fashionable 'S' shape. She faced the camera, one arm raised to a wide-brimmed hat, the crown encircled with a dark sash. 'Her nephew, Sebastian, took part in the cross-country, which is why she was there. He's on the far right.'

'Who else is in this photograph?' Flora asked, mildly disappointed when he reeled off some names, which meant nothing to her.

'Her lady companion is there, but not the man she brought with her. Mater says she always has some young chap escort her to all the best parties, if for no other reason than to shock people. There was a scandal attached to her a few years back. One of her young men stole a diamond bracelet from her, then disappeared.'

'I thought you said Lady Egerton was a family friend?' She cast a teasing eye upon him.

'Oh, she is, but it doesn't stop Mater gossiping.'

Ed appeared at the door with a loaded tray he caught against the door frame, rattling the crockery. 'Whoops, sorry about that.' He set the tray down next to the teapot. 'Not still looking at Arnold's rogues' gallery, eh, Flora? Surely you must be bored with those by now?'

'Not at all.' Flora sliced him a rueful look. 'They're more interesting than you think.'

'I don't mind.' Arnold began the ritual of pouring tea and handed round sugar and milk. 'It's a while since anyone has asked about them.' He offered Flora a bis-cuit decorated with icing sugar and parma violets from a distinctive green decorated box she recognized as being from Fortnum's. 'Delighted as I am to meet you at last, Flora,' he held a theatrical finger beside his cheek. 'Something tells me this isn't purely a social call.'

'Whatever makes you think that?' Ed's self-conscious shrug made her wonder what he had confided during their sojourn in the kitchen.

'Stinky called in last evening for a sherry and said he had received a telephone call from you, Ed, with instructions for Lady Jocasta should she call. He was to confirm Ed was staying with him.' Arnold inserted an air of conspiracy into his voice. 'Are you on the trail of another murderer by any chance?'

'I see there's no fooling you, Arnie.' Flora accepted a biscuit and placed it on her saucer. Had Arnold's mater been present, she would no doubt have insisted he used plates.

'Comes from spending so much time in bed as a child.' Arnold dipped his biscuit into his tea. 'I know the difference between coincidence and correlation. What with Ed's jumpiness since his arrival, I assume the latter.'

'How astute of you, and in fact I am investigating a suspicious death.' Arnold's eyes brightened, and she smiled at how murder horrified some people and yet fascinated others. 'I had an idea about Albany, and Ed suggested you might help.'

'I'd be happy to, although I have no idea how.' Arnold sloshed milk into his tea, ignored the various chairs and sofas and, instead, perched on the low window ledge, crossed one spider leg over the other and fixed Flora with an attentive stare. 'Fire away.'

'I'm looking for an army colonel, possibly retired, who might live here.'

'Retired army colonel, eh?' Arnold's prominent Adam's apple bobbed as he swallowed a mouthful of tea. 'You've described about eighty percent of the residents.' He blushed and looked down at his shoes. 'I, uh, don't know if Ed mentioned it, but the rule here is we don't discuss who lives here. Not done, you see.'

'Surely this is different, Arnie?' Ed shot him a conspiratorial look. 'A murder has been committed.'

'You don't think the old colonel is involved do you?' Arnold straightened in alarm.

'No, but he might know something about the circumstances.'

'I see, well.' He cleared his throat, but his deep flush persisted.

'Look, Arnie.' Flora set down her cup, prepared to leave rather than compromise this charming young man. 'If it makes you uncomfortable —'

'It does.' He nodded, clearly conflicted.

'Which could be a problem.' Flora shot Ed a hard look, which he returned with a shrug. 'If this man has a set here, I was hoping you might introduce me to him. I need to speak to him. It's important.'

'Hmm, well then, I'll have to think about it. What's the chap's name?'

'Amery Hunter-Griggs,' Flora replied.

'Ah.' Arnold waved the remains of his biscuit in the air. 'I know him. We've shared a sherry or two since I moved in. He lives with his former batman in C12 at the end of the Rope Walk.'

'What's the Rope Walk?' Flora asked, pleased with herself at having guessed correctly regarding the Colonel's address.

'The newer part of the building is in two parts linked by a covered walkway which runs down to Vigo Street.' Arnold uncrossed one bony ankle to the other and placed his cup on a low table between them. 'There's a garden at the end with a fishpond. I don't make much use of it, but the old chaps like to sit there on sunny afternoons.'

'Do you think the Colonel would talk to me?'

'I don't see why not. Nice old chap, and he has all his marbles too, unlike some of the old dodderers round here. He's the type who might forgive me for introducing you, seeing as you're an attractive young lady.' Arnold held out the box of biscuits again, which Flora declined. 'I'll warn you though, he's no fool, and if he thinks you're trying to pump him for information as opposed to being friendly, he might clam up.'

'I've considered that.' She appreciated Arnold's sharp mind, which was at such odds with his fragile appearance. 'I thought I could claim to be an aspiring journalist for a women's periodical.' Flora nibbled her biscuit, more from politeness than hunger. 'Small circulation, elite staff sort of thing. I'll say I'm writing a story about military life in the last century.'

'Good plan. He served in the Hussars in India, so I expect he has a few tales to tell.' He cocked his head to one side like a friendly robin. 'What exactly is this all about?'

'Go on, Flora. Arnold won't tell.' Ed's guarded look conveyed he would prefer her to miss out the part about him being a suspect.

'A body was discovered on a train a few days ago. I'm trying to discover who killed him and why.'

'The one at Paddington that was in all the papers?' Arnold straightened, alert. 'You think Hunter-Griggs might be connected? Wait though, the papers said the body hadn't been identified.'

'The police haven't yet released the deceased's name to the newspapers.' Ed wiped crumbs from his upper lip, while avoiding his friend's eye.

'Excellent.' Arnold rubbed his hands together. 'All a bit hush-hush, then? What's your interest, might I ask?'

'I cannot say at this stage,' Flora glanced briefly at Ed, who blushed. 'If it turns out I'm mistaken, I wouldn't wish to alarm an old man. I'm sure you understand.' Not only did she want to protect Ed, but she also didn't want to put Arnold into an awkward position if questions were asked later.

'Quite right. I see your predicament. When do you wish to talk to him?'

'What about now?' Ed asked before Flora could answer.

'Ed, it might not be convenient,' Flora said. The photograph had convinced her the real Leo Thompson was dead, a fact she didn't want to let slip to the Colonel without meaning to.

'Don't see why not,' Arnold rose and tugged down his jacket. 'He doesn't go out much and, as far as I'm aware, has few visitors.'

'What's wrong, Flora?' Ed urged when she had not moved. 'Isn't this why we came?'

'I suppose so.' His aversion to the photograph still worried her, though with both of them so enthusiastic, what reason could she give for a change of heart? 'All right then, we'll go now.'

'Word of warning,' Arnold said as they stood in the sparse lobby and waited for him to lock his front door.

'You must acknowledge no one walking the grounds or the Rope Walk.'

'Why?' Flora asked, confused.

'It's considered poor form,' Ed added. 'Even if you've been introduced. Eye contact is also taboo.'

'Then how do you become acquainted with your neighbours?' Flora asked.

'You don't unless they wish you to. On coming across another resident, one gives them a brief nod before passing on. Later, it's polite to send them a written invitation to drinks or dinner.'

'Again, why?' Flora asked, confused.

'Simple. If we don't acknowledge one another, then we haven't seen them. If you see what I mean.'

'I see,' Flora said. 'In which case, I'll try to remember to cut anyone I see.'

'Trying's no good, Flora,' Ed instructed, her sarcasm evidently lost on him. 'Or Arnold could be reprimanded by the trustees. Oh, and whistling isn't permitted either.' At her startled expression, he added, 'I'm not joking. Whistling is strictly forbidden by the trustees.'

She bit back an acerbic comment, resigned to the fact the upper classes ran their entire world as if it were a massive boarding school.

Arnold led the way back to the ground floor and

along the main hallway, where Arnold pushed open a rear door onto an open-sided walkway Flora assumed must be the Rope Walk where Chinese-style railings rose to a tented ceiling of narrow boarding, reminiscent of a garden party. At the bottom of a short flight of steps, a pathway ran between two blocks of white stucco-faced buildings three storeys high.

'Here we are.' Arnold halted beside a door on their left, two-thirds of the way along and waved them inside. 'The Colonel has the ground-floor set.'

'Ed,' Flora waylaid him as he was about to knock. 'I think it would be best if you waited in the motor car.'

'Why? I've come this far. Besides, Colonel Hunter-Griggs won't know me from Adam.'

'Maybe,' Flora said slowly, suddenly awkward. She needed time to think through what her new knowledge of Leo Thompson's identity meant. 'Suppose he mentions to Inspector Maddox we were asking questions about Leo?'

'Ah, yes. Could be tricky. What about you? He told you to keep away, didn't he?'

'I know, but let me worry about that.' He had a point. She would have to hope the doorman's discretion applied to everyone, including the police.

'Right-oh. I'll leave you here then. But I expect to

be told everything when you've finished.' Ed aimed a brief, if reluctant wave in their direction before loping down the central pathway towards the gate at the far end into Vigo Street.

Flora watched him go, doubt clouding her mind for the first time since Ed had arrived at Eaton Place. Could he have had a reason to kill an old school friend and then pretend not to know him?

19

'Ah, good afternoon, Toombs,' Arnold greeted the slight man who answered his knock. 'Is your master at home? I've brought a lady friend of mine to meet him if it's convenient.'

'For you, sir, naturally.' He regarded them with a mild but friendly enquiry from unblinking, close-set eyes. 'Perhaps you would like to await the Colonel in the sitting room?' He stepped aside, his head inclined in invitation for them to enter a room crammed with heavy furniture designed for a much larger establishment. A glass-fronted bookcase took up the entire far wall, together with an oversized Georgian dining table and four stout chairs. Another pair of well-worn armchairs completed the seating arrangements, all giving off an unidentifiable but homely smell, reminiscent of biscuits and furniture polish. But no sign of the Colonel.

'He's taking a nap at present. I'll tell him you are here.'

'Please don't disturb him,' Flora pleaded. 'We could return at another time.'

'He welcomes visitors, madam, and wouldn't forgive me if I failed to inform him. I shan't be a moment.' He bowed and backed out of the door.

While they waited, Flora toured the room, taking care not to knock over any of the many china ornaments that covered every surface.

'So far, so good,' Arnold whispered at her shoulder, his hand cupped theatrically at the side of his mouth. 'Do you want me to ask him anything? Should I jump in with an acerbic question here and there to try to catch him out?'

'No, thank you.' Flora suppressed a smile. 'As far as I know he isn't a suspect. If you would make the introductions, then leave me to ask the questions.'

'Then I'll choose my moment and make an excuse to withdraw.' He tucked his hands into his pockets as if afraid to move. 'This room always makes me jumpy. I'm always afraid I'll break something.'

'I know what you mean.' Flora's eye caught a sepia

photograph in a silver frame. The image faded round the edges; the subject a pretty woman in her twenties with fair hair who glanced sideways into the camera with a winsome smile. Another depicted a handsome young soldier in a dress uniform she assumed was the Colonel as a young man. He held his fur-trimmed shako tucked under one arm, the trademark of gold embroidery in an elaborate triangle covering most of his chest.

'Here we go.' Arnold drew her attention to a tall, yet spare silver-haired man who leaned heavily on a cane. The cuffs of his burgundy velvet smoking jacket were decorated with a gold braid. His bushy moustache and neatly trimmed old-fashioned side whiskers gave him a distinguished appearance.

'Welcome, welcome.' He took Flora's hand in a firm, warm grip and brought it to his lips. 'Colonel Hunter-Griggs, retired. Rarely I'm graced with the presence of such a lovely lady.' His pale grey eyes alighted with mischief as they settled on her companion. 'You surprise me, young Arnold. Didn't think you had it in you.'

'I don't, sir. I mean, Colonel. I—' Arnold's complexion turned from milk-white to a deep raspberry-red.

'Just toying with you, my boy. No need to flush like

a virgin. Sit down, sit down.' He waved them into two midnight blue velvet chairs before shuffling over to a leather wing chair with worn shiny patches on both arms and at head height. Tapping his cane on the floor, he rotated full circle like a dog preparing to lie down, bent painfully from the waist and collapsed onto the squab.

'What was your name, my dear?' He laid the cane across his knees. 'Toombs told me, but the chap's such a natterer. I rarely listen to him these days.'

'It's Flora, Flora Harrington, and I apologise for intruding on your time.'

'No need, no need. I hate taking naps, but Toombs insists. I suspect it's less for my health than to give him an hour of freedom.' He chuckled delightedly and twisted the end of his moustache with a thumb and forefinger. 'Now, how can I be of service?'

'I would like to interview you. If you are agreeable, of course.'

'I've never been interviewed before. What's your interest?'

'I'm hoping to be a freelance journalist, for which I'm researching the military life of British soldiers who served abroad.' She nodded at the photograph she had spotted earlier. 'I see you were in the 11th Hussars.'

A mixture of surprise and admiration entered his eyes at the mention of his regiment, which she did nothing to dispel. 'Yes indeed. Light-brigade man all the way. Not smart enough to be in the infantry, and before you ask, I was too young for Balaclava.' His rich chuckle ended in a cough. 'Ah excuse me, touch of bronchitis, but I'm getting over it.'

'I'm sorry. I wasn't aware you were unwell.'

'It's nothing at all, really.' He waved her away. 'I had what the medicos call "an incident" last winter. The old ticker, you know.' He patted his chest with emphasis. 'Quack told me I ought to get my affairs in order as I might not last the year, but as you can see, I'm still here. Fella obviously got it wrong.'

'Can't always trust these doctors.' Arnold glanced up from his perusal of a magazine and grinned before going back to the page. 'They put me through a barrage of treatments in childhood. Few of them helped.'

'You must be very relieved,' Flora addressed the Colonel, noting his slight breathlessness when he talked.

'Relieved? I was furious. The blackguard cost me in lawyers' fees to sort out my assets when I didn't need to. Ah, well it's done now I suppose.' A small frown appeared between his thick eyebrows and he changed the subject. 'Freelance, did you say?'

'Er, yes. I need articles to impress an editor. It's so difficult for a woman to break into a profession considered a man's domain, but I'm determined to try.'

'Must say I don't approve of women earning a living. Home and hearth is the best place for a lady, but, well, times have moved on, I suppose. See women all the time in town serving in shops and restaurants. Some even train to be doctors. What do ye think of that, eh?'

'I find it admirable,' Flora replied without apology. 'Mrs Garrett is one of my inspirations, as is her sister, Millicent Fawcett.'

'The suffrage woman?' He upended his cane onto the floor with a bang. A liver-spotted hand gripped the silver top. 'Not sure I would go that far. Votes for Women indeed. Who's to say what they would do with them if they had them? Makes me an old curmudgeon to a youngster like yourself, I expect.' Before she could either agree or refute this remark, his expression lightened. 'What about you, Arnold? How do you feel about women having the vote?'

'Me?' Arnold blinked. 'Actually, I approve. I don't have a clue what to do with it other than vote the way my father and grandfather have always done. Perhaps it's time to let the ladies have a say? Not to mention the forty percent of working men who are also denied a choice in how the country runs.'

'Good grief, boy, didn't expect a lecture.' The old man grinned, but a hint of disapproval sat behind it. 'Now, young lady, have you got your notebook ready?'

'I have.' Flora withdrew a bound notebook and a pencil from her capacious handbag, a pencil poised above an empty page. 'How old were you when you joined the army, Colonel?'

'This is my cue to make myself scarce.' Arnold left his chair and backed away, rubbing his hands together. 'I hope to see you again, Mrs Harrington, Flora. I'd be interested to hear the... er... outcome of your research.'

Flora gave him a weak smile, suddenly nervous.

'You off, Arnold, old chap?' The Colonel peered up at him in mild confusion. 'Bored with hearing my stories, eh?' He delivered a slow wink at Flora.

'I'd listen to your account of the Gordon relief of Khartoum any day, Colonel. Only I hoped to have a chat with Toombs. He had an idea about how I might remove a boot polish stain from my bedroom carpet. If Mater sees it, she'll send her housekeeper round to bully me, and I can't have that. She thinks I cannot look after myself and makes noises all the time about my going home to Kensington.'

'I understand. A man needs his privacy. What?' He cheerfully waved Arnold off before turning his attention back to Flora. 'Now, the regiment.' He scratched his white side whiskers as an aid to thought. 'I went in as a lieutenant at twenty-one in the days before the Cardwell Reforms put a stop to buying commissions. I suppose my father assumed I couldn't get promoted on my own.' His rich chuckle held no resentment at his parents' lack of faith. 'Surprised him no end that I became a Major before he died. It was called the 11th Dragoons back in the 1830s. Before my time, of course.' He seemed not to require any involvement from her and appeared happy to talk, which suited her perfectly.

'The regiment was sent to Dover to escort Prince Albert when he came to England, you know? Impressed him enough for him to adopt them as his own and he converted the regiment to Hussars.'

'I had no idea, how interesting.' Though she didn't have to pretend, and wrote it all down.

'Impressive uniforms we had, as you see.' He pointed his cane at the photograph that had drawn Flora earlier. 'Fur busbies, crimson bag and blue dolman and pelisse. Our red trousers had double yellow stripes taken from the Saxe-Coburg livery. Lord Cardigan commanded them then, calling them

Cherry-Bums. Then later it changed to Cherry Pickers.' He sighed and his gaze moved away from her as if recalling old memories.

'Because of the red trousers?' Flora broke off from her assiduous note-taking. Despite the subterfuge, she found the old boy's account fascinating.

'Strangely enough, no. That came later, during the Peninsular War, a troop were forced to hide in cherry trees to avoid the French.' He chuckled with delight. 'As I said, before my time.'

'I would like to hear about your time, Colonel,' she prompted.

'I left Kent for Bengal in '66, then on to Bombay a few months later. It was a good life during peacetime, as the army took care of everything. Accommodation, travel, servants, transport, et cetera. It's tougher on the wives, of course, having to manage in a strange city with unfamiliar customs. Bombay had a large contingent of British families, so every need was catered to. Couldn't do much about the disease though, and there was a lot, with deaths from heatstroke to dysentery. Probably still is.'

'How did your wife manage in such a tropical climate?'

'Marguerite loved the army life, and all Bombay offered. She was an excellent hostess with the ability to converse with everyone, from my commanding officer to the lowliest foot soldier. When the regiment returned to England, I stayed on in the Bombay Army. Retired in '93, the same time as Sir Arthur Lyttelton-Annesley, my commander. Fine man, fine man.'

'Is that your wife?' Flora pointed to the photograph she had noticed earlier.

'That's my Marguerite. Quite a beauty, wasn't she?' He smiled gently at the picture, his head on one side. 'She died of fever, leaving me with two small children.' Before Flora could offer her condolences, he continued, 'The life doesn't suit all women. Sylvia hated India. The hierarchy and expectations of military wives, the heat and the insects.'

'Sylvia?' Flora tried not to sound too eager.

'My second wife. She had a rough time having our boy and came home to England as soon as she could bring the little chap with her. We've had brief contact since.'

'I'm sorry to hear that.' Flora's voice cracked slightly. If she was right, this kindly old man had no idea his youngest son lay on a mortuary slab in a police station. Nor did she intend telling him. Inspector Maddox could claim that privilege for a second time.

'Sylvia felt out of her depth.' He released his breath with a long sigh. 'My fault, really. I'm afraid we married too soon after Marguerite's death. Sylvia was my children's nurse, you see. The twins were only three when Marguerite died, and almost nine when she left. Everyone told me to send them back to Sussex to live with my sister, but I didn't want to part with them. Selfish, I suppose, and the pair of them went wild with only amahs to look after them. Made them too dependent on each other as well.'

Flora noted how his voice softened when he mentioned his first wife, whereas 'Sylvia' was spoken with no emotion behind it.

'It must have been a difficult time for you all.' Her mouth dried as she crept closer to why she had come. 'What happened to your younger son?'

'Leonard?' He smoothed his silver moustache down with a thumb and forefinger. 'I didn't return to England for some years, but even then, Sylvia refused to allow me to see the boy. Said we'd been separated too long, and I had nothing to offer him.' He sighed. 'Perhaps she had a point. I supported them both for years. Even paid for Leonard to go to Marlborough College. Better education than I had.'

'That seems unfair,' Flora said, her sympathy mainly with Leo having grown up without his father. She wrote Marlborough College in bold script and underlined it twice.

He shook his head. 'She didn't count on the boy's own feelings on the subject. Sylvia died recently, after which, Leonard came knocking on my door. He said he had always wanted to see me, even as a lad. I've been given the chance to get to know him again after all this time.' He stared off again, deep in thought, and murmured, 'Sad thing about his mother.'

'Yes, very sad.' She wondered if Leonard had known about his father. Sylvia might have told everyone she was a widow but told Leo the truth and insisted he kept it to himself?

'Ah well, condolences are misplaced,' the colonel's voice broke into her thoughts. 'I hadn't laid eyes on the woman in years.'

'Does your son live here with you?' Flora asked, knowing it was unlikely a young man's belongings would fit amongst the jumble of army and Indian memorabilia jostling for position in the compact space.

'No room, as you can see, and I can hardly turf Toombs onto the kitchen floor.' He issued a low chuckle, apparently visualising this concept. 'He's been living at a hotel we own in Bloomsbury since January, like my other children. I say children, but they're thirty now and neither of them married.' His eyes took on a faraway look. 'Frederick never considered it, although Francis came close once. Ah well. Anyway, they run the hotel very well between them.'

'This hotel you own?' Flora hoped her contrived innocence wasn't beginning to pall. Arnold had been right about the old man being sharp, although he seemed happy to talk about his family. 'I know Bloomsbury well. I might have heard of it.'

'The Dahlia Hotel. Named it after their mother's favourite flower.'

'Ah, no, I don't know it.' Flora fidgeted and ducked her head to her notebook. 'Your younger son appearing after all this time must have been unexpected?'

'It was, though he found the twins first, and they brought him to meet me.' He steepled his fingers beneath his chin. 'The lad's rough round the edges, and dresses like a dandy, but I'll make a gentleman of him, given time.'

'I'm sure you will.' Flora stared at her hands, reminded that the real Leo had already been a gentleman. It was unlikely the man at The Dahlia had been anywhere near Marlborough College. 'Will Leonard take a role in the hotel?'

'He's expressed no desire to, although he'll inherit a third of it when I go, of course.' He eased forward in his chair. 'Between you and me, my dear,' he lowered his voice, although there was no one to hear him unless Toombs had a penchant for eavesdropping, 'I'm hoping Leonard might rein the twins in a little. They inherited their mother's tastes and spent too much on the renovations. I had to call a halt. No more money until the place pays its way.' He balanced his cane on the floor, both hands crossed over the polished end. 'Talking about Leonard. Odd thing, I had a visit from a police inspector recently. The chap tried to tell me Leonard was dead.'

'How awful.' She adopted a suitably sympathetic expression. 'Whatever made him think that?'

'Something about a body on a train and a witness. This policeman chap admitted the body had no papers on him, so they couldn't be sure. Fella got it all wrong, and I told him so. Leonard is perfectly healthy.'

'I'm glad to hear it. How could the police have made such a mistake, though?'

'Ach! Incompetence, I imagine.' His disdainful snort told her all she needed to know about his opinion of the police. 'I can't recall the chap's name. Madley, Masham, or something similar anyway.'

'Maddox,' she said without thinking. At his start of surprise, she added, 'We've met. He's quite tenacious about his cases. I'm sure he'll get to the bottom of it.'

'Cases, you say?' His eyes sharpened with intelligence, reminding her he might be elderly, but there was nothing wrong with his mind.

'Um, yes. I've had some dealings with the inspector in the past.' She groaned inwardly, so busy trying not to reveal her suspicions she had blundered into territory she had hoped to avoid. 'I hope to make a name for myself in crime reporting.'

'Strange occupation for a gel.' His bushy eyebrows knitted together in a mixture of bemusement and suspicion. 'I would have thought there were more genteel ways to occupy your time between the schoolroom and marriage.'

'Do they have any idea who the victim might have been?' Flora attempted to divert him from his views as to a woman's natural role in life.

'None. This inspector said they found the body on a train at Paddington, would you believe?' He snorted as if the location were as unbelievable as the crime. 'He wanted me to identify the body, but I put a stop to that. Sent the chap off with a flea in his ear too.' He burst into loud laughter, making Flora's pencil jump in her hand, leaving a long mark on the page. 'I feel sorry for the poor chap they found, of course.' His eyes clouded as he pondered the question. 'Odd that Inspector chappie thought it was Leonard.'

'I gather you've seen your son since the policeman called?' Flora asked, carefully. 'For your peace of mind, I mean?'

'What?' He jumped slightly. 'Oh, yes, yes, of course. Freddie and Leonard dropped round last evening for a nightcap. I told them what the police said, and we had a good laugh about it.'

The Colonel settled back in his chair, his eyelids drooping. Flora debated whether she could ask another question or withdraw discreetly. When Arnold reappeared at the door, an 'is everything all right?' expression on his face.

Flora nodded, returned her notebook and pen to her bag and rose, pressing the old man's hand on the arm of the chair. 'Thank you for agreeing to see me, Colonel.'

He jumped and stared round as if he had forgotten where he was. 'What? Oh, not leaving already? Shame.'

'I've taken up far too much of your time, and I promised Arnold I wouldn't monopolise his afternoon. Oh, please don't get up,' she added when he tried to lever himself up with the stick. 'I'm sure Arnold knows the way out.'

'Nice of you to call,' he reverted to a clipped

manner of speech as if full sentences tired him. 'Good luck with your career.'

'My what? Oh, yes, of course. Thank you.'

'Well?' Arnold prompted once Toombs had shown them back onto the Rope Walk. 'Did you find out what you wanted?'

'Partly. There are still some unanswered questions. Maybe I could come to tea again when this is all over and I'll explain it to you.' She didn't relish the idea of recounting what promised to be a very sad story, but she owed it to him. 'How did you get on? Has Toombs sorted out your boot polish problem?'

'What?' His brow furrowed for a moment. 'Ah, no I made that up. Good thinking, eh?'

'Very good thinking, and thank you again, Arnie, for being so obliging. This must strike you as a very odd way to behave.'

'Not at all. I find it exciting. I always believed I'd make a good detective. I always had plenty of time on my hands to think things through.'

'You could well be right.'

20

Flora was several feet from the motor car when Ed poked his head out of the window. 'Well?' he demanded. 'Did you find out anything?'

'You could at least let me get inside first before questioning me.' She slid into the seat beside him and waited for Timms to close the door; an automatic reaction, but a redundant one. Their chauffeur knew almost as much as they did. 'Nothing we didn't know.' She adjusted her hat in her reflection in the window. 'The Colonel is charming, although he's adamant his son Leonard is alive, well and living at The Dahlia Hotel in Bloomsbury. I might call on Inspector Maddox to see if he's found out anything more about the man on the train.'

'Oh, I wouldn't do that. I'd rather go straight home if it's all the same to you.' He eased his collar away from his throat, swallowing. 'We don't want your inspector knowing I left the house without permission. Besides, don't you and Bunny have a wedding to go to later this afternoon?'

'Oh yes, I almost forgot you are under house arrest, and we do indeed have a wedding, but there's plenty of time, as the ceremony isn't until later. And he isn't *my* inspector.' Flora tapped the chauffeur lightly on his shoulder. 'You heard his lordship, Timms. Back to Eaton Place.'

'As you wish, madam.' Timms pulled into the heavy traffic moving towards Hyde Park Corner, the silence in the motor car broken by the chunter of the engine and the clatter of hooves from carriages and tradesmen's carts that crowded the road.

'Albany is a strang— er, unique place isn't it?' She could do without insulting Arnold's home when he had been so obliging. 'Though I wish you'd told me about that odd rule of silence regarding other residents.'

'I'd forgotten it, actually. But it turned out all right, didn't it? What did you think of Arnie?'

'I really liked him.' She fully intended to raise the subject of the photograph again while they were inside the car so he couldn't avoid answering. 'What an intelligent young man he is, and so talented. Those photographs he took are excellent. The one of the cross-country race presentation particularly interested me. Strange that you weren't in it. I remember distinctly your mother telling me how hard you trained for it throughout the Easter holidays.' She sneaked a look at him, but he continued to stare straight ahead, his profile impassive.

'Um, Flora.' He tugged his collar away from his throat but still did not look at her. 'Before we, or rather you, do anything else, there's something I need to tell you.'

'Go on, I'm listening.' Her senses prickled, the motor car swaying as Timms manoeuvred into the traffic flowing swiftly past Green Park.

'I wanted to tell you before, but—' His gaze slid to the windshield and widened. His lower jaw went slack, his eyes widening as he yelled, 'Look out, Timms!'

A Harrods delivery van had taken a sharp turn and cut right across their path. Muttering a colourful curse, Timms braced his arms on the steering wheel and stamped down on the brake.

Time seemed to slow as they sped towards the van, the company name growing larger with each drawn-out second as the flat side of the van loomed inches away from the motor car bonnet.

The driver of a hansom approaching from the opposite direction gaped in horror at the van coming straight towards him. At the last second, before a collision between all three vehicles seemed inevitable, the cabbie hauled on the reins.

Ed gave a yell of fury and frustration, at the same time throwing himself at Flora, who gasped as his arms closed round her, pinning her to the seat. She made a grab for the leather handle above the window just as the screech of brakes and the grind of wooden wheels were followed by a hard jolt as Timms had expertly steered the motor car between the van and the hansom. Braking hard, he came to a shuddering halt at an angle on the road.

The hansom rumbled past them with a clatter of hooves, the horse's fearful snort scattered foam flecks on the glass before the driver halted twenty feet farther along the road.

The van carried on in its chosen path as if nothing had happened, the driver oblivious and staring straight ahead.

'Goodness, that was close!' Flora unclenched her fingers from the grab handle and brought them against her bodice to still her thumping heart.

'The crazy driver, he didn't even look!' Ed glared at the miscreant through the rear window. 'There should be rules about people like him being on the roads.'

'Are you all right, Timms?' Flora asked as the van disappeared round a corner.

'I'm fine, madam.' He twisted to face her, one arm spread across the back of the seat, his face pale. 'Is anyone hurt?'

'Not me. What about you, Ed?' Though her enquiry was perfunctory as Ed continued to complain loudly.

'A bit shaken, but not hurt, and well done, Timms. Excellent driving.'

'Thank you, my lord. I'll just make sure the hansom driver is all right.' He slid out of the driving seat and loped across the road to where the hansom stood. The driver had climbed down from his perch and was busy calming his spooked horse. Several passers-by stood to watch the small drama unfold, some of whom shook their heads at Timms as if the fact he drove a dangerous contraption must put him at fault.

'Are you sure you're all right, Flora?' Ed's gaze roved Flora's face and came to rest on her forehead. 'Did you hit your head?'

'I'm all right.' She fingered a sore spot above her

left ear, but decided it wasn't worth making a fuss over.

After exchanging a brief word with the cabbie, Timms circled the motor car, aiming the odd kick at a tyre and polishing a fender with the sleeve of his jacket. Apparently satisfied no damage had been incurred, he retrieved the starting handle and yanked the engine into life again.

'Is the horse all right, Timms?' Flora asked.

'The cabbie seems to think so.' He climbed back into the driving seat and released the brake handle, slowly pulling back onto the road. 'The poor animal had a fright. I think he'll be finished for the day.'

'Good. I always worry about those poor animals. They always look so tense and far too thin. Their life on the roads is so hard and many die too soon.' She picked up her bag from the floor where it had fallen and settled it in her lap.

'I agree,' Ed propped his elbow on the sill and stared out of the window. 'I think horses should get fat on hay and run free in green fields, not be forced to dodge the traffic in city streets.'

'Quite. Now, what did you want to say to me, Ed?'

'I beg your pardon?' Ed's bemused frown was almost comical.

'You were about to tell me something.'

'Was I? Ah, well, it wasn't important. Forget it, we're almost home now.'

* * *

While Ed joined Timms in a last check to see the motor car had sustained no damage, Flora let herself into the house, where from the hall table, she retrieved a lilac envelope addressed to her.

A series of rapid footsteps across the hallway tiles announced Stokes' arrival. 'Mr Harrington asked for you, madam.' He gave the closed study door a long, knowing look. 'I wasn't sure what to say regarding your whereabouts.'

Flora's stomach lurched. She had hoped she and Ed would have got home before Bunny returned.

Ed bounded up the front steps but had only one foot across the threshold when Flora shoved the letter hurriedly into her bag with one hand, grasped his arm with the other and propelled him towards the stairs. 'Go upstairs quickly. Bunny's home.'

'Lawks, how did that happen?' Ed shoved his coat into Stokes' waiting arms just as the study door opened.

'Too late.' Flora held her breath as she watched

Bunny stride along the hall towards them, his furious gaze aimed at Ed before sliding to her.

Stokes ducked his head and made a discreet withdrawal.

'I wondered why the staff avoided all my questions about where you were this afternoon.' Bunny's voice was tight. 'You have them well trained, Flora.'

'Thank you. I mean, no, I've done no such thing. And before you get too angry,' she began, taking a deep breath, 'I needed Ed with me today, but we were discreet.' She removed her coat and hung it on the row of hooks in the vestibule. 'You'll never guess where Colonel Hunter-Griggs lives. Well, you might, but I claim sole credit for having thought of it first. However, without Arnold Baines we would never have—'

'Who the devil is Arnold Baines?' Bunny interrupted, his eyes hard behind his spectacles.

'Um, he's a friend of Ed's.' Flora widened her eyes. Bunny never used such language, especially in front of her.

'A friend, eh?' Bunny's uncompromising gaze shifted to Ed. 'One you admit to knowing, or did you denounce him too?'

'Cripes,' Ed muttered from beside Flora, easing behind her as Bunny withdrew an envelope from an inside pocket, this one a thick, creamy bond.

'This arrived by the second post. It's quite enlight-ening.' He paused, his gaze going to each of them. 'Don't you want to know who it's from?' He opened out a page covered with bold looped handwriting on evenly spaced lines: the hand of a man of confidence.

'All right, we'll do this your way.' Flora swallowed, taking in her husband's set jaw and stiff shoulders. 'Who's the letter from?'

'Funny you should ask.' He adopted a false, sar-castic tone. 'It's from Reverend Bell.'

'Ah.' Ed stared at the page as if it might bite him, his face drained of colour. 'Um, perhaps I'll go up-stairs and leave you two to talk.' He sidled past them towards the staircase.

'Oh, no, you don't.' Bunny's free hand fastened onto his shoulder. 'You have some explaining to do, young man.' He jerked his head towards the sitting room door.

'Better do as he says, Ed.' Flora gave him a push before following.

Bunny took up his master-of-the-house pose be-side the fireplace while Ed chose the sofa the farthest away, his forearms on his knees and his head down.

'Would someone explain?' Flora broke the tense silence. 'Who's Reverend Bell?'

'He's my old headmaster at Marlborough.' Ed

sneaked a look at Bunny, who raised a sardonic eyebrow, adding, '*Our* old headmaster.'

'No longer,' Bunny said. 'He retired a couple of
years ago. I wrote to ask if he could he tell me anything about Leo Thompson's time at Marlborough
College.'

'How long have you known Leo Thompson went
to your old school?' Flora regarded Bunny steadily. *She
had only found out herself an hour ago. Had he been
keeping secrets from her?*

'When Maddox was here last, he asked if the
words *Deus Dat Incrementum* meant anything to us.'

'I remember.' Flora nodded. 'In fact, I was going to
ask you about it but something distracted me and it
went out of my head. Why is that significant?'

'It's the Marlborough College motto,' he replied.
'One Corinthians, chapter three, verse six. "God gives
the Increase."'

'It means,' Ed muttered, shifting his feet. 'That we
all do our part to make things grow but at the end the
improvement is down to God.'

'What a strange concept.' Flora shrugged. 'Why
make any effort at all when the ultimate result is decided at the whim of—'

'That's irrelevant, or irreverent, whichever you prefer.' Bunny cut her off with a sartorially raised eye-

brow. 'What matters is that the chances of anyone other than a Marlburian having that verse on his person is unlikely. That's how I knew. Leo must have had it written somewhere among his things.'

'Leo also said something about a spark to Ed. Did he have that written too?' Flora asked as the memory returned.

'I've no idea, but according to Reverend Bell's letter,' Bunny waved the paper briefly while enunciating each word to control his anger, 'Ed and three other young reprobates caused Leo Thompson a good deal of trouble at school.' When Flora made no comment, he raised an eyebrow in enquiry. 'You don't look very surprised, Flora?'

'I'm not, although I didn't find out until this afternoon that Leo went to Marlborough. As for trouble, perhaps Ed ought to tell us what he did?'

'We didn't do anything!' Ed insisted. 'Nothing serious, anyway. We played jokes on each other. Hiding Leo's books and sports kit, that sort of thing. He did the same to us!' Ed clenched his fists on his knees, his boyish indignation dissolving beneath Flora's stare. 'I tried to tell you in the motor car just now but lost my nerve.'

'Go on, Ed. We need to know all of it.' Bunny placed one foot on the fender, his arms folded across his chest and the incriminating letter dangling from one hand.

'It's not as bad as you think.' Ed loosened his tie, keeping his gaze averted. 'Leo was two years ahead of me and had a reputation for treating the first years like his personal servants.'

'It's called fagging, Ed,' Bunny interrupted him. 'It's normal. We all did it.'

'I know that, but some prefects treated the commoners worse than others. Leo picked on one small, skinny little chap. Got him carrying things he could barely manage. Some of the other boys and I did something about it.'

'That sounds pretty noble to me.' Flora held Bunny's gaze in challenge. 'Did *you* make smaller boys work for you?'

'For simple things like cleaning my shoes, running errands, that sort of thing.' Bunny shrugged. 'It's traditional, reminiscent of the relationship between squires and knights in medieval days. It symbolises service between ranks. Everyone has to go through it.'

'Exactly. It's medieval.' Flora shuddered at the thought of Arthur having to endure being treated that way at school by some smug, entitled aristocrat's brat.

'Yes, well, sometimes boys get carried away.' Bunny

had the grace to blush. 'I never caned mine, although some of the other chaps did.'

'That's what I meant,' Ed interjected. 'Leo pushed it too far. He made his fag clean his boots at midnight when he should have been in the dorm. Got him a detention for it, too.'

'I have to agree,' Bunny said, chastened. 'That was above and beyond.'

'Why didn't the boys complain to the housemaster?' Flora asked.

'And get punished for being a sneak?' Ed snorted. 'Not likely.'

'Oh.' Flora fell silent for fear of compounding her ignorance of what the English upper class regarded as a normal childhood for their sons. Daughters had no better bargain as once released into the world, men still had the upper hand.

'I expect Ding-Dong told you all about the race?' Ed stared at the page in Bunny's hand.

Flora bit her bottom lip to hide a smile at the nickname attributed to their former headmaster. 'Why don't you tell us about the race?'

'Thompson organised the cross-country race on sports day, which is when he paid us back for all the japes us chaps played on him.' Ed twisted his hands in his lap, reverting to the habit of referring to other pupils by their surname. 'He fixed it so Stinky, another two boys and myself would start. Pettigrew and Farley, in case you're interested.'

'Not particularly,' Bunny snapped. 'Keep talking.'

'Leo must have had the signposts changed as we were sent off on a longer route over rough ground.' His upper lip curled. 'Very rough ground.'

'I see.' If Leo's treatment of younger boys was anything to go by, Ed should be applauded for not ignoring it. Had one of these young men chosen to take their revenge years later? 'What happened next, Ed?'

'Exactly what Thompson hoped would happen. We got lost and walked in circles for hours. Pettigrew fell into a gully and sprained his ankle, so we had to carry him. It rained and by the time we got back to school, we were wet, cold and exhausted. And because we were out after curfew, we missed supper.' His voice notched up an octave at the memory of this last humiliation.

'That's why you acted so strangely when I pointed out the photograph at Arnold's?' Flora said. 'When I asked you why you weren't in it, you couldn't leave the room fast enough.'

'What photograph was this?' Bunny demanded.

'Arnold took it after the race. Which is how I discovered they went to the same school. And if you had explained the motto thing, I would have known sooner.'

'I wasn't sure at that stage, which is why I wrote to Bell,' Bunny said apologetically.

'Yes, well.' Ed ran his hands up and down his thighs. 'We were still clambering over fallen trees and climbing ravines when that photo was taken.'

'There aren't many ravines in Wiltshire, if memory serves,' Bunny interjected. 'Chilmark perhaps, but it's miles from Marlborough.'

'It jolly well felt like it when we were soaked through, freezing cold and covered in nettle stings.'

'Topography aside, let's get back to the other night,' Bunny said, losing patience. 'When Inspector Maddox said the man on the train wasn't Leo, why didn't you speak up and contradict him?'

'How could I? I had already claimed not to know him.' Ed slipped further down into the sofa squab as if he wished himself invisible.

'What possessed you to lie?' Bunny snapped. 'You must have known the truth would come out?'

'Maddox already thinks I'm a murderer. If I had told him about the feud at school, he would think I had a reason to kill Leo.'

'Because of a race?' Flora said, aghast. 'That's the

most ridiculous thing I've ever heard. And what do you suppose he'll think of you now?'

'I daren't think,' Ed mumbled into his hand.

'Is that what happened on the train, Ed?' Bunny asked. 'Did Leo laugh about the way he had sent you and your chums through mud and undergrowth until you were exhausted, bleeding, and lost? It must have been frightening in the dark, miles from anywhere with an injured comrade?'

'It was.' Ed shuddered. 'But we found our way back, eventually.'

'I don't think you're being very fair to—'

'Let me finish, Flora,' Bunny interrupted. 'Ed needs to hear this. It must have rankled that Thompson shamed you in front of the entire school? I'll wager he let everyone know what a dog's breakfast you had made of a simple race? A bitter defeat when you had always been good at sports. Always top of your class in academic subjects too?'

'Yes!' Ed rocked back and forth on the edge of the sofa. 'All right, it was hard.' He looked so despondent and beaten, Flora longed to comfort him, but Bunny would only criticise her for taking Ed's side. 'We stopped the tricks and practical jokes after that, so Thompson got what he wanted.' Ed lifted his chin, defiant. 'He stopped bullying the smaller boys too, so it was a victory all round. Neither of us bore a grudge.'

'Perhaps that was true until you saw him on the train? Then the day of the cross-country race came flooding back. You didn't intend to lose your temper, but Leo goaded you. You snapped, picked up a sharp instrument someone had left behind on the seat and plunged it into his chest.'

'Bunny!' Flora couldn't help herself. She had never seen him so lacking in empathy.

'No! That's not what happened!' Ed rose from the sofa, his fists clenched at his sides.

'It's quite understandable,' Bunny continued, oblivious to Ed's distress. 'A sudden, uncontrollable and isolated impulse. You were shocked by what you had done, but he was obviously dead. The train had arrived at Paddington, so you slipped the spike into your pocket and positioned him so he would look as if he slept.'

'I cannot believe you're saying this.' Ed held his arms out, palms upwards.

'Bunny, please stop—' Flora began, but he ignored her.

'When the guard accused you, fear made you bolt, but you knew who to go to for help. Flora knows something about murder investigations and I'm a solicitor. We couldn't possibly think you were capable of murder.'

'That's enough!' Flora slid closer to Ed and wrapped an arm around him.

'Sit down, Ed.' Bunny's voice softened. 'And, Flora, I know this is upsetting, but I know what I'm doing.'

'How can you *say* that?' She brought her head up to stare at him, horrified. 'Look at him, he's shaking with fear.'

'Necessary, I'm afraid. Look Ed.' Bunny placed a gentle hand on Ed's shoulder. 'I know you didn't murder anyone. But don't you see? If this gets to court, the Prosecution will subject you to far worse than this.'

'Court?' Ed gasped. 'I'll have to appear in court? But I didn't do anything!'

'I know.' Bunny straddled the arm of the sofa. 'Now, Ed. What *did* happen on the train? The truth this time. All of it.'

'Apart from claiming not to know Thompson, everything I told you was true.' Ed sighed and tugged at a loose thread on his shirt cuff. 'I recognized him straight away, but felt awkward seeing him again. I was debating whether to move carriages when he saw me. He stared at me for a moment, then laughed. He said he remembered the state we were in when we stumbled back to school with our clothes torn and covered in mud. He asked me how much running I had done since, and when I said none, we both ended up laughing like drains. After that, it wasn't awkward at all. We even shook hands. In fact—' Ed broke off and swallowed. 'When I think of what happened afterwards, I'm glad I had the chance to apologise to him.'

'Oh, Ed. I'm so sorry.' Flora hugged him closer. No wonder he had been so distressed the other night when she visited his room.

'I didn't mean it to get so serious. It never occurred to me anyone would really think I had killed him, so when Maddox asked if I knew him, I kept quiet. I just didn't think.'

'You didn't think murder was serious?' Bunny demanded.

'No! I mean yes. When I saw him slumped against the window – dead, I panicked.'

'Which is how it all begins, Ed. You tell one lie, which leads to another, until no one will believe anything you say.' Bunny closed his eyes and massaged his forehead with one hand. 'What a mess.'

'Do you have to tell Inspector Maddox about Ding-Dong's letter?' Ed asked.

'Yes, we do!' He brought his fist down on a lamp

table at his elbow, almost toppling a Meissen figurine. 'And don't keep using that name. He's a respected man and doesn't deserve to be made fun of.'

'I'm sorry.' Ed sniffed. 'Didn't think.'

'I'm sure Ed only kept silent this long because he was afraid to tell us.' Flora discreetly moved the china ornament out of Bunny's reach. 'But he has admitted it now, and—'

'It's not good enough, Flora,' Bunny interrupted. 'I'm professionally bound to pass on any information coming into my possession.' He patted the pocket where he had placed Reverend Bell's letter before sitting down. 'We solicitors rely on the goodwill of the police.'

'Do you have to tell Inspector Maddox straight away?' Flora began carefully. 'I mean, he probably knows by now Ed went to Marlborough and nothing has really changed.'

'And I'm still a suspect,' Ed muttered.

'I'm afraid so.' Bunny sighed. 'Leo's body is on a slab in the mortuary and you were the last person to see him alive.'

'We're not obliged to do Maddox's work for him if it makes matters worse for Ed,' Flora said.

Bunny bit his bottom lip, which told her he was considering what she said.

'Only for a day or so,' she wheedled. 'Until we find out more about the man at The Dahlia who is pretending to be the Colonel's youngest son.'

'Please, Bunny,' Ed pleaded. 'Give me a chance to clear my name.'

'I've an awful feeling I'm going to regret this.' Bunny sighed. 'All right, but just for a day or so.'

21

Once Ed had retreated to his room, Bunny came to stand behind the sofa where Flora sat, his hands braced on the upright behind her head, one hand resting on her shoulder.

'You realise you've verbally abused a viscount and accused him of murder?' Flora twisted on the sofa to face him. 'I'm only glad his father wasn't here to witness it. He would have had you horsewhipped.'

'I found it strangely satisfying actually, and how many members of the nobility does a solicitor get to harangue?'

'More than you might imagine, I should think. And I'm sorry for taking him out of the house without telling you.' She slid her hand over his and squeezed.

'You're forgiven.' He planted a swift kiss on her temple. 'I'm angrier with Ed for lying than I am with you. When I read Reverend Bell's letter, even I wondered.'

'It's certainly made things more complicated.' Flora didn't like to admit Bunny's tirade had shaken her own confidence in Ed's innocence, if briefly.

Bunny rested his forearms on the sofa back, his gaze level with hers. 'Was he really about to tell you the truth? Or was it another of his inventions?'

'No, I think he was about to, but then—' She pushed their near miss in the motor car away. 'This means that the man calling himself Leonard Hunter-Griggs at The Dahlia is definitely not Leo Thompson.'

'And what do we do with that information without getting Ed into further trouble?'

'Hope Maddox will find it out by himself? The Colonel said—'

'Wait, a moment.' Bunny straightened. 'You've spoken to the Colonel?'

'Um – yes. That's why I took Ed with me. He came to live at Albany when he returned from India a few years ago. Ed's friend has a set there, so I asked him if he knew the Colonel.'

'Ah yes, Arnold Baines. Ed has mentioned him. I think he's going to ask Earl Trent if he might have a set there when he leaves university. That was clever of you to think of that, Flora.'

'I don't understand the attraction. The place is like an army barracks and the sets are tiny. They discourage women too.'

'That *is* the attraction. What's he like, this Colonel?'

'A really nice man, if ridiculously old-fashioned. He was obviously devoted to his first wife, although had little to say about Sylvia.'

'No wonder she left him, taking young Leo with her. Incidentally,' he squatted lower so his eyes were level with hers. 'How did you get a stranger to talk about his family?'

'Er... I expect he took a shine to me. I can be charming when I choose.' His steady stare unnerved her, and she gave in. 'I pretended to be a journalist doing an interview about the army, but that isn't relevant.' She slid her arms round his waist and rested her head on his shoulder. 'Oh, Bunny, it's so sad. He was thrilled Leonard came to find him after Sylvia died. It gave him a chance to get to know him again. I sat six feet away from him pretending to take notes about some spurious article, knowing his actual son lay on a mortuary slab and whoever is masquerading as Leonard at the hotel is an imposter.'

'It's the price you pay for digging into people's lives.' Bunny hugged her tighter, his breath warm on her forehead. 'We unearth a lot more than we really want to know. You're sure he said Leonard came to find him, not the other way round?'

She pulled back enough to look up into his face, nodding. 'One of the twins brought them together. Frederick, I think he said.'

'Interesting.' He adjusted his glasses with one hand. 'What else did the Colonel tell you?'

'A little about his time in India, and how Sylvia hated it, which might have been her main reason for leaving him as he stayed there for some years after-wards. In fact, I have a theory.' She patted the vacant space on the sofa beside her, inviting him to sit. 'No, don't look at me like a solicitor about to cross-examine me. Listen.'

'Barristers do that, not solicitors.' Bunny skirted the sofa and took the seat Ed had vacated beside her.

'I stand corrected, but you can stop scowling at me. We know Sylvia had no contact with her es-tranged husband, but when Leo grew up, it's reason-able he would want to know about his father.'

'Even if Sylvia told him he had died?'

'More so, I would have thought. Amery Hunter-Griggs was a soldier. What young boy wouldn't want to know everything there was to know about him? Especially if his mother had woven some elaborate story for his benefit.'

'It's possible. Would Sylvia have known he had returned to England?'

'She might have if the bank who paid her allowances had informed her. Even if she didn't tell Leo, the twins were eight or nine when Sylvia left, old enough to be aware Leo existed. They could have gone looking for him.'

'I think I know where this is going.' Bunny's brow creased in thought as he threw his analytical mind into the riddle.

'I knew you would.' She snuggled closer, resting her head on his shoulder. 'The Colonel was seriously ill last year and was encouraged to sort out his affairs. He probably wrote a will, or he rewrote one. The twins discovered they might lose part of their hotel to a half-brother they hadn't seen for years. A hotel they had spent all their money renovating and worked hard at every day to make successful.'

'I can see how that might create resentment,' Bunny mused, frowning. 'To kill off their half-brother is pretty extreme.'

'Families are tricky at the best of times. When inheritances are involved, they can be malicious. Suppose the twins employed someone to impersonate Leonard in order to charm the old man into believing he was his son?'

'To what end?' Bunny shrugged. 'If they planned to dispose of the half-brother, why use a substitute? They've simply replaced one problem with another. Besides, Sylvia Thompson knew Leo was the rightful heir.'

'True, but Sylvia wouldn't be a problem if she was already dead,' Flora said. 'Suppose the twins sent that woman to the shop to cut Sylvia's hand?'

'Ah, we're back to your lady in the red coat, are we? Sylvia Thompson died from blood poisoning. Had Dr Grace suspected the injury resulted from foul play, she would have insisted on a post-mortem.'

'If you remember, she suggested one be carried out, but Leo refused. Sylvia died at Christmas and Leonard came to live at the hotel in January, so they might have prepared the way for him to take his place at The Dahlia.'

'But Leo wasn't killed until April. Why did they wait so long?'

'A good question.' Flora had to admit there were holes in her theory, but she wasn't prepared to let go of it just yet. 'With Sylvia dead, no one would con-nect Leo Thompson living in Cheltenham to a

Leonard Hunter-Griggs in London. Everyone we have spoken to insists that Leo had no idea his father was alive, therefore he wasn't likely to come looking for him.'

'Hmm. Strangely, that makes a sort of convoluted sense.' Bunny relaxed his head against the sofa back and stared at the ceiling, deep in thought.

'Something must have changed, making the real Leo a threat.' Flora chewed her bottom lip as she ran through scenarios in her head. 'Maybe he discovered his father was alive and came to the hotel to meet him.'

'Hmm, I'm following. Go on.'

'They already had a Leonard Hunter-Griggs staying at the hotel and didn't want another spoiling their plans, therefore they had to get rid of the real one.'

'Strangely that all makes sense. But it's still speculation. Inspector Maddox won't want to hear unfounded theories about what might have happened.'

'Like my lady in the red coat?'

'Exactly.' Bunny's lips curled into a wry smile, which fell short of outright dismissal. Her enthusiasm dissolved. He was right. She had taken a few bare facts and twisted them into a conspiracy.

The door clicked open and Stokes appeared in the

doorframe. 'Would you and madam require afternoon tea, sir?'

'No thank you, Stokes. We've no time.' He grasped Flora's hand and pulled her to her feet. 'You need to get changed, Flora. Had you forgotten, we have a wedding to go to later?'

22

Flora curled her fingers over the edges of the roll-top bath and relaxed in the silky water scented with rose oil. A fire had been lit in the grate of the generously proportioned bathroom, making the room so comfortable that the tension left her neck and shoulders. She released a contented sigh, intent on enjoying Lydia's wedding without a head crowded with murder, metal spikes, and an amiable colonel whose heart would inevitably be broken.

The water had grown almost cool and her fingertips wrinkled when she left the tub, patted her skin dry with a towel and slipped on a silk negligee. Tugging the clasp from her hair, she let it flow over her shoulders and entered the bedroom.

The House of Joel had delivered her gown for the ceremony which Sally had hung on the front of the wardrobe door. Flora admired the full skirt that flowed in gentle folds from a pinch-waist bodice in fabric so fine, the layers beneath glimmered through in varying shades of blue and lilac. The full-length sleeves and high neckline with a row of tiny covered buttons fashioned from matching coloured lace gave the impression it might float away on a puff of wind. Flora had rarely experienced such heady anticipation of owning a dress as exquisite as this before. She hoped the afternoon would remain mild so she could discard her coat and show it off.

Her gaze fell on the drawstring bag which Sally must have brought up from the hall table where Flora had left it earlier. As she moved it to the dresser, a rustle from within reminded her of the letter she had put there on her arrival home.

Upending the contents on the bed, she picked up the lilac envelope and slid a thumbnail beneath the seal and withdrew two pages of closely written handwriting in a spidery, sloping script.

Dear Mrs Harrington,
What a surprise to receive your letter, and naturally I remember you from your time at

Cleeve Abbey, having a passing acquaintance with Lord and Lady Trent. I hope you have fully recovered from the dreadful murder of Mr Maguire three years ago, an event which I believe altered your circumstances considerably. How gratifying it must be for you to be received as part of Earl Trent's family.

Flora smiled at her way of saying she had graduated instantly from butler's daughter to Lord Trent's niece.

Sylvia Thompson and I were indeed close friends, however, she was always reluctant to discuss her life before she came to Cheltenham, so forgive me if I cannot provide you with the information you seek.

Being a military widow myself, I often liked to reminisce about my dear late husband, whereas Sylvia preferred not to discuss her years overseas at all. What I know is her husband served as an officer somewhere in the tropics, but I never learned exactly where.

I believe he died of fever when their son was a toddler, prompting her to return to England, where she lived with her parents in the Glouces-

tershire countryside. Her father died within two years, which is when she and Leo moved to Cheltenham with her mother and purchased the shop, which they ran together until that lady's death.

A delicate creature, Sylvia had always been ill-equipped for life, emotional and inconsolable at the simplest of crisis. Nor did she handle illness well, so I'm afraid, at first, I failed to treat the injury she suffered last year with sufficient seriousness. Thus, I was as shocked as anyone when she contracted blood poisoning.

However, I digress, as you asked specifically about Leo, a young man of whom I am very fond. Leo was very close to his mother and always deferred to her. She suffered greatly when he went away to school, which seemed odd when we have one of the best day schools in the town. Once, she lamented at having no choice but to send him to boarding school, a statement which puzzled me a good deal.

Leo is a charming young man, but he did not enjoy the same affluence as his boyhood contemporaries. Perhaps he harbours a certain resentment which prompted an interest in politics,

which Sylvia strongly disapproved of. I believe
they had some disagreements about it and the
fact Leo had embarked on what she referred to as
his 'Foreign studies'. Not being a political person,
I can shed no light on what any of this signified.

It wasn't until I received your letter, did I re-
alise I hadn't seen Leo since early February. I
called at Thompson's Haberdashery yesterday,
only to be told by Mrs Drake that he had left for
London again and planned to be away for a
while. I will happily mention your enquiry to him
when he returns, and, of course, give him your
condolences regarding his mother.

Yours very sincerely,
Katherine Tilney

Flora summoned Sally, then refolded the letter,
uncomfortable with the knowledge Mrs Tilney could
never fulfil her promise. Despite the length of her reply, she had not revealed anything Flora didn't already
know, apart from a vague reference to Leo's political
interests. The knowledge that Leo's schooldays might
have been tainted by Ed and his friends sat like a
stone in her chest. Ed had always been a sunny, generous child, which had not changed as he grew into a

young man, making his behaviour so much harder to believe.

Bunny often spoke of his happy days at Marlborough College and always said when Arthur was old enough, they would send him there as well. Flora had found the subject easy to avoid with their son still a baby, but what of the future? What if his classmates discovered his mother had once been a governess? Being Earl Trent's niece might compensate to some extent, or would her past become something her son came to be ashamed of?

Her troubled thoughts were sharply interrupted as Sally burst into the room, breathless from the three flights of stairs.

'Sorry for being so long, madam.' She dropped the pile of towels she carried onto the bed. 'Abel had a slight mishap with a saw when he was cutting wood for a vegetable frame.'

'Oh, dear, I hope he isn't badly hurt.' Flora placed the letter in a drawer and slid it closed.

'The blade slipped and sliced his forearm,' Sally added. 'Clumsy great thing.'

Flora grimaced. 'That sounds painful.'

Sally removed the muslin covering, lifted the dress from the hanger and held it out by the shoulders. 'Oooh, madam, this dress has turned out lovely. Now, best be getting you into it or you'll be late for Miss Lydia's wedding.'

'Has Abel gone to the hospital?' Flora stepped into the cornflower blue silk, her back turned while Sally fastened the long row of covered buttons.

'Hah! Not him. He'd rather be fussed over by me and Mrs Cope. Me with the water and bandages and her with the tea and cake. In his element he was. Who would have thought a strapping young man like Abel would be such a baby about a bit of blood?' Sally kept up a stream of enthusiastic chatter over Flora's shoulder. 'Not that he would keep still so I could clean the wound. I told him I did. Soil in cuts are dangerous. Many furry creatures use the garden as their privy. But would he listen? Would he heck? Squirmed about like a kid with an earache. Shall I tie the sash in a bow at the back, madam, or would you prefer it draped round your waist and pinned?'

'Draped and pinned, I think. Trailing sashes always make me feel like a schoolgirl.'

Once Sally had finished arranging the gown to Flora's satisfaction, they took their places at the dressing table.

'Madam?' Sally met her eyes in the mirror, hairbrush in hand. 'Is there something funny going on at that hotel you went to?'

'Why? Has Timms been gossiping over cups of tea in the kitchen?' It shouldn't surprise her that her and Bunny's activities would cause interest among their staff. She would have to suggest Bunny have a quiet word with them to ensure none of it went beyond the house.

'Timms doesn't gossip, but I heard Mr Bunny ask him to see what he could find out before you went. The Dahlia, wasn't it?' Her focus appeared to be on winding conker-coloured hair round her fingers into sausage curls on Flora's head.

'I'll tell you, but only to stop you eavesdropping,' Flora began, resigned. 'The two owners and their father might be involved in the murder, but I need to find out more.'

Sally's hand stilled; a curl held in mid-air. 'They ain't hardly likely to admit anything to you, are they?'

'I'm not sure.' Mr Frederick didn't strike her as a killer, but there was always his brother Francis, whom she had not yet seen.

'Lots of interesting things happen in hotels. What about the chambermaid Timms spoke to? She might be up for a bit of extra dosh for some idle talk.'

'Did he tell everyone in the servant's hall?' Flora inwardly groaned.

'Course not, madam. He knows you and I do these

things together, so it stands to reason he would tell me. Only, the minute you poke about in a hotel where you have no business, someone is going to notice and ask what you're up to.'

'I could pretend I'm a chambermaid looking for work?'

'What, you, madam?' A wry smile tugged at her lips. 'You'd have to dress down a bit. Pretty chambermaids aren't popular in posh hotels as they cause trouble.'

'What sort of trouble?' she asked, appreciating the compliment.

'Attention from men. Those what like it and those what don't, both of them trouble in their own way.'

'I see, I think.' Flora frowned at her reflection. Even after three years in her service, Sally's turn of phrase could be confusing.

'I'll hang about the back door chatting to the chambermaids, if you like? A few shillings might loosen some tongues.'

'A kind offer, but absolutely not.' Flora recalled the trouble they had got into the last time she had involved Sally in an investigation. A villain had drugged her and locked her up on a barge intent on selling her to a brothel in Kentish Town. Fortunately, she and Bunny had rescued Sally in time, but she didn't want a repeat of the horror she had felt at being responsible for Sally's fate.

'How's about we make up a story and ask one of the staff to help us?'

'What kind of story?'

'We could say your husband is having it away with a girl and you want to catch them at it.'

'Sally! What *are* you suggesting—?'

'I'm suggesting nothing, but the chambermaids would sympathise with a jealous wife, if you see what I mean. They must see that sort of thing all the time.'

'I'm not sure The Dahlia is that sort of hotel.'

'*All* hotels are that sort.' Sally sniffed. 'Some aren't so blatant about it, but most turn a blind eye to a well-dressed woman going to a gentleman's room, never to be seen again.'

'Would Inspector Maddox be interested in hearing about this?'

'Not likely.' Sally shrugged. 'Chances are his lot takes backhanders to keep out of it.'

'What a cynical view of the police, Sally.' Flora bit her lip to prevent a laugh at the idea of Inspector Maddox taking a bribe. Or was she being naïve?

'You don't know the half of it,' Sally muttered. 'And toms make good coppers' informants. How else can a Whitechapel girl raise herself out of the gutter?'

'Isn't that a contradiction?' Flora bent her head so Sally could fasten her necklace. She had a pretty good idea what 'tom' meant, but refused to ask Sally and show her ignorance. 'Doesn't that sort of work lower a woman's status in society?'

'Depends which way you look at it.' The tip of Sally's tongue appeared between her teeth as she concentrated on the fiddly clasp. 'A girl on our road worked for four years as a tom, then she packed it in and bought a share in a teahouse in Clapham.'

'I had no idea such a trade was so lucrative.' Flora met Sally's knowing eyes in the mirror.

'You'd be surprised. Not all girls ply their trade on street corners. She worked in the hotels as well. The porters take commission and the girls don't even have to provide the room.' Sally stepped back, her head tilted as she studied the finished effect. 'You look beautiful, madam.'

'Thank you.' Flora adjusted her hat a fraction of an inch. 'Remind me never to dismiss you, Sally. You make my life so much more colourful.'

'When I marry Abel, he might not want me to carry on working. Especially a lady's maid hours.'

'Is this your way of telling me I work you too hard?' She checked the clock, and realising the time, collected her bag and gloves. Bunny would pace the floor in the hall. He hated being late.

'Ask yerself,' Sally swept a pile of discarded linens from the floor and made for the door, 'why would I want to help undo your corsets at midnight, when Abel could undo mine?'

Flora laughed softly as Sally left. But she had a point. Short of booking in as a guest at The Dahlia, how could she wander round in the rooms without being challenged?

23

In the muted gold light of a late spring afternoon, Flora strolled the short distance to Eaton Square on Bunny's arm. St Peter's Church dominated the west side of the square, its Ionic columns, white Portland stone façade and neat clock tower like a painted toy at the end of a railed garden.

Timms, handsome in his uniform cap, had been waved off by the kitchen maids, a buttonhole pinned to his lapel by a blushing housemaid. Bunny's motor car had left an hour before, having been pressed into service to transport the bride; the bonnet artfully festooned with sprigs of cherry blossom, white freesias, and pink sweet pea tied with white ribbon.

'Either we're very early, or Harry's family carried

out their threat not to attend.' Flora slid into a pew on the left side of the nearly empty church to the faint strains of organ music. Posies of ruffle-headed carnations and foliage were attached to the end of each pew, their heady scent making her nose twitch.

'It would be a poor show if they did,' Bunny flicked up the flaps of his frock coat and sat, nudging aside a prayer cushion with his foot. His glance slid to the parcel wrapped in tissue paper on Flora's lap. 'What did you say we had bought them for a wedding present?'

'I didn't, because you never asked.' She rolled her eyes. 'And I bought them a silver pierced marriage box.'

'Ah, yes.' Frowning, he leaned closer. 'What exactly is that?'

Flora tried not to sigh. 'A trinket box engraved with their names and today's date.'

'Harry will appreciate the reminder, no doubt.' Bunny grinned. 'I'll be sure to react accordingly when she thanks me. By the way, Inspector Maddox called when you were having your bath. That spike I handed over *was* the murder weapon. He's sending an officer round to collect Ed's jacket.'

'That might make things worse for him.'

'Perhaps not. I didn't mention Reverend Bell's

letter to him, either, but don't assume he hasn't discovered for himself that Leo Thompson was the real Leonard Hunter-Griggs. Or that Thompson and Ed attended Marlborough at the same time.'

'Inspector Maddox isn't a fool, despite his smug attitude. He'll be trying to find out who the imposter is at The Dahlia.'

'Either that or he thinks he's got enough evidence to convict Ed and won't look any further.'

'No.' Flora shook her head. 'He wouldn't do that. It makes sense the imposter is the more likely suspect.'

'But without more evidence there's no proof Ed didn't do it.'

'Then we'll have to find some for him, won't we?' Flora glanced back down the aisle, to where a group of guests had entered the church.

'Looks like the Flynns have arrived.' Bunny followed her gaze to where a gaunt woman with dead eyes and a mouth puckered in disapproval strolled slowly down the aisle; a single white ribbon tied round the crown of her hat the only relief in a deep purple gown.

'She looks as if she's wearing mourning.'

'Perhaps she is.' Bunny's chuckle was abruptly cut off by Flora's nudge to his arm.

Flora craned her neck to get a view of a portly,

bald man who strutted at her side, leaning heavily on a cane. 'Lydia has spoken about them,' Flora murmured into his sleeve. 'We've never met. It looks as if I was spared an unpleasant experience.'

'Those anaemic-looking creatures are Harry's sisters,' Bunny referred to two girls in their late teens, both dressed in pastels which leached colour from their already pale faces.

'They barely acknowledged anyone,' Flora observed the group take their places at the front of the church.

'Perhaps they're still suffering from shock that their son is marrying a schoolteacher,' Bunny said.

'Lydia's not *just* a schoolteacher.' Flora's hackles rose on behalf of her friend. 'She's the headmistress of a prestigious Ladies' Academy. She has three earls' daughters and those of several members of Parliament among her pupils. They should admire her achievements, not be so critical.'

'You don't have to convince *me*. I'm a staunch advocate of Lydia. In fact, any woman who forges a career.' Flora shot him a look, and he shrugged. 'Not in *that* way, obviously. She's very accomplished. Like you. But not as beautiful, naturally.'

'Good recovery.' Flora resumed her study of the

groom's family, who had spread themselves out across the pew as if to discourage any interlopers.

In a previous murder case of Flora's, Lydia's long-standing friendship with the victim's fiancé had blossomed into love, a development which surprised no one.

The groom, an attractive young man with fair hair, twisted in his seat to greet his family. His glance swept past them and caught Flora's eye, gave a delighted start, then waved. His parents and sisters exhibited no curiosity at this exchange and sat with their backs rigid, their gazes fixed stoically to the front.

'Harry looks happy enough.' Flora waggled her fingers at him in a restrained wave.

'As do they.' Bunny tapped Flora's shoulder, his chin cocked towards the church door where William and Alice had paused on the porch, where an usher consulted a list. Alice wore a wide lapelled jacket in a shade of olive-grey over a primrose gown, a matching wide-brimmed hat with a primrose sash wound round the crown in soft folds arranged at an artistic angle on her ash blonde curls.

Released from the usher's attention, the pair progressed down the aisle arm-in-arm. William's intense, penetrating stare alighted for a few seconds on each face, making the men nod in approval and the women dimple prettily at being the focus of his attention, if briefly. Alice glided rather than walked, her ankle-length gown swaying gently, a shy smile directed at those who acknowledged William's greetings.

'Looks like your plan to get them here together worked.' Bunny's lips twitched.

'More Lydia's than mine, but they look good, don't they?' Flora watched them with possessive pride.

Alice's gaze swept the half-empty church before she paused beside their pew. Her head dipped to brush her lips against Flora's cheek. 'Where is everyone?'

'Dissension among the families,' Bunny whispered, his hand thrust out to shake William's. 'This union has not received the seal of approval from the Flynns.'

'My favourite kind of wedding,' William said as they settled in the pew behind them, plucked Alice's hand from her lap, and laced his fingers with hers. 'Will it get interesting later?'

'I sincerely hope not.' Heat suffused Flora's face, and she swung back to face the altar, strangely uncomfortable with their easy intimacy. An emotion which confused her when she had worked so hard to bring them together again.

'What are you thinking about?' Bunny said. 'You've gone all wistful.'

Having to witness my parents behaving like moon-struck youngsters. She flicked a look behind her, but the pair seemed engrossed in conversation. 'I was... er... just thinking about the woman in the red coat.'

'I'm not even going to tell you how I feel about that subject,' Bunny said.

'You just have.' Flora flicked him a wry look. 'I know it might sound obsessive, but the coat keeps nagging at me.'

'We'll not solve this case by chasing red coats. We ought to concentrate on finding out how the imposter knew about Leo's connection to the Hunter-Griggs to perpetrate his fraud.'

'I've given that some thought, too.' Flora didn't like him to think she focused on the trivial and ignored everything else. 'Perhaps Sylvia told the woman who helped her when she hurt herself?'

'What brought you to such a conclusion?'

'It's not a conclusion, just an idea. Dr Billings said Sylvia appeared near hysterics when she arrived at the surgery. Maybe the woman with her tried to calm her, put her at ease by mentioning she lived in London and Sylvia may have said what a coincidence, her husband did too but she hadn't seen him for years. Sometimes people reveal things in a state of high emotion that they wouldn't normally. She might have mentioned in passing that her husband had been in the army and this woman was devious enough to wheedle more out of her?'

'Hmm. And this woman, whoever she is, uses this snippet of information to devise an entire scheme to deprive Leo of his inheritance? It's very tenuous.'

'Perhaps not a chance encounter, then? Could a relative of the Colonel's – one we know nothing about – be greedy enough to dispose of the son of the disapproved of second wife to clear the way for the elder two? He said he had a sister in Sussex.'

'Who is most probably dead by now?' Bunny's sceptical, almost comical sideways look made her shrink back against the pew.

'Oh, all right, I agree it's far-fetched. But I'm speculating and I wanted to hear your opinion.' She winced as the organist played a wrong note.

'I think you're letting your imagination run wild, Flora.'

'All right, dismiss this aspect for the moment, but whatever is going on, I'm convinced it's connected to the hotel.'

'The Aspidistra?'

'You know very well it's The Dahlia. Sometimes I think you aren't taking this seriously.'

'I'm taking it all seriously, but could we forget it for one afternoon? We're at the wedding of two friends who have been through a great deal to reach this day. Could we simply enjoy their happiness?'

'What a sentimental soul you are, Bunny Harrington.' Smiling, Flora bumped his shoulder with her own.

A teacher Flora recognized as being from the Harriett Parker Academy exchanged greetings and small talk on the way to her seat. She had barely passed on when a young woman from the suffragist society meetings Flora infrequently attended in Victoria Street stopped to ensure Flora intended to go to their next meeting. Having promised to be there, the woman moved away and Flora's thoughts returned to the former problem.

'We still don't know how this imposter found out Leo was Colonel Hunter-Griggs' long-lost son? No one knew. Not even the woman who worked for Sylvia.'

Bunny sighed. 'If you insist on discussing this now, and evidently you do, then I suggest you ask yourself how frail *is* the Colonel? Is his demise impending?'

'Now there's a thought. I cannot be sure. His skin looked sallow and his mind wandered a little. He almost fell asleep when we were talking as well. Do you think the plan is to kill him, too?'

'Not necessarily. They might not have to. Whoever the killer was, he could simply let nature take its course. Then no one will be suspicious when the imposter claims his inheritance, as he has already staked his claim to the family.' Bunny clapped a hand to his forehead. 'Now look at me, even I've lumped the twins into the role of murderers.'

'But what happens to the imposter? Do they pay him off or kill him as well?' Flora sighed. The more she thought about it the more questions she came up with. 'Inspector Maddox isn't likely to tell us if the fake Leonard was seen on that train. We'll have to find out for ourselves. And don't ask me how, I have no idea. I'll have to think about it more.'

'Well, we cannot spend any more time on it now,' Bunny said as the opening bars of Wagner's 'Here Comes The Bride' echoed through the church. 'The bride has arrived.'

24

The couple's exchange of vows was intimate, emotional and lovely, marred only by the stoic faces of Harry's parents and sisters, all of whom refused to crack so much as a smile throughout the ceremony.

Harry made his declaration in a firm voice, while Lydia's responses echoed clear but soft in the sunlit church. Her blonde delicacy was enhanced by a cream silk gown, her petite figure laced into the fashionable 'S' shape that accentuated her tiny waist. Gigot sleeves puffed out at the shoulders, tapered to points over her wrists, a garland of yellow and white flowers inter-twined with spring greenery encircled her head like a fairy queen. A wedding band collar embroidered with rows of tiny seed pearls was so rigid, it was a wonder she could bend her head at all.

As the reverend delivered his sermon on the sanctity of marriage, Bunny groped for Flora's hand, his grip strong and almost painful. Taking their seats again amongst shuffling of feet and muffled coughs, Flora met his gaze, unsurprised to see his eyes were wet.

With the register signed, the smiling bride and groom sauntered back down the aisle to Mendelssohn's rousing 'Wedding March', emerging onto the porch in a hail of rice, rose petals and happy laughter, where a photographer struggled to marshal guests into specific groups before the light faded.

The guests adjourned to the reception on foot in a good-natured, chattering crocodile of colourful hats, flowing skirts and handsome men in frock coats; a procession, the groom's family declined to join and, instead, sat bolt upright in their carriage and stared ahead as they swept past.

On their arrival at Lydia's neat villa in Kinnerton Street, the guests filed in to the parlour and formed into groups in a room where yellow and white flowers with hints of mauve filled the ground floor with the scent and colours of spring. China pots and glass jugs of all sizes had been pressed into service along a long table, in the centre of which stood a two-tiered cake of pristine white sugar paste topped with a swathe of artfully arranged yellow freesias.

Once the speeches had been performed, and the cake cut, Lydia was freed to mix with her guests, making a beeline for Flora. 'I do so hate being the centre of attention.'

'How could you not be? You look exquisite.' She brushed her lips across her friend's cheek.

'Are you sure my entering the church alone didn't look strange?' Lydia asked. 'My father died years ago, and it seemed wrong for anyone to take his place.'

'Not at all,' Flora replied, and meant it. 'Anyone who knows you would understand perfectly.'

'That makes me feel better, and by the way, Flora, I love your dress. Such a simple yet elegant cut, and I've never seen such fine stitching.' Lydia's grey gaze swept the cornflower blue confection with open admiration. 'If I didn't know you better, I would think you were trying to outshine me.'

Flora sought her reflection in the oval mirror over the fireplace and took a few seconds to preen. 'I thought today warranted something special. But no one should talk about *my* clothes to a bride as lovely as you, Lydia. Your own gown is exquisite yet understated, much like you.'

'It is rather lovely, isn't it?' Lydia glanced down at herself. 'Harry insisted I engage this dressmaker his cousin frequents in Bond Street. He said he wasn't going to let his mother heap more criticism on the fact we had had a simple wedding.'

The way society weddings appeared in the press in such lurid detail was well known, and Flora sympathised with Lydia's aversion to having her history being the subject of journalistic fodder. There was also the unspoken issue that Harry's two sisters would have made the ugliest bridesmaids in England.

'We planned to hold the reception at the new house in Kensington,' Lydia interrupted Flora's train of thought. 'Only the renovation isn't finished and Harry refused to postpone again. He said we had waited long enough.'

'This house is lovely, and perfect for the two of you,' Flora gazed round at the neat little house, which had benefitted from some decoration since her last visit. 'You'll be working at the academy most days.'

'Which is yet another aspect of my life the Hon. Darnley Flynn and his wife disapprove of.' Lydia's smile wavered as her gaze went to the groom's parents, who huddled in a corner, staring into their champagne glasses as if suspicious they might have been poisoned. 'They wanted me to resign, but the academy has never been in such demand and I refuse to hand it over to a less dedicated headmistress.' Lydia's gaze strayed to her new husband who stood amongst a group of sleek, well-dressed young men that included Bunny, all of whom exuded wealth and privilege. 'Do you think Harry might have been happier with Evangeline?'

'How could you even think such a thing? Especially today.' Flora suppressed a groan. She had hoped they had buried the spectre of the sainted, beautiful and wealthy Evangeline Lange some time ago.

'The Flynns wanted him to marry an heiress, not an orphan whose father had once been employed in a Bermondsey factory.'

'Fate evidently had a different plan,' Flora insisted. 'Harry was being the dutiful son when he agreed to marry Evangeline Lange. He's grown up since then and is so much happier with you.'

'I certainly am.' Harry appeared, his face wreathed in a wide smile, apparently having heard her last remark.

Behind him, Bunny gestured with his glass to show Harry might have imbibed a little too much, confirmed when the groom swayed into one of the hired waiters, putting a platter of sandwiches briefly at risk.

'The custom of marrying only inside one's social circle is ridiculously outdated,' Harry declared. 'Bunny here is a prime example. Look how happy you and Flora are.' He slapped Bunny's shoulder, threatening to spill his champagne.

'I regard Flora as my equal in every way, Harry, and always have,' Bunny placed his glass in his other hand and shook droplets off his fingers, lowering his voice to a whisper. 'You might be wise to change your perspective, or you might find yourself an exceedingly unhappy man.'

'Don't take me wrong, old boy.' Harry frowned, genuinely perplexed. 'I couldn't imagine life without Lydia now, but we must acknowledge times are changing. The classes should mix more. We have so much to learn from each other.' His glance shifted to a point over Bunny's shoulder. 'Ah, I spy my Uncle Randolph over there.' His waving arm swung his glass a fraction of an inch from Bunny's chin, sending him back a pace. 'I must introduce Lydia to him. He's stinking rich and a bachelor. I need to inform him he's been selected as godfather to our firstborn.'

As Lydia was borne away, she turned and mouthed an apology over her shoulder.

'Don't think too badly of him,' Bunny said in response to Flora's frown. 'The best man just told me he was so nervous, he was sick three times before the ceremony.'

'Were you nervous before our wedding?'

'Of course not.' He paused. '*I* only threw up once.'

'It's not like Harry to be so careless with his opinions.'

'Maybe the champagne has made him uninhibited enough to voice his true feelings,' Alice said from behind them.

'Alice! I didn't see you there.' Flora turned to where Alice stood, her cheeks suffused with high colour.

'I doubt Harry did either.' Alice drained her glass and set it down on a nearby surface without checking where it landed.

'You weren't offended by Harry's remark about marrying beneath him? He didn't mean it. If I thought that, I would have had something to say to him myself. Their entire courtship has been a trial for both of them, what with his family objecting so strongly. For Harry especially.'

'Flora, hush. You don't have to defend him.' Alice cupped Flora's chin gently. 'He's only saying what most people still believe. That you should never marry outside your social class.'

Flora frowned. 'You don't think people will think the same about you and William, do you?'

'It's ridiculous, I know, but I cannot help it.' Alice clamped her lips together, distress not for away. 'I'm hardly a prime candidate for an earl's brother-in-law. A former lady's maid who bore him a child twenty-five years ago, married another man to salve my reputation and then ran away, leaving that child. They'll say he's only being kind to me now, for your sake.'

Bunny's cheeks flushed red, and he backed away. 'Excuse me a moment, there's someone over there I need to – um.'

'Coward,' Flora mouthed as he retreated. She grasped Alice's hand and pulled her to one side, away from the curious looks they had attracted, although, unlike Harry, at least Alice did not appear affected by the champagne. 'I hope this isn't a bout of self-pity on your part. It doesn't become you.'

'Is that any way for a daughter to speak to her mother?' Alice's eyes sparkled with mischief. 'I've never cared much what people think of me, but somehow things have changed. I worry too that William has been a bachelor too long to consider marriage now.'

'You've discussed it already?' Flora asked. 'But it's only been a few days.'

'Seeing as it's a day for secrets,' she slid her hand

into Flora's and squeezed, 'I'll let you into one of mine.'

'Another one?' Flora raised an eyebrow. 'You seem to have a penchant for those.' Alice's eyes darkened and Flora added quickly, 'I'm sorry, I didn't mean that.'

'I wouldn't blame you if you did.' Alice's smile held no malice. 'A week after the child abduction case, William saw me coming out of your house at Eaton Place.'

'He saw you?' Flora inhaled sharply. Their careful plan to ease Alice back into William's life slowly had gone awry. What had she just said to Lydia about Fate?

'I'm afraid so.' Alice's eyes glittered above her sheepish smile. 'He waved down my hansom and said he knew it was me immediately but had to make sure he wasn't imagining things and had to speak to me before I disappeared. He climbed in beside me and ordered the driver to circle Hyde Park three times. It was all quite romantic.'

'Are you telling me my surprise dinner party was no such thing?' At her slow nod, Flora gaped. 'Why didn't you tell me?'

'I wasn't sure how you would feel, or even how William and I felt. And, besides, we didn't want to spoil your evening by admitting we had been meeting for some time.'

'Now I know why you've been so happy these last months. And *I* thought it had something to do with me and Arthur.'

'You know I'm thrilled to have you back again. I have a beautiful grandson and the handsomest, kindest son-in-law anyone could imagine. Naturally, I'm happy. And now there is William too.' A smile played round her mouth. 'Since seeing him again, he's all I can think about. Does that sound ridiculously sentimental for a woman of my age?' Before Flora could respond, Alice nudged her, 'Look out. Lydia is coming back. Remember, for now it's our secret.'

'I had to come and apologise for Harry.' Lydia insinuated herself between them. 'He never drinks, but that oaf of a best man plied him with brandy, as he was shaking with nerves.'

'Bunny told me,' Flora said. 'And honestly, Lydia, there's no need to explain.'

'My first wifely lecture will be a stern talk about inadvertently offending his guests.'

'I might do that myself.' Flora said, eliciting a laugh from Lydia.

'There's no need, either of you.' Alice pleaded through her watery smile. 'Let's not spoil such a lovely day with things which don't matter.'

'You're very gracious, Alice. Now I've been dying to

ask you how the dinner party went.' Flora glanced at Alice, who shrugged.

'Oh dear, have I been indiscreet?' Lydia brought a hand to her mouth. 'Did it not go well? Only I assumed—'

'You assumed right, but it turns out it wasn't as much of a surprise,' Flora said. 'We were talking about William just now in fact.'

'You know I couldn't help noticing how comfortable you two are with each other,' Lydia said, laughing. 'Therefore, I'm not in the least surprised.'

'You've met my friend, Lydia, haven't you, Alice?' Flora laughed. 'Not much gets past her. She's a better detective than I am.'

'It doesn't take much more than intuition. I've seen the way William looks at you.' Lydia swept a glass of sherry from a tray offered by a passing server. 'He's quite a different man from the overly serious diplomat I met when Flora first came to London.'

'I agree, he is,' Flora said. 'William has always regretted allowing his sister to persuade him not to marry Alice. And I'm not making that up, he told me himself. He's worth waiting for, and I'm not saying that because he's my father. I've got to know him this last year, and he's a very special person.'

'He always was.' Alice's smile held a world of memories and maybe even some more recent ones.

'I've known Harry for years and yet I still had to convince him we were suited,' Lydia said. 'Men find change unsettling. It's up to us women to tell them what we want and they'll capitulate rather than risk change to the status quo.'

'Not all men are like that,' Flora said, feeling slightly smug. 'For months after the SS *Minneapolis* docked, Bunny bombarded me with letters, flowers and gifts saying he couldn't live without me and we must become engaged as soon as possible.'

'Then he's the exception. Harry needs persuasion for most things.' Lydia sighed. 'He prevaricated about joining the Labour Party for so long. I told him that if socialism was too far to jump, he should join the Liberals.' She gave a sly wink. 'I'm easing him into it.'

'Talking of politics,' Alice began, taking a sip of champagne. 'I was thinking of joining the National Union of Women's Suffrage Societies. I assume you both attend meetings?' The look she gave Flora dared her to dissemble.

'Not as often as I should,' Flora admitted, sheepish. 'But Lydia is a dedicated member and if anything important happens, she'll keep me informed.' Aware this was yet another subject Lydia's in-laws would count against her, Flora cast a nervous glance at where they had formed a tight circle near the front bay window, alert for any interlopers.

'They can tut over me all they like.' Lydia drained her champagne glass. 'My activities are nothing compared to Harry becoming a Liberal.'

Alice choked on her drink and Flora slapped her back hard.

'I'm a little disappointed in our society, truth be told,' Lydia said when Alice had recovered. 'Millicent Fawcett has been campaigning for over forty years, but with over forty percent of adult men having no right to vote, no wonder the politicians feel women's rights are a low priority. Perhaps we should concentrate on male suffrage first and let society develop naturally to include women.'

'It will take a war to do that, which isn't something we should wish for.' Flora regretted having broached such a subject at a wedding of all things, but William's talk of the situation in Russia had stayed with her. Maybe revolution wasn't as far away as they hoped.

'War aside, I agree things must change.' Lydia placed her empty glass on a tray carried precariously by a passing server. 'There's such poverty in London and the child mortality rate is scandalous. Two out of three children born south of the river die before their first birthday. It's a disgrace.'

Alice nodded sadly. 'It's something St Philomena's has been fighting for years. Until something is done to ensure they have clean air, clean water, and children of ten don't have to work ten hours a day in a factory, nothing will change.'

'Harry's concern for the plight of the less fortunate is what I most admire about him. A majority of his class simply don't care.' Lydia's eyes shone with pride for her new husband, then darkened. 'His ability to handle alcohol notwithstanding.'

Flora joined in with the resultant laughter, but her thoughts remained squarely on William. If only she could be sure he would stay out of harm's way. For Alice's sake and her own. She drained her glass with a shaking hand, but barely tasted the excellent champagne.

25

Extricating herself from a one-sided conversation with an elderly relative of Harry's, Flora went in search of William. She found him in the walled courtyard, his hands in his pockets and a glass of wine balanced on a bench beside him. Pots, urns and metal buckets crammed with spring flowers crowded the flagstones of the immaculate yard where vines and early-flowering plants hid the red-brick walls.

'You look lovely today, Flora.' His gaze travelled from her feet to her hair, finally settling on her face. 'Harry's great-uncle appears to have put colour into your cheeks. I saw you talking to him just now.' He aimed a brief nod at the room behind her.

'Is that who he is? He waylaid me to expound an

opinion on women's role in the world. He thinks Harry should rein in Lydia like an unbroken filly now they are married. He regards the female sex as being too intellectually weak to be trained to do anything more taxing than counting linens or mixing cake batter.'

'He was born before the old queen came to the throne, in the days when Chartists were transported.'

'You might have stepped in and saved me.' Gathering her skirt round her, she prepared to take a seat on the bench when William held her off with one hand, moving his glass to one side with the other, and drew a handkerchief from his pocket and dusted off the slats.

'Thank you.' Flora sat. 'Have you forgiven me for springing Alice on you the other night?' She held up a finger in mock surprise. 'Oh, that's right, I didn't. You've been seeing each other since last year.'

'Ah,' His lips drew back in an embarrassed grin. 'Alice told you, did she? I'm sorry, but we weren't sure how we would feel about it and neither of us wanted to get your hopes up. Things didn't end well when we last saw one another.'

'I'm not a child any more, and I'm delighted you and Alice have found a – connection again, but neither am I unrealistic. I was prepared for a less than satisfactory ending.'

'And yet we are enjoying each other's company again. We took tea at the Prince's Skating Rink last week.'

'You took me there during the Lange case if you remember?'

'Which made my nostalgic visit symbolic. New beginnings and all that.'

'Did she tell you why she ran away from Cleeve Abbey all those years ago?'

'She told me everything. Her story must have been a shock for you, Flora.'

'It was.' She summoned a shaky smile. Having everything she had always believed about herself swept away was still hard to accept.

'When she mentioned Lydia and Harry had invited her to their wedding, it made practical sense we should attend together.'

'Practical,' Flora sliced him a sideways look. 'Is that how you choose to look at it?'

'Maybe not.' His eyes softened, and he stared at his feet with a ghost of a smile.

'Bunny will be horribly smug when he finds out. He told me not to meddle.'

'I'm sure he'll not dwell on it. Bunny never crows.

Now, lovely as it is to chat with my daughter, I suspect you sought me out for a reason.' William retrieved his glass and took a sip of champagne. 'I suspect you want to ask me what I was doing at The Dahlia Hotel.'

'Ah, you saw us?' She twisted to face him, taking care not to pull the sheer fabric of her dress on any stray splinters. 'I hoped we had been discreet.'

'Hah! The pair of you shot out of there in such a hurry I could hardly miss it.' His right eyebrow rose a fraction. 'Do I make a good Russian?'

'Passable, at least to anyone who doesn't know you. I assume you were there because of the Congress?'

'I was, but fail to see *your* interest.'

'The newspapers blame Russian émigrés for everything from unemployment to growing slums and the breakdown of society. Some scandal sheets claim bomb-throwing anarchists exist on our doorstep.' She broke off as a group of guests entered the courtyard, their voices raised in enthusiastic chatter.

'Inflammatory rubbish!' William's upper lip curled in disdain. 'I agree the sweatshops and slums south of the river attract activists and propagandists, but they aren't violent. They want what any reasonable working man wants. Enough food, education for their children and a roof over their heads they can afford.

Most of them aren't interested in deposing the government.'

'And Vladimir Lenin? What does *he* want?' At his sharp look, she added, 'Bunny pointed him out to me.' Since she had first heard of a foreign revolutionary on British soil, the concept had fascinated her.

'You understand I can't say too much.' He gave the other guests a swift look before continuing. 'He's a militant political activist determined to bring down the Tsarist regime. He's here with his wife, Nadya, and members of their party to discuss a strategy.'

'A strategy for what?' she asked, surprised he would tell her anything. 'It sounds serious.'

'It is, and I hope it never happens. The Okhrana sentenced Vladimir to prison for three years in Siberia, which is probably the equivalent of ten in an English prison. And that's all I'm prepared to say about him.'

'Who are these Okra— whatever it is, people?'

'Okhrana. The Department for Protecting the Public Security and Order,' William recited in a monotone. 'The Russian Secret Police who monitor the activities of their revolutionaries abroad. Lenin is a serious threat to the Imperialists, and he's watched constantly. By both governments.'

'Oh dear. Any government organisation operating in secret strikes me as sinister.' She shuddered.

'I agree. Lenin sees their spies everywhere, for good reason. It wasn't easy getting him to accept me into the party.'

'I imagine not.' There was no one more sartorial or upper class than William.

'Strangely enough, it was my expertise with printing presses.'

'Printing presses?' Flora frowned. 'I had no idea you had any experience of those.'

'I don't, but I received some fast tuition before setting off for St Petersburg.' He took another sip from his glass. 'The party newspaper is being published here in London.'

'Newspaper,' Flora murmured, a memory returning. 'What's it called?'

'*Iskra*, it's taken from a poem, I believe. Something about "The spark will kindle a flame." Lenin calls his elite group of comrades "The Spark" as well.' He lifted his glass away from his mouth. 'What made you ask about *Iskra*?'

'I heard the word somewhere.' A thrill of excitement ran through her. Could that have been the publication Inspector Maddox found in Leo Thompson's luggage? Could Leo have been a member of the

Russian Socialist party? 'I assume the Russian government would prefer this newspaper didn't exist?'

'Definitely.' William snorted. 'They destroy the presses whenever they find them and anyone connected with them is imprisoned. Printing them here keeps them out of Okhrana's hands, but also makes it easier to supply our government with copies.'

'Do you provide the Okhrana with copies too?'

'Not exactly.' He glanced away quickly, mildly uncomfortable. 'We're more inclined to let them find out for themselves. It's called diplomacy. With the way things are going in Russia, our government must appear neutral in order to leave us free to negotiate with whichever regime prevails.'

'Neutral? That's so duplicitous. Suppose this Lenin person finds out you're as English as crumpets? Someone you know might see you. I did.'

'I'm being careful, I promise.' He massaged her shoulder gently. 'Now, why're you asking me all these questions?'

She hesitated, recalling Bunny's warning not to mention Ed, but if she wanted William's help she had no choice. 'Did you read about the body found in a train compartment at Paddington earlier this week?'

He nodded slowly. 'Stabbed, as I recall. The newspapers didn't identify him.'

'He had a copy of *Iskra* on him.'

William eased closer, his shoulder pressed against hers, forming a close circle of intimacy between them. 'Go on.'

'From what you've just said, it occurs to me this man's death might have something to do with the Party. It might be worth informing Inspector Maddox about the newspaper.'

'Good Lord, *Maddox* is investigating?' At her nod, his expression darkened. 'Hmm. I could do without the inspector crashing through the hotel in his size tens, making everyone panic. If he sees me, things might get sticky.'

'Which is why I mentioned it.'

'I appreciate it. So, tell me, Flora, how are you involved with a dead body at Paddington? This isn't one of your amateur investigations, is it?'

'My amateur investigations usually turn out very well. But no, this one is a little different.' She hesitated, debating how much to reveal. 'The young man discovered bent over the body when it was found is the police's prime suspect.'

'Sounds like a reasonable assumption. If Maddox is handling the case, why not leave it to him?'

'Because...' Flora hesitated. 'I suppose you'll find

out before long. The young man in question is Edward.'

'My sister Letitia's Edward?' William almost choked on his drink. 'How is that possible?'

'Shush.' She flapped her hands to quieten him. 'It's complicated, but I assure you he didn't do it.'

'I should think not!' He pushed a hand into his hair, creating narrow partings in the carefully applied pomade. 'The poor chap must be scared rigid. How's he holding up?'

'Frightened, frustrated.' She had no intention of mentioning he had almost sabotaged his own story. 'Inspector Maddox has allowed Ed to stay with us at Eaton Place until further enquiries are made. But if no fresh evidence comes to light in the next couple of days, he'll have no choice but to arrest him.'

'My God, poor Edward.' He stroked his chin thoughtfully. 'I gather you and Bunny have taken it upon yourself to find out who the murderer is?'

'Did you think we wouldn't?'

'No.' His eyes softened. 'And I'm sure my sister will appreciate your efforts. But what led you to The Dahlia?'

'Before he – died – this man told Ed he was going there, although the staff at the hotel claim they weren't expecting him.'

'I see. Doesn't sound as if you have much to go on.'

'We don't. But you mentioning this *Iskra* makes me think the victim might have had something to do with this conference you're involved with. He had a copy of *Iskra* in his luggage and was planning to stay at that hotel. Or rather, he *is* staying there.'

'I'm sorry, I don't follow.'

'It's complicated, but if I could establish a connection between this man and the conference, I might get somewhere. Could you find out if he was on the delegate list?'

'The chap who was on the train?' At her nod, he added, 'Of course, if it helps prove Ed is innocent. What was his name?'

'Leo, Leo Thompson.'

'Thompson!' William's eyes widened. He said something else but broke off, his face splitting into a wide smile as Alice glided towards them.

'There you are! I might have guessed I would find you two together. The bride and groom are preparing to leave. You must come and say goodbye.'

26

Flora joined the crowd of wedding guests who spilled into the street like colourful butterflies crowding round Harry's motor car to bid the happy couple an enthusiastic farewell. Someone had arranged for a local chimney sweep to shake the groom's hand and offer a token kiss to the bride to guarantee the couple's future prosperity. Neighbours smiled from their doorways, while children gathered up dropped rose petals and scrambled for the handful of coins Harry had thrown through the motor car window as they pulled away.

Declining William's offer of a ride back to their house, Flora and Bunny took the short walk back to

Eaton Place. The evening air was cool but not uncomfortable as dusk fell slowly in a mackerel sky to the sound of birdsong in Belgrave Square. Flora loved the city at this time of year, when the damp oppressive fog was long forgotten and blossoms appeared in the garden squares, peppering the verges with tiny pink and white petals.

'You were right about William and the Russian conference.' She linked her arm with Bunny's and leaned closer.

'I guessed as much. His recent trip to Russia was too coincidental.'

'He also told me "Iskra" means "Spark", which is also the name of—'

'The Russian Socialist Party Newspaper,' he finished for her.

'You knew?' She glanced up at him, frowning.

'You aren't the only one good at this detecting stuff. It's interesting that Leo Thompson had that pamphlet in his suitcase. It answers the question of why his mother disapproved of his friends.'

'Mrs Tilney replied to my letter.'

'Sylvia Thompson's friend?' Bunny halted to let a cat streak across their path into a nearby garden, followed by a scuffling in the hedge. 'The one Amy Coombe told us about?'

She nodded. 'I meant to tell you earlier, but we were distracted. She said Leo spent a good deal of time in London. William agreed to finding out if Leo was on the delegate list for me. If so, we'll know he was a party member.'

'That might tell us more.' Bunny pushed opened the front gate, which brushed against a lilac bush, releasing the evening perfume into the air.

Stepping aside to let Flora through first onto the mosaic pathway. They had barely climbed the steps before the front door opened to reveal Stokes.

'You have a visitor, sir, madam.' He hurried forward to divest them of their coats.

'At this hour?' Bunny adjusted his spectacles, looking up as Ed clattered down the staircase.

'It's Inspector Maddox,' he said, breathless. 'He's been in the study for half an hour, but I hid upstairs until you got home before speaking to him.'

Flora exchanged a fearful look with Bunny. Had he come to arrest Ed?

'We'd better get this over with.' Bunny herded them along the hallway towards the study, one hand on Flora's lower back, the other gripping Ed's shoulder.

Inspector Maddox occupied Bunny's chair; a studded leather contraption with a mechanism which allowed its occupant to half recline. Maddox had taken full advantage of this facility and sat with both feet inches off the floor, his slender, almost feminine hands folded flat over his midriff.

'I see you are having a knot garden installed.' He swivelled the chair a half-turn away from the window, facing them. 'An authentic design, if I may say so. Unfortunately, it's too late to enjoy the spring flowers, but perhaps the summer display will be impressive.'

'They'll no doubt delight us next year.' Bunny's expression tightened, as if he resisted the urge to order the man out of his chair; a liberty even Flora hesitated to take without permission.

'My, you look very elegant this evening, Mrs Harrington.' Maddox's gaze travelled slowly over her cornflower gown. 'Nice to see the reappearance of lighter clothes in springtime colours. Quite lifts one's spirits after a cold winter.'

'Er, thank you, Inspector.' *Compliments from the inspector, whatever next?* 'We're sorry you had to wait, but we've been at a wedding.' She rubbed her upper arms at a sudden chill, debating whether to summon a maid to lay the fire, but decided against it. Hopefully Maddox wouldn't stay that long.

'No matter.' Maddox smoothly set the chair in its upright position. Too smoothly, which told Flora he had been experimenting during their absence, as the thing always stuck on the first try. 'Ah, Lord Trent, join us.' He smiled and gestured to Ed, who stubbornly remained by the door; an act of defiance not lost on the inspector, whose eyes glinted with amusement.

'What have you come to tell us, Inspector?' Bunny asked, taking charge of the conversation. 'I assume this isn't a social call' He too pointedly remained standing.

'It is not.' Maddox cleared his throat. 'First, the body on the train has now been formally identified as that of Leo Thompson, born Leonard Hunter-Griggs.'

Ed cleared his throat and Flora chewed her lip nervously, not daring to look at Bunny or Ed.

'Ah, I see this is not news to any of you.' The policeman directed a speculative look at each of them. 'I assume you know what it means.'

'That the man staying at The Dahlia Hotel is an imposter,' Flora replied, relieved to say it aloud.

'Exactly.' Maddox shifted on the leather, making it creak. 'Since his mother's death, Mr Thompson must have reverted to his birth name.'

'Or he didn't,' Flora said. 'It was the imposter who is using it. Leo never did.'

'True.' His steady gaze swivelled to Ed. 'Do you

still maintain you were not acquainted with Mr Thompson, sir?'

'I uh... I have an apology to make, Inspector.' Ed inched forward. 'I haven't been as straightforward as I should have been.' He licked his lips nervously. 'We weren't friends, but we both attended Marlborough College. It was there an incident occurred which—'

Maddox held up a hand to silence him. 'If you are referring to a certain cross-country race, I already know about it.'

'You know?' Ed gaped. 'But how?'

'I'm a professional, my lord. I have my ways of—'

'It was the Marlborough College tie, wasn't it?' Flora interrupted what she suspected was going to be one of his lectures about their being amateurs. 'That's how you made the connection?'

'Uh, yes, well. As I was saying...' The inspector cleared his throat. 'My line of enquiry included a visit to that establishment, where a schoolmaster recalled a long-standing feud, between Viscount Trent and Mr Thompson.'

'It wasn't a feud! Well, not really.' Ed's scowl displayed more shame than disapproval. 'It was two years ago.'

'Even so.' Maddox raised an enquiring eyebrow. 'Are you sure there was no lingering resentment between you when you met again by chance last Tuesday?'

'Not at all. We even shook hands that day he... on the train.'

'Shook hands?' Scepticism stood in the policeman's eyes. 'After the dreadful prank he played on you? Sending you and your friends off on a false trail so you got lost for almost an entire day? The way I heard it, when you and your chums finally returned, it was to open ridicule from the entire school which lasted the rest of the term.'

'Not the entire school,' Ed protested. 'Only our year.'

Flora sighed, irritated that Ed still felt the need to keep secrets, while Bunny's jaw clenched and he studied the ceiling. Maddox rocked gently back and forth, making the chair creak, oblivious to their combined discomfort.

'Or,' Maddox seemed determined to prolong Ed's humiliation. 'One or more of your friends sought their own revenge on Mr Thompson? Perhaps I should ask them?'

'You can't question the other chaps about this.' Ed's voice rose in panic. 'I'd never live it down. Besides, they weren't involved in Leo's murder. How could they have been? I was the only one on the train.'

'Is that a confession, my... lord?' He dragged out Ed's title in open disrespect.

'Of course not!' Ed gasped.

'Inspector, surely you don't suspect this was a conspiracy between four young men to murder an ex-schoolmate over a prank?' Bunny said.

Maddox narrowed his eyes at Ed. 'I've already been misled as to the details of this case; therefore, I intend to examine every possibility.'

'Are you going to arrest me?' Ed backed against the wall beside the door as if preparing for a physical onslaught.

'Not yet, but believe me, I will if I have to.'

'What about the man at The Dahlia Hotel?' Flora demanded. 'You know he's an imposter, so why haven't you locked *him* up?'

'A small thing called proof, Mrs Harrington. I have to be able to prove the imposter was on the train with Mr Thompson to make a case for murder. At the moment, I can only charge him with fraud and deception.'

'Isn't that enough?' Bunny crossed his arms over his chest, frowning. 'Surely you aren't going to risk this individual getting away?'

'Have you even interviewed him?' Flora fidgeted. 'Do you know his real name?'

'No, on both counts.' Maddox sighed, evidently unaccustomed to being questioned. 'And to make things more complicated, this man has an alibi for the day of the murder.'

'Is it a strong one or can it be broken?' Bunny asked with the confidence of someone who knows how the police operate.

'Not without showing my hand.' Maddox shook his head. 'The person calling himself Leonard Hunter-Griggs was recovering from a heavy bout of late-night revelling on the day of the murder. The staff all claim he didn't leave the hotel all day and the chambermaid who cleaned his room said he was sleeping.'

'Which means he couldn't have killed Leo.' Ed's shoulders slumped in disappointment. 'Which still leaves me as your chief suspect.'

'For the time being, it would appear so. However, I have more enquiries to make.'

'Enquiries with my former classmates, which will embarrass me no end when this gets out.'

'A situation of your own contrivance, my lord.'

'Are the Hunter-Griggs twins aware this man is pretending to be their half-brother?' Flora interrupted, her frustration mounting, though she had

some sympathy for the inspector. He couldn't ignore
Ed's part in the affair even if he wanted to.

'Not as yet. He's done a thorough job of ingrati-
ating himself with the family. They've formed an at-
tachment to the man. It won't be easy convincing
them he is not who he claims to be.'

'You might find it easier than you think, Inspector,'
Flora said. 'Especially if they have employed this man
to impersonate their half-brother?'

'Employed him? To what purpose, Mrs Harrington?' Maddox heaved a resigned sigh.

'The Colonel cut off the money they wanted to
renovate the hotel. Perhaps they thought bringing the
Colonel and his youngest son together again after so
long would soften him towards them. To make him
more amenable to their demand for money.'

'I shan't ask exactly *how* you obtained this information, Mrs Harrington. However, we have no evidence Frederick and Francis Hunter-Griggs are
involved, any more than is the Colonel.' He released a
slow breath, slapped both hands on the chair arms
and pushed himself to his feet, signalling the interview was over.

'I'm sorry if you feel we've misled you, Inspector.'
Flora rose, blocking his path to the door. She suspected he had got what he came for. 'But please un-

derstand, Ed means a lot to us and we couldn't just stand by and let this misunderstanding ruin his life. Could you answer me this? How did this man know Leo Thompson was Colonel Hunter-Griggs' son if the family had no contact with him for years? Ed didn't know, did you Ed?'

'No.' Ed splayed his hands in a gesture of surrender. 'I knew him throughout school as Thompson.'

'It's possible this case is far simpler than you imagine?' Maddox adopted a patronising tone. 'In my experience, villains are like magpies who see something shiny and reach for it without attention to the consequences. This man saw a chance to pass himself off as a wealthy man's long-lost son and took it. Sylvia Thompson might have told her son about his father, who told others.' He narrowed his eyes again at Ed. 'And I'm still not convinced his lordship didn't have a personal grudge against Mr Thompson, which turned into a fierce argument on that train.'

'That's ridiculous! Our meeting was amicable.' Ed placed his foot on the fender of the tiny fireplace and glared sullenly into the empty grate.

Flora was about to defend Ed again, when Bunny's warning look and the slight shake of his head changed her mind. 'I intend to find out the truth of this matter.' He turned a hard look on Flora.

'I'll bid you all a good evening.' With a sad shake of his head, he headed off down the hallway to where Stokes had positioned himself beside the open front door.

'Do you think he paid any attention to what we had to say?' Ed asked, looking more despondent than when they arrived.

'Don't underestimate him.' Bunny replied. He slid an arm around Flora's waist and guided her back along the hallway to the sitting room. 'I suspect he knows more about this case than we do, but isn't prepared to reveal it. He still regards us as amateurs.'

'He's the most frustrating man,' Flora snapped.

'I need a sherry.' Ed strode past them heading for the sideboard. 'Anyone care to join me?'

'Good idea,' Bunny replied.

Flora followed them inside, where Ed had made himself comfortable in a wing-back chair beside the fireplace, a large full glass of Bunny's vintage Fino in one hand.

Catching her expression, Ed smiled sheepishly. 'I hope you don't mind, but that entire conversation was stressful.'

'Don't take it to heart, Ed.' Bunny handed a glass to Flora. 'If Maddox believed you guilty, he would have arrested you by now.'

'Perhaps we should have shown him Reverend Bell's letter?' The evening had turned cool, so she sat on the sofa closest to the fire which Stokes had thoughtfully prepared.

'I doubt it would have made a difference, Flora.' Bunny hefted the decanter in his hand, and plucked a glass from the tray. 'He has all the information we do regarding the school.'

'I wish he would hurry and find out what really happened.' Ed slung one leg over the arm of the chair, making it creak. 'I'm a bag of nerves waiting for the axe to fall.'

'I suspect he's closer to a solution than we think, Ed,' Bunny said. 'Or why wasn't he angrier at your deception?'

'Suppose Leo planned to attend the conference at the hotel knowing nothing about the Colonel being his father?' Flora sipped her sherry, savouring its yeasty, nutty undertones on her tongue. She had drunk champagne earlier, so perhaps it was not a good idea, but what harm could it do?

'Then why did the imposter have to kill him?' Ed asked.

'Fear of being found out and having all his plans disrupted?' Flora shrugged, beginning to feel warmer and slightly light-headed. 'He couldn't take the risk that even if Leo was ignorant, he might not stay that way.'

'Or,' Bunny began. 'Someone didn't like the idea of Thompson spreading Bolshevik propaganda among the good folk of Cheltenham. That copy of *Iskra* he had with him was telling.'

'What's "Iskra"?' Ed's brow furrowed. 'Maddox said something about that the first time he came, but it made no sense.' Ed slung one leg over the chair arm. 'And what does all this have to do with anything?'

'Er, let's not get side-tracked.' Flora caught Bunny's warning expression and winced. She had almost forgotten her promise not to tell Ed about William's involvement.

'I'm going to my room,' Ed announced, placing his empty glass on a table at his elbow. 'I might as well get used to being confined for the immediate future.'

'Stop feeling sorry for yourself.' Bunny slapped Ed playfully as he passed. 'There's still a good chance we can solve this. Provided there's nothing else you've kept from us?'

'I've told you everything, I promise.' Ed halted and looked back at them from the door. 'Look, I know I've been pretty stupid about all this, but it was only because I was scared.'

'We understand, Ed. Truly.' Flora rested her head

on the back of the sofa and arched her neck to look at him.

'I'm sorry. I didn't even ask how the wedding went.'

'You didn't get much chance,' Flora said, softening towards him. 'Lydia was the perfect bride. Harry drank too much, and your Uncle William was the handsomest man in the room.'

'What about me?' Bunny peered at her over his newspaper.

'You always look handsome.' Flora blew him a kiss.

'I'm glad.' Ed smiled for the first time since they arrived home. 'You both deserve to enjoy yourselves. I appreciate everything you're doing. I didn't mean to bring all this trouble to your door. I'm aware I would be in a cell right now if it weren't for you.'

'That's enough apologies, Ed, and you're welcome. See you in the morning.' Bunny waved him away. 'I hope his faith in us isn't misplaced.' Bunny released a long sigh as the door closed behind Ed.

'So do I,' Flora murmured, biting her lip.

Was Maddox right and this affair was simpler than they imagined? Her theory that the Hunter-Griggs twins might wilfully deceive their elderly father in such a way would be unnaturally cruel. Despite her only having met him once, she couldn't help liking

Frederick Hunter-Griggs, and was reluctant to assign him to the role of a killer. Perhaps his brother Francis, whom she had yet to meet was the more ruthless of the two? As she had discussed with Sally, she would need to pay The Dahlia Hotel another visit. The answer had to be there.

27

Flora propped her elbows on her dressing table, her chin cupped in her palms as she stared at her reflection. Weariness settled on her as she listened to Bunny humming to himself in the dressing room next door. Where was the enthusiasm for the chase she had always experienced in previous cases, together with the anticipation of unearthing facts which threw light on an otherwise confusing puzzle? All she felt now was despair that a member of her own family was immersed in a murder. One which they were no closer to solving. She couldn't even fathom who was guilty of what. Murder, impersonation or both?

She reached to unfasten her diamond pendant, but her fingers wouldn't grip the clasp.

'Here, let me.' Bunny emerged from next door and rushed forward. The chain slipped from round her neck and he dropped it into her open jewellery box.

'Don't lose hope, my love.' He massaged her shoulders with both hands. 'Remember you aren't responsible for what happens to Ed.' The firm pressure of his fingers on her knotted muscles was painful at first, but rather than discourage him she gritted her teeth. As the knots in her neck loosened, she relaxed, melted into his touch, and rolled her neck in a circle.

'I know, but failure would be the worst thing to happen to us. To all of us. You, me, the Trents, not to mention Ed.'

'Inspector Maddox is more than capable of unearthing the truth. He'll sort this out, you'll see.'

'I hope so, but it's so much more than that. My theory doesn't even make sense. Why would the twins kill their half-brother only to replace him with a fake? Is it about money or something else? Perhaps Colonel Hunter-Griggs expressed a wish to see his son before he died, so the twins deceived him because they didn't know where to locate the real one?'

'More likely, it's about the old man's estate. Didn't you say he wasn't well last year and put his affairs in order?'

'He said as much, yes.'

'Perhaps the twins plan to pay off this chap when the old boy dies. Although I don't fancy their chances if their tame villain gets greedy and won't go quietly.'

'If I were them, I would claim I had no idea their stooge was an imposter.' She arched her neck to look up at him over her shoulder. 'Then he'll hang for killing Leo and they will not only be in the clear but still inherit all of their father's estate.'

'I didn't know you could be so ruthless?' He smiled while running a hand across her neck making her shiver. 'Or Maddox is correct, and the imposter was working alone?'

'Alone how? He would have to know all about the Hunter-Griggs' family situation.' She was still convinced the twins knew more about the fraud than they claimed.

'What's this?' Bunny plucked a letter from the bedcover, and slid a thumbnail beneath the flap.

'Oh, I forgot, it arrived earlier. I assume it's from your mother.' The envelope had the words Burlington Hotel beneath an embossed emblem of a square building.

He angled the pages towards an oil lamp placed on a chest of drawers, his brow furrowed as he read.

'Oh, dear, I know that look.' Flora slowly removed the pins from her hair and dropped them onto the surface of the dresser. 'Is she not enjoying the delights of Eastbourne?'

'Something of the sort.' He lowered the page and sighed. 'I knew there would be trouble when Cousin Arabella proposed a holiday of bracing walks on the seafront.'

'Does Beatrice dislike walking?' Flora's hairbrush halted in mid-air.

'Hah! Mother hasn't been on a bracing walk since next door's dog chased her round the garden when I was ten.'

Flora smiled at the image this conjured inside her head. 'Who goes to the south coast in April, anyway? The weather is bound to be awful.'

'It's not the weather she's complaining about, for once. It seems the company is not what she had hoped.'

Bunny's mother shared a villa in Chiswick with her widowed cousin, Arabella, with whom she got on famously and enjoyed frequent holidays together. 'Listen to this,' Bunny read aloud, '"There are insufficient persons of consequence staying at our hotel. I would insist we move to the Cavendish had that awful pianist fellow and his paramour not taken up residence there."'

'What "awful pianist" fellow?' Flora asked. 'And who says "paramour" these days?'

He read further down the page. 'Debussy, apparently. That Frenchman who ran off with the wife of some Parisian banker. Her son was once his student.'

'Claude Debussy isn't a pianist. He's a composer and a very good one,' Flora corrected him. 'Didn't his wife stand in the Place de la Concorde and shoot herself when he left her?'

'Did she?' He stared at her briefly. 'Odd thing to do.'

'She survived,' Flora said. 'But the scandal alienated Debussy from his friends.'

'Which I suppose is why he's now ensconced at the Cavendish Hotel with his mistress?'

'Probably.'

Bunny chuckled, his gaze scanning the page. 'Here's something interesting. "That dreadful Lady Egerton is here with one of her young gamblers. They monopolise the dining room straight after supper and play card games into the night."'

'Lady Egerton? I've heard that name. Now where was it?' Flora tapped the hairbrush against her opposite hand.

'Mother seems to know everyone. She goes on to say, "At least this particular suitor has the decency not to flirt with Lady Egerton openly in public, not like that Eric Paige character who stole a family heirloom at one of her parties and disappeared."' He glanced up from the page. 'Why on earth she thought I would want to know this, is beyond me.'

Flora gasped. 'Lady Egerton! Of course. Arnold Baines mentioned her. Her nephew went to Marlborough. There was something about a diamond bracelet being stolen. And something about a cross-country race.'

'A diamond bracelet was stolen at the race?' Bunny frowned at her reflection in the mirror.

'No, not then.' She twisted on her stool to face him. 'Lady Egerton is a society lady who likes to entertain young men. I'm surprised your mother has never mentioned her before. She homes in on such scandals like a bat.'

'Are you calling my mother a flying mammal?' Bunny glanced up from the page in mock-horror.

'As if I would dare.' Flora smiled at him in her reflection as she pulled the brush vigorously through her hair. 'But we've been looking for connections and this could be one.'

'What *are* you talking about?' Bunny refolded the letter and stuffed it haphazardly back into the envelope.

'I'm not sure yet, although perhaps the Soviets regarded Leo as a threat to the Bolshevik party? Stabbing a man on a train was the sort of thing a Russian activist would do.'

'What has that to do with stolen bracelets and gigolos?' Bunny held her gaze steadily in the mirror, his eyes softening. 'Have I told you, you outshone the bride today, Flora?'

'No.' She swivelled on the stool to face him. 'But there's nothing stopping you now.'

'You're right. There isn't.' He tossed the letter aside, caught her hand in his and hauled her off the stool and onto the bed.

She gave a half protesting squeal as the silk coverlet slid halfway onto the floor on impact and bunched beneath her hips as she landed, face up.

'Bunny, quiet. Ed will hear us.' She slapped him away, but there was no genuine conviction behind it. 'Is this really a good time?'

'I don't care.' He laced the fingers of her left hand through his and nuzzled his lips into her neck, nipping gently at the skin behind her ear. 'Let him hear. He might learn something.'

* * *

At breakfast the next morning, Bunny had already left for the office when Stokes entered and handed Flora a note. 'This came by messenger just now, madam.'

'Thank you.' She replaced her butter knife on her plate and examined an envelope which bore no markings other than her name on the front in William's writing. She slid a thumbnail under the seal, withdrew a thin sheet of paper and began to read his flowing masculine script.

Flora,

I have some information for you. I'll be at the flowery place later this morning. Don't ask for me, I'll find you. W

'Who's it from?' Ed asked through a mouthful of sausage.

'Nothing important.' Flora folded the page and slipped it into her pocket. 'I might pay another visit to The Dahlia Hotel and see what I can find out.'

'Not a bad idea. You could seek this Leonard and trap him into revealing himself. It's not as if your inspector chap is trying hard to establish my innocence.'

'You shouldn't underestimate Inspector Maddox, Ed. He has rules to follow, whereas we don't. We shall have to tread carefully.' Not that she planned to confront the imposter, simply take another look at him 'I might take Sally with me.' It wouldn't do to be visiting a hotel alone without raising eyebrows.

'Let me come, Flora?' Ed whined. 'I'm sick of being here all day.' Ed wiped the butter from his lips and threw his napkin on the table. 'I'm more likely to spot suspicious persons than Sally.'

Flora's maid had a canny sense for reading people and could spot what she called a "wrong'un" on first sight. 'I don't think so. Bunny is already annoyed with me for allowing you out of the house.'

'Aw come on, Flora. Since when did you ever do what's expected? Remember that year at Cleeve Abbey during the heaviest snowfall in years? You and Jocasta wanted to meet friends at the Pump Rooms when everyone said it could be dangerous, but you both went anyway.'

'How did you remember that? You were only about eight. And it was mainly Jo's idea. We came out to find all the trams cancelled due to ice, so we walked all the way home in a blizzard. My dress was frozen solid from my knees and Jocasta caught a severe cold and was sick for days.' She propped her chin on her hand. 'I've never regarded snow as romantic since.'

'There, you see. Rebel Flora.' He grinned.

'Hmm.' She softened; aware she was being manipulated. Then an image of William dressed as a Russian floated into her head and she straightened. 'No, Ed. I can't risk it. I'll tell you if I find out anything when I get back.'

'Will Timms drive you?' he asked sulkily, drawing a fork over the tablecloth, creating indentations on the linen.

'No. Enough people in this house know my movements already. I'll take a hackney. If you would like to be helpful, ask Stokes to order one for me. I'll visit the nursery before I leave.'

'Excuse me, madam,' Stokes hovered at the door. 'You have a visitor. I explained it was too early for morning calls, but—'

'It's all right, who is it?' Flora hadn't even heard the doorbell ring.

'A lady, madam, name of Billings. She claims to be a doctor. I imagined such a case to be unlikely and asked her to leave, but she became quite insistent.'

'She is indeed a doctor, and an excellent one.' Flora pushed back her chair and rose, trying not to show her annoyance. 'Show her into the sitting room. I'll be there directly.'

'If you say so, madam,' he murmured darkly as he withdrew.

'Ed, you stay here and finish your breakfast while I talk to her.'

'I wasn't going to suggest anything else.' Ed spread a thick layer of butter on another roll.

* * *

'This *is* an unexpected pleasure, Dr Grace,' Flora glided forward to shake her visitor's hand. 'Please excuse my butler, he's a little old-fashioned where women are concerned. There are times I too feel his disapproval.'

'Most gentlemen of my acquaintance are the same. I'm in London for a couple of days to attend a meeting of the British Medical Association.' Dr Grace resumed her seat in the wing-back chair in which she looked immediately at home. Her business-like skirt and jacket were a soft grey and plain to the point of masculinity, the hard lines softened by a white, high-necked blouse and a string of pearls. 'I see you have eschewed the dark brown and forest greens prevalent in so many houses these days.' Her shrewd gaze surveyed her surroundings like an auctioneer. 'This wallpaper is delightfully light and pretty. Is it hand-painted?'

'It is, yes.' Flora stared at her in mild surprise. 'It's

based on a Morris design called Hyacinth, but less busy.' She loved the soft blues and greens of the intertwined flowers and leaves and had asked the artist to add a few birds for interest. 'Might I offer you some coffee?'

'No, thank you. I enjoyed a very satisfactory breakfast at the hotel.' At Flora's look of enquiry, she added, 'Since your visit to the surgery the other day, I haven't been able to get Sylvia Thompson out of my mind. Knowing I was coming to town, I got your address from Kitty Tilney.'

'I hope you don't think I cast doubt on your abilities as a doctor by questioning you about Sylvia's illness?'

'No, no, not at all. Only I've been over my notes several times since your visit, and there's something not right about the incident that did not occur to me before.'

'About Mrs Thompson?' Flora eased forward in her seat, her pulse racing.

'Not Sylvia. The woman who accompanied her to the surgery that day. Now I think about it, Sylvia showed more anger than distress.'

'Anger towards the woman?'

'Yes. Her remark about being clumsy was directed at the woman with her. Not herself. I only wish I had pursued it, or at least asked the woman's name.'

'I doubt she would have revealed it if she was up to no good. Not her real name, anyway.'

'Ah, that hadn't occurred to me.' She frowned. 'There was something else. Do recall I told you Sylvia's hand was bound when she arrived?' At Flora's nod, she continued, 'The cloth used didn't belong to Sylvia. When I cleaned and redressed her hand, I offered it back to her. Sylvia denied it was hers and said to throw it away.'

'And did you?'

'I'm afraid I did, yes. I didn't see any importance in it.'

'Dr Grace,' Flora began, 'Is it possible this woman injured Sylvia deliberately?'

'By cutting her hand?' She laughed; her eyes sparkled. 'If I was going to hurt someone I would have aimed for something far more vital. Like an artery.'

'Sepsis can occur anywhere in the human body, can't it? Not necessarily in a vital organ?'

'Ah! now I know what you are getting at.' She fell silent for a moment. 'The cloth. But who would wish Sylvia Thompson harm? She was the proprietor of a haberdashery shop and lived a quiet life.'

'It wasn't her present life which mattered, but her

past,' Flora said, half to herself. 'Dr Grace, does it not strike you as odd that in a town where Sylvia is known, both her son and her assistant are coincidentally absent when she is hurt, leaving a stranger to come to her aid? I have no actual proof, but—'

'And I haven't brought you any. I'm so sorry.' Dr Grace's face fell and Flora rushed to reassure her.

'This might be my misinterpretation of events. Sylvia Thompson's death could easily have been an accident.' Not that she believed it for a moment, and Dr Grace's presence in her home showed she didn't either.

'I was in two minds whether to repeat this, but your mention of Sylvia's past has decided me.' Dr Grace cleared her throat. 'Mrs Tilney visited the surgery yesterday – for no other reason I could see than to gossip, as she has always enjoyed rude health. During our somewhat protracted conversation, she said you had written to her asking about Leo Thompson.'

'Yes, I did. I hope it didn't put you in an awkward position?'

'I don't see why it should, unless things have changed since we last saw one another?'

'Initially, there was some confusion about the identity of the young man on the train.'

'Confusion? Ah, I see.' Dr Grace pondered a moment. 'That could explain what Kitty told me, with some relish, I might add, that Mary Drake was summoned to London to identify Leo's body. She was sworn to secrecy because the police appeared reluctant to release his name to the public.'

'The police were being cautious, but Leo was definitely dead. Murdered. The inspector in charge feels if the villain realised the details, he would disappear and be almost impossible to catch.'

'Then perhaps it's as well I didn't mention our concerns about Sylvia's death to Kitty. She's not the most discreet of persons.' Dr Grace tore her gaze from Flora's with a small sigh of relief. 'Is Lord Trent still a suspect?'

'Officially, yes, although the situation is complicated.'

'Well,' Dr Grace sighed, 'I don't pretend to understand what's going on, but I hope everything is sorted out soon, for the young man's sake.'

'What was it you were about to tell me about Mrs Tilney?' Flora reminded her, mildly impatient.

'Oh yes, of course.' Dr Grace set her capacious handbag on the floor at her feet. 'Since hearing of Leo's death, Kitty recalled an incident she had not included in her letter to you, but now feels she should have mentioned it.'

'And yet she came to tell you specifically?'

'I got the impression she wanted to tell someone, and a doctor's office encourages confidences. I'll recount her story and let you decide if it's relevant or not.' Dr Grace eased forward in her chair, creating a sense of intimacy. 'It happened about four years ago, when Kitty took Sylvia to Bath to visit Kitty's eldest daughter and her husband. Whilst there, they went on a tour of the Assembly Rooms, where something happened which Kitty said struck her as exceedingly odd. Those were her words, not mine.'

'In what way odd?'

'A rather grand lady arrived with her maid and a group of friends, all talking loudly and attracting the attention of everyone present. You know the sort of thing. The grand lady greeted Sylvia in a loud, booming voice, claiming to know her. According to Kitty, Sylvia was mortified, which Kitty put down to her being shy. This woman claimed they had met in Bombay while their husbands served in the army there. She wittered on about Sylvia's son, Leonard, and how he must have grown into a handsome young man by now if he was anything like his father. Sylvia denied knowing the lady at all. Rudely, I understand.'

'Now, that *is* interesting. Sylvia and her husband were estranged, but he is still alive and lives here in London. I met him the other day.'

'Goodness, you *do* surprise me. Well, as I was saying, according to Kitty, Sylvia became upset, and insisted they return to Cheltenham the same afternoon.'

'Did Mrs Tilney know who the grand lady was?'

'Not at first, but the woman was disarmed at having upset Sylvia and sent her maid out to apologise. Kitty overheard her say that Lady Egerton is very sorry for having upset her.' Dr Grace's mouth curved into a coy smile. 'I can see by the look on your face this means something to you.'

'More confirms a suspicion,' Flora mused. The pieces of a frustrating puzzle had come together, though they still didn't quite fit. 'I don't suppose Mrs Tilney remembered the maid's name?'

'Let me think.' Dr Grace tapped her lower lip with a finger. 'The woman introduced herself to Sylvia. Now what was it?' She tapped her lower lip with a finger. 'It began with an "A"... Anne, perhaps, or it might have been Agatha. No, sorry, it's gone.' She glanced up at the ormolu clock on the mantel as it chimed the quarter hour. 'Goodness, is that the time? I must go or I shall be late for my meeting.' Gathering her bag and gloves, she adjusted her hat in the mirror over the mantelpiece. 'Since Mrs Garrett Anderson's retirement, I'm the only female doctor at meetings these days. I like to shock them by accepting a cigar and a brandy after dinner.'

'I would enjoy witnessing that.' Flora's admiration for the good doctor increased tenfold. 'I appreciate your coming to see me, especially when you could have put all this in a letter.'

'I was in town anyway so, a slight detour was no trouble.' She slung her bag over one arm and made for the door.

'Perhaps you'll call again when you're next in town? And hopefully not because I have a murder to deal with.'

'I should love to. It will give me an opportunity to appreciate this beautiful house.' She gave the room a sweeping glance before striding purposefully into the hall. 'That's all right, my man,' she waved off Stokes who had arrived to show her out. 'I'm quite capable of finding my way to the front door. However, if you wish to be of use, you can direct me to where I might locate a hackney.'

ANITA DAVISON

28

Flora perched on the edge of the forward-facing seat in the hackney that took her to Coptic street, her bag gripped tightly on her lap into which she had placed a small revolver. Their previous case had culminated in her and Bunny being threatened by a murderous doctor whom he had disarmed, after which the gun had been forgotten. Flora discovered it at the bottom of a drawer in Bunny's study and sought a discreet gunsmith on Bond Street from whom she purchased ammunition. The proprietor had admired the compact Webley Bulldog, even showed her how to load and fire the weapon; a skill she hoped she would never need. She had debated endlessly whether to bring it along, but if whoever killed Leo was at the hotel, either alone or with the twins' cooperation, she would be prepared.

'Are you sure you won't require me with you, madam?' Sally had enquired a third time while helping Flora dress.

'Not this time, Sally.' She met her maid's disappointed face in the cheval mirror. 'The next time I visit Bond Street, I'll be sure to take you with me.'

'That's kind of you, madam. I should enjoy that.' The maid's reply was innocuous enough, but her frown persisted. Sally could be discreet when she chose, but Flora did not want to have to explain what William was doing at the hotel dressed as a Russian Bolshevik.

Before the hackney had rolled to a complete halt in Coptic Street, Flora eased forward on her seat and grasped the door handle, only to have it yanked out of her hand as the door was flung open.

Ed's smiling face appeared at the window, sending her back into her seat.

'Might I be of assistance, missus?' he said in a mock East End accent, his free hand extended to help her down.

'What are you doing here?' she gasped. 'How did you get here so quickly? I left you back at the house.'

'Er, perhaps I shouldn't go into that.' He tugged his collar away from his neck.

'You will tell me, or you can get into this cab and I'll take you straight home.'

'Oh, all right, but you mustn't blame Timms.'

'Timms? What do— Oh, no, you took Bunny's motor car!' Several scenarios occurred to her at once. None of them was less than a disaster. 'Ed, suppose you had crashed, or hit someone, or—'

'I didn't. I'm an excellent driver. Now stop panicking. The Berliet will be back in the mews in an hour. Bunny will never know.'

'I cannot believe Timms simply let you take it.' She waved him aside and climbed down onto the road, slamming the cab door behind her.

'Er – he didn't exactly let me, but I left him a note.' At Flora's horrified stare he added, 'Don't panic, Flora. It's quite safe. I parked it round the back of the hotel. Look, I'm here now, so let me come with you.'

'I don't even know what I'm looking for.' She groaned, aware that making him take the motor car back to the house could be equally hazardous.

'We could look together,' Ed pleaded. 'I'm good at talking to people.'

Flora huffed a breath, defeated. 'Since you're here, you can pay the driver.'

'Um... that could be a problem. I gave my last shilling to the boy I asked to mind the motor car.' He made a show of rummaging through his pockets, shrugging. 'I don't suppose—?'

Flora rolled her eyes, withdrew the coins from her bag and dropped them into his hand, pushing the revolver into the bottom with her other hand.

The man tipped his hat in acknowledgement, and with a cheery, 'Walk on' the horse pulled into traffic with a rumble of wheels.

Ed took her arm and guided her over a crossing cleared of manure and rubbish, dodging carts and horse-drawn buses that approached at speed from both directions. 'If Maddox reaches the same conclusion you have, he might arrive to arrest this imposter chap. If so, he won't be best pleased to see us.'

'You've given this some thought, then? You didn't simply steal Bunny's motor car on impulse?' Flora summoned a smile for the benefit of the doorman who sprang forward to open the hotel's double doors.

'I borrowed it, which is entirely different. I've been thinking about Leonard's alibi all night. Perhaps we could talk to that maid?'

'What maid?' Flora thought for a moment. 'Oh, the one Maddox said gave Leonard an alibi? Good thinking, Ed, but we have to be very careful. The police don't take kindly to having their witnesses harassed.'

'I wasn't going to harass her. Suppose she got the time wrong, or she could even have lied about seeing him that day?'

'As long as you are careful. Making accusations won't get you very far.'

The lobby was crowded, but there was no sign of William or any Russians. She hoped if he saw them first, her father was as good a diplomat as he claimed and would keep out of sight.

'Ed, while we're here,' she whispered. 'We need to be discreet, so promise to do what I say. If I tell you not to look at something, you obey me. Understood?'

'If I'm already looking at something, how can I *unsee* it?' Ed handed his hat to a bellboy, along with the coin Flora had provided.

'Never mind. Just do as I ask.' Ed could infuriate; even when he was in serious trouble, he found time to answer back.

'All right, but you aren't making much sense.' He halted inside the main door and stared round at the opulent entrance lobby. 'This isn't quite what I imagined. All this silver and black is most unusual. It's exotic somehow, a bit like some Turkish bordello.'

'What do you know about Turkish bordellos?' She

cast him the sideway look she had perfected during her governess days, but he appeared not to have heard her, his attention caught by something.

'I say, is that an ascending room over there? I wouldn't mind taking a ride in it. What are the chances, Flora?'

'We aren't here to entertain ourselves. We came to find evidence which might clear you.'

'I know that, but seeing as we're here, it wouldn't hurt to look around.' He set off towards the gate, leaving her to follow.

She had only taken a few steps when she spotted William beneath the curve of the cantilevered staircase. His height and build marked him out from the crowd, even without his unshaven chin and oversized coat that flapped round his ankles.

He had not yet seen her, his focus on the man whom she assumed to be one of his Russian associates. Not Mr Lenin this time, but a smaller man with sandy hair squashed beneath a soft canvas cap. He appeared to be doing most of the talking. William nodded at intervals, but contributed little to the conversation.

'I've got it!' Ed exclaimed suddenly. 'If Maddox turns up and demands to know what we're doing here, we can say we're going to the Trafalgar Exhibition.'

'What exhibition?' Flora grabbed his arm, so he had no option but to halt with her.

'The one at the British Museum to celebrate the centenary of the battle. I read it in the newspaper. I haven't had much else to do these last few days but read.'

'Perhaps your temporary incarceration has done you some good?' Still holding tight to his arm, she eased him firmly round in a half-circle so his back was towards William and his companion.

William caught Flora's eye over Ed's shoulder, cocked his chin at a door to his left in a gesture so swift, he barely interrupted his conversation with his companion.

'Um, Ed,' Flora placed a hand on his arm to get his attention. 'I could really do with a cup of coffee. Would you mind sorting out seats for us and ordering?'

'Oh, er, all right. What are you going to do?'

'I'm going to take advantage of their facilities.'

'What sort of facilities?'

'This hotel provides comfort rooms for ladies.' It still surprised her how the innovation of ladies' conveniences confused and sometimes annoyed some men. Possibly because they resented the fact women could spend more time in the outside world as opposed to being confined at home.

'Oh, yes, of course.' He broke off with a contrived cough. 'I'll see you back here in a few moments, then. Or however long it takes to, uh—'

'Ed, just go.' Flora gave him a gentle push, her gaze on his back as he passed the end of the staircase. When she judged him unlikely to turn back, she hurried through the door marked 'Private'.

* * *

Flora entered a windowless hallway decorated with yellow paint and chocolate brown skirting. A row of gaslights hissed at head-height, casting an incipient gloom in marked contrast to the stark electric lighting proliferating in the public areas.

The hairs on her neck prickled as a figure stepped from the shadows. She gripped her bag tighter, comforted by the weight of the small revolver.

'You got my note?' William loomed in front of her. As well as the long black coat, a misshapen black leather cap and a faded woollen scarf completed his ensemble, despite the mild weather.

She took a slow, calming breath and tried not to wrinkle her nose at the stale tobacco smell emanating from him. William never smoked, not even cigars after dinner. 'The flowery place?' She raised an eyebrow. 'Really?'

'Too obvious, eh?' He scratched his chin. 'I was trying to be obscure in case that nosy maid of yours read it.'

'I doubt our boot boy could have failed to crack *that* code. What's this information you have for me?'

'We can't talk here.' He gave the hallway a swift but thorough glance. 'This way.'

He guided her through a door marked 'Function Room', which held a square oak table surrounded on four sides by rows of chairs Flora assumed was used by the congress for their meetings, the air heavy with the smell of beeswax overlaid by the tang of old food.

'Why did you bring Ed with you? Isn't he supposed to be under house arrest?' He pulled out a wheel-back chair and gestured for her to sit.

'I couldn't stop him. He's scared and angry, so he wants to be a part of clearing his name.' A half-lie, but she wasn't going to admit Ed had outwitted her.

'I can appreciate what he's going through, Flora, but I'm not simply passing the time here. This congress is important to our government. These men are incredibly suspicious. If they discover you're my daughter, and he's my nephew, I could be in trouble.'

Instead of taking a chair, he straddled a corner of the table, his arms folded across his chest.

'Isn't the fact he's a murder suspect equally important?'

'Yes, yes, of course.' He lifted the unflattering cap and scratched his head before replacing it. 'How's the investigation going?'

Watching him, Flora squirmed at the idea of what the cap's previous owner might have left behind. 'I believe the twins employed someone to impersonate their brother, but when presented with the possibility of their proper brother arriving at the hotel, they killed him. Ed was unfortunate in that he was in the wrong place at the wrong time.'

'Hmm, half-brother, eh?' He stroked his chin thoughtfully. 'I think I've seen this chap strutting round the hotel. Everyone calls him Mr Leonard, then cast him evil looks behind his back. Do you have an idea who he really is?'

'Possibly, but I need to prove it before Maddox arrests the imposter or they'll get away with it.' Her confidence did a small dip, but what her mother-in-law had said in her letter seemed perfectly logical.

'Why would the twins put a fake in their half-brother's place? Wouldn't disposing of him have been enough?' William asked.

'Bunny said the same thing. It puzzled me too, but Maddox said criminals weren't the cleverest of people so perhaps their mistake will be what exposes them in the end?'

'If Maddox knows about this imposter, why isn't he here instead of you?'

'I'm not sure Inspector Maddox trusts my theories. Anyway, I'm here because of your note.' It was a lie, but if he knew she had come to reveal the man masquerading as Leonard Hunter-Griggs as a killer, he would send her home immediately.

'Maddox is a good policeman, and can be insightful.' William stroked the stubble on his chin with one hand before transferring it to her shoulder. 'But you are better.' He gave her shoulder a squeeze, which sent warmth through her.

'I don't know about that, I—'

'No, I mean it, and you were right about Thompson. I checked the delegate list and Leo Thompson was expected to attend the Congress as you suspected.'

'He was a member of the Russian Labour Party?'

'He wanted to be.' William ran his hands up and down his thighs, both feet splayed. 'For two weeks in March, Leo stayed at the King's Cross lodgings of a woman called Apollinariya Yakubovna and her husband.'

'I'm pretty sure I would have remembered a name like that had I heard it before. Who is she?'

'A Marxist revolutionary and one of Lenin's acolytes. Rumour has it, Lenin asked her to marry him at one time, but she refused. He subsequently married Nadya, but she and Apollinariya are friends, or they used to be. She and her husband fled from Russia and have lived here in London for the last five years.'

'Poor Nadya. It can't be comfortable for her to have this woman present knowing her husband's feelings for her.' Flora had never met her, but any woman who did not command her husband's heart earned her sympathy.

'She doesn't need your sympathy, Flora.' William seemed to read her thoughts. 'Any woman who escapes from a Siberian prison and travels the seven thousand miles to London undetected is strong enough to take care of herself. She and her husband hold debates in the East End on the principles of Russian socialism. Thompson attended some of them and had been distributing *Iskra* both here and in Cheltenham, which explains why Maddox found a copy in his luggage.'

'Should we inform the police about Leo's loyalties?'

'I'd rather not have any of the delegates questioned until we have more evidence—' William jumped to his feet, approached the door carefully and opened it a crack, his free hand held up to warn her to be silent.

Flora's heart thumped uncomfortably in her chest as a male voice called out, followed by another, then the sound of a door being slammed and finally silence.

'It's all right, they've gone.' William relaxed again, closed the door gently and resumed his seat on the table.

'Are we likely to be discovered here?' Flora asked, concerned.

'I hope not. It would make things exceedingly awkward for me to have to explain your presence.'

'I'm thinking Bunny's right and this case is too complicated. Sometimes it looks straightforward, but what with Thompson's involvement with Mr Lenin, maybe I should leave it to Inspector Maddox.'

'This isn't like you, Flora. I thought you loved to get your teeth into a good mystery?'

'I do, normally. But there's more at stake here for

Ed, and now you. I'm worried the responsibility is too great.'

She couldn't believe what she had just said. Bunny was always telling her the same thing, but she never listened to him.

'Don't lose confidence now.' William massaged her shoulder gently with one hand. 'I wish I had taken more of an interest in Leo. He was supposed to arrive here on Tuesday, when we might have learned more if—'

'He hadn't been murdered,' Flora interrupted him. 'I know. What else did he do apart from handing out newspapers?'

'He took part in a protest a few weeks ago to support the new Aliens Act.'

'The Aliens Act,' Flora repeated slowly. 'But that restricts immigration? Thousands of Russians came here to escape the pogroms in the eighties, so why would they want to prevent that? And don't stare at me like that. I'm not totally ignorant.'

'I didn't say you were, my darling.' His eyes, which had resembled scraps of flint as he talked, softened. 'Foreign workers are paid less than their English counterparts, which squeezes the labour market. The Labour Party here would like to protect jobs for our own countrymen. The Tory factory owners take full advantage of cheap labour. The protest caused a riot outside a church hall in Southwark last month. Three people died and thirty-five were taken to hospital.'

'Leo sounds like quite the rabble rouser. I assume he was learning to speak Russian too?' At William's enquiring look, she added, 'Why would he have a copy of *Iskra* in his luggage unless he could read it? But whether we disagree with his politics, he didn't deserve to be stabbed to death.'

'No, he didn't.' William sighed. 'There's also a possibility our own government was aware of Thompson's activities and viewed them as detrimental to our country.'

'What are you saying?' She lowered her voice to a fierce whisper. 'That our own government might have disposed of him?'

He shrugged. 'It's not unknown for the authorities to deal with potentially embarrassing situations. Why hold a public trial which could be embarrassing, when a problem can be solved by simpler methods?'

'I see.' Flora refused to contemplate the full meaning of what he was saying. Could a former governess ever be cognisant of what went on in the hallowed halls of government to keep the population safe? Did she want to know? Probably not.

'The Bolsheviks are more than a few fanatics

throwing bombs at carriages. My task right now might be straightforward information gathering, but there are those in positions of power who would welcome the collapse of the Imperialist regime. It could take years, but eventually there *will* be a revolution in Russia. An American financier called Schiff has already provided the party with substantial funds to be used for propaganda. Germany is also making encouraging noises towards the socialists.'

'And the British Government? What's their stance on this revolution idea?'

He held her gaze for a long moment, but before she could discern what sat in his eyes, he removed his watch chain and consulted his half-hunter. 'I ought to go. Vladimir will wonder where I am. We're meeting at The Crown in Clerkenwell later. I'm not looking forward to feigning enthusiasm for his turgid diatribes against the Imperialists. He—' At the sound of voices from the hall outside, William straightened and slid off the table.

Flora joined him at the door, their heads head cocked to listen.

'Have you seen a young woman in a blue coat and hat?' Ed's voice echoed along the corridor.

'It's Ed!' Flora lowered her voice to a fierce whisper.

'No, sir, I haven't,' a low, but distinct female voice answered.

'She was on her way to the facilities,' Ed continued. 'But I cannot imagine they are down this way.'

'No, sir. You'll need to go back the way you came to the lobby, and—'

'Stay here and I'll go out and talk to him.' Flora gestured to William behind the door, so as not to be seen from the hallway. 'William?' She halted with her hand on the doorknob. 'If America and Germany want this revolution, where does Britain stand?'

Instead of an answer, he planted a swift kiss on her forehead and opened the door just wide enough for her to slip through. 'You'd better go.'

29

Flora emerged into the hallway in time to hear Ed thank a woman in a severe black gown for her help. She carried a thick ledger and wore a chain at her waist from which hung several keys. Something about her struck Flora as familiar, but before she could work out what it was, the woman hurried away.

Ed must have sensed Flora's presence behind him because he swung round. 'There you are.' He stood with his head tilted and arms held out at his sides. 'You were gone for so long, I came to look for you. What are you doing back here?'

'I took a wrong turning.' She cocked her chin at the departing figure. 'Who was that woman you were speaking to?'

'I've no idea. She must work here, as I heard her giving instructions to a kitchen maid. Why?'

'I'm not sure. She looked familiar, but I doubt we've ever met.'

'You probably saw her when you came here with Bunny.'

'Possibly. Have you ordered our coffee?' she asked, dismissing the woman from her mind.

'Er – no, I didn't, sorry. But I haven't been idle. I've located a very talkative maid.'

'The one who gave Leonard his alibi?' She cast a sideways look at the meeting room door, visualising William pacing back and forth behind it.

'Not her, the one Timms spoke to: Libby. She told me the chambermaid who cleaned Leonard's room that day was a girl called Maisie Cook. Libby's going to arrange for me to talk to her.'

'How much did *that* cost you? If I recall, Timms paid handsomely for Libby's cooperation.'

'Nothing, yet.' He revealed his teeth in a sheepish grimace. 'I don't have any cash on me, so I said you'd pay her.'

Flora halted mid-step. 'Did you indeed?'

'On come on, what's a few shillings in exchange for my freedom?' He had carried on a few paces and stopped, forced to retrace his steps to where she stood. 'You know you would have done the same thing.'

'All right.' Flora sighed and resumed walking. 'How do we find Maisie?'

'Libby said to meet her near the kitchens and she'll take us to her.' Ed led her through a green baize door into a space more shabbily appointed than the last. The clatter of metal pans and shouts could be heard behind a double door with porthole windows; a savoury smell of cooked meat made her mouth water.

A few feet beyond the kitchen door stood a fair-haired girl in a white apron complete with bib and frilled shoulder straps. She leaned against the wall, her arms folded and one foot tapping to a rhythm inside her head. When she saw them, she pushed away from the wall with a deep sigh. 'Hurry, I ain't got all day.'

Flora raised an eyebrow at the girl she assumed must be Libby, but before she got any closer, the kitchen door swung open, sending her a pace backwards. A waiter with a loaded tray balanced on his shoulder crashed through.

'Have a care, Reg,' Libby tutted, grimacing.

Reg gave Flora and Ed a swift, bemused look and Libby a longer one before he swept along the corridor and out of sight.

'This way.' Libby gestured for them to follow her to another double door farther along the hall, which opened on silent hinges, releasing a wave of hot, humid air which could only be the laundry. Two metal vats belched clouds of white steam, where young girls in pinafores and caps heaved dirty linens from waist high wicker baskets. A row of smoothing irons strung from leads hung from the ceiling were being wielded by similar maids over snowy white bed-sheets laid out on tables.

Libby halted beside the open door of a cupboard lined from floor to ceiling with wooden shelves, where a dark-haired girl crouched on her knees arranging piles of bedsheets onto the bottom shelves.

'This is Maisie.' Libby's voice held an air of triumph at a job well done.

The girl sat back on her knees and stared up at Flora and Ed. Her mob cap spilled black curls onto her forehead above wide green eyes, her angelic features marred by a suspicious scowl. 'Who are they?'

'No need ter get all uppity, Maisie.' Libby flicked a look behind her, though no one in the bustling laundry paid them any attention. 'The lady and gent jest want ta talk to yer about Mr Leonard.'

'What 'bout him?' Maisie rose slowly from her crouch, drawing herself up to her full height, but barely reached Flora's chin. She heaved a pile of dirty linens from the floor and tossed them into the nearest basket.

'Good day to you, Maisie,' Flora began, unsure how she might question this girl without accusing her of lying. 'I believe you spoke to the police the other day.'

'S'right.' Her eyes narrowed. 'What of it?'

Flora sighed. They had hardly begun, and the girl was already defensive. Would they get anything of use out of her?

'You told the police you saw Mr Leonard on Tuesday,' Ed interjected. 'That he was asleep in bed when you cleaned his room?'

Her green gaze slid over Flora and settled on Ed. Her face instantly softened, and she peered up at him through dark lashes. 'Might have done.'

Flora bit back a sharp retort and left him to do the questioning. Maisie might look sweet and innocent, but she knew exactly what her attractions were, and how to use them.

'Did you actually see Mr Leonard in his room on Tuesday?' Ed asked.

'He were in bed,' She folded her arms across her diminutive chest. 'Like I told the copper.'

'You're sure?' Flora urged. 'Did you see his face?'

'What choo implyin'?' Maisie's eyes glittered, the look of someone used to being on the defensive.

'We're not accusing you,' Ed said quickly. 'But might someone else have been in the bed pretending to be Mr Leonard?'

She shrugged. 'Dunno. I only stayed long enough to clean the washroom and change the towels.' She split a hard look between them. 'Look, what's this all about? Who are youse anyway?'

'Watch your cheek, Maisie.' Libby nudged her with an elbow. 'They'll pay yer for the truth. Long as it is the truth, mind.'

'Flora.' Ed nudged her with an elbow, his hand held out, palm upwards.

Flora tutted, resigned, slid a hand inside her bag and located a handful of silver coins which she handed to Ed.

'I can't change me story,' Maisie eyed the coins greedily. 'Not now, I've told the filth. They'll 'ave me for purging.'

'I think you mean perjury,' Flora corrected her.

'They'll do that anyway, if they find out you was lying,' Libby said, her voice lowered. 'Think about it, Maisie, we get blokes here all the time who drink all night and sleep till teatime. It could easily have been one o' them. Well? What do you say? Wrong room and a quid, or right one and get done for purging?'

'Perjury,' Ed and Flora said together.

Maisie hesitated; her mouth puckered as she thought it over.

'Ed, put the money away, we're wasting our time here.' Flora started to leave, pulling Ed with her.

'No, wait!' Maisie shouted, halting them.

'Well?' Flora prompted. 'Was Mr Leonard Hunter-Griggs in that room all day on Tuesday, or not?'

'He weren't,' Maisie mumbled, reddening. 'He paid me five shillings to say he was, but I didn't know it was the coppers who would be asking. I figured he wanted to keep outta the way of his gambling friends. I didn't mean no 'arm. When the constable came asking questions and said I had to make a statement, it scared me rigid.'

'Then that's what you tell them.' Flora plucked the coins from Ed's hand and slipped them into Maisie's apron pocket, where they made a satisfying clink. 'That you were too afraid of losing your job to defy Mr Leonard so said what he told you to.'

'I ain't going to no police station.' Maisie slid a hand into her pocket and fingered the coins. 'If they come back, I'll tell them, but not otherwise.'

'Then we'll have to ensure they come back,' Flora

said, confident Inspector Maddox was too much the professional to ignore the girl's story. She would bet he had left her questioning to one of his younger officers. Maddox would have seen right through her flimsy lies.

''Ere. What about me?' Libby cocked her chin at Ed. 'He promised me five shillings.'

'Of course he did.' Flora sliced a look at Ed and slid a crown into Libby's hand from her diminishing pile. 'And thank you for your help.'

'Pleasure.' Libby pocketed the coin. 'I'd show you out, but I'm behind with me work already. Go back the way you came and turn right at the end.' Without waiting for a response, she hurried away, leaving Maisie to return to the linen cupboard.

'We'll let Maddox know Mr Leonard's alibi is no good and make sure he comes back to question Maisie,' Ed chattered happily as they retraced their steps along the dingy hallway. 'If she does what she promised, I'll be safe.'

'*If* she does,' Flora muttered. 'I hope the fact we paid her won't count against us when this gets to court.'

Entering the lobby felt like stepping from a dark cupboard into a fairyland of bright lights in a grand hall where elegant ladies in enormous hats and uniformed staff swept by. She half expected the conversations to pause and everyone turn to stare, but no one appeared to notice them. In her eagerness, she almost ran into the woman she had seen talking to Ed earlier.

'Oh, excuse me.' Her apologetic smile faded at the woman's hard, penetrating look as she swept past without a backward look. Flora stared after her. 'If she *is* staff, then she ought to change her attitude to customers.'

'Never mind her,' Ed said, irritated. 'Aren't you pleased we now know Leonard Hunter-Griggs wasn't in the hotel the day Leo was killed?'

'I am, Ed, honestly.' She didn't like to remind him that Maisie's story didn't put Leonard's imposter on the train. Nor could she banish her uneasiness about the woman in the black dress. Where had she seen her before?

* * *

'Where were you earlier?' Ed asked Flora as they traversed the lobby arm-in-arm. 'The woman I spoke to in the corridor told me the facilities are nowhere near the function rooms. She couldn't think why you were there.'

'Really, Ed, what an inappropriate question to ask

a lady.' Flora avoided his gaze. 'I've already explained I took a wrong turn.'

'Don't tell me then.' Ed huffed a breath but dropped the subject, much to her relief as they entered the crowded lobby where patrons sat drinking coffee and chatting. 'I meant to say hello to Dr Grace this morning,' Ed continued as they paused beneath the curve of the staircase, complete with its white marble treads and black wrought-iron balusters. 'But she had gone by the time I had finished breakfast.'

'She couldn't stay long. She had a meeting to attend.' Flora searched for a recognisable face amongst the crowd.

'Did she have anything new to add about what happened to Leo's mother?'

'Not so loud, Ed. And no, not really. She confirmed most of what we already knew, although there was one thing. She mentioned Lady Egerton.'

'I know that name. Her nephew Sebastian attended school with me. What about her?'

'Do you know if Leo and Sebastian were friends?'

'What? Yes, I suppose so. They were in the same year. Why do you ask?'

'It might mean nothing at all, but the name keeps cropping up.' Flora stiffened at the sight of the young man she had seen on her first visit. 'Ed.' She pulled him into the overhang of the stairs. 'Leonard Hunter-Griggs is heading for the porter's desk.' She nodded to where a young man shoved a guest abruptly aside and took his place. The porter ducked his head in apology at the guest before reluctantly addressing the interloper.

'That fellow?' Ed pursed his lips. 'I suppose he has a look of Leo, but that garish blue suit is a giveaway. No one educated at Marlborough College would wear their tie like that, either. He's giving that porter quite a set-down too. No manners, obviously.'

'He behaved similarly the first time I was here. Have you seen him before?'

'No, I haven't. But I didn't see everyone who was on the train that day. He might have been there.'

The altercation with the porter came to an abrupt halt when Leonard Hunter-Griggs pounded the desk with a fist, then swivelled on an angry heel before disappearing through a door on the other side of the lobby.

'I wonder what that was about?' Ed mused.

'I've no idea, but we got what we came for, so perhaps we shouldn't tempt fate and leave now. Inspector Maddox can follow up on Maisie's story.'

'It's Miss Harrington, isn't it?' A masculine voice said at her elbow.

Flora spun around to where a handsome man in a black frock coat and a perfectly tied cravat appeared. 'Er... yes it is, I...' She swallowed nervously, unsure which of the Hunter-Griggs twins stood before her, and certainly she had not given her name on her previous visit. 'It's Mrs Harrington, actually.'

'Mrs Harrington.' He shook her hand in both of his. 'My father described you perfectly. He said a charming lady journalist by the name of Harrington called on him at Albany requesting an interview.'

'The Colonel... uh, mentioned me?' Flora squirmed. He had not released her hand, and she debated how to withdraw it without offending him.

'He did. And I'm glad to thank you. You brightened up the old boy's day. He isn't in the best of health and doesn't get about as he used to, so he becomes easily bored. Actually,' his eyebrows rose into his low hairline. 'Haven't we met before?'

'You have an excellent memory, Mr Hunter-Griggs.' She relaxed, smiling at the realisation this must be Mr Frederick. 'On that occasion, you were distracted by an awkward guest.'

'A good memory for names and faces is an advantage in the hotel business. Is your husband not with you today?' He aimed a vague, enquiring look towards Ed.

'Er... not today. However, allow me to introduce my cousin.' She tugged her hand firmly from his. 'Edward, Viscount Trent. Viscount Trent, Mr Frederick Hunter-Griggs.'

'Pleased to meet you.' Ed thrust out his hand, which the older man took with a polite but bland inclination of his head showing the name meant nothing to him. 'To what do we owe the pleasure of your visit today?'

'We were on our way to the exhibition at the museum,' Ed replied without missing a beat. 'We stepped in here for some refreshment beforehand. I'm told it's a fascinating display.'

'How interesting. I haven't yet seen the exhibition, which is remiss of me being as it's merely yards away.' Mr Frederick nodded slowly. 'Actually, there's someone I would like you to meet. If you aren't in a hurry to get to the museum, of course...'

'Well, we really ought to—' Flora stammered.

'Oh, say you can spare a few moments. My sister, Francis, would love to meet you.'

'Your sister?' Flora said weakly. *Francis is a woman?* Why didn't she think of that before? Francis was also a woman's name, and often spelled the same way.

'My twin sister, yes.' He stared round the crowded lobby, searching faces as he talked, oblivious to her growing disquiet. 'As a woman of business herself, Francis expressed a keen wish to make your acquaintance. She's interested to hear all about your journalistic ambitions. In fact, she should be back from her appointment at any moment.' His darting gaze finally shifted to a point past her shoulder. 'Ah, there she is now.'

A striking young woman entered the hotel and greeted a guest, giving Flora time to study her: tall, slender, with dark hair swept into a loose arrangement of sausage curls beneath a pert burgundy felt hat with a vertical black feather. Her skin was flawless and porcelain pale, with symmetrical features in a face which drew all eyes towards her; a phenomenon of which she appeared unaware.

Her conversation ended, and she swept the room with wide cat-like eyes, finally settling on her brother. Her perfect lips curled into a warm smile as she glided towards them.

'Frederick.' She greeted him with a brief press of her lips on his cheek before her gaze slid to Flora and Ed, with a look of enquiry, as she waited for an introduction.

Flora's throat dried and found she was staring. However, it wasn't Francis Hunter-Griggs' classic looks which affected her, but the woman's burgundy red coat with its row of black chevrons encircling the flared skirt below knee-level.

'Francis, my dear.' Frederick drew her closer. 'This is the lady Father told us about. Mrs Flora Harrington, and her cousin, Viscount Trent.'

'How wonderful you should be here!' She clasped her gloved hands together, her lips parted, displaying perfect, even white teeth. 'When Papa told me he had been interviewed by a lady journalist, I was entranced. When he mentioned you were an admirer of Mrs Millicent Fawcett, I begged him to give me your name and address, but he seemed to know very little about you.'

'Well, I'm not actually a journalist, er—not yet.' Flora summoned a weak smile, while she resisted every nerve ending which told her to run.

'Don't be so modest,' Francis placed a hand on Flora's forearm. 'A journalist *and* an advocate for women's rights. I'm sure we will have so much to talk about.' She gave the room a swift, critical sweep with her startling eyes. 'But you don't want to sit here with all these people coming and going. Why don't we adjourn upstairs to my sitting room?' Without waiting for a response, Francis placed a firm hand on Flora's back and guided them both towards the ascending room.

'Perhaps we might postpone this visit for another

time?' Flora halted in front of the gates. 'I'm not fond of enclosed spaces, I'm afraid.'

'I didn't know you were claustrophobic?' Ed rubbed his hands together, oblivious to her frantic eyebrow dance. 'I'd *love* to try it out. I've never been in an ascending room, only those escalator things they have at Harrods, which aren't the same at all.'

Had he not been so far away Flora would have stamped on his foot. Instead, she groaned inwardly as the gates clanked open and she was ushered inside. That's all she needed; to be trapped in a cage with a murderess.

30

'These contraptions have always fascinated me.' Ed kept a steady stream of chatter on the short but tense journey inside the metal box up to the fourth floor. 'Ever since my grandmother told me about the one at the Crystal Palace Exhibition when she was a girl.'

'They've been refined somewhat since then.' Miss Hunter-Griggs turned the full heat of her beautiful eyes on him. 'More and more hotels are installing them, which is a shame. I'm sure many of our guests book a room here primarily to enjoy the novelty of our ascending room.'

The lift jerked slightly. Flora reached for the handrail that ran around three sides of the enclosed box, the other pressed against her midriff.

'Are you all right, Flora?' Ed ducked his head close to hers to be heard over the loud grinding of gears. 'You look pale. Don't you find this exhilarating?' His enthusiastic nudge to her ribs and cheerful smile made her want to slap him.

'Please don't be unduly worried, Mrs Harrington.' Miss Hunter-Griggs laid a reassuring hand on Flora's forearm, her eyes darkening in concern. 'This is an Otis safety elevator. Should the cable break, which I assure you it will not, a device engages knurled rollers which lock the guides.'

Flora smiled and nodded, refusing to play the nervous female regarding the lift, although she kept a tight grip on her handbag. The sight of grey blank walls and building struts gliding past on their way up made her slightly queasy.

The lift bounced to a stop, the gates dragged open with a noisy screech by the attendant, releasing them into a semi-circular hall with three doors leading off a curved wall.

Miss Hunter-Griggs approached the left-hand door, which she unlocked with a key attached to a fob in the colours of the hotel. 'Welcome to my domain,' she stepped to one side and gestured them inside with an expansive wave of her arm.

'This is lovely.' Flora couldn't help but admire the

spacious sitting room decorated in shades of teal and pale cream. She had not known what to expect, but the use of colours and textures were beautifully combined to make Flora envious.

'I'm so glad you like it.' Miss Hunter-Griggs tugged off her gloves, revealing slim fingers with oval pink nails.

Ed wandered to the window and braced his palms on the sill. 'There's quite a view from up here. I can see the entire front of the British Museum.'

'This side of the building faces the street but is far enough up to be quiet.' Miss Hunter-Griggs dropped the gloves on a nearby table. 'My bedroom is through there, together with a private bathroom, complete with water closet.' She gestured to a set of double doors opposite the window. 'You'll probably think I'm spoiled, but when Frederick and I were forced to sell our house in Bloomsbury, I insisted everything here be arranged exactly as I wanted it.'

'You were forced to sell?' Flora laid her bag carefully down on a champagne-coloured silk couch with spindly gold legs.

'Yes, and it was such a blow. I loved that house.' She sighed. 'But we needed the funds to complete the hotel renovations. Father had been generous enough and Frederick and I agreed we had to raise the money ourselves.'

Flora made no comment, having gleaned a different impression from the Colonel. Either Miss Hunter-Griggs was an accomplished liar, or the twins had accepted their father's decree without resentment. 'Frederick and I are delighted with the hotel, which is doing well.'

'It's most elegant.' Flora's gaze stayed on the coat that she had draped carelessly over a chair.

'In fact, I hardly miss the house at all now,' she went on. 'The only drawback being the staff call on me at all times of the day and night with problems to sort out, not to mention the odd irate guest.' She paused on her journey across the room and tilted her head. 'Make yourself comfortable, both of you. Might I offer you some refreshment?'

Ed looked about to accept, but at a swift glance from Flora he clamped his mouth shut.

'That's kind, but no thank you.' Flora sank into the upholstery of a blue velvet sofa she had assumed, wrongly, offered more style than comfort.

'Ah, well, if you're sure.' Their hostess's smile dissolved as she took a chair in the same rich blue velvet. 'I'm sure Frederick has done so already, Mrs Harrington, but I wanted to thank you for being so kind to my father.'

Deprived of an opportunity for food, Ed restored to a slow tour of the room, his hands clasped behind his back while examining a display of china ornaments and paintings.

'I didn't see it as kindness.' Flora hoped her lie wasn't too transparent. 'I genuinely asked him to help me.' Not that she was about to explain with what.

Miss Hunter-Griggs sighed. 'He gets few visitors, and after his health upset last winter, he's been ordered to rest more.'

'He's been ill?' Flora recalled the Colonel had mentioned some recent trouble with his heart. 'He appeared well during my visit. I hope nothing has changed?'

'Oh, Father's as strong as a horse. A carthorse.' Her light tinkling laugh filled the room. 'Frederick doesn't trust doctors and was convinced he told us Father had a heart problem to increase his fee.'

Ed paused in his examination of a painting of a gloomy landscape to give a long, admiring look at Miss Hunter-Griggs.

Flora suppressed a sigh, although his interest in such an attractive woman was understandable. What was more unnerving was the fact she too liked this woman.

'Tell me about your career in journalism, Mrs Harrington.' Miss Hunter-Griggs wiggled back in her seat and arranged her skirts round her as if settling in for a long chat. 'I so admire you, a married woman and yet determined to follow your own path. You must have a very obliging husband?'

Ed gave a snort of laughter, which he changed into a cough. 'Sorry, frog in my throat.'

'The journalism idea is very new and experimental.' Flora briefly narrowed her eyes at Ed. 'I don't know if it will turn into anything, but my husband heartily approves. In his view, if I'm happy and fulfilled, then he can only benefit.'

'How wise of him. I was engaged once, but I broke it off, much to Father's chagrin. I prefer life as a businesswoman to that of a wife. I would love to know how you combine the two. Do you have children?'

Flora swallowed, her gaze going back to the coat. The less this woman knew about her the better. 'Um, no, not yet.'

Ed aimed a puzzled frown in her direction but did not contradict her.

'Well, I'm sure you'll handle that as efficiently as you obviously do everything else.' Miss Hunter-Griggs rose and swept the incriminating coat from the chair. 'Let me put this away and then we can have our talk.' She disappeared inside the bedroom just as a streak of black shot past her into the room while emitting a high-pitched wail and dashed under the sofa where its mistress had sat.

'I hope you're not averse to animals?' she asked, reappearing minus the coat.

'Er, no, not although I have none of my own.' Flora eyed the animal that looked ready to attack any second.

'We have gun dogs in the country.' Ed replaced an expensive looking Chinese vase onto its plinth, enabling Flora to breathe again. 'Cats too, to keep the rats down, but they're feral and I never know how many there are.'

'I couldn't be without my Mr Brody.' Miss Hunter-Griggs bent, hooked an arm under the sofa, and swept the bundle of fluff into her arms. 'Have you been fighting again, you naughty boy?' She pursed her lips and nuzzled the soft fur. 'I keep him inside most of the time because he battles with the street cats.' The animal rubbed its nose along her jaw, mewing gently. 'My poor darling always comes off worse and suffers so.' She resumed her seat and propped the cat on her lap. Mr Brody scrunched up an already flat face and kneaded her skirt with its claws, circled twice, stretched a pink mouth in a yawn, and settled on her knee.

'Your father mentioned you had recently reconciled with your half-brother,' Flora ventured, having unwittingly entered the lion's lair. She might as well find out what she could whilst she had the chance. 'He said you hadn't seen him for many years?'

'That's right.' Her fingers teased the animal's fur gently. 'I shouldn't speak ill of the dead, I know, but Frederick and I resent Father's late wife for having kept Leonard from us for so many years. I'm sure she must have poisoned his mind against Papa. Not that we would ever speak disrespectfully of her in Leonard's presence. He's very loyal to his mother's memory.'

'Your father mentioned she had died. Was it recent?' Flora asked.

'Last year, yes.' She kept her attention on the cat as she spoke but seemed quite matter-of-fact. 'I hadn't seen her since I was a child, so cannot pretend to feel anything more than mild regret. She was our nurse, mine and Frederick's. Between you and me, I think it's why Papa married her. As a widower with four-year-old twins serving in India, he found himself somewhat at a loss.'

'How did you come to meet Leonard after so long? Your father didn't give me specific details.'

'It was all quite unexpected.' The cat stretched its limbs as an invitation to stroke the soft curls on its belly, and she obliged. 'Leonard visited us and explained who he was.' She dimpled prettily and brought a delicate hand to her mouth. 'Taking the word of a complete stranger sounds naïve, doesn't it?'

'I didn't mean to imply—'

'Oh, no, I'm sure you didn't. And *we* didn't. Take his word for it, I mean. Frederick was diligent and put him through some rigorous questioning. Leonard knew all about Father's service in India, how Sylvia had deserted Father and went running back to her parents in England taking him with her. She opened a haberdashery shop, of all things. Can you imagine? No wonder Leo couldn't wait to meet his real family.'

'Did Leonard remember anything about you or his father?' Flora asked.

'He claimed to have an unusual intellect and could remember things from when he was about a year old. Since I've got to know him, I've thought he fudged it. He's not the smartest person I've met, if you see what I mean.' She directed a knowing smile at Flora, which she transferred to Ed, who flushed. 'He had always known who he was, of course, but was reluctant to contact us out of respect for his mother. When she died, he no longer felt the need to keep away.'

Flora searched for inconsistencies, but the story flowed easily and with unexpected candour. Nor did she appear to suspect why Flora asked so many questions. If Francis Hunter-Griggs were guilty, then she was also a consummate actress. The prosecution would have a difficult time with her.

'Where had Leonard been all these years?' Ed placed one foot on the fender and tucked his thumbs into his waistcoat.

Flora bit her lip to prevent a smile. Bunny often stood just like that when he was pontificating on a point of law or sifting through scenarios. Ed must have studied him to mimic him so accurately.

'He grew up in Cheltenham,' Miss Hunter-Griggs said. 'Which is in Gloucestershire, you know. Not that I've ever been there, but I'm told it's an attractive town.'

'I know, and it is. I once lived there,' Flora said.

'I still do,' Ed added.

'Really?' She stared at each of them in what appeared to be genuine surprise. 'You didn't know Leonard or his mother, did you?'

'Well, I—' Ed began.

'No, I'm afraid not,' Flora cut him off sharply,

studying Francis for signs of guilt or anxiety, but saw none. 'It's quite a large town.'

'Oh, yes, of course, how silly of me.' Her girlish giggle was interrupted by a discreet rap at the door, which opened to reveal the woman in the black dress Flora had seen on the ground floor.

'I'm very sorry to bother you, Miss Francis,' she said in a flat, bored voice with no discernible accent. 'There's a problem in the kitchens.'

'Can't Mr Frederick handle it?' Still cuddling the cat, Miss Hunter-Griggs stood and drifted towards the door.

'He's not available. I told the delivery man he must have got the order wrong, but he insists it's correct.'

'I'm always being interrupted.' Miss Hunter-Griggs sighed, placed the cat on the floor, which scampered back under the sofa. 'I'll have to see to this, I'm afraid, but I won't be long.'

'Don't let us keep you from your work.' She gestured to Ed it was time to go. 'We'll leave you in peace.'

'I wouldn't dream of your going so soon.' She strode forward and guided Flora firmly back into her seat. 'We were having such a pleasant talk. I wouldn't want it to end so abruptly.' She gave a bright smile on each of them, the door catch clicking loudly as she closed it behind her. Was it Flora's imagination, or was there a sinister edge to Miss Hunter-Griggs' insistence they stay?

* * *

Flora waited until their footsteps had receded along the hall, then ran forward and gave the door handle a firm turn.

'What are you doing?' Ed broke off from his contemplation of a semi-nude painting on the wall.

'I wanted to see if it was locked.'

'And is it?'

The catch gave, and she released a relieved breath. 'No.'

'Then what's wrong? You've been jumpy ever since we came up here. Why don't you relax and sit down? She'll be back in a moment.'

'That's what worries me. Ed, listen. Everyone referred to the Colonel's children as "the twins", so I assumed Frederick and Francis were both men. It never occurred to me Francis could be a woman.'

'I don't see what the problem is.' Ed shrugged. 'I find her charming and quite beautiful.'

'Which hasn't gone unnoticed.' She sliced him a disdainful sideways look. 'I've been searching for a woman in a red coat, and she's been in front of me all the time.'

'Coat? Yes, of course, she was wearing one with those black embroidered things you spoke about. A bit of a coincidence she should own one like it, don't you think?'

'Don't be dense, Ed. It's hardly a coincidence.'

'Are you sure? I'm afraid I didn't put much store by it since Bunny and the inspector didn't either.'

'You don't have to remind me.' She worried a thumbnail between her teeth. 'They both made me feel stupid for even mentioning it. Dr Grace told us the woman who brought Sylvia Thompson to her surgery was wearing a coat like that. One exactly like it was delivered to this hotel last year. Do you still think it's all pure chance? Are you sure you don't recognize her from the train or on the concourse when you were leaving?'

'I think I would have remembered Miss Francis.' Ed shoved his hands in his pockets, his brow furrowed. 'I don't believe she's a killer, and anyway, she said she's never been to Cheltenham?'

'Oh, well, if she *said* so.' Flora lost patience. 'Because a beautiful woman couldn't possibly tell lies or kill anyone? Ed, you're such a man.'

'I can't help *that*.' Ed fidgeted, his neck an uncomfortable red. 'Are you sure you've got this right, Flora? She's convinced that the chap downstairs is Leonard, so if she and Frederick didn't kill Leo, who did?'

'I'm uncertain of anything at this point.' She had to admit Miss Francis had convinced her, too. Maybe Frederick was the one who was in cahoots with Leonard or whatever his name was? They might have kept Francis in ignorance as an integral part of their plan.

'Well?' Ed demanded. 'What do we do now?'

'I'm not sure, but now we're here, you can help me search. You try in here and I'll look in the bedroom.' She opened the inner door to an even more opulent room decorated in deep pink and pale green. A gilt-framed cheval mirror set at an angle across one corner reflected the light from a window with the same view as the sitting room.

'Search for what?' Ed jumped back as the cat ran between his feet and scooted under the silk-covered bed.

'I need to find something which links Miss Francis to Sylvia, or even Leo. Lady Egerton's diamond bracelet might be a good start. I don't know what it looks like, but I doubt there's more than one.' She strode towards a bureau and started pulling out drawers which contained little but handkerchiefs and small boxes of cosmetics.

'What does a bracelet have to do with anything?' Ed called through the door from where he crouched in front of a red and gold lacquered Chinese cabinet from which he pulled out a row of shallow drawers.

'It's complicated. But I have an idea that the Leonard downstairs was one of Lady Egerton's card-playing young men who stole one from her.'

'I have no idea what you are talking about.' Ed poked his head round the cupboard door, a hank of hair flopping over his forehead.

'Never mind, just keep looking.'

Apart from the detritus of cosmetics in delicate pots, a powder puff and various trinkets on Francis's dressing table, sat a photograph album Flora would have loved to browse through, but resisted. In a shallow drawer below it, lay a pile of postcards from seaside towns, a few handkerchiefs and pencils.

'It's the only connection I have made between Leo, Marlborough and the coat.'

'Sounds thin to me.' Ed sat back on his knees. 'Should we be doing this?'

'Yes, we should. Keep looking, we don't have much time.' She bundled everything back where it was before attacking another drawer, her nerves jumping at every noise.

'There's no jewellery box here.' Ed clambered to his feet and dusted off his trousers. 'Not even one of those velvet-lined cases jewellers use.'

'No, you're right. It doesn't seem to be here.' Disappointed, Flora replaced the double drawers she had pulled out of a small desk containing notepaper and pens, but no letters or anything remotely personal. 'Francis might have sold it. She said they had run out of money for the hotel renovations.'

'Huh! Then it's probably languishing in a pawn-shop somewhere.' Ed's voice softened as he wandered to a bureau in a corner of the sitting room.

'You're not helping, Ed.' Flora muttered to herself, attempting to coax the cat from beneath the bed without success.

'Hey, look at this. It's just like the one you bought in Cheltenham the other day.'

'What is?' Flora gave up on the cat and scrambled to her feet. Ed stood at the bedroom door, a rectangular wooden box in both hands, the lid angled to reveal a design of white painted peonies.

She gasped. 'Where did you find it?'

'On the bureau over there by the door.' His face

took on an animation that had been lacking until now. 'Are you thinking what I am?'

'Possibly. Let me see inside.' Her heart thumped as she eased open the lid, revealing a neat row of instruments nestled into grooves in the velvet lining.

'There's a space where the stiletto should be.' Ed pointed, his eyes wide. 'Oh, Lord. Miss Francis killed Leo?'

'That settles it. We're leaving.' Flora slammed the lid and shoved the box towards him. 'Put it back where you found it. We need to find Inspector Maddox.'

The sooner they got out of there, the better.

31

Flora checked the drawers had all been replaced as she had found them, replaced the stool under the dressing table and re-entered the sitting room where she stared round at the chaos. Drawers had been ransacked and left open, magazines and books pulled haphazardly from the shelves, and piles of embroidered cushions tossed onto the floor.

'Ed! What on earth—?'

'Find a bracelet you said, and those things are small. You can't expect me to do that tidily. I've put the box back where I found it.' He wore a bemused, half-contrite expression identical to his thirteen-year-old self when stating the obvious.

'We can't leave the room like this!' Her horrified

gaze skimmed the walls. 'You've even moved all the pictures.'

'I thought there might be a safe behind one of them.' He shrugged, sheepish.

'Which you wouldn't have been able to open, anyway. Come on, help me clear up before someone comes.'

'No time, Flora. If Miss Francis *is* involved, we must let the police know.' Ed made for the door as he talked. 'I saw a sign in the lobby showing the way to a public telephone. I can move faster than you, so I'll take the stairs while you tidy up in here. Use the ascending room when you're finished and wait for me in the lobby. Lose yourself in the crowd. I'll come and find you.'

Flora was about to protest, but she could already hear his footfalls receding along the corridor. She had to admit he was right about one thing: he could cover more ground than she could in her cumbersome skirts.

Sighing, she gathered papers and books, straightening pictures as fast as she could, all the while amazed at the way he had taken charge of the situation and of her. Anyone would think coming to the hotel was his idea. Having spent a fruitless few minutes trying to coax the cat back into the sitting room, she gave up and giving the suite a quick, appraising glance to ensure everything was as they had found it, pulled the door closed behind her and set off along the hallway Ed had disappeared down minutes before. Where the stairs and lift met at the end, she pressed the button which summoned the lift. A few stressful moments passed with no mechanical sounds, until finally, the elevator appeared in a slow-moving beam of light and creaked to a halt. The gates slid open with a clang of metal to reveal a single occupant.

Flora's breath caught at the sight of the man calling himself Leonard Hunter-Griggs.

'Well?' He leaned a shoulder against the edge of the gate, his voice slow and mocking. 'Don't you wish to go down, Mrs Harrington?'

'Er, shouldn't we wait for the attendant?' Flora's thoughts raced, alarmed to be addressed by her name.

He stepped away for a moment. 'But I can operate the machinery. I've done it a dozen times.' His manner of speech sounded forced, as if he had spent hours in front of a mirror perfecting it.

Flora hesitated. 'Miss Hunter-Griggs—'

'Won't be returning, I'm afraid. She asked me to inform you she's been called away.' Before Flora realised what was happening, he had grasped her wrist, gave it a painful twist as he hauled her inside the lift and closed the gates, which made an ominous clang. The momentum of his push flung her against the velvet-covered bench at the rear, which hit the back of Flora's knees. She bounced off and tumbled to the floor, dropping her bag.

'You ought to know the police are on their way.' Panic filled her chest, though she forced herself to sound calm. 'They might already be here.'

How long had Ed been gone? Long enough to telephone Maddox?

'And yet you're here, and they are not.' His upper lip curled as he swung the handle that denoted the floors until the red arrow pointed to the embossed letter 'B'.

Grinding gears brought her gaze to the ceiling as the motor above whirred into action and the lift moved. Bile rose in her throat as they glided downwards, her chances of escape diminishing with each second.

'In case you're wondering,' his low, menacing tone made her pulse race. 'I recognized your companion when you arrived. Frederick told me you've been here twice. Been asking questions about me, haven't you?'

Flora swallowed, not daring to deny it, even though she had only suspected him recently. Nor did she ask what, if anything he had done to Ed. She wouldn't give him the satisfaction of pleading with him.

'I've done nothing to him,' he added as if reading her thoughts. 'It's her he needs to watch out for. She's not in a good mood.' He turned his back on her, his fingers laced through the diamond pattern of the closed gates.

Slowly, she reached for her bag and slid it out of sight beneath her. What did he mean? And who wasn't in a good mood? Was he talking about Francis? Pushing herself gingerly onto her knees, she rose.

'Stay where you are!' he snapped without looking at her. 'She was right.' The arrogance seemed to have flowed out of him, leaving uncertainty.

'Right about what?' Flora sank slowly back onto the seat, the solid outline of the gun in her bag pressed against her thigh.

'When the police turned up and questioned the staff, she said we should get out. I should have listened to her. We could have been halfway to Waterford by now.' He seemed to talk to himself, his voice tight.

'You were there weren't you? On the train when Leo Thompson was killed?' She couldn't be sure whether he was responsible for Leo's death, but the man seemed to unravel. Perhaps he thought she knew more than she did.

'That wasn't me! And you can't tell them it was.' He leapt for the handle and slammed it into the 'Stop' position.

The lift screeched and jerked to a halt between floors, sending Flora off the edge of the seat. She righted herself quickly, her bag concealed beneath the folds of her skirt. 'What happened to Leo?'

He swivelled to face her. 'I was supposed to knock him on the head and push him out of the train when it reached Pangbourne. But I didn't do it.'

'Why there?' She didn't really care, but keeping him talking struck her as the right thing to do while she inched her fingers into the bag's silk lining.

'There's a steep slope that runs from the rails down to the river. She said everyone would think it was an accident.' He snorted again, annoyed with himself. 'He saw me on the train, didn't he? That young chap with you. Isn't that why you're here?'

He didn't appear to expect a response, so she didn't give one, her mind racing as she tried to re-member the name her mother-in-law mentioned in her letter from Eastbourne. Paget was it? Payne? No Paige. Eric Paige.

'She told me to do it, anyway.' He seemed to have forgotten she was there, his focus on the weak light in the lift ceiling, and made a derisive noise, something between a snort and a chuckle. 'I said no. That it was too risky, but she wouldn't listen.'

'What then? You had to improvise?' Flora's fingers closed around the rough surface of the metal grip. 'You waited until Leo was alone in the compartment, then stabbed him with the only thing she had to hand – the needlework stiletto. Isn't that right, Mr Paige?'

'How did you know my—?' he broke off, his mouth working but no sound came. 'Not that it matters,' he snarled and swung the handle to the last notch on the wheel.

'Where are you taking me?' she demanded, her panic mounting. The gun now sat, solid and heavy in her hand, but would not be easy to pull free of the bag.

'Somewhere no one will find you!' Paige growled. 'Not until we've gone, anyway.'

The lift started moving again, and she released the catch on the top of the gun. The bullet entered the chamber with a tiny metallic click. Releasing a slow breath, she slid her finger behind the trigger. A large painted "L" on the brick wall slid into view, showing they had almost reached the lobby. With a strangely steady hand, Flora freed the weapon from her bag and pointed it at his back.

'Stop the lift, Mr Paige! Now!'

He swung round to face her, his lips curved into an arrogant tilt ready to deny her. His gaze settled on the gun and he froze, his eyes widening.

You didn't expect that did you?

The lobby ceiling came into view through the gates. Her hand tightened on the gun, hoping she wouldn't have to pull the trigger, but she couldn't let him take her into the bowels of the building.

The floor dipped a few inches past the lobby, where several eager faces appeared beyond the diamond lattice arrangement of the gates.

'I said. Stop the lift.'

Fury entered his eyes, followed by resignation, and he swung the handle to the 'Stop' position.

The lift screeched to an abrupt halt with a jolt that threw Flora off balance. Her grip on the gun loosened as she staggered but regained her balance just as the lift bounced and settled.

Paige threw open the gates and leapt into the crowd, waiting to go in. 'Everyone get down! She's got a gun!' Paige yelled and shoved a stocky man with both hands hard enough to send him staggering backwards into the couple behind him. They stumbled into each other, the three of them blocking the doors and preventing any chance of Flora following. The woman regained her feet, her eyes locked onto the gun in Flora's hand, and she screamed. A high-pitched cry of terror loud enough to draw all eyes towards her as far as the front desk.

Flora watched helplessly as Paige took off at a run through the crowd and across the lobby, shoving by-standers aside among gasps of indignation and screeches of alarm.

Frustration made her want to scream as she strained on tiptoe, moving her head from side to side to keep Paige in sight.

A young porter eased his way through the cluster of people, arms outstretched and palms held down. 'Miss, I think you should put that down.'

'What? I—' Flora stared at him in confusion, then her gaze went to the gun in her hand, and she groaned.

He eased closer, a hand extended. 'Give me the weapon, miss.'

The couple who had unwittingly helped Paige escape regained their feet, their eyes wide with alarm.

Flora sighed and addressed the eager young porter. 'I know you think you're being very brave, but it's not me you should be worried about.' By this time Paige was little more than a glimpse of a blue jacket weaving through the lobby and out of sight. 'Oh, for goodness' sake, he's gone now.' Flora lowered the Bulldog, clicked the safety catch on and returned it to her handbag. 'And no, I'm not giving it to you,' she snapped at the hovering porter, who couldn't have been much older than Ed. 'It's safer where it is.'

The crowd around the lift backed slowly away, apparently deciding she was no longer a threat, their faces showing more irritation than fear, while one or two scowled at her and tutted in annoyance. Flora debated what to do first. 'I need to call the police,' she addressed the porter, enunciating each word as if she was speaking to a child. 'Where's the hotel telephone?'

'Going to turn yourself in, are you?'

'No, that isn't— Look.' She pointed her hand at the far end of the lobby, creating a murmur of panic through the small crowd, though her hand was empty. 'That man who rushed through here a moment ago is the dangerous one. He's wanted by the police. Now, where's the public telephone?'

'Er,' the porter frowned as her calm request seemed to flummox him. 'There's one in the corridor leading to the function rooms for the use of guests.'

'Thank you. I hope you haven't just helped a murderer escape,' she snapped in a combination of relief and tension.

'I fear you are mistaken, madam.' The porter recovered himself and peered down at her from his un-usual height. 'The man you pointed your weapon at is Mr Leonard Hunter-Griggs, a part owner of this hotel.'

'No, he isn't. I mean I know who he is, but— Oh, never mind.' She had barely gone three steps before the main doors crashed open and several policemen surged through in a wave of navy blue, helmets bob-bing as they took up places inside the doors and the front desk. Once in position, they produced guns from their belts while shocked murmurings went up among the crowd that milled inside the doors, spreading rapidly across the lobby.

Inspector Maddox, in his ubiquitous mustard check suit and bowler hat, pushed through to the front desk and addressed a shocked clerk. 'I'm looking for a man named Eric Paige.'

Flora exhaled in relief and turned an imperious gaze on the porter. '*Now* do you believe me?' She eased sideways through the crowd at the lift, most of whom had stopped staring at her as if she might grow horns, their attention on the irate man at the front desk.

'I... I don't know of such a person,' the clerk stam-mered, his gaze transfixed on the sea of blue invading the lobby. He pulled a large ledger towards him and ran a finger down the list of names. 'We... we have no Paige in the hotel.'

'I'll handle this, Reeves.' Mr Jessup, the manager, appeared and shoved the clerk to one side. 'There must be a misunderstanding, Inspector. If you'll just wait here a moment, I'll inform my employers.'

'I won't argue with you. I have a job to do.' Maddox glared at Mr Jessup before gesturing towards his men with both hands, sending them in all directions. 'Paige is here somewhere. Spread out and guard the doors. No one leaves.'

'Inspector,' Flora said, easing to his side.

He glanced down at her, his glare still in place. 'Mrs Harrington?' His eyebrows took up residence in his hairline. 'What are *you* doing here?'

'The same as you. Trying to flush out Leo Thompson's killer. I was right, wasn't I? It's Eric Paige?' She leaned closer, not intimidated by his furious expression.

'Yes, it is,' he lowered his voice to a fierce whisper. 'But I thought I warned you—'

'I remember all your warnings, Inspector, but never mind that now. I cannot find Ed. Paige said he recognized him from the train and now I don't know where he is.' She stared frantically round the lobby, which was crowded with both anxious and interested guests, several policemen and staff, but no sign of Ed.

'Lord Trent?' Maddox's face fell, and he propped both hands on his hips beneath his unfastened overcoat. 'Don't tell me he's here as well?'

'Isn't that what I just said?' Flora snapped. Why was he being so slow? 'Ed went to find a telephone to call you a few minutes ago. And pardon me, Inspector, I doubt you work that fast, so I assume you were already on your way here?'

'I'll ignore that.' Maddox's upper lip curled briefly. 'This is a carefully planned operation.'

He nodded to where his officers had spread out through the ground floor, and one mounted the stairs.

'Then where *is* Ed?' Flora's gaze swept the lobby again, greeted only by fearful and interested faces. 'And where is Paige? He took off through the crowd just before you arrived. I didn't see where he went.'

'You've seen him?' The policeman gave her his full attention. 'Which way did he go?'

'I'm not sure. He disappeared beneath the curve of the staircase and I lost sight of him. But the function rooms are in that direction, and the dining room which leads to the kitchens.'

'You.' He tapped the shoulder of an officer beside him. 'Take two men and go where she said.'

From the corner of her eye, Flora spotted the porter who had demanded she hand over her gun at the lift. Keeping his steady gaze on her, he shoved through the crowd, halting beside Inspector Maddox.

'I think you ought to be aware, officer,' He pointed an arrogant finger at Flora. 'This lady is armed.'

'Armed?' Maddox's penetrating gaze swivelled towards her. 'Is that true?'

Flora rolled her eyes. 'It's only a small revolver. Nothing like the ones your men are carrying.' She nodded to where at least three policemen used their weapons to wave the crowd back into the lobby.

'Hand it over.' Maddox waggled the fingers of one hand, sighing.

She was about to refuse, but the combined scrutiny of the clerk and that of Mr Jessup, as well as the critical stares directed her way, changed her mind. Sighing, she retrieved the Bulldog from her bag and slapped it ungraciously into his open palm.

'You realise you might have scared off Eric Paige?' Maddox examined the little gun minutely. 'What were you doing with something like this in a public place?'

'*I* scared *him*?' Flora gaped. 'I'll have you know. He trapped me in the ascending room and was taking me goodness knows where. I only got out by producing...' She made a vague gesture at his hand, where the gun looked impossibly small and harmless.

'Really?' Maddox raised one eyebrow. 'But you have no idea where Paige is now?'

'I *told* you; he ran off. But he's probably still somewhere in the building as you got here a few minutes after he left the lift.'

'Let's hope so, for your sake, madam. My men have orders not to let anyone leave the hotel until Paige is in custody.'

'Then will you please send someone to find Ed?'

He stared at her for a tense moment before exhaling in a sigh and signalled to a nearby officer.

'Tell Hicks to make a search for Lord Trent. Nineteen years old, sandy hair, arrogant expression and a penchant for meddling.'

'Thank you, Inspector.' Flora could breathe again. 'Now, may I have my gun back? I promise I won't use it.'

'Hah! Not likely.' He clutched at his pocket as if she might try to retrieve it herself. 'The last thing I want is a civilian running around the place with a dangerous weapon. Especially a woman. Leave this to my men. They're armed and well trained.' He pointed at another of his men. 'You stay here and keep an eye on Mrs Harrington. She gets into trouble if left to wander.' He aimed a slow wink in her direction. 'And move these people back would you, Constable? I need some space to manoeuvre and could do without the flapping of idle ears.'

The officers dashed away in all directions, while alarmed and curious onlookers were ushered to the rear of the lobby, leaving the main doors and the staircase clear. The police presence with all its frantic activity should have reassured her, but Flora still felt helpless, with nothing to do but watch.

32

The guests already inside the hotel were ordered to stay where they were, while those attempting to pass through were subjected to scrutiny before being turned back. Confined to a square yard of carpet by a stern officer who glared at her at intervals, Flora fretted, searching every face for Ed, but there was no sign of him.

With her nerves stretched to the limit, she spotted William on the far side of the lobby. The sight of a familiar face made her heart jump almost painfully as she watched him conduct a brief but intense exchange with the policeman who guarded the door. For an anxious moment she thought he would not be allowed past, but finally, the policeman lowered his arm and allowed him through the crowd towards her. Tears welled, her hands twitching as she resisted the need to throw her arms round him.

The policeman set to guard her blocked his way just as he reached her, one hand pressed against William's chest. 'Excuse me, sir, but you must step back.'

'Inspector Maddox knows me,' he whispered, elbowing the man aside. 'Are you all right, Miss?' he asked in a falsely bright voice, then more urgently, 'What happened? There are armed police everywhere.'

'Miss?' His eyes widened pointedly, and she caught on. 'Oh, yes, of course, thank you – sir. Just a little shaken.' She wanted to hug him but resisted, whispering, 'Not *my* doing this time.'

As if at the sound of his name, Inspector Maddox appeared. His gaze slid over William without interest, then he did a double take, his jaw dropping in disbelief. 'Good God, Mr Osborne, is that you?'

'I would appreciate it if you kept your voice down, Inspector,' William's fierce whisper silenced him. 'I'm not here, if you get my drift.' He tapped the side of his nose with a finger. 'My, er, associates observed your arrival and were understandably concerned. I volunteered to investigate. This young lady appeared distressed. Is everything all right?'

'I assume your – *associates*,' Maddox put mocking emphasis on the word, 'are most likely holed up in a back room expecting to be rounded up at any moment. I imagine that happens a lot where they come from?' He chuckled at his own joke, then in a stage whisper, said, 'You can inform Mr Lenin he's quite safe. I've not come for him or his Bolshevik friends.'

'His Boll... er, thank you, Inspector, I'll let him know. Erm... how did you know they were here?'

'In this hotel, or this country?' Maddox chuckled again at William's obvious bewilderment. 'You don't think a group of socialists would be on *my* patch without my knowledge? They were here two years ago, and we kept them under surveillance then, too.'

'I meant the hotel, and you're quite right, Inspector. Your intelligence is obviously as extensive as ours at the Foreign Office.' William's gaze swung to a point over their heads to where Vladimir Lenin and six swarthy men pushed their way through the crowd towards them.

'Oh, blast,' he muttered under his breath. 'I told him to stay in the meeting room. Flora, make yourself scarce, would you?'

'Do I have to? He doesn't know me, and I'd be interested to meet him.' She raised herself onto her toes to get a good look in the pressing crowd.

'Yes, you do. Now go.' He gave her a firm shove.

Sighing, she eased beneath the curve of the cantilevered staircase, taking care to stay close enough to observe the exchange between Maddox and the Russians.

'Mr Lenin, sir,' Maddox grasped the Russian's hand and gave it a hearty shake, forestalling whatever apology William had been about to offer. 'Welcome back to London.'

The Russian's cat-like eyes narrowed even further. 'I had no idea the British police were so interested in my travels.' Lenin said in good, though heavily accented, English.

'The Metropolitan Police are aware of *everything*, sir. As guests in our country, your welfare is important to us.' He waved an arm at the chaotic room. 'I apologise for the disruption, but I'm in pursuit of a murderer at present, therefore I would ask you to remain here while we apprehend him.'

'Are you referring to the man who killed a member of my delegation a few days ago?' Mr Lenin withdrew his hand slowly from the policeman's grip, his steady gaze fixed on Maddox's face.

'Yes, sir. A Mr Thompson. Found stabbed on a train,' Maddox replied.

'Mr Osborne told me of this.' He nodded first at William, then approached his fellow Russians, who immediately closed into a tight circle and began talking loudly over each other in their own language.

A young policeman arrived at a run and halted beside the inspector. 'Sir! One of our men thinks he saw Paige near the owners' suites on the fourth floor ten minutes ago.'

The indistinct murmur escalated into a muted roar as this news spread rapidly throughout the lobby, including the Russians who talked faster and louder.

Maddox gestured to the two policemen. 'You two! Get up there and try to flush him out. I'll have men standing by down here.'

Flora emerged from under the stairs and crept back to where the inspector stood.

'It was the newspaper that brought you here, wasn't it, Inspector?' she whispered at his elbow. 'The one Mr Thompson had in his suitcase.'

'Still here, Mrs Harrington?' Maddox's narrowed-eyed stare told her he would have preferred otherwise.

'Where else would I be? You have all the doors locked and guarded.' She nudged him gently. 'I'm right, aren't I? The paper was a copy of *Iskra*.'

'It was, although not the most taxing part of the investigation.' He sighed, resigned. 'Once we established the connection between that publication, this hotel, and the Hunter-Griggs, it wasn't too difficult to put together. At first, I was unhappy about those Bolsheviks. I wanted to round up the bunch and drag them down to Cannon Row, but my superiors instructed me to abandon that idea.' He nodded to where William stood with Mr Lenin, their heads close together in urgent discussion. 'And you don't have to look so worried. I obeyed the order.' His upper lip curled into a ghost of a smile. 'Wouldn't want to upset Whitehall, now, would we? And it turns out the Russians had nothing to do with it.'

'That was my conclusion as well.' Not that he would give her any credit. 'I don't mean to tell you your job, Inspector, but are you aware he isn't working alone? There's also a woman who—' she broke off as Frederick Hunter-Griggs pushed his way through the cordon of police.

'What's the meaning of all this?' he demanded. 'Some flatfoot just told me there's a murderer on the premises.'

The manager, Jessup, appeared from another direction, his hands clasped tightly in front of him. 'It's all most irregular, sir. The inspector appears to think

Mr Leonard is a person of interest to the constabulary.'

'There must be some misunderstanding!' Mr Frederick insisted. 'My brother can be headstrong, even reckless, but surely you cannot suspect him of murder? If you'll allow me to send for him, I'm sure this can all be cleared up in a matter of moments.'

'Our information says otherwise, sir,' Maddox said. 'Besides, it appears your "brother" has made a run for it. If you would allow us to do our job, everything will become clear.'

Frederick's confused gaze slid from Maddox to Flora. 'My dear Mrs Harrington, how did you get caught up in this fiasco? Weren't you upstairs with my sister?' His gaze swept the crowded lobby. 'Incidentally, where *is* Francis?' The quick nervous movements of his hands showed discomfort at having lost control of the situation.

'I... er, haven't seen her since the police arrived.' Flora hesitated, unsure if he was complicit in the deception or not. His agitation certainly seemed genuine, as did an involuntary tick beside his left eye.

'I assure you, Mr Hunter-Griggs,' Maddox replied, 'I have everything under control.'

'I beg to differ, Inspector. What with your men

dashing about in all directions with guns. Most upsetting for my guests.'

There was still no sign of Ed among the worried guests, harassed hotel staff, and the half-dozen serious-faced policemen. Her stomach knotted with worry, and she debated what to do next when a loud crack echoed round the lobby, followed by the tinkle and whoosh as the bevelled glass in the dining room door shattered.

Instinctively, Flora covered her head with her arms and dropped into a crouch behind a pillar. Heads swivelled towards the source of the noise, women screamed, men threw themselves upon their female companions, who cried out in alarm as a wave of shining crystals rained over them. Slivers of glass speared arms and faces; the scene magnified and reflected by the array of mirrors on the walls.

From among the chaos, a figure dived through the space where the glass had been, arms braced over his head to protect his face. Revolver in hand, he landed with a crunch of glass, staggered, but stayed on his feet, then let off another shot, which punctured the pillar beside Flora. More screams sounded, and he waved the gun wildly in case anyone was reckless enough to approach him as he headed for the main doors.

Paige.

A policeman let off a shot from near the stairs, which missed its mark but pinged off a metal urn, while the next exploded a vase of flowers into a colourful rainbow, showering purple irises and pink chrysanthemums in all directions.

'Don't they practise with those things?' Flora muttered, more annoyed at how chaotic everything had become and yet no one seemed concerned for Ed. Guests, staff and policemen dived to the floor. A man hit by flying glass toppled into a pedestal dislodging a five-foot-high plaque on the wall that crashed heavily onto the floor and disintegrated into chunks of jagged plaster.

Still on her knees, Flora poked her head out from behind the pillar just as Paige reached the entrance. One of the still standing policeman was about to raise his revolver, but it barely skimmed his waist before Paige punched him squarely in the face. The officer crumpled to the floor, dropping his gun, which discharged, shattering a plate-glass window that overlooked the street; the destruction greeted by more panicked screams from inside the lobby and the road outside.

Paige's own gun had also been knocked from his hand by the falling policeman. It sailed through the broken window and skittered across the pavement into the road. An urgent car horn sounded while passing pedestrians who were visible through the broken front window scattered as Paige leapt through the jagged edges of the glass that still clung to the frame.

'Don't just lie there, go after him!' Maddox yelled from his hiding place behind the front desk. 'I thought he was upstairs?'

'Apparently not, sir.' An officer scrambled to his feet and brushed off his jacket with both hands. 'He came from the corridor where the public telephone is located.'

'The telephone!' Flora planted her feet squarely in front of him. 'Did you see a young man with sandy hair in that corridor? He's a little taller than me and wearing a dark blue suit with a mustard tie?'

'No, Miss, I saw no one of that description. And there's no one there now. The hallway's empty and it's a dead end, which is probably why Paige ran through the lobby. There's no way out back there.'

'I see. Thank you.' Disappointed, she backed away, leaving him to set off after the other officers who had all scrambled to their feet and dashed into the street. The policeman who had been punched in the face hunted for his gun, which he found under a chair and took off after his comrades. Another pulled himself into a sitting position, a hand to his neck where he had been hit by flying glass.

'See to that man, someone!' Maddox waved vaguely at the injured man. A distressed woman helped her middle-aged companion to his feet, his hat knocked askew, a line of blood on his cheek. Though shocked, he seemed relatively uninjured. In fact, other than a few superficial cuts on shocked and bewildered faces, no one appeared badly hurt.

And still there was no sign of Ed.

Had he made it to the telephone, or had Paige told Francis about Ed and she had done something to him? Was he lying somewhere hurt, or worse?

With the lobby devoid of blue uniforms, frightened and blood-splattered guests either demanded help for the injured or explanations for the ensuing chaos. Hotel staff, maids and bellboys darted in between with bags, or delivered messages in response to the barrage of questions thrown at them.

The Russians had joined the exodus towards the main doors, apparently bent on joining the chase when Maddox's outstretched arms held them back. 'Please remain here, sirs, where it is safer.'

'We should do as the inspector says, Vladimir,' William tried to coax him back the way he had come.

'I suggest we return to the meeting room until the police have done their job.'

'*Nyet!*' Lenin shrugged off William's hand and raised his fist. 'In my country, we leave nothing to the police.' He shouted something in Russian, which was greeted with firm nods of assent, before they headed for the entrance. William tried to block their way, but they surged round him and hurtled across the lobby out into the street.

'Oh, hell, now what do I do?' William tipped his shapeless leather cap farther back on his head and blew a breath between his lips.

'There's nothing you can do unless you plan to go with them.' Flora watched as, coats flying, they disappeared across the road. 'Suppose they find Paige first? They're not armed, are they?'

'Uh – possibly.' William grimaced, lifted his hat, and scratched his scalp before replacing it.

'William. Forget the Russians for a moment. I've lost Ed. Maddox sent two policemen to look for him, but they haven't come back.'

'If he's still in the building, they'll find him.' He reached a hand towards her shoulder but thought better of it. 'I doubt even Ed is impetuous enough to show himself with bullets flying about.'

'Paige recognized him from the train, and I'm worried.'

William's perplexed frown hardened 'Tell me exactly what happened.'

'He had me trapped in the lift earlier, which is why I pointed the gun at him, and—'

'You brought a *gun* with you?' This time his hand came down hard on her shoulder, his eyes narrowed.

'I don't have it now, so it's irrelevant.' She shrugged off his hand. 'Are you really going to stand here and tell me off, or are you going to help me find Ed? He could be hurt!' *Or worse*.

'Of course, I am.' He inhaled a deep breath. 'Now, where was Ed the last time you saw him?' He pulled her to one side to make room for two porters who attempted to upright an upturned sofa.

'He left me upstairs while he went to telephone the police. Maddox claimed he received no such call and was on his way here, anyway. Ed was supposed to meet me down here, but then the shooting started, and I haven't seen him at all.'

'Wait here. I'll find out if the police have located Ed first, then we'll decide what to do next.' He lifted his arms as if to give her a hug, but changed his mind and instead went to talk to the nearest policeman.

'I wish everyone would stop telling me to wait,' Flora muttered.

* * *

Feeling abandoned among chaos, Flora stared round at the porters who swept broken glass into manageable piles and righted overturned furniture. Chambermaids in black and white uniforms bobbed about like penguins, collecting shards of broken china and scattered flowers. The matron Flora remembered from her first visit sat on a sofa, a hand to her head, her eyes closed, being comforted by a maid who held a bottle of smelling salts to her nose. The woman's ferret-like dog had discovered something interesting in a tall pot plant and frantically dug earth onto the floor with its front paws.

Frederick had regained his composure enough to command attention in the centre of the lobby. His hands spread wide to encompass the room, he apologised for the inconvenience to all the hotel's guests, assured them there was no longer any cause for alarm and that complimentary tea and coffee would be served directly. That he had remained to restore order showed he was an innocent man, or confident his 'imposter' had escaped.

Then there was Francis, who had still not made an appearance? Would she emerge when it was all over and tearfully claim to know nothing? Or had she too escaped with her partner in crime?

'Think, Flora,' she muttered to herself. Paige was in the rear hall, so had he seen Ed there when he was making the call to Maddox? Or had he warned Francis the police had arrived, and she intercepted Ed? As she tried to work out where the most likely place to search would be, the porter who had approached her when she emerged from the lift appeared to have appointed himself her unofficial guardian in the police's absence. His gaze left her as he was accosted by an irate elderly gentleman who waved a knotted cane in his face, demanding he be allowed to use the ascending room, as his legs weren't strong enough to climb to the second floor. The porter patiently explained the lift was out of service, and as the discussion grew more heated, Flora took her chance and slipped past them and up the stairs. She reached the second landing with relative ease, but her steps slowed on her way up to the fourth floor, her corset not designed for such exertion. She paused at the top to catch her breath. One hand braced on the balustrade, the other pressed to her midriff where a whalebone dug into a rib.

The signs of a struggle were laid out in the hallway; a toppled aspidistra plant, a rucked-up carpet and a bullet hole gouged into the wall. She cocked her head to listen but could hear no sound. Straightening, she crept along the thick carpet to Francis's suite. If Ed had been taken there, perhaps Francis had not thought to lock it?

A door halfway along the corridor stood ajar. Pressing her back against the wall, she poked her head round the jamb, and froze at the sight of Francis perched on the end of an unmade brass bed, Mr Brody curled on her lap.

Was she aware Paige was being chased by the police? Or was this his room, and he had packed his things and bolted without her? If so, it explained why she looked so bewildered.

'Mrs Harrington?' Francis glanced up from stroking the cat's silky fur. 'I didn't realise you were still here. Have you seen Miss Sharpe by any chance?'

'Um, no I don't think—' the question came out of nowhere, leaving her flummoxed.

Flora entered a room not merely empty but abandoned. The wardrobe stood open, with nothing but wooden hangers and disarranged shelf liners. A sheet of old newspaper lay on the bottom. Each drawer in the dresser had been pulled open, all bare but for similar paper liners, as if someone had packed in a hurry.

'Agnes Sharpe, my housekeeper,' Francis said. 'She's packed all her belongings and gone. There's nothing left of her here.' She gestured vaguely at her surroundings. 'I don't understand it. Why would she just leave?' Her abrupt movements disturbed the cat that leapt to the floor with a barely discernible thump and ran off down the hallway.

'She's gone?' Flora asked, confused. Then the pieces of the puzzle she had struggled to put together over the last week shifted in her head. Agnes Sharpe was the woman in the black dress she had seen talking to Ed in the hallway. The same one in Arnold Baines' photograph which contained Lady Egerton and her companion.

'We were friends.' Francis's voice developed a slight whine. 'Why would she leave without explanation or even a goodbye?'

'Has she taken all her things?' The answer was blindingly obvious, but it was all Flora could think of to say.

'Apart from the needlework case she left in my sitting room. Agnes is a marvellous seamstress and went nowhere without some mending or embroidery to keep her occupied. She must have forgotten it.'

Or left it there to implicate you. It was Agnes who injured Sylvia Thompson.

'Miss Hunter-Griggs.' Flora tamped down her growing urgency and slid onto the bed beside her. 'This might sound like an odd question, but did Agnes ever borrow your coat? The one with the chevrons?'

'That *is* an odd question.' Francis's eyes widened. 'How could you know such a thing?' Her languorous way of speaking increased Flora's impatience.

'She expressed a particular liking for it, though it was only a copy I had made by a tailor in Fulham. Why are you asking questions about my coat? Does it have something to do with the police van parked outside the front doors?' Her eyes swivelled towards the window.

Flora chose not to answer. If she knew the police were crawling through her hotel, why was she up here, and not demanding to know what was going on?

'In case you're wondering,' Francis seemed to guess what she was thinking. 'When I returned to my suite, you and your cousin had gone. I saw the police van arrive through the window and was on my way. When I saw Agnes's door was open and her room was like this. Then I heard this strange noise, like a crack and a whistling sound. I entered the hall to see what it was when I was almost mown down by a policeman who came running out of Leonard's room at full pelt. He had a revolver in his hand. I was so shocked; I ran back in here. Then you arrived. What is happening?' Her clear, intelligent eyes met Flora's with both confusion and fear, but no guilt. Francis Hunter-Griggs was no killer.

Flora slid from the bed. 'I'll explain later, but I need to find Viscount Trent.' At her deepened frown, Flora added, 'I mean Ed, my cousin. We got separated before the furore downstairs happened and I've no idea where he is. I'm horribly afraid he might be in trouble, so please excuse me. I must find him.'

'Mrs Harrington!' Francis's raised voice halted her. 'We don't know each other well, which I sincerely hope will change in time. However, I can see you're frightened. Why is it so urgent you find your cousin? He's not a child and quite able to stay out of harm's way.' She rose from the bed and smoothed down her skirt, calmer now. Flora hesitated, and she added, 'You can tell me. I'm good with secrets. Are you both in trouble with the police?'

'Definitely not.' A laugh bubbled up in Flora's chest at the idea, as ludicrous as that seemed in this situation. 'At least not in the way you think.'

'I see. Well, I haven't seen your cousin. But before the policeman ran by, I heard noises I assumed were workmen moving furniture. After a few shouts and bangs, everything went quiet.'

'Could you tell where these sounds came from?'

'Not really. We could search the guest rooms if you wish. The master key is kept downstairs in the lobby.'

'That will take too long.' Flora's thoughts whirled until an idea came to her. 'Miss Hunter-Griggs, apart from this room, is there anywhere else in the hotel where Agnes spent her time?'

'Agnes? Well, there's her office. It's three floors down off the rear staircase. Practically in the basement.'

Where Paige had intended to take Flora in the lift.

'Thank you. I'll try there.'

'Wait!' Francis halted her again. 'It might be locked. You'll need the key.' She delved into a pocket of her gown and withdrew three keys held together by a metal ring. 'I keep all the office keys with me. I never know when I might need them.'

Flora made to take the keys, when Francis clutched them to her chest.

'I'm coming with you. It isn't easy to find and, besides, I want to know why you're so interested in Agnes.' She brushed past Flora and set off towards the main stairs, past an aspidistra that lay on its side, a trail of earth on the carpet. She ran a hand across a ragged end of wallpaper. 'Goodness, is that a bullet hole?' Her eyes widened. 'Exactly how much excitement did I miss?'

'A lot, actually. You should see the lobby,' Flora murmured. 'Did you hear nothing?'

'Apart from the noises I told you about? No, nothing. Mind you, these walls are thick, so sound doesn't travel well.' She paused beside an alcove tucked into one side of the galleried landing. 'These are the old servants' stairs.' She gestured Flora through. 'We don't use them much, but they come in useful occasionally.'

Flora peered over a plain bannister to where narrow wooden steps twisted away to a lower level, narrowed and disappeared into the dark. The smell of damp and ancient dust irritated her nostrils as she picked her way down the shallow treads.

'What's that strange sound?' Francis paused a few steps down, her head cocked, listening.

'It sounds like banging,' Flora descended to join her, and the sound came again. Once, twice, three times in succession. It stopped for a few seconds, then resumed in the same rhythm. 'It's not a mechanical sound. The ascending room has been locked open on the ground floor, so it's not coming from there.'

'It could be a pipe, or—' Their eyes met.

'Ed!' they said together.

33

Flora clattered down the wooden steps, at the bottom of which an arched hallway ran off to one side, the gloom barely lifted by a row of gaslights on one wall.

'This building is a lot older than it looks.' Francis led the way to a door at the far end, her steps slowing as she spoke over her shoulder. 'This section juts into the building next door. The façade was rebuilt about eighty years ago, but the foundations were still sturdy, so we didn't change anything. At first glance these hallways look like dead ends, but there's a rear staircase that connects them.'

'That might explain a few things,' Flora muttered, straining to locate where the banging was coming from. The sounds grew more insistent, but farther apart; as if whoever made them was tiring.

'It's a strange place for an office.' Flora wished she would hurry. She rubbed her upper arms as she walked to warm them from the chill that leached from the stone walls.

'Agnes chose this room.' Francis located a key on the metal ring and inserted it into the lock. 'She liked to be away from the bustle and chaos of the kitchens and cellars.'

'I'll bet she did,' Flora muttered under her breath. Then another thought struck her. Suppose she had miscalculated, and Agnes waited on the other side ready to pounce? She took a step backwards, debating with herself.

'Is there something wrong?' Francis's hand stilled on the key. 'Mrs Harrington, you can trust me. If Agnes has harmed your cousin, I'll never be able to forgive myself.'

Flora hesitated, searching her expression for signs of deceit, but saw only sympathy. 'All right. Open it.'

The lock clicked gently, and the door swung inwards on well-oiled hinges. Flora barely took in the room, her gaze going straight to where Ed was tied to a spindly wooden chair which leaned against one wall; his hands secured behind him and his ankles tied to the front legs with hemp ropes. A strip of cloth had been jammed into his mouth and knotted behind his head. The stark fear in his eyes changed to relief when he saw her.

Flora crouched beside him, hooked her fingers beneath the cloth and tugged it down over his chin.

'Thank God it's you, Flora.' He hunched forward, setting the front legs back on the floor, dislodging a hank of hair that tumbled across his forehead.

'Who did this to you?' Francis rushed to his other side.

Flora stared round in search of something to release the ropes. The office contained only a square desk set in front of an inset fireplace, a pile of ledgers strewn across the scarred surface.

'Your brother did!' Ed's voice became a furious growl as he continued to struggle uselessly against his bonds. 'At least that's what he's calling himself.'

'I assume you mean Leonard, because Frederick would never do something like this,' Francis protested. 'What exactly has he done?'

'I will explain, but first we have to get Ed free.' Flora was surprised she had not tried to defend the man she thought was her younger brother. 'I'll need something to cut these ropes. Is there anything on that desk I could use?'

'I'll look.' Francis left her side, but after a good deal of rummaging shook her head. 'There's nothing sharp enough. Only a useless pair of scissors and a butter knife. You'll have to wait until I fetch someone or try to untie them yourself.'

'Hurry!' Ed tossed back his head and wriggled. 'Get me free before Paige comes back.'

'Keep still, Ed,' Flora snapped. 'You're making it worse. The more you pull, the tighter the knots become. You don't have to worry about Paige. He's either languishing in a police van or halfway along the Ratcliffe Highway by now.'

'I don't understand.' Francis paced the room. 'Who is this Paige person, and why would Leonard tie you up and leave you down here?'

Flora sighed as she wrestled with the bindings, wishing she could defer the explanations to another time, but Francis was evidently not going to give up; a sentiment Flora understood perfectly.

'All right, I'll give you an edited version. Eric Paige has been impersonating your half-brother for months. I'm afraid the real Leonard was murdered.'

'Murdered?' She halted, her eyes welling with tears. 'No. It cannot be true! You must be mistaken!'

'It gets worse, I'm afraid.' Flora tugged at an especially tight knot. 'Agnes is involved too.'

'How... how did my brother die?' Francis's voice hitched in genuine distress.

'Perhaps this isn't the time?' Flora gritted her teeth as the rope fibres scratched her skin like tiny needles. 'There'll be time for all that later.'

'I want to know everything.' Francis loomed over them. 'Please, tell me what happened?'

'Leonard was murdered on a train to Paddington,' Ed gabbled, ignoring Flora's frantic eyebrow signals.

'On a train, you say?' Francis's gaze slid off into the distance. 'I think I read it in the newspapers.' Her eyes darted round the room as she fought to compose herself, her mouth working soundlessly. 'I... I'll need some time to think about this. Not that I think you're lying. I mean, why would you? But I just—'

'Look, Miss Hunter-Griggs,' Flora spoke firmly, but grimaced as the ropes chafed her fingers. 'Why don't you inform the police that Viscount Trent has been found?' Having something to do might help her focus. 'Ask for an Inspector Maddox.' She hoped he would still be there and had not called his men off and returned to the police station.

'Frederick will be devastated about Leonard,' Francis drifted off again. 'He was so thrilled to have him back in the family again.' She closed her eyes and took a deep breath. When she opened them again, she seemed calmer. 'What was I doing? Oh, yes.' She paused at the door and turned back. 'I'll be back as soon as I can rouse someone. And, Lord Trent, I'm so sorry about what Leonard has done.'

'It wasn't your fault,' Ed mumbled, then louder, 'Miss Hunter-Griggs. Do you think you might call me Ed?'

'Ed, then.' Francis smiled at him over her shoulder as she left.

'She's too old for you,' Flora said, once the door closed.

'I know.' His sigh held regret. 'How are you doing with those knots? My wrists are sore, and my head really hurts.'

'I'd work quicker if you'd stop squirming.' The more he struggled, the tighter the knots became. 'What happened exactly, Ed?' Flora tried to distract him. 'How did you end up here?'

'I reached the telephone cubicle when that chap stuck a gun in my back and forced me down the back stairs. Did you say his name was Paige?'

'I did. Eric Paige.' His shoulders relaxed, and she loosened the rope that held his hands together. 'What then?'

'When he was tying me up, he said he was going back for you, so I brought the chair leg down on his foot and grabbed the gun, only he was much stronger than me and he took it back easily. I should have stopped him, but – well, I froze. That's when he hit me across the head with the handgrip.'

'There's no need to be ashamed. It's probably a good thing you didn't struggle with him. You would probably have come off worse.'

'I was groggy, so I didn't put up much of a fight. Then something must have spooked him because he left. A noise on the street, I think. Shouting and such. I cannot believe I had that gun in my hand and did nothing. I was completely useless.'

'Mine didn't get me anywhere either,' she muttered under her breath. 'Then what happened?'

'I scooted the chair over to the wall.' He nodded to where a long dent in the plaster showed where he had made contact. 'I banged it for ages but wasn't sure anyone could hear me.'

'It was good thinking because Francis and I both heard it.'

'Did I hear you tell Francis he had got away? Paige?'

'Don't worry, the police went after him, assisted by a group of Russians.' She smiled at an image this created in her head. 'I doubt he'll get far.'

'Russians? Where did they come from?'

'Er... I'm not entirely sure.' Gritting her teeth, she tugged at a stubborn knot. 'Ah, I've got it.' The bindings fell away, pooling onto the floor in a continuous brown snake.

'That's a relief. I was getting a cramp in my arms.' He flexed his shoulders, leaned his forearms on his knees, and rubbed each wrist. 'By the way, I told you Miss Francis wasn't guilty.' He angled his head towards her, grinning.

'All right, I admit I got it wrong.' Flora sighed. 'The most important thing is, you'll be exonerated, and I haven't publicly accused two innocent people.'

'Two?'

'I assumed Frederick was complicit, but I've changed my mind about that as well.' She reached to brush dust from his hair, revealing a two-inch wound on his forehead that oozed red. 'Ed, you're bleeding!'

'Am I?' He brought a hand to his head and frowned. When he brought his fingers away, they were stained with red.

Flora got to her feet and started round the room. A half-sized butler sink occupied a corner, above which sat an old-fashioned pump. On the wall above was a row of hooks, each with a neatly labelled fob. It took a moment for Flora to register the room had no window, only a glass-covered metal grille set above shoulder-height, which threw a rectangle of daylight onto the floorboards. The click of footsteps and rumble of wheels beyond told her the main street lay on the other side. She approached a brass-bound trunk in a corner, which to her relief wasn't locked. Though heavy, the lid came up easily. Inside were piles of sheets and blankets, most of which were darned and frayed, most likely intended for sewing or tearing up into dusters. She grabbed a faded pillowcase, tore it deftly in half and carried it to the sink where she pumped the metal lever a few times.

'Now hold still, this will be cold.' She tilted his chin up and dabbed at the drying blood on his forehead.

'Ouch, that hurts.' He ducked away from her touch like a schoolboy avoiding a wet hankie.

'Keep still.'

'Flora,' Ed submitted, wincing while she cleaned the blood away. 'Was it my imagination, or did you say you had brought a gun with you?'

'Yes, I did,' she replied, refusing to apologise. 'It's a Webley Bulldog. Small but effective.'

'Not for you, evidently,' Ed probed the lump on his forehead with his fingers.

'Leave the cut alone, or you'll make it bleed again.' Flora slapped his hand away. 'I always rush into these situations without thinking of the consequences, so this time I wanted to be better prepared.'

'Where is this gun, then? Did you lose it?'

'I did not lose it. Inspector Maddox took it from me.' She rose and threw the bloodstained cloth into the sink, annoyed with herself. 'Could we please drop the subject?'

She had never harboured a desire to shoot someone, but for a moment in the lift she had felt in control. The raw fear on Paige's face when she had pointed the gun at him had given her confidence.

'Can you stand on your own, or are you still giddy?' she asked Ed.

His eyes looked cloudy, but he seemed to understand her. Wincing, he staggered to his feet; stretched each leg and rolled his shoulders.

Flora tucked her arm beneath his and eased him to his feet. 'Let's get out of here and see what's happening upstairs.'

The door opened with a high-pitched creak before they reached it. 'You weren't very long,' Flora said, her focus on the floor as she supported Ed. 'Did you find William?' She looked up, her smile fading as she saw Agnes Sharpe in the door frame, her expression as cold as her eyes.

'I've no idea who William is,' Agnes said from the

doorway. 'But I couldn't leave without ensuring you get what you deserve.' In her right hand sat a revolver somewhat larger than the Webley Bulldog.

* * *

'You know who I am, don't you?' Agnes adjusted her grip on the revolver, raising it higher.

'Me, no I don't think we've met, I—' Ed stammered.

'Not you,' she snapped, her aim swinging at Flora. 'Her.'

'Not until about half an hour ago, no.' Flora's voice rose, and she found she could barely breathe. The hole at the end of the barrel seemed to grow and recede. 'I've seen your photograph, though.'

'What are you talking about?' Agnes tilted her head, her eyes narrowed.

'An acquaintance of ours took it during a sports event at Marlborough College three years ago. You were there that day with Lady Egerton.'

'I wondered why you were so interested in that photograph,' Ed murmured, shifting from foot to foot. 'But what's it got to do—'

'That's where you met Eric Paige,' Flora said, ignoring him, her gaze fixed on Agnes. 'He was one of her young men. Lady Egerton sacked you for stealing her bracelet.'

'You think you're so clever, don't you?' The gun trembled in Agnes's hand. 'My bad luck about the bracelet. I thought her ladyship had forgotten she had it, let alone noticed it was missing.'

A voice in Flora's head told her to be quiet, but her need for the truth overruled her common sense. 'Either it was a coincidence, or you went looking for the Hunter-Griggs family. You took the position as housekeeper and befriended Francis. It didn't take long for you to discover the shy boy you had met at the Marlborough Sports Day with Lady Egerton two years ago was Colonel Hunter-Griggs' estranged son, Leo. You persuaded Eric to pretend to be Leonard Hunter-Griggs. You disposed of Leo Thompson. I doubt Eric would have used a needlework tool to kill him, so I assume it was you.'

'Well, you're quite the little busybody, aren't you? I might admire your skills of deduction had you not brought the police here.'

'And yet you avoided them.' Where was Francis? And the police? Belatedly, Flora remembered most of the officers had rushed off after Paige. She didn't even have a scary Russian she could call upon.

'I know all this building's secrets.' Agnes administered a swift kick to the door, which sent it back into its frame with barely a sound. 'I told Eric we should leave days ago, but he didn't listen. He wasn't going to give this life up easily. He was always greedy, that man. I don't intend to wait and see if he'll keep quiet about me to the police.'

'You're abandoning Eric?' Flora swallowed and her stomach clenched. If she had no one to protect, it made her more dangerous.

'Why not? I expect he'll say those killings were all my doing.'

'If you have a way out of here the police don't know about, just go!' Ed pointed to the door. 'We'll give you a head start, won't we, Flora?'

'Of course.' Flora admired Ed's quick thinking. Unfortunately, Agnes didn't look willing to take advantage of the offer.

'How obliging of you.' Her eyes narrowed, giving them the cat-like quality Dr Grace had mentioned as she jerked the gun at Flora. 'I'll bet it was you who told that Russian downstairs to call the bluebottles. Why were you talking to him, anyway? He didn't know Thompson.'

'What's she talking about, Flora?' Ed whispered. 'What Russian?'

'Hush.' Flora nudged him into silence. 'Actually,

Leo knew him. He came here to take part in the Russian Socialist Congress. Leo knew nothing about you or Eric. He didn't even know he was the Colonel's son.'

'He didn't come here to meet his father?' Her gaze shifted to the middle distance as if she were talking to herself. 'Then we messed everything up for nothing! Eric and me, we would have made a good life in this place. He knows how to fleece the rich who lose more on the turn of a card than I ever earned in a year. Now everything is ruined, and it's all his fault.' She levelled the revolver at Ed's chest. 'Now stand aside.'

'Oh, cripes, Flora, I think she means it.' Ed's face paled.

'What good would it do to kill him?' Flora wanted to say Agnes wasn't lost, that there was a way out for her, but it would be a lie. She had killed two people. 'Look, why don't you do what Ed suggested and just go?' She stepped sideways, partly blocking him. 'No one knows you're involved except us.'

'Liar!' The gun shook in Agnes's hand. 'You'll yell for the coppers as soon as I'm out of the door.'

'Why *did* you kill Sylvia Thompson?' Flora couldn't curb her curiosity any longer, despite the danger she was in. 'She and her husband hadn't spoken for years, and Leo thought his father was dead.'

'I hadn't bargained for the Colonel living beyond New Year. When he was ill last winter, he re-wrote willing the hotel to his three children. When Frederick said they didn't know where Leonard was, well—'

'The twins trusted you to help find him, didn't they?' Flora said, marvelling at the woman's duplicity. Though if she hoped to appeal to the woman's better nature, she was wasting her time. Agnes had planned everything in the last detail. Except the part that meant killing Leo.

'Why wouldn't they? I often sat with the twins in Miss Francis's sitting room of an evening when Frederick would join us. They stopped noticing little me sewing away quietly in the corner. They wanted to put things right before the old man died. Couldn't have that, could I?'

'That's when you went to Sylvia's shop in Cheltenham.'

'And made sure Sylvia wouldn't be in any fit state to accept an invitation to London. Worked better than I thought. I knew it would make her ill, but I didn't count on her dying. Bit of luck, that was.'

'Not for Sylvia,' Ed snorted.

Flora nudged him into silence, though Agnes seemed not to notice as she appeared to enjoy her chance at self-congratulation. 'Is that when you had the idea of Eric pretending to be his son, Leonard? Even though Leo was alive and living in Cheltenham?'

'You said yourself Leo had no idea his father was alive. He didn't even know his real name. Sylvia made certain of that. The plan was when the old man died, Eric would inherit part of the hotel. Then, in a few months, Leonard would announce he didn't like hotel work and get the twins to buy him out. Then he and I would be off, and no one would be the wiser.'

'Ah, now I see. But Leo wrote a letter saying he was coming to The Dahlia, and you panicked, thinking he had found out about his family?'

'Why else would he come here? There are hundreds of hotels in London.'

'But the only one in which the Russian Labour Party Congress was being held.'

'What's that got to do with anything?' Agnes's features twisted with frustration and anger.

'But what happened to Frederick's letter? The one he wrote to invite Sylvia to London?' Was it possible Leo found it after his mother died, which was the real reason he chose that hotel for his stay in London?

'My luck held there. He had only just begun

looking for Sylvia when he received a notice from the bank saying she had died.'

'That wasn't luck. You killed her!' Ed blurted.

'All you had to do then was handle Leo?' Flora filled in the gaps. 'Who had no idea his half-brother and sister wanted to see him?'

'Eric did a great job of playing the grieving son who had always wanted to see his father again, but Sylvia would never allow it. He claimed he even wanted to take his real name again as a tribute to his old dad. Nice little drama, that was.' Agnes's upper lip curled into a parody of a smile that made Flora shudder. 'You should have seen it. Eric gave a fine performance.'

'You appear to have thought of everything, Miss Sharpe.' Flora tried to work out how long they had kept the woman talking. Surely long enough for Francis to have found someone and told them where they were. But then Francis thought they weren't in any danger, so might have simply waited for them to join her.

Forcing herself not to stare at the gun still pointed at Ed, Flora asked, 'What about the real Leo? Why wait until now to kill him if he hadn't contacted the twins or the Colonel since Sylvia's death? Didn't that tell you he knew nothing about them?'

'That's what I thought, but then that letter came. Why would he come here if it wasn't to see his father and the twins again? I couldn't take the risk.'

'What's she talking about, Flora.' Ed fidgeted, his gaze darting around the room. 'She's not making any sense. How did she know about Leo and his father?'

'Yes, she is,' Flora whispered, then louder for Agnes's benefit. 'You were Lady Egerton's companion when Sylvia pretended not to know her that day in Bath. She told you she had known Sylvia in India. Then, in the cross-country race, you saw Leo, and remembered what she had said about the family rift. Couldn't you and Eric make enough at her card parties, so you had to think of something else?'

'You're better than the coppers, aren't you?' Agnes's harsh laugh matched the sheer fury in her eyes. 'It was a sweet deal until Eric stole that bracelet. He had to disappear, and I found the Hunter-Griggs and got the job here. Took me over two years to plan all this, and now you come along.'

'And once Sylvia was out of the way, you sent Leo the train ticket. It wasn't only Eric on that train, but you were, too. Which explains why you had to kill him with a stiletto.'

'*She* put that thing in my pocket?' Ed's voice was a hushed whisper.

'You're too clever for your own good,' Agnes said before Flora could answer.

'Not clever enough,' Flora murmured. 'Which is why I'm down here looking into the barrel of your gun.'

'It was a perfect plan. No one would have put it all together if it weren't for you two.' Agnes's arm wavered, her eyes losing focus as if she had forgotten where she was.

'What are you going to do, Agnes?' Flora's voice sharpened, hating the fact they were at this woman's mercy. 'The police will have caught Eric by now and will be back here for you before long. We can't stand here all day. What are you going to do?'

'Flora!' Ed's voice rose in panic. 'She didn't mean it, Miss Sharpe. Take all the time you need to decide.'

'Stop talking! Both of you!' Agnes raised her arm and took aim at Ed. 'I should have done this the minute I first saw you.'

Flora had no time for thought. It was as if she watched herself from above as she lunged across the room straight at Agnes.

'Flora! No!' Ed shouted as she flung up her arm to knock the weapon away at the same instant a loud, sharp crack erupted into the room.

34

A roaring expanded inside Flora's head as a stinging sensation exploded beneath her left breast. She brought a hand to the spot where a burning intensified and hot wetness welled. She glanced down to where a trickle of red squeezed between her fingers.

'My God, no!' Ed's arms encircled her tightly, his warm breath on her cheek.

Her vision blurred. Weakness flooded her legs, which refused to support her weight. She crumpled to the floor, taking him with her.

He held her head on his knees, one arm beneath her shoulders, the other hand cradling her face. 'What do I do?' Ed pleaded. 'Tell me what to do!'

'Agnes?' she whispered through rapidly drying lips. 'Where—?'

'She ran out.' His voice hitched. 'My God, Flora, I was convinced she was going to kill us both.'

'I'm still here, Ed.' She tried to laugh, but it hurt as much as talking.

'I'll... I'll get someone to help.' He released her hand, which collapsed to the floor as if boneless.

'No, don't leave me!' Panic filled her at the thought of being alone, even for a moment.

'I have to get something to stop the bleeding until help arrives.' He eased her head down onto the floor and scrambled to his feet.

Her throat constricted at the void he left, though the click of the trunk lid told her he not gone far. In seconds, he was a dark shape above her again.

'You have blood all over your skirt, though I expect Sally will get it out for you. Not that you care much right now, I... oh, what am I saying?' His voice came rapid and jerky, so she had to concentrate to understand him. 'I'll wad up this sheet and press it onto the wound. This might hurt. Well, it's bound to, but I can't help it. Forgive me.'

A crushing weight made her cry out as pain exploded into her side and spread upward into her chest so she could hardly breathe.

'Sorry, sorry.' Ed swiped a hand across his face, drawing a streak of red across his cheek, the crumpled, blood-soaked sheet in his other hand. 'It's not working!'

The room darkened round her as pain forced her to take short, shallow breaths that made her giddy. She tried to raise her hand to the square of light behind his head, but her arm felt too heavy and flopped back onto the floor.

'What is it, Flora?' Ed asked, his breathing fast and shallow as her own. 'What are you trying to say?'

'Grille. Police. Call... through... it.'

'Right. Yes, yes, of course. What am I thinking?' He ran to the grille and rapped on the glass covering. 'Hey! Is anyone up there? We need help. Someone is hurt.' The murmur of distant voices responded, which he answered in panicked monosyllables. In seconds he loomed above her again, his face blurry but intense. 'They're coming. Hold on, Flora. Stay with me.'

'Bunny.' Cold enveloped her, and she shivered. She tried to lift her head, but her vision darkened and her head spun, bringing panic. 'Please... fetch... Bunny.' She strained upward to push her urgency home, but could barely raise her shoulders from the floor and flopped back down.

'Keep still, Flora.' Ed grasped her hand again, his

fingers slick. With the other he refolded the sheet and applied it to her side again. 'Each time you move the wound spurts more blood.'

Craning her neck, she glanced down and to the side, where her left arm lay in a pool of something shiny and dark. 'Is that—?'

'Don't look,' Ed's voice cracked. 'Oh, hell where are they? Hold on, please. They'll be here soon. Flora, can you hear me?'

'I'm... sorry, Ed,' she said with a sigh.

'*You're* sorry?' His voice was strangled and high. 'I'm the one who insisted on coming. I let that thug Paige catch me and bring me down here, so you had to come and rescue me. It was my fault. What have I done?'

'No, Ed... it was me. I shouldn't have... goaded Agnes.' The room dimmed as she fought the pull of oblivion. 'I treated it all... like a... game. Bunny warned me. I... wouldn't... listen.'

'Flora, listen!' He gripped her hand harder. 'I can hear footsteps! They're coming.'

The London sky beyond the grille above Ed's head had darkened since she first looked – how long had she lain there? Minutes? Hours? The shivers quickly worsened into uncontrollable shuddering. Why did she feel so cold?

The light shimmered and flickered out as she sank into oblivion.

* * *

A voice was calling her name, over and over. A woman's voice. Familiar. Alice? No, not Alice. Someone else. Someone she knew. The cadence and volume became intrusive, which sent her burrowing into the cocoon of softness that surrounded her.

'Flora!' The voice came louder and more persistent, accompanied by a firm shake of her shoulder.

Reluctantly, she prised her eyelids open, an arm raised against blinding daylight, but froze as agony lanced through her back and side. A face loomed into view, indistinct features that sharpened into those of Dr Grace Billings, her hair swept into a soft bun, a crisp white blouse buttoned to the neck worn with a plain black skirt.

'How are you feeling, Flora? No, don't try to move.'

'Dr Grace?' Blinking awake, she stared around at what was clearly a hospital room. She lay in a half sitting position, supported by a stack of pillows in a metal bed, a plain electric bulb and shade hung from the ceiling directly above her. A small table with metal legs on her right side held a pitcher and an empty glass, a plain wooden chair and a window half covered with a translucent blind gave the room a sterile feel. The only spot of bright colour was a small glass vase on the windowsill, bursting with tiny pastel blue flowers.

The click of rapid footsteps, hushed voices and the rumble of trolley wheels sounded from somewhere beyond a half-glazed door about fifteen feet from the bottom rail of the bed.

'I'm not sure how I feel. What are you doing here?' Wherever here was. Her voice came out croaky, her lips dry and cracked.

'You're at The Royal Free Hospital.' Dr Grace poured water from the pitcher into the glass. 'I was giving a lecture to medical students when you were brought in. This being the only hospital willing to train female doctors.' Her feelings on the matter were clear in her clipped speech as she held the glass to Flora's lips.

Flora's eyes slid closed again as she let the cool, soothing liquid glide down her throat. Never did water taste so good.

'I admit to a certain excitement when I discovered it was a female with a gunshot wound,' Dr Grace went on, enthused about what she evidently saw as a professional opportunity. 'When I found out your name, I said you were a patient of mine, so your surgeon was kind enough to let me assist in your operation.'

Flora's eyes snapped open again. 'Operation?'

'Do you remember what happened?' Dr Grace's penetrating gaze searched her face.

'I was shot, wasn't I?' Memory returned in a series of stark images, each one more distressing than the last, followed by questions that swirled in her head until one took prominence. She tried to sit but winced as pain flooded through her. 'Ed? Is he all right?'

'Viscount Trent is fine.' She took the glass from her hand, then eased Flora gently back against the pile of pillows. 'And your husband is here. He's been making a nuisance of himself demanding hourly reports from any member of staff he encounters.' Her indulgent smile conveyed more sympathy than complaint. 'However, I want to know how much pain you are in before I allow anyone through that door. Even him.'

'I'm not sure – yet.' She took inventory of the discomfort between her knees and shoulders, which ranged from being stiff and sore to agony each time she moved. 'What happened at the hotel? Has Agnes Sharpe been found?' An image of the woman's vengeful face made her shudder.

'I'm afraid not.' Dr Grace sighed. 'Miss Sharpe disappeared from the hotel within minutes of the shooting. As far as I know, she hasn't been seen since.'

'Did they catch Paige?'

'He was apprehended, yes. In fact, his pursuit through the British Museum by the police and several irate Russian gentlemen was headline news in *The Morning Post*, although it only made page five of *The Times*. He was finally cornered amongst a display case of Nelson's uniforms, which was in danger of being toppled at one point, much to the chagrin of the curator. Bunny has kept a copy of both articles for you to read. An artist drew some suitably dramatic sketches of the incident which were included in the report.'

'I'm glad they caught him.' Flora straightened. 'Wait! Newspaper? How long have I been here?'

'Two days.'

'What?' She jerked upright, then halted, releasing a groan as her body violently protested.

'Try to keep still.' Dr Grace gently eased her down against the soft pillows. 'The incision is still raw, and you don't want the sutures breaking.'

'Are they likely to?' Flora stared down at herself to visualise what had happened to her. 'I've never been stitched before. How do they work?'

'Similar to sewing, but clumsier. Short lengths of catgut are soaked in iodine to avoid infection. We'll keep a close eye on them as catgut dissolves unpredictably in some patients.'

'Which ones?' Flora was not reassured.

'Don't worry about it. Hopefully, they'll hold until the wound has healed.' Dr Grace plumped up her pillows unnecessarily. 'You've been unconscious for most of the time, and there are anxious people outside eager to know you're awake.'

'Really? Who?' Flora asked, distracted. Her mind was still on the sutures.

'Besides your husband? Your parents are here, also a young woman with a lot to say for herself who goes by the name of Sally Pond.'

'Dear Sally, I imagine she's been anxious about me?'

'Not to mention vociferous. I wouldn't let her in, so she planted herself on a bench in the visitors' hall and refused to move. She was complaining about a stiff neck the last time I saw her.' She nodded to the lonely vase of tiny blue flowers. 'The myosotis was her gift to you. I disapprove of flowers in sickrooms, but she was insistent.'

'Forget-me-nots. My favourite.' Flora smiled. She must have bought them herself, as there were none in the garden at home.

'I suppose such devotion should be acknowledged.' Dr Grace's mouth lifted at one corner but failed to develop into a smile. 'I'll allow her in if you wish.'

'I... I don't suppose my husband brought Arthur with him? If he hasn't seen me for two days, he must be fretting. He's too young to understand why I'm not there.'

'It's against rules to bring infants into the hospital, I'm afraid.'

Flora bit her lip as tears threatened, prompting Dr Grace to squeeze her shoulder gently. 'However, I'm not without influence here. I'll see what I can do.'

'Oh, thank you.' Emotion clogged her throat. 'I would appreciate it.'

'Miss Francis Hunter-Griggs also made an appearance yesterday,' Dr Grace went on. 'She says she'll return when you're strong enough for visitors.'

'That was kind of her, especially when I feel so terrible about suspecting her of being a murderess.'

'She doesn't strike me as the sort to bear a grudge.'

'No, I don't think she would.' Flora squeezed her eyes shut but opened them again quickly when Agnes's face appeared behind her eyelids. How could she forget the raw hatred in the woman's eyes? 'Dr Grace, is it possible the cut on Sylvia Thompson's hand was deliberately contaminated?'

'It's plausible, but difficult to prove after all this time. Why do you ask?'

'I had this really vivid dream which keeps coming back to me.'

'That's not unusual after an anaesthetic. Was it disturbing?' Dr Grace looked up from where she draped a blanket on the bed.

'More strange than disturbing. There was a cat staring at me. Then Sally arrived with a bloodied cloth talking about shovels.'

'That sounds disturbing to me.' Dr Grace straightened. 'Now, is there anything else you need?'

'Lots of things, including a more comfortable bed and something to stop every inch of me from hurting.' She wiggled backwards into the stack of pillows, grimacing as the bindings across her ribs pulled.

Dr Grace moved round the room, a silent shadow in Flora's peripheral vision as pieces of the puzzle of what Flora would always think of as The Bloomsbury Affair swirled in her head. Fragments came together to form a whole, and suddenly it all made sense.

Wearing Francis's red coat, Agnes had contrived to cut Sylvia's hand then insisted on taking her to the surgery and remaining, where, in the ensuing chaos of Sylvia's hysteria she contaminated the wound, possibly with something Francis's cat had brought home from one of its fights. It wouldn't have surprised Flora if Agnes had let the creature out on purpose, knowing it would get into a fight with the obvious result; a cat bite that would inevitably turn into an abscess.

Had Agnes channelled her intellect into something less evil, the woman could have made a success of her life, not ended up a murderess. But then she hadn't yet been caught, and who knew if she would be?

Flora shuddered at the thought Agnes Sharpe might at this moment be looking for another opportunity to improve her life at the expense of some unwary soul.

'Are you cold, Flora?' Dr Grace loomed above her.

'Er no, not at all.'

'Then you rest awhile.' She retrieved the glass Flora still clutched in her hand, replacing it on the table. 'I hope you'll be kind to your inspector. Maddox, is it? He was mortified that he had failed to protect you. When his men reported Agnes Sharpe's room had been cleared out, he never imagined she might still be in the hotel. He blamed himself for sending all his men after Paige, leaving a lone officer outside the front of the hotel. Your husband threatened to report him to the Commissioner for incompetence.'

'Poor Inspector Maddox, though in fairness, what happened was largely my fault.'

'There will be time to dissect the details later. Now,' Dr Grace squeezed Flora's hand, 'I expect you'll want to see your husband?'

'Oh, yes, please.' Flora's eyes welled, her heart thumping as Dr Grace strode to the door and ushered Bunny into the room.

Relief, frustration and love each took a turn on Bunny's face as he approached the bed, his face blurred through her tears.

'Don't move, you mustn't move.' He spread his hands, hesitating as he reached for her, as if terrified to touch her.

'From what Dr Grace said, I expected to see a distraught lover in a rumpled suit with two days' growth of stubble.' Flora observed his immaculate dark suit, his slicked-back hair darkened by pomade and sharp white cuffs fastened with the diamond cufflinks she gave him on his last birthday. She liked to think he had chosen them specifically.

'I've been here since you were brought in. Until two hours ago anyway, when Dr Grace insisted I go home and change. Just as well, I suppose. I'm sure the porters must have thought I was some sort of vagrant.' He gazed down at himself and up again with a sheepish shrug. 'And now I look if as if I've just had luncheon at my club.'

'Is that where you've come from? Luncheon at your club?'

'No, of course not.' His features crumpled like a child wrongly accused of a crime. 'How could you think such a thing?'

'And how can you still not tell when I'm teasing you?' A laugh bubbled into her chest, abruptly halted by a wave of agony that cramped her side. Gritting her teeth, she took a shallow breath to control it. 'Are you furious with me?'

'I should be. And I was, but not now. Well,' he chewed his bottom lip, 'maybe a little.' He slid onto the bed and took Flora's hand in both of his, massaging her fingers. 'I don't understand why you went to The Dahlia without telling me. And to take Ed with you. What *were* you thinking?'

'I didn't exactly take him,' she replied, but chose not to explain and risk getting Ed into trouble. 'I had no idea it would turn out the way it did.' She took a deep, shuddering breath. 'Once we persuaded Maisie to change her story, we were about to leave, then Mr Frederick spotted us and introduced us to Francis. She was wearing the coat, the one with the chevrons, so I assumed she was Paige's accomplice. She insisted we go to her suite, and although I wanted to refuse, I thought it might have alerted her. Then Ed was wittering on about the ascending room and, after that, everything happened so fast. Ed and I split up so he could call the police and the firing started and—' Her breath caught in her throat as memory flooded back for the second time since waking. She tried to inhale, but her chest contracted with pain, and she couldn't breathe.

'It's all right.' Bunny shifted higher on the bed and wrapped his arms around her, his lips against her hair. 'It's over now. You're safe.'

'I keep hearing those awful cracks.' She pressed her head into his shoulder, her fingers latched onto his upper arm. 'The way the window shattered was like an explosion, showering everyone in the lobby with shards of glass like tiny arrows. I froze and ducked, hoping for the best, but some people were hurt.' Sudden dizziness made her feel sick, and she couldn't get enough air into her chest, her breaths coming fast and shallow.

Dr Grace appeared above Bunny's shoulder and pressed the fingers of one hand against her wrist. 'Look at me, Flora. Breathe in gently. Now hold it for five seconds. That's right, now exhale slowly. And again.'

Flora obeyed, relieved to find her panic slowly receding. Her rapid heartbeat settled into a less frightening rhythm and the room stopped spinning.

'What's wrong with her?' Bunny's eyes filled with anxiety.

'A moment of panic, that's all. Perfectly normal after what she has experienced.' Dr Grace patted his shoulder on her way to the door. 'I'll leave you two alone. If you need me, I'll be right outside.'

'Are you sure you're all right?' Bunny asked when she had gone. 'Sorry, that was a stupid thing to say.' He raised her palm to his cheek and held it there.

'No, but I'm much happier now you're here. How did you find out what happened? Did Inspector Maddox send for you?'

He shook his head. 'William telephoned me at the office to say you were at the hotel and that the police were searching for Ed. He had put a policeman to watch you, which is why I thought you were safe and everything was under control.'

'For a while, that was true. Then I'm afraid I gave him the slip.'

'Which is what I was told when I arrived at The Dahlia, fully intending to give you a stern talking-to before bringing you straight home. I—'

'When did *that* ever work?' Her brief laugh developed rapidly into a cough that made her gasp with sudden pain.

'I have to keep up the pretence I have my wife under control.' He planted a kiss on the back of her hand to show he didn't mean it. 'Hush, I haven't finished. When I arrived at the hotel, it was to be greeted by William, who informed me you had been shot and were being brought here. I'm sorry to say I became quite upset, but I didn't mean to tear his suit.'

'Wait. You tore William's suit?'

'Not his, Maddox's. He kept telling me to calm down, which made me furious, so I grabbed his lapels and shook him. I demanded he explain how he could have allowed it to happen and – well, one of them came off in my hand. Shoddy workmanship, if you ask me.'

'He's on a policeman's salary. What can you expect? Did he uh... tell you everything?' The Webley Bulldog sprang to her mind.

'He explained how Francis told him you and Ed were in the basement. He and William went straight down there but didn't know you had been hurt until they got there.'

'Then how did he miss running into Agnes?'

'Maddox is still trying to work that part out. The basement is a maze of old tunnels dating back to the sixteen hundreds.' He shrugged. 'While they were loading you onto a makeshift stretcher to bring you here, Timms comes rushing in brandishing Ed's note and looking terrified.'

'Ah.' Flora licked her dry lips. 'I know what that was about.'

'Precisely. Did Ed actually drive the Berliet here?'

'Yes, and although I take responsibility for everything that happened, I never imagined he would take the motor car. I assume you found it?' Timms must have been frantic to have turned up at the hotel looking for it.

'Do you honestly think I would go looking for the blasted motor when you were—?' Bunny flushed, sheepish. 'No, I left Timms to locate it, and came with you in the ambulance. In case you're wondering, the manager located the Berliet for me. It was exactly where Ed had left it. In an alley down the side of the hotel. Undamaged, thank goodness.'

'Unlike your wife,' Flora added, taking a minor triumph from his embarrassment. 'Did William tell you what happened?'

'I got most of it from Ed, but as he was euphoric and concussed it took a while to get the story straight. Did you really stop Agnes shooting him?'

'I don't remember it being quite like that, but she

was quite determined to make him pay for having ruined her nice little scheme.'

'It was courageous of you, but jolly reckless. Naturally I'm relieved Ed is safe, but, my God, Flora,' his voice caught with emotion, his grip on her hand tightening. 'I almost lost you.'

'But you didn't.' She returned the pressure of his hand, the only part of her which did not hurt, her eyes tightly closed against the memory of lying on the floor of Agnes's office in agony, terrified at the thought of leaving everything she knew.

'Are you in a lot of pain? And don't say no, because you wince every time you move.'

'As a comparison, I would have to say being shot wasn't as bad as having Arthur.'

'My goodness, really?' His voice choked again, and he turned his lips into her hand, his breath hot on her skin.

'How *is* Ed? The whole thing must have been a terrible shock for him. Is he all right?'

'He suffered a concussion, but he's on the mend. Or he will be when Jocasta stops ranting at him for getting both of you into this mess. She only draws breath long enough to burst into noisy tears, then hugs him until he complains he can't breathe.'

'She *is* pregnant, so you have to make allowances.'

'Ed's pretty proud of himself for having helped you foil a double murderer's escape.'

'But we didn't. If Paige is to be believed, it was Agnes who killed Leo and Sylvia, and she's still out there somewhere.'

'Semantics. Paige conspired with her, so he'll certainly hang. It's only a matter of time before they catch up with Miss Sharpe.'

'I hope you're right. I feel so sorry for Colonel Hunter-Griggs. He was so pleased to have reconciled with Leonard after all these years.'

'Miss Francis was also worried about how the news would affect him, but after the initial shock, she said he's been remarkably stoic.'

Dr Grace reappeared at the door. 'Your parents are outside. Shall I explain you need to rest and ask them to come back tomorrow?'

'No, please, I want to see them,' Flora said. 'But you'll have to give me a moment or two to make myself respectable. I must look a fright.' She disentangled herself from Bunny's arm and slowly, carefully, eased upright. 'Is there a mirror here?'

'Er... no,' Dr Grace threw Bunny an oblique look. 'But I could brush out your hair.'

Their combined uneasiness told Flora all she needed to know about her appearance.

'Let me do that.' Bunny took the hairbrush from Dr Grace and applied it to Flora's hair. 'I passed Sally dozing on a bench in the visitors' room. I doubt she'll leave either until she sees for herself you're all right.'

'That's what Dr Grace said.' Flora bit her lip as tears threatened, this time from the harsh treatment to her scalp.

'She's helped with Arthur while you've been here, although I don't think Milly is impressed to have her role usurped.' He leaned closer, his breath on her cheek. 'I would have brought flowers, but Dr Grace disapproves.'

'You don't need to bring me anything. After you, the only thing I need is Arthur. How is he? Does he miss our after-breakfast playtimes and bedtime stories?' She hoped Bunny would say yes but didn't want Arthur to fret. Not then. There wasn't anything she could do about it. Children weren't allowed in hospitals unless they were ill.

'He cannot voice his displeasure yet in anything more than grizzles, which tells me he wants his Mama back. He's being thoroughly spoiled too, as my mother has been calling in every day to fuss over him.'

'Your mother's home from Eastbourne?' If a visit from Beatrice was imminent, she ought to warn the hospital staff.

'She says April is too cold for a coastal holiday.' Bunny said.

'I could have told her that. Had she asked,' Flora murmured, her teeth gritted as another knot came away.

'Not bad, even if I say so myself.' Bunny stepped back to admire his work as Dr Grace finished bathing Flora's face with a cool cloth. By the time William and Alice were ushered in, she felt almost human again.

___

35

'Flora, I've been frantic.' Alice hugged Flora gently but awkwardly, tipping her pert hat further over one eye. Flora returned her embrace as she inhaled jasmine and starch, a fragrance she now associated with her mother. 'When they brought you down from surgery, you were still unconscious and I was only allowed in the room as a professional courtesy. Since then, Dr Grace has kept me at bay.' She shot a hard look at her fellow medic, which did not make so much as a dent in the doctor's composure.

'As a nurse, you of all people shouldn't complain about hospital rules.' She pressed a hand against her midriff to hold down a laugh that threatened.

'I know, but it's different when it's your own flesh

and blood. I had no idea how terrifying the waiting could be.'

'You gave me a fright when I returned to the lobby to find you had gone, Flora.' William reached across Alice and tenderly smoothed the hair from Flora's forehead.

'I'm sorry, I know I should have stayed where you told me, but—'

'Never mind all that now.' Alice flapped her hand at him. 'What matters is that Flora is going to be fine. Also, while we awaited news, I've caught up on what's been going on in the Trent family during the years I have been away.'

'Jocasta came to visit us at Prince Edward Mansions last night and stayed for supper,' William replied to Flora's unasked question. 'The two of them gossiped for hours.'

'She hasn't changed at all,' Alice said, laughing. 'Jocasta is as spirited and outspoken as she was as a child and hasn't she turned out lovely? I cannot believe she's a mother and about to have a second child.'

'She *told* you?' Flora asked, surprised. 'Well, don't say anything. She hasn't made an announcement to the family yet.'

'No, she didn't, but as you said yourself, I'm a nurse. I have an instinct for these things.'

'Inspector Maddox sends his apologies.' The bed dipped as William perched level with her knees. 'He had to go back to Cannon Row but wanted you to know he's delighted you're making a good recovery. He also said he has something of yours which he'll return later. I asked him what he meant, but he wouldn't explain.'

'I'm sure it's something and nothing.' She waved him off, hoping Maddox would keep quiet about the Webley Bulldog. The way her body felt right then, she hoped never to see the thing again.

'Do Lord and Lady Trent know what happened?' Flora changed the subject.

'I wired the ship, explaining briefly what had occurred.' Bunny nodded. 'Couldn't have them walking into this with no warning. Not when they're bringing Lady Amelia and the children back with them.'

'I'll warn you now. Jocasta is likely to invite you both to the house party. If she hasn't done so already.'

'By which time, Alice and I will be married.' William grasped Alice's hand on the coverlet and brought it to his lips. 'We can all go to Gloucestershire together.'

'William,' Alice nudged him, indignant. 'You promised *I* could tell her.'

'You were taking too long and I couldn't wait.' He

pinched her chin gently between his thumb and forefinger.

'And I kept my mouth firmly shut, as instructed,' Bunny added, hands spread in surrender.

'You knew?' Flora stared at him, blinking away welling tears.

'Don't be cross with him, Flora, we swore him to secrecy,' Alice said.

'I'm not cross. I'm delighted, but it's happening much faster than I imagined.' Flora smiled up at them. 'I will attend the wedding, won't I?'

'We're having a civil ceremony at Caxton Hall in mid-May. You have just over three weeks to recover.'

'Then I'll book my bath chair now,' Flora said, determined not to miss something as momentous as her parents' wedding.

'I'm also giving up the Foreign Office,' William added. 'Secret government work is palling.'

'I won't pretend I'm not thrilled about that.' Flora wondered if her remark about the government funding foreign revolutions had struck home. 'What will you do instead?'

'I'm considering buying an estate near George and Venetia in Gloucestershire. Cirencester perhaps, or Tewkesbury. Not as large as Cleeve Abbey, of course, but somewhere you and Bunny can bring Arthur to stay for the holidays. Anyway, there's no rush. I want to get used to being a married man first.' He pulled a reluctant Alice to her feet. 'We should go. Leave Flora to rest.'

'We'll call again tomorrow.' Alice threw her a kiss over her shoulder from the door.

They had barely quit the room before a commanding female voice sounded from the hallway.

'Indeed, I heard you say Mrs Harrington isn't receiving visitors, but I very much doubt she meant *me*.' Lady Jocasta Fitzhugh glided into the room, her still slender figure draped in a layered sapphire blue coat over an amber-coloured gown and a matching wide-brimmed hat which trailed amber ribbons artfully arranged on her abundant sausage curls. She not only looked but sounded so much like her mother, Lady Trent, Flora was quite taken aback.

'How are you, Flora darling?' She bussed Flora's cheek, the smell of face powder and perfume subsuming the antiseptic smell that overpowered the room. 'What a dreadful thing to happen. I nearly fainted when that charming inspector told me you'd been shot. And when you were saving my wretch of a brother too,' she said as if it were a daily occurrence. 'Oh, darling, you have horrible purple bruises beneath your eyes.' She bent and traced a line on Flora's face with a gloved finger.

Dr Grace appeared with a glass of something pale amber which bubbled, her face a picture of disapproval which was lost on Jocasta.

'No, thank you,' Jocasta airily waved her away. 'I'm about to have luncheon.'

Dr Grace rolled her eyes behind Jocasta's back, and Bunny hid a smile behind his hand.

'It wasn't Ed's fault.' Flora grimaced at the bitterness of the liquid on her tongue. 'The situation developed out of a set of unfortunate circumstances.' She was feeling sleepy again but knew at the first sign of a yawn, Dr Grace would dismiss them all.

'When Papa hears the full story, he'll be livid you took a bullet for a Trent. How will he hold his head up at White's after this?'

'I hope that was a joke.' Jocasta's coy smile left an element of doubt. 'I'm sorry I couldn't tell you at the beginning, but Ed didn't want anyone to know.'

'Just as well you did. I would have been worried sick, if I wasn't sick enough already.' Jocasta hunched her shoulders and giggled, a protective hand on her abdomen. 'Alice has agreed to come to the house party after the wedding, so, between them, she and Dr Grace can oversee your return to health.' She grimaced as she realised what she had said. 'Oh dear, there I go again when William asked me not to mention it. Sorry.'

'He told me about the wedding a little while ago, so you haven't spoiled the surprise.' Flora's voice hitched as a wave of emotion combined with weariness overwhelmed her.

'Why are you crying? You never cry. Aren't you pleased?' Jocasta pouted again.

'Of *course* I am. It's the best news I've heard for days.' Flora swiped a hand across her wet cheek and blinked away tears.

'That's all right then.' Jocasta's eyes brightened. 'I'll travel down to the Abbey at the same time with Mabel. Jeremy can join me later when the House rises for the summer recess. I'm longing to see Amelia again; it's been five years since she went off to America to get married. I've missed her terribly.' She stared off for a moment. 'You don't think my big sister will have become too grand, do you? What with living with all those wealthy Americans at their summer cottages the size of Buckingham Palace?'

'Whatever gives you that idea?' Flora blinked back welling tears, fighting to remain calm.

'Emerald does. She said a title was an asset, but no one can compete with that sort of wealth.' She sniffed

delicately. 'I'm fortunate in that marriage has mel-
lowed me.'

Flora exchanged a swift look with Bunny, who
backed away a step, hands held up in surrender.

'Oh, I almost forgot.' Jocasta's pensive frown trans-
formed into childish delight. 'I met Miss Francis
Hunter-Griggs. What a charming woman and certainly the newest advocate to the Flora Harrington
appreciation society.'

'Don't be flippant, Jo. She's recently discovered her
family has been cruelly duped.'

'Yes, and what a scandal!' Jocasta ignored Dr
Grace's admonishing sigh. 'Now – I must go.' She adjusted her hat, gave the room a sweeping glance but,
finding no mirror, abandoned the idea. 'I'm having
luncheon with Milly Soames and her sister-in-law,
whose name I can never remember. Marianne Apsley
will be there and that insipid friend of hers, Liza,
something or other. I can't wait to see their faces when
I tell them my cousin was shot apprehending a killer.'

'It wasn't quite like that, Jocasta.' Flora's eyelids felt
heavy, but she forced herself to stay awake. Though
she knew she was safe, she dreaded the thought of
being left alone. The sound of Agnes's gun dis-
charging still echoed inside her head.

'Oh, darling, no one really cares about the tiny details. It's close enough.' Jocasta blew her a kiss from her fingertips before floating out of the room on a cloud of perfume.

'She's right, you look tired,' Bunny said when she had gone.

'It must be these nasty bruises under my eyes,' Flora muttered dryly. 'I'm exhausted but cannot sleep until I'm sure Ed is all right. Please let him in, even if it's only a minute.'

'Five minutes only.' Bunny nodded curtly towards Dr Grace, who offered no further protest as she disappeared into the hallway. She returned in seconds with Ed, his face wan but smiling, and a rumpled white bandage encircling his forehead.

'Gosh, Flora, you look terrible.' Ed pressed a kiss on her cheek, the smell of antiseptic and lemon verbena from his cologne bringing fresh tears to her eyes.

'Thank you, although it looks worse than it is and Dr Grace says I'm healing well. How's your head?'

'No one's taking *my* injury seriously.' Ed fingered the bandage as he slid onto the edge of the thin mattress, making the bed dip slightly. 'Not after the drama over yours, anyway.'

'Now that's untrue!' Bunny cuffed him lightly. 'Concussion is nothing to be dismissive about.'

'The doctor says I won't even have a scar when the

swelling goes down.' He gestured vaguely at the space between her throat and her waist. 'I'll bet you'll have something to show for all this excitement?'

'Gunshots are no joke, Ed,' Bunny snapped. 'Flora almost died.'

'Sorry. Didn't mean to make it sound trivial.' His eyes rounded. 'I thought for a while there she *had* died.'

'It's Leo's death I regret most of all,' Flora said, forestalling Bunny's protest. Ed's way of dealing with upsetting situations was to make light of them.

'So do I.' Ed's smile faded. 'In the end, he died for nothing.'

'Most of us do, Ed.' Flora sighed, a heaviness settling onto her chest, which had little to do with the tight bindings.

'You know, Flora, I've been thinking.' He shifted position on the bed, sending shock waves into her hip. 'We're good at this detective stuff. Why don't we open a private agency in Mayfair with "Viscount Trent, Fighter of Crime", etched in gold on the door? I'll hire a secretary and buy one of those typewriting machines. What do you say, Flora?'

'I think I prefer "Harrington and Trent"?' Flora suppressed a smile. 'And what would you tell your father?'

'Ah, didn't think of that.' Ed stroked his chin with one hand, thoughtful but not at all discouraged. 'I could still sit in the House when the time comes?'

'That's enough now, Ed. Flora's getting tired.' Dr Grace eased him firmly into the hallway, directing a swift but firm nod at Bunny in a silent signal Flora didn't understand. Following Ed from the room, she pulled the door closed behind her, leaving them alone. Bunny dragged the chair closer to the bed and sat, plucked Flora's hand from the coverlet and laced his fingers with hers. 'I need to talk to you.'

Her stomach flipped as she looked into his eyes, unable to discern what she saw there.

'Do you recall the last thing Inspector Maddox said to you before he left Eaton Place?'

'I should. It's his favourite litany where I'm concerned. That I should forget chasing villains and stay at home to look after my husband and baby.'

'Considering what has happened, is it such an unreasonable expectation?'

'When there are so many bad people ruining lives? Someone has to stop them.' Bunny's jaw went slack, and he opened his mouth to speak, but Flora forestalled him. 'I'm joking, silly. Although, without us, Ed could face murder charges. Although Maddox solved this one pretty much on his own.' She ran a finger along his clean-shaven cheek, waiting for him to broach what was really on his mind. Bunny was a master of deflection.

'You've had close shaves before,' he whispered. 'But this could have been the end for both of us. I cannot risk it happening again. It's my duty to look after you, which I cannot do if you're running around town chasing criminals. I need you. Arthur needs you, and—'

'Suppose I *do* stay at home? Won't that spoil everything?'

'What do you mean? What could be spoiled?'

'Us.' She ran her thumb over his palm, avoiding looking at him as her throat constricted. 'When we met, it was over a dead body on a steamship, which set the pattern of our lives together in a chain of murder, robbery, spies and fraud. We enjoyed those cases, didn't we? Finding out who killed Riordan when everyone said it was a riding accident. And then there was the Evangeline Lange case where we exposed that Serbian spy. And the children who went missing? What will happen to you and me when we have no mysteries to solve?'

'There are always crossword puzzles.' He tucked in his chin, his lips pursed as he peered at her over the top of his spectacles.

'I'm being serious.' She would have nudged him, but the threat of more pain prevented her. 'If all I had to discuss with you over dinner was Mrs Cope's beef being tough, or Arthur having learned a new word, wouldn't you get bored with me?'

'What a strange girl you are.' He left the chair and slid onto the mattress, his arm around her shoulders. 'You've never bored me in the entire time I've known you.' She contradicted him, but he silenced her with a finger to her lips. 'Which has nothing to do with your crime-solving skills. I rather think it's despite them.'

'Are you sure? You won't start dining at your club every night and going off for shooting weekends without me?'

'That will never happen.' He leaned against the mountain of pillows supporting her shoulders, his lips against her hair. 'Flora,' he whispered, 'I have to tell you something.'

'What is it?' A frisson of alarm ran through her, aware he had been working up to whatever it was he planned to say since he arrived. It couldn't be Arthur, or he would have mentioned that immediately.

'Dr Grace told me the bullet has done some... damage.'

'I know, I can feel it.' She summoned a smile; he did not return. 'But don't worry, the surgery was a success and I'm a quick healer. I shall have a wonderful story to tell about my battle scars when I'm your mother's age.'

'Flora,' he tilted her chin with his finger so she was looking straight into his eyes.

'Hmm?' Her gaze focused on a speck of dirt on his spectacles.

She reached to brush it away, but her hand stilled as he said, 'There will be no more children.'

Her hand dropped nerveless onto the coverlet, a heavy silence stretching between them as she waited for the surge of denial, shock and rage at fate's unfairness to rise inside her in a maelstrom of despair. Nothing happened. Had Dr Grace's potion addled her brain so she couldn't think straight?

'Flora, did you hear what I said?' His brow furrowed as he searched her face. 'I know this is awful news for you, but you'll get over it.'

'*I'll* get over it? What about you?' Her voice cracked. 'Aren't you horribly disappointed?'

'In *you?*' He shook his head, incredulous. 'No, how could I possibly be?'

'We never discussed it. But I always imagined we would have a large family someday.'

'Flora, my love. I had a wonderful childhood not having to compete for attention. You were a singleton too. Did you feel you suffered from not having siblings?'

She shook her head. It was true. She had always loved the fact it was only her and Riordan in their cosy apartment on the top floor of Cleeve Abbey. Being able to command his exclusive attention had always made her feel special.

'Arthur is all I could have imagined in a child,' Bunny whispered. 'I'm more than content to be a father of one. How do *you* feel about it?'

'I don't know yet. A little sad, maybe.' Where was the grief and regret for what might have been? 'A bit like a present I always looked forward to but will never have.'

Fast on these thoughts came the one she had never admitted aloud. That she doubted her ability to love another child the way she did their beautiful little boy. Now she would be spared the guilt of having a favourite.

'Get some rest. I'll be right here when you wake up.' Bunny brought her hand up to his lips, his breath warm on her fingertips. 'And before you say it's not allowed; I defy even Dr Grace to stop me.' He tenderly adjusted the coverlet over her and smoothed the pillow behind her head. Her eyelids fluttered closed as fatigue engulfed her, lulled by the touch of his hand holding hers.

Had he suppressed his own disappointment to spare her a sense of inadequacy? Would the subject be forever avoided to spare them pain, or would they have the courage to broach it again in the future?

In the place between wakefulness and oblivion, she recalled something Eric Paige had said about being halfway to Waterford. Wasn't Holyhead where the ferry to Ireland left from? She must remember to tell Inspector Maddox to alert the Garda Síochána in the morning.

ACKNOWLEDGEMENTS

I would like to thank the brilliant team at Boldwood, specifically Caroline Ridding for her vision in helping me bring Flora to life. My thanks go to Isobel Akenhead, Sarah Ritherdon, Sue Lamprell and Debra Newhouse, and also to Boldwood's creative department for the stunningly beautiful covers.

ABOUT THE AUTHOR

Anita Davison is the author of the successful Flora Maguire historical mystery series.

Sign up to Anita Davison's mailing list for news, competitions and updates on future books.

Visit Anita's website: www.anitadavison.co.uk

Follow Anita on social media here:

ALSO BY ANITA DAVISON

Miss Merrill and Aunt Violet Mysteries

Murder in the Bookshop

The Flora Maguire Mysteries

Death On Board

Death at the Abbey

Death of a Suffragette

Death by the Thames

Death on a Train

Poison & Pens

POISON & PENS IS THE HOME OF
COZY MYSTERIES SO POUR YOURSELF
A CUP OF TEA & GET SLEUTHING!

DISCOVER PAGE-TURNING NOVELS FROM
YOUR FAVOURITE AUTHORS &
MEET NEW FRIENDS

JOIN OUR
FACEBOOK GROUP

BIT.LYPOISONANDPENSFB

SIGN UP TO OUR
NEWSLETTER

BIT.LY/POISONANDPENSNEWS

Boldwood

Boldwood Books is an award-winning fiction publishing company seeking out the best stories from around the world.

Find out more at www.boldwoodbooks.com

Join our reader community for brilliant books, competitions and offers!

Follow us
@BoldwoodBooks
@TheBoldBookClub

Sign up to our weekly deals newsletter

https://bit.ly/BoldwoodBNewsletter